Man In The Woods

Jon Hill

Banzai Press

VISIT www.jonhillwrites.com and join the mailing list for your free novella! This story is not available anywhere else! It is exclusively for those who sign up on the mailing list! (huoh-huoh-huoh!)

It's that time of year again, that row of calendar boxes we all spend the winter months looking forward to. Summer vacation. A chance to escape the daily grind, to relax, unwind, reconnect, and get some sun.

For Jeff, those days have always been spent in Cape May, New Jersey, and this year is no exception. But a terrible surprise awaits those vacationing in Cape May County this year, and beachgoers soaking in the rays will be forced to turn their attention from funnel cake and tan lines to simply surviving the rest of the week.

Note From The Author

Thank you for picking up this second installment of the Jack and Stacey Green series. If you haven't read the first book, *Man In The Water*, you may want to start there, as it is essential for understanding the rest of the series.

As for this book, I just want to mention that I have taken creative liberties with the terrain of certain actual locations while completely making up others. I also wanted to incorporate the Appalachian dialect in the dialogue, but after studying the topic a bit, I concluded that doing so would probably have the opposite effect than the one intended. There is a strong "hillbilly" stereotype surrounding the people of Appalachia, and I did not want to feed into it by not getting the dialogue perfect—which I don't think I would've been able to do (just look up books that take place in that area and read the reviews left by the people who actually live there). In my research, I discovered that the mountain dialect is not a broken and distorted version of today's English, as many believe, but rather it is an archaic sort of Scottish-flavored Elizabethan English held intact from when the Scottish-Irish settlers first arrived. The story of how the Scottish arrived in Appalachia is for another time and place, but it is fascinating all the same. With that said, however, I did want the reader to have some sense that the people talking spoke differently than our main characters, so I tweaked the dialogue just enough to remind the reader of who the characters were and where they came from. But in no way is this dialogue an accurate representation of the Appalachian dialect. This is not the sort of story for that. And since our main Appalachian characters are bad guys, they are in no way meant to be representative of all Appalachian peoples.

So, with all that out of the way, I hope you enjoy book two and will stick around afterward for what's coming up next!

For Uncle Teddy
Woodsman, godfather, and my dad's best friend. Thanks for everything.

HAM LOOKED UP FROM the map that was spread across the table. A cloud of dust was rising in the distance, suddenly obscuring his view of the mountains. He picked up the short glass that had been holding down the map and brought it to his lips. The liquid slid down the back of his throat like lava, and he stifled a cough. The moonshine that his neighbor Bud had delivered as a way to pay off the debt he owed was top shelf around here for sure. Ham used to guess at the old fool's formula until he figured it was probably best not to know. Didn't the Good Book say something about not asking your host if what they were serving had first been offered to idols? Wasn't this the same sort of thing? He figured it was. He drained what was left and thought, *Amen.*

He stood, and the chair slid back across the wooden floor. He hobbled over to the sun-bleached curtains and pushed them aside with a large but steady hand.

Yup. They were back, no doubt about it. He sighed. Picked the smoldering cigarette butt off the windowsill where he'd left it before the phone call and the moonshine and the map, and took a long drag. When he exhaled, a cloud of smoke filled the air. "Sons of bitches," he mumbled. The words set the smoke around his head into a dance, and he squinted over the tops of his black-framed glasses, at the clock in the other room. Noon. He hadn't been expecting them back for another three hours.

He made his way to the door. Picked up the revolver he kept loaded and resting on the table beside it. Then he returned the cigarette to his mouth so he could use both hands to get the gun into the side pocket of his overalls. He swore, angry that he needed two hands to do such a simple thing. His late wife, Lilly, had been right. He was getting too damn fat. That was why she had started calling him Ham. And that was why she was buried in the backyard. Still, the name had stuck, as names did around here, and he didn't have the energy to go around killing everyone who used it.

With the pistol finally in place, he reached down with a groan and wrapped his hand around the grip of his trademark axe, Joanna. That was what he'd named it, after the girl who'd split his heart in half when he was twelve years old. She hadn't been able to help herself, and neither could this fine tool he'd crafted in her memory. Though, truth be told, he really had no business falling in love with a high school senior who had plans for a life beyond the mountains in the first place.

He swung her up onto his shoulder. As he stared out the little window in the door, he tapped the cigarette and sent ash fluttering to the floor. He tried to imagine what might have gone wrong. Though with this crew, he knew there was one reason more likely than all others.

Taking one last breath of smoke, he ran his fingers through his graying beard, opened the door, and flicked the butt into the grass with the rest. He grabbed the railing, took the short steps to the ground, and waited.

THE OLD PICKUP CAME down the dirt path like a dog with its tail between its legs—knowing it had to come, but knowing what the coming meant and not wanting any part of it.

The driver—John Tyler, he was certain—was not in a hurry. There was no one bleeding out in the bed of the truck, that was for sure. Yet there was a sense of urgency in the way he was navigating the uneven terrain. Like the news he didn't want to deliver would just make things worse the longer it was delayed.

Ham turned his head and spit as the truck rolled to a stop in front of him. He twirled Joanna, her blade catching the sun.

The doors swung open, and three of his gang hopped out. Three more jumped out of the bed.

James and Michael, the two brothers, walked side by side, leading the others while John Tyler and Theodore hung out in the back. This let Ham know all he needed to know about what had happened. But he asked anyway.

"What happened?" He perched his left hand inside a suspender strap.

James stopped a few feet in front of him. "Things got a little outta hand, is all." He stated it matter-of-fact, like that was all there was to say about it.

Ham looked at Michael, and Michael averted his gaze, staring at the ground instead.

"What does that mean?" Ham asked, meeting James's eyes again.

Everyone knew that James would soon be the leader of the pack (once Ham finally suffered the impending heart attack), and most seemed okay with that. James could probably take over right now if he wanted. Just a flick of his wrist would be all it would take. Spill Ham's guts all down the front of his trousers. But James wasn't one to mutiny. Still, he wouldn't let anything happen to his younger brother, as wild and crazy as Michael might be at times.

"It ain't nothin'," James said.

Ham looked past them, past Lawrence and Colt, and found what he was looking for in the body language of Theodore. The guy developed a nervous twitch when he was stressed. And high. Ham could tell that he was both right now. He pushed past the brothers and went to the truck.

Theodore stepped away from the truck bed, fidgeting. "He went all crazy, Ham. Started sayin' about goin' to the police. Michael just done did what was needed is all."

Ham leaned over the back of the truck to get a glimpse of whatever it was they were all too afraid to just come out and say. He let the axe fall off his shoulder, and the big head thudded on the ground beside his square-toed boot. "You know he was never going to any authorities. Just wanted more time."

"He don't have what he owes," Lawrence said, twirling his mustache.

Ham turned to looked at him and had to squint through the sun reflecting off his bald head. "Well, I can certainly believe that. But he could've gotten it. And more."

Colt stepped forward. He was covered in tattoos, but it was the US Marines tattoo on his arm that got most people's attention. That and the crossed M16s on his back that referenced the name he'd been given while on a sandy tour half a world away. "Need to send them a message, Ham."

Ham shook his head. Ran a hand through his overgrown crew cut. It was no secret that he and Colt didn't like each other. "Colt, if I wanted people to be scared to death of doin' business with me, then I'd have gone and cut up most of the region by now." He sighed. "Be that as it may..."

Theodore, John Tyler, and Michael all looked uncomfortable, not sure of what the boss was going to do. Of what punishment he would measure out. James, Laurence, and Colt, on the other hand, knew that this crew was the best one Ham had and that it wouldn't be worth his time fighting over something as stupid as this.

Ham looked into the truck again. At the guy all tied up in twine and with a bloody burlap sack over his head. "How bad is he?"

A grin stretched Michael's lips, appearing beneath the shadow cast by the brim of his cowboy hat. "Won't ever walk again."

Theodore started to giggle. "Won't ever hump again."

Ham saw that the guy's arms were bent the wrong way at the elbows. "Won't be pitching for the Yankees neither."

They all laughed at that. Except James. He just watched, chewing on a toothpick and studying things as he always did.

"All right," Ham said. "Use the chainsaw. Spread him around." Then he walked over to Colt. Got so close that his boulder of a belly was touching him. "You and I gonna have a problem?"

Ham was six feet three and had to look down at Colt, but they both knew that with his military training and his combat experience in the Middle East, it would only take a moment for Colt to kill Ham. But they both knew Colt would never dare try. James might, if he'd had it in him, because he had support. He was a natural born leader. Not Colt. He was a loner. There would be no one in his corner. If he tried anything, he would be the one in the truck and cut into pieces. If not by the rest of this crew, then by one of Ham's others. That or he'd either have to kill everyone or flee. He didn't feel like doing much of either.

"No, Ham. We ain't got no problem."

"Next time, do what the hell I tell you to do."

Colt nodded, but his eyes were balls of ice.

Ham shot a warning glance at Michael, which was all he was willing to do. He didn't need to give James a reason for wanting more than he had, which meant putting up with his little brother's episodes. "Good," he said to Colt. "Now c'mon. We got a job to prep for."

Lawrence came up beside him. "A job?"

"Yup."

"For who?"

Ham put Joanna back up onto his shoulder. "Didn't ask. It came through a middleman."

"Not the Jennings gang?"

"No. Not them for sure. They don't get into this sort of stuff."

"What sort of stuff you talkin' about, then?" John Tyler asked. They were getting more comfortable now that it seemed they'd made it out of this with only a verbal rebuke.

"Stuff we don't talk about. Stuff we don't even like to think about. Abomination stuff."

They all fell silent.

"When you're done with him"—Ham nodded to the truck —"meet me back here. We got a lot of plannin' to do." He turned and started for the front door of the cabin. Then stopped as if he'd thought of something else. "Oh, two more things."

They waited.

"You're gonna be working with the Baker boys—"

Lawrence interrupted him with a curse, turning away and throwing a punch into the side of the rusted truck.

But John Tyler started laughing, a look of insanity coming over his bearded face as spittle flew from his mouth and caught the sunlight.

"Ham," James said evenly, "why you gotta bring them into it?"

"Those guys are insane," Colt added.

Ham looked at Theodore. Watched as he began twitching, no doubt replaying in his half-baked brain the last time they'd had a run-in with the Baker boys.

"It ain't my call. Was a condition of the job. It'll be fine," Ham assured them. Then he looked at Michael. "As long as people keep their cool and get along."

James stepped forward and talked softly. "They're right, you know. Those guys are—"

"Tougher than you?"

James shook his head. Looked down at his feet. When he raised his eyes, they were filled with conviction. "They ain't got souls, Ham."

Ham laughed himself into a coughing fit. "Ain't got souls? And you all are saints, aren't ya?" Then he lowered his voice and leaned close. "Keep 'em together, James. I'm puttin' you in charge of this one. It's probably not somethin' we believe in, but the money's too good to pass up."

"Thirty pieces of silver, then?"

Ham frowned. "Don't get all self-righteous on me. As I recall, we both got things buried in our backyards, and that makes us at least parallel, don't it?" Then he looked up and shouted out the second thing he'd thought of. "You ever go against my orders again, and you won't just be sawin' up whoever you brought back. You'll also be drawing straws. One person for the cuttin' and the other for the fallin' apart. You understand me?"

They nodded and went to take care of business.

Ten minutes later, Ham was back to studying the map with a refill of moonshine as the sound of a chainsaw and a man's screams rode the mountain breeze outside.

2

JACK GREEN STOOD IN the driveway behind the black RAV4 and stared at the backup plan he'd packed into the trunk. Two coolers filled with food and drink, two duffel bags of clothes, and another bag of random items he thought they might want in the event things went sideways (and if he was honest with himself, he was sort of hoping they would). He went down his mental checklist one last time. Most of the stuff he wouldn't need. Maybe none of it. But it was always better to be looking at it than for it.

Satisfied, he closed the trunk and turned. Leaned against the bumper. As he watched the mid-June sun dip beneath the horizon, he checked his new watch. 8:34 on Sunday. He worked the buttons on the side and set an alarm for 7p.m. He'd want to keep in mind what time the sun set while they were out there, and he thought an hour and a half reminder should be enough to wrap up whatever it was they might find themselves in the middle of.

The urge to smoke struck him like a freight train, and he frowned. He'd taken up the habit about a year after the cruise ship incident when a guy at a bar had offered him one of his cigarettes. He then spent the next three years wishing he'd turned it down. But he eventually overcame the habit and could only hope he'd stopped in time to avoid any long-term damage. He wanted to be around for any grandchildren. Plus, the fact that secondhand smoke racked up more victims per year than gun violence sort of made him feel like a dick. So wanting one now, seemingly out of nowhere, was interesting.

He went inside.

HE WALKED INTO THE kitchen and stood at the table. Stacey was in front of the stove, her back to him. He stared at her, studying her figure as she sipped from a wineglass, her mind somewhere else. She still looked great, and though there were times he missed her blond hair, he liked her as a brunette even more. He loved the way she was wearing it now. Long, down her back, the blond highlights like feathered flames. She knew he loved her hair like that, and after being married for more than a decade, he was pretty certain what it meant. He looked at his watch again and decided that he'd better finish up. He sure didn't want to run out of time.

She turned, leaned against the stove, and tilted her head. "Almost done?" she asked, taking another sip.

He nodded. "Think so." Yup, there was no doubt about where this was going. Hair + wine + questions about bedtime + trip tomorrow morning = some mommy and daddy alone time.

She pushed off the oven and walked to the table. She looked down at the equipment that covered it and smiled.

"What?" he asked.

She picked up the survival guide he'd ordered a few months ago and flipped through the pages. "Nothing."

He snatched the book out of her hands.

"That's a lot of underlining," she said.

"I'm like Anthony Hopkins in *The Edge*." He tapped the side of his head. "It's all up here now."

"Mmm...book smarts in the wilderness. What could go wrong?" Another sip. "Why are you taking it if it's all—" she tapped her head in mock fashion "—up here?"

"Because I might forget which berries nourish you and which ones kill you."

"You definitely don't want to mix up your berries."

"I sure don't."

"Could ruin the week."

"Could ruin my colon." He sighed. "I hate the woods."

Stacey looked toward the steps in the other room. "Shhh..."

"I know. I know. Boy would be searching the classifieds for a new father before breakfast if he heard me say that."

"Think you can fake it?"

Her question, as innocent as it was, touched an old nerve, and he had to bite his tongue to keep from responding with some smart-ass comment.

She seemed to notice but didn't say anything, and the moment passed just as they always had over the last eight years. So much subtext. So much innuendo. So many elephants in the house. But it was their unspoken agreement not to drudge up the past that had allowed them to keep moving forward.

She walked around the table and kissed him. "Don't stay up too late. There's something I want to give you before you go."

"Should only be a few more minutes."

She walked out of the room.

He scratched his unshaven face as he swept his eyes over the stuff scattered across the table. Then he turned and looked into the living room, at the stuff he had piled on the floor in there too. He checked his watch again. He figured he had a half-hour window before Stacey fell asleep and he missed out on whatever it was she had for him. He got to work.

First, he picked up the knife. Held it up to the light.

Everything he'd read said that the belt knife was the most vital tool because it could be used to recreate most other things. It was recommended that it be kept on your person at all times, preferably in a leather sheath with a flap that snapped shut over the handle. Leather because whatever lubricant was used to protect the knife from rusting would end up in the leather and be applied to the blade whenever it was inserted. The downside was that leather held water when it got wet. Which was why he'd followed someone's suggestion and waterproofed it by soaking the sheath in olive oil, letting it drip dry over the last twenty-four hours. Stacy had smiled at that too.

He'd gone with a six-inch full-tang blade made of high carbon steel and a Scandinavian grind. It took him the better part of three months to settle on it—to find one that could send off a shower of sparks when struck against the right material. That meant finding one with a sharp ninety-degree edge that wasn't factory coated. He'd coated the blade with olive oil himself. They said it was preferable to the petroleum-based lubricants if you were going to use the knife to process food. He didn't have any such plans, but he couldn't rule it out. Anything could happen in the wilderness.

The full-tang design meant that the knife was one solid piece of steel, the handle screwed to either side of it so that there was no danger of the blade falling apart. If the handle broke, he could fashion another one easily enough.

But the toughest decision was on which grind to choose. He'd narrowed it down to either convex or Scandinavian, ultimately deciding on the latter. A convex blade was more resilient but harder to maintain in the wild and more difficult to use for finer tasks. So they said. What did he know? Scandinavian seemed to him a good compromise between the resilience of the convex and the brittleness of the sharper but thin hollow grind.

The knife felt good in his hand. Seemed a natural fit, like it was made for his grip alone. Maybe he and Joseph would come up with a name for it this week. He slid it into the sheath and snapped it shut. Put it aside.

Next he picked up the axe. He had been as meticulous in choosing the eighteen-inch hunter's axe as he had been the knife. It had a Scandinavian head and a hickory handle with a straight grain all the way through. It was considered one of the best compromises for all-around use; and since he had no idea what he was getting into, he figured "all around" was his best option. Joseph had helped him burn lines into the handle every half inch so that it could also double as a measuring stick. Not that he planned on doing a lot of measuring, but who knew. Maybe he'd try to build one of those shelters that were in the book.

He folded the leather axe mask over the head and set the tool beside the knife.

He shook his head. The last time he'd been to the woods (not counting the nearby lake that he and Joseph occasionally fished) was eight years ago when Agent Johnson had stuck him in that cabin in the mountains. That had been enough wilderness to last him the rest of his life. But he reminded himself that this was for Joseph. And a week of camping wasn't such a big price to pay for some quality father and son bonding. Not when taking into consideration what the boy had been through. What they'd both been through.

It took him five minutes to arrange all the equipment into categories—pockets, belt pouch, haversack, and pack. The stuff that he would carry in his pockets and the things that would go on his belt he put into a backpack. He'd put them on his person when they reached the campsite.

He went to the living room and folded the eight-by-eight-foot oilcloth tarp that was spread across the floor into thirds. Then he folded a queen-sized wool blanket in half and placed it on top of the tarp. Folded a twin-sized wool blanket in half and laid it over the queen. Then he began to place items on the blanket that wouldn't be immediately needed and could be rolled up inside the pack. Stuff like rope and stakes and spare socks.

He rolled it up and set it aside.

Next he packed the belt pouch with things like a waterproof flashlight and matches. Then the haversack. He set them beside the blanket roll and stole another glance at the time.

Fifteen minutes before Stacey was asleep.

The rucksack was made of canvas and had a small number of pockets. The books had warned against getting a backpack with too many zippers and compartments, because it could take too long to remember what you put in each pouch. Keep it simple, stupid.

He'd gotten the pack (most of the stuff, actually) at a military surplus store. With cash, of course. He didn't know if they were still on anyone's watchlist, but he didn't need any red flags going off by putting knives and axes on his credit card.

The waterproof bag went in first to keep the equipment from getting wet. Then it was one item at a time, each one getting crossed off his list as it went in. Folding saw, bush pot, skillet, notebook and pencils, hemp rope, repair kit, whetstone, parachute cord, first aid kit...

When he was all done, he tied the blanket roll to the top of the pack. Then he stood and looked over his work. *Jerry packed all this crap*, he thought.

Jerry.

No one had called him that in a long time. But it was that part of him that was always imagining some post-apocalyptic scenario where he'd have to live off the land (or some other, more realistic reason that would cause him to go off the grid) that wanted to see if he could do it. So he decided to pack for more than just setting up a tent and roasting marshmallows. Maybe an EMP would go off next week, and he and Joseph would have to survive on their own for the next ten years. Not a pleasant thought.

And neither was how fast Stacey's window was closing.

He started taking the equipment out to the car, beginning with two exercise mats and Joseph's little backpack the two of them had packed before dinner.

It took four trips, and on his last one, he saw Stacey's face appear in the bedroom window above the driveway. And then the upstairs lights went out.

He quickly finished arranging everything, making sure that Joseph would have plenty of room in the back seat, and shut the door. He ran inside.

In his haste, he hadn't noticed what he knocked off the passenger seat and out of the car while shifting the gear around.

JACK WENT UP THE stairs, hitting light switches off as he went. When he reached the top, he found a melodic whisper traveling down the hall and followed it to Joseph's room.

Joseph had started listening to movie scores at night a few years ago. Said it helped him sleep. Right now it was the late James Horner who was composing the soundtrack to his dreams. The Jackie Chan *Karate Kid* remake.

Jack bent over to turn off the bedside lamp and paused. The light was washing over Joseph's face in such a way that he seemed to be glowing. Jack straightened. Studied his boy. The way his hair was coming down over his eye (against Stacey's wishes, they were having a hair-growing competition). The slow, methodical way his chest rose with each breath. He wondered what he was dreaming about, if it was as climactic as the music.

"I love you, Joe," he whispered. He pulled the blankets up a little higher so that they reached his small shoulders and then kissed his head. "We're gonna have a great week."

Then his eyes drifted, as they often did, to the scar.

And every time it took him back to that moment, to Vadim holding Joseph in front of him and dragging the knife across his neck. He wondered if Joseph remembered anything about that day. He hoped not, which was why he never asked. Best not to stir the pools of memory if the memory wasn't already floating there on the surface.

He turned the bedside lamp off, and Luke Skywalker's blue lightsaber glowed from the wall clock across the room. According to Luke's saber, he only had two minutes left.

He was about to turn the soundtrack off, but then thought better of it. As he walked out of the room, he instead turned it up a couple of notches.

A smile spread across his face as he walked down the hallway. The music following after him was from a training scene, and in the present context it made him feel like he was in a parody. He felt like loosening up, taking a couple of jabs, doing some neck rolls.

When he entered the bedroom, he thought he could see Stacey under the covers, lying on her side, asleep. His heart sank. But then a voice sounded from behind him.

"About time," she said.

He turned and could just make her out in the light coming from the hallway. She was in a new black lace teddy, complete with garter and stockings.

For some reason the lace made him think of the lingerie he'd found while looking for something to wear in Donny's drawer.

The engagement ring...

It had taken years, and maybe a few cigarettes, to get over Donny's death, but every once in a while, the sting of it still surfaced, as it was starting to now.

Until Stacey stepped forward and started to unbutton his shirt.

YOU THINK YOU'LL MAKE it the whole week?" Stacey asked.

They were lying on their backs and staring up at the ceiling in the dark.

"I'm planning on it. But the shelter is just a little over a half mile from the campsite. If things get uncomfortable, we'll just pack up and hike there." He turned his head toward her. "Are you gonna be okay?"

"Yeah, I think I can manage here on my own."

"You know what I mean."

She turned onto her side. "No, I don't know what you mean."

He returned his gaze to the ceiling.

"What?" she pressed.

"Nothing."

She propped herself up onto an elbow as the elephants came parading into the bedroom. "Are you talking about—"

"Forget it. I'm sure you'll be fine." He reached his hand over and placed it on her thigh. She still had the lace on.

But she wouldn't let it go. Not now that the subject was broached. "What are you thinking?"

He sighed. "I'm thinking this is the first time that I'm leaving you. That you'll be alone."

"Is this Jerry I'm hearing?" she asked, amused and a little surprised.

"Maybe."

She put her hand on his chest. "It's been a long time since I've heard anything from him."

"I've been keeping him in the basement."

He looked over and saw the white of her teeth and knew she was smiling. It made him smile too. And he thought that maybe that was why the urge for a cigarette had come back—a subconscious reflex meant to keep his conspiracy theorist alter ego at bay. Because he knew what getting back into that mindset would mean, what it would do to his peace of mind. If people had named him after Mel Gibson's character in the *Conspiracy Theory* movie before, what would he be like after everything that had gone down eight years ago—when he'd found himself at the center of a CIA false-flag operation? No, ignorance now wasn't just bliss, it was essential. His wife was the daughter of KGB agents, ex-wife to a rogue SVR operative, and herself part of a CIA black op. Convincing Big Brother that they were happy to live normal, ignorant American lives was crucial to their being left alone. Hitting up the independent websites at 1a.m., checking out books on other American-made false-flag events, signing petitions to limit the scope of the NSA's surveillance system, and sharing WikiLeaks posts might just nudge them into the liability column. So he'd put Jerry in the basement and out of sight.

"If you're thinking what I think you're thinking," she said, lightly raking her fingernails over his skin, "I don't think you need to worry about it. I haven't spotted any activity in years."

"Would you tell me if you had?"

Silence drifted over them; her hand paused. "Depends," she finally said.

He nodded, able to appreciate her honesty.

She moved closer, putting one leg over top of his and an arm across his chest. "I can't believe you're going camping for a week." She nibbled his earlobe. "In the mountains."

"I know."

"What if there are bears?"

"As long as they aren't carrying AK-47s, we should be okay."

"What?"

"Kidding." But then he wondered if he was.

"Snakes, mountain lions, poison berries..." She giggled. "I'm sorry. I so can't see you out there. I give you three days max before you're going to the shelter or coming home."

"Think Joseph would be disappointed."

"No doubt."

"Okay, it's a bet."

"What is?"

"That I make it the whole time."

"And the stakes?"

He thought about it. Then lifted up the covers and pretended to look beneath them. "I can think of a few things."

"Okay. And if you don't make it, you need to start on the deck."

"What deck?"

"Exactly."

He groaned. "Fine."

Her teeth appeared again. "We'll have to change your name from Jerry to Jeremiah."

"As in Jeremiah Johnson?"

She ran her hand over his coming beard. "You're practically halfway there."

He laughed. "Yeah, right." Then he asked, "How do you know about that movie?"

"My mom had a thing for Robert Redford."

"Really?" He wondered if the Kremlin would been okay with one of their spies having the hots for an American actor, but didn't want to dampen the mood by bringing up the Motherland. He'd been very delicate when speaking about Viktoriya, mostly for Stacey's sake but also out of respect for the Russian countess. The last twenty minutes of her life had completely reshaped his view of her, and he thought the two of them could have gotten along just fine after clearing the air and taming all their elephants. Though he wasn't sure how things would have played out between her and Stacey...

He fell asleep and, for the first time in years, dreamed of bears.

3

MONDAY MORNING STARTED OUT with the coffee not being right. Either the ratio was off, or the machine needed cleaning or the beans weren't fresh, or the water filter needed replacing. It wasn't a huge difference, not enough to make you spit it out, but Jack could tell. Maybe he'd woken up with a brain tumor that was suddenly affecting the way things tasted. Wouldn't that be fun?

He brought the mug to his lips and sipped some more, each taste moving him further along the road to adaptation. By his second cup, he'd be used to it. By his third, he wouldn't even remember what it was supposed to taste like.

He was in the kitchen, leaning against the door frame that led out back. The morning was cool, so he'd opened the sliding glass door and watched the sun rise above the big oaks at the edge of the neighbor's property. Listened to the birds sing their songs, not a note out of key. The verse about God's eye being on the sparrow came to him, as it always did when he took the time to notice them, and as always it brought back a certain context with it. A context comprised of dilemmas.

After the events of eight years ago, he'd felt that he owed it to his grandmother and to God to finally pursue some kind of resolution to his spiritual conflict, a conflict that had felt like a pair of concrete shoes while he was treading water in the middle of the ocean. They say there are no atheists in foxholes, and he hadn't even been an atheist. So he'd started checking out some of the nearby churches and re-familiarizing himself with the Bible. But all he got out of the services was a sore back and an intimate knowledge of the guy's cowlick sitting in front of him.

The message all seemed to be the same. Try hard to be a good person, and in so doing you will earn God's blessing. But they never said how, and he was pretty sure he remembered Grandmom saying something about not being able to earn God's favor anyway. Something to do with faith and righteousness and atonement and an indwelling Lord. But he couldn't remember and only got more frustrated the more he went. So he'd accepted a cigarette at a bar instead.

An oriole flew across the yard and landed on the swing set. Its black and orange colors were vibrant in the rising sun, and Jack marveled at its beauty.

Beauty. It was the metaphysical note that kept getting stuck in his head and drawing him back into the magic. He remembered quoting the Song of Solomon to Stacey on the cruise ship. *Thy two breasts are like two young roes that are twins, which feed among the lilies...* He smiled, took another sip, and looked at his watch.

He'd gotten the watch for about four hundred bucks. It had all the features: pedometer, heart rate monitor, elevation tracker, compass, military-grade durability, synchronization to his smart phone, compatibility with satellite networks and global emergency response, and so forth and so on. To access the latter features, he'd needed a satellite communicator and a subscription, but that was a bit more than he was willing to get into for just a week-long camping trip a couple of hours away. What he did do, however, was get a satellite Wi-Fi hotspot that would pair with his phone and enable him to call, text, and access the internet. He'd already been using the watch via the phone for the last few days. With the solar phone charger he'd packed, he didn't anticipate a time that he wouldn't be "connected" to the outside world. Not that he'd need to be, but... Bears.

It was a couple of minutes after six, and a second cup of coffee was calling him. He closed the sliding door and got another mug out of the cabinet. It was a Temple University mug —his alma mater. He topped off his cup and filled the Temple one, then walked them both through the living room and up the stairs. Stacey had said she wanted him to wake her before 6:30.

When he got to the top of the stairs, he stopped. The hallway stretched away from him in both directions, each ending at a door. The door to his left, perpendicular to Joseph's bedroom, was closed. He turned, faced it, and stood entranced as the two porcelain mugs quietly ejected clouds of steam into the stillness.

The door was always closed.

Most of the time it was a subliminal detail that never stood out as they went on with their lives. But it had a subtext that was always there, buried beneath layers of scarring. Whether they realized it or not, it was present...living, breathing, moving. And every once in a while, like right now, it had a way of jumping out at you, turning into an exclamation mark in their house, screaming that it was present. That it was always present.

The mugs trembled in his grip, and some of the hot liquid slipped over a rounded edge, burning his hand. He hardly noticed, the door and what should have been behind it these last seven years making him numb to anything else. Sadness, loss, confusion—there seemed to be no rhyme or reason as to when or why they'd show up, unannounced, unprovoked, and unwanted. Sometimes it was just a quick jab of sorrow, like a needle. Other times it was more like a stabbing pain in the gut. Yet there were times when it was a doubled-barreled shotgun blast to the chest that dropped you to your knees in mid-step.

He took a deep breath, blinked a tear away, and turned his back on the past.

JACK SET THE COFFEE on the nightstand and lightly kissed Stacey on the forehead. Then he went into their bathroom and turned on the shower. As he waited for the water to warm, he stripped out of his shorts and stood in front of the mirror. He took a sip of coffee while running a hand over his torso. He was as fit as he'd ever been in his life, thanks to Stacey's insistence that he beef up and train. Just in case. So she'd taught him what she'd learned from her own CIA training days, hitting the mats hard, no punches pulled. It was preparation for any retribution that either side might throw their way, but it was also a way to work out the pain of almost losing a child...and losing one.

Even as things settled down (Jack no longer paying attention to the world scene, and Stacey confident they were in the clear), he didn't give up this new part of his life, still hitting the weights and practicing the self-defense maneuvers every week. He'd even taken some martial arts training from a place down the street and joined a flag-football league mostly made up of twenty-year-olds, managing to earn their respect by demanding double coverage on every offensive snap. It'd been a couple of years since he played football, but he was still invited to the annual Thanksgiving games. Last Thanksgiving he'd had six touchdowns before rolling his ankle. Joseph had cheered him on from the sideline the entire time.

He threw his head back and finished the coffee, then stepped into the shower. He thought of the week ahead and for the hundredth time hoped he knew what he was getting into.

WHEN HE WALKED BACK into the bedroom, wrapped in a towel, Stacey was sitting up in bed, and Joseph was next to her, his ankles crossed. She had a T-shirt on, but he could see the black strap beneath it running over her left shoulder. He hoped she'd gotten the lingerie covered in time. A twelve-year-old boy could be scarred for life by something like that. And he had enough scars as it was.

"Hey, buddy," Jack said, walking over to the bed. "You ready?"

He nodded, and his hair fell into his eyes. He brushed it away with the back of his hand. "Are you?"

Jack laughed and shot a look at Stacey while raising his eyebrows and sucking air through his teeth. He looked at his watch. "I want to leave in twenty minutes, okay?"

Joseph grabbed his own camping book he'd apparently been showing Stacey again and hopped off the bed.

As he went past him and out of the room, Jack patted his head. "Kid's hair is getting long," he said to Stacey.

She threw the covers off and swung her feet onto the floor. "Yeah, you two will fit right in with the Sasquatch."

"Sasquatch?"

She pulled the T-shirt up over her head and tossed it on the bed. "Bigfoot."

Jack feigned concern as he took a few steps backward and kicked the door shut with his foot. For Joseph's sake. "You think there's Sasquatch?"

"Your campsite is off the Appalachian Trail. Isn't that where all the sightings are?"

"I have no idea."

"Hmm." She pulled open a drawer and took out a pair of sweatpants. "I thought you would've looked into that...Jerrymiah."

He smiled. "Cute." Then he sat on the edge of the bed and watched her get out of the lace. Of course she made a show of it, and now he was wishing they had more than—he looked at his watch—sixteen minutes. But apparently that was her whole game, which became apparent by the way she smiled at him on her very naked way to the bathroom.

"You're cruel," he said.

"Just reinforcing the stakes of our bet," she said.

"I thought you wanted a deck."

"I want our son to have the time of his life."

She closed the door, and he heard the water go on in the shower. He decided he should take her the coffee still on the nightstand.

He pulled the curtain aside and leaned against the tiled wall, watching her. Her back was to him, and when she turned around, her eyes were closed and she was running her hands through her hair. He was debating whether to say "boo" or "hi there" or just stand there and enjoy the view, when she opened the eye closest to him. The way she did it—the bored manner in which her eyelid separated, the green iris already focused on him —told him that she'd already known he was there. Spies...they took the fun out of everything.

He raised the Temple mug in offering.

"It's gross," she said, and turned her back to him again.

He stared down into the black liquid, contemplating it. Then he took a sip of his own and shrugged. "No tumor, then." He left the bathroom and went to the clothes he'd laid out the day before and got dressed.

Then he went to see how Joseph was making out.

TWELVE MINUTES LATER, THEY were standing at the top of the driveway and saying goodbye to Stacey. Joseph squeezed her tight. Jack kissed her.

"You're sure you're going to be okay?" he asked.

She gave him a look that was clearer than any words. It said, "We both know who should be worried about whom here."

He kissed her again and took a step back, his fingertips on hers, neither wanting to let go. But then he took another step back, and their arms swung back to their sides. "I love you."

She smiled and gave her best Han Solo impersonation. "I know."

A lopsided grin spread across his face, and he turned toward the loaded RAV. "Okay, Joey, let's load up!"

"Aye-aye, Capt'n," he said in a pirate accent.

Jack raised an eyebrow. "We're going camping, Joe, not scallywagging."

Stacey mouthed "scallywagging" back to him in a question, and he shrugged.

Joseph climbed in the back seat and buckled himself in. Closed the door.

Jack looked at Stacey over the roof of the car. "We'll be back."

"In a week," she reminded him.

"We'll see," he whispered, and then got behind the wheel.

"You packed my bag, right, Dad?" Joseph asked.

"Yup, it's right behind you." He turned the key and brought the engine to life. He rolled down the windows, but Stacey was already back on the porch. His watch buzzed. He looked down and saw the text: LUV U.

"Here we go," he said, backing out of the driveway. He joined Joseph in waving out the window as he hit the gas and moved them toward a new adventure.

4

YOU HUNGRY?" JACK ASKED, stealing a glance at Joseph in the rearview mirror.

"Yeah," he said without looking up from his book.

"Me too. How 'bout that place we went to with Mom on Mother's Day?"

"Yeah, sure." This time he did look up from his book. "Dad?"

"Yeah, sport?"

"Do you really want to go camping?"

Jack laughed at what he pretended to be an absurd question. "Of course I do. Look at this!" He held up his arm so that Joseph could see the watch. "Do you know how much I paid for this thing? It's got GPS and everything. You saw my knife, right?"

Joseph smiled. "And your axe."

"That's right. I've been planning this trip for a long time." When he came to a red light, he turned around in the seat and faced his son. "But I do have a little secret." He feigned embarrassment. "I am a little nervous."

"Why?"

"Because I've never been camping before, and I don't really know what to expect. Plus, we'll be in the wild."

"I know. It's gonna be awesome."

"Yeah, but to tell you the truth...I'm kinda scared of—"

"Of what?" And a "you've-got-to-be-kidding-me" look came over his face. "Not of bears."

Jack shrugged and looked away. "Weeeeell..."

"Are you serious?" He laughed in genuine incomprehension. "Dad, black bears are the only bears in the east."

"And black bears are friendlier than the brown ones?" The light turned green, and he turned his eyes back to the road.

Joseph put a hand to his forehead and shook his head in disbelief. "Uh, yeah, considering that in the United States the brown bears are grizzly bears."

"What about Russian Bear?" he asked in his best Russian accent while making a muscle. He knew that Joseph wouldn't get the reference, but he didn't care. He got pleasure out of it just the same.

"What are you even talking about?"

He laughed. "It was a commercial on TV when I was growing up."

"Okay..." He looked up at the rearview and made eye contact in the reflection. "Seriously, though, black bears aren't that big of a deal. They might come into camp looking for a snack—from a backpack, not you—but you can just hang our stuff up in a tree if it makes you feel better."

"It might."

"And if you see one, just don't run."

"Don't run. Got it."

"If you slowly back away, it should do the same. If it doesn't, try changing the direction you're walking in."

Jack scratched at his jaw. "And if it's still coming at me?"

"If it's still coming at you, especially if its starts huffing and waving its paw around, then you want to start screaming. Throw rocks at it."

"Really? And that won't just piss it off?"

"You have to intimidate it. Make yourself seem bigger."

"Would you recommend that for, say...a polar bear?"

"Yeah...no. If it's a polar bear, you better hope you're not alone and that you're faster than the other guy."

"Nice."

They drove over Scudder Falls Bridge and into Pennsylvania.

"Besides," Joseph added, "you have the bear spray, right?"

"Yup. Never leave home without it."

Joseph smiled.

HMM… THINK I'M GOING with the triple stack of French toast, two eggs, bacon, and hash browns," Jack said, staring at the menu.

"Holy crap, Dad."

Jack looked up. "What?"

"You know you're gonna have to dig a hole for that."

He sat up straight and deepened his voice. "I plan on filling many holes, my son."

Joseph shook his head and looked back to his menu. "I think I'm gonna get what I got last time."

"You remember what you got last time?"

"Pancakes."

Jack thought about that. They'd only been here once last Mother's Day. Over a year ago. But he supposed it wasn't all that surprising that most twelve-year-olds could probably remember stuff from when they were ten and eleven. *But could they remember when they were four?*

Jack nodded his approval. "How many?"

"Five."

"Five? Do you remember how big those pancakes were?" *Do you remember the feeling of cold steel slicing through your throat?*

He used his hands to answer the question, indicating a circle about as big as a dinner plate. Then he smiled. "I'm gonna fill more holes than you."

"That sounds like a challenge."

"Oh, it is."

"Alright, Joey Crapper, what do you think of this?" He started moving his hands across the table, creating a visual. "I read that if you're going to be in one spot for a little while, it's better to dig a trench and fill it in as you go."

Joseph thought about it. "Makes sense. Okay, then the longest trench wins."

"You're on."

"Good thing Mom's not here."

They both laughed.

After the waitress took their orders, Jack pulled a piece of paper from his back pocket and unfolded it. It was a printout of a map. Then, out of habit, he quickly took note of everyone else in the restaurant. Thanks to Stacey's training, he knew what to look for. And thankfully, he found none of it here.

When his eyes returned to Joseph, he found that his son was staring at him with something akin to suspicion on his face.

"What?" Jack asked.

Joseph squinted as if trying to solve some kind of mystery and then looked around the room himself.

Jack immediately thought of the show *The Americans* that coincidentally came out just after the events of eight years ago. Thought about how the husband and wife KGB team had tried to hide their true identity from their kids. How their daughter had begun to grow suspicious of certain aspects of their lives that stopped making sense once she was old enough to notice. He wondered if Joseph was similarly beginning to pick up the scent of elephant crap in their own lives.

"Why do you do that?" Joseph asked.

"Do what?"

"Look at everyone in the room. In the parking lot. Like you think one of them might have a gun or something."

Jack blinked. *This just happened.* He thought about what to say. Shrugged. "I don't know what you're talking about."

"Denying it just makes it more intriguing."

"Intriguing?"

Joseph leaned forward and whispered across the table, "Did you, like, rob a bank or something a few years ago?"

"What?" Jack blurted.

"Whenever we go anywhere, you're always looking at everyone like you're afraid someone's gonna arrest us or shoot us."

"Yeah, well, the world's a crazy place."

"Are you a crazy person?"

Jack blinked again, unable to find immediate words. He knew the day would come when he'd introduce his son to Jerry, but he always imagined it would happen over a high school homework assignment on the Vietnam War or the Bay of Pigs or the JFK assassination. Not over breakfast with a twelve-year-old. He could almost hear the next question: *And how did I really get this scar on my neck anyway?*

"Do you think I'm a crazy person?" Jack asked.

"Nah. Just paranoid."

Damn straight. "Maybe a little."

"Why?"

"I'll tell you what. Why don't we continue this conversation around a campfire?"

"Okay."

"Good. Now"—he pointed at the map—"this is where we're going, to this campsite."

"What's that?" Joseph asked, pointing half an inch northwest.

"That's a shelter. It's about half a mile from the campsite, so if we need to, we can stay there."

"Why would we need to?"

"I don't know. Polar bears, tsunamis, Sasquatch, mountain lions."

"Mountain lions are extinct in these parts."

"Really?" Jack asked. "I'll have to tell your mother."

"Think we can hike some of the Trail?"

"The Appalachian Trail? Sure. We'll be right next to it."

"What if we hiked all the way to Maryland?"

Joseph's eyes lit up with such a sense of adventure that Jack actually considered it for what probably amounted to a whole nanosecond. "Yeah, I don't know about all that. Maybe we could hike north a few miles though." And he saw some of the adventure fade from Joseph's eyes. It was the idea of walking into another state that had excited him. Walking further north into Pennsylvania was no big deal. "Well, how far is Maryland?" The map was a zoomed-in printout of the area they were staying, but the legend had made the cut, as did a little of the area beneath Pennsylvania. He put his thumb next to the legend, the line about the length of his thumbnail, and then added up how many thumbnails it took to get from the shelter to the state line. "Dude," he said, looking up. "That's like sixteen miles."

"So?" But it was obvious from his expression that he knew it wasn't going to happen.

"I'll tell you what. If this trip goes well, and we don't get Sasquatched—"

"Is that a thing?"

"Oh, yeah... Happens all the time."

"That's what the axe is for?"

"I'm like Abraham Lincoln Vampire Hunter with that thing. You have no idea. But seriously," Jack continued, "if this is good, maybe we come back someday just to hike the Trail. Maybe do a couple states."

Joseph stared at the map. "Someday, I want to do the whole thing. All 2,193 miles, all fourteen states."

"Really?"

"Dad, it's the longest hiking path in the world. Who wouldn't want to walk the whole thing? It's like climbing Mount Everest."

Jack thought he'd rather kill himself, but he just nodded instead. "You'd have to do some serious training for that. Could take a person seven months to complete the whole Trail." The thought of spending seven months out in the wilderness, crapping in holes and trying to start fires every night, almost gave him a panic attack right there in the restaurant.

"Only about a quarter of the people who try it actually make it," Joseph said.

"How do you know so much about it?"

"It's called the int-er-net." He said it as if he were speaking to a cave man.

Jack threw a sugar packet at him. "If you like the woods so much, why don't you work for the Bureau of Forestry when you grow up?"

"There's a Bureau of Forestry? Like the FBI for forests?"

"Yup. The FBF. You know what their primary objective is?"

"What?"

"Investigating Sasquatchings."

Joseph threw the sugar back at him.

"No," Jack explained, "I think it's a state job. At least in Pennsylvania. Not sure if Jersey has one or not."

Joseph seemed to think about it. "I could be a park ranger."

"Yes, you could."

At that point, the waitress came over with their food, and Jack folded up the piece of paper and stuck it back into his pocket.

As they dug into their breakfast, Jack thought about shooting a secret text to Stacey under the table, letting her know that their son was onto them, but he wasn't sure he'd get away with it. Seemed his son had a bit of his mother in him. Next would be school papers on spycraft. Jack would have to steer him away from Joseph Green Secret Agent and toward Joseph Green Park Ranger instead.

"When did you start to like the woods, anyway?" Jack asked through a mouthful of French toast.

"Think when I was seven or eight. When I saw *The Revenant*."

Great, Jack thought, *the kid remembers when he was seven?* That was only three years removed from what he hoped would take a lot of hypnosis sessions to bring back. "You saw *The Revenant*?"

"Yeah, at Gordon's house."

"You have a friend named Gordon?"

"That's his last name, but everyone calls him that."

"Everyone as in all your seventh-grade classmates?" He reached for his coffee. They'd only just crossed the Delaware, and he felt like he was already getting an education in how much he didn't know his boy. But then, that was what this trip was for, right? "I don't think I started calling friends by their last names until college."

"Well, they say kids grow up a lot faster these days."

"That's what they say, huh?"

Joseph nodded. "Pretty soon, I'll be older than you." He shoved a sausage link into his mouth.

"Now isn't that a thought." Then he pointed his fork at him. "You know you'll be seeing that sausage again, right?"

Smiling, he nodded and ate another.

Suddenly, the color went out of Jack's face, and he sat up straight. "What are we gonna do about toilet paper?"

Joseph stopped chewing. "What do you mean?"

"Can we bury toilet paper in a hole?"

"Are you serious?"

"I've never been more serious."

"Your book didn't say anything about toilet paper?"

"I don't remember." He dug his phone out of his pocket and managed to find an answer in two minutes. "Says to bury TP deep, but they recommend packing it so that animals don't dig it up." He wiped his brow with the back of his hand. "That was close, pal. Don't know if I could take rubbing poison ivy all up in there."

"Why would you use poison ivy?"

"I wouldn't. Not on purpose."

"You don't know what poison ivy looks like?"

Jack picked up a piece of bacon. "It looks like your face."

Joseph laughed. Jack laughed. Things were off to a good start.

"Here, look at this," Jack said, sliding his phone across the table.

"What the heck is that?" Joseph's grin seemed to swallow his entire face. He tapped the phone and brought back from antiquity the Russian Bear commercial.

They laughed harder.

JOSEPH CLIMBED INTO THE back seat, and Jack closed the door for him. Then he walked around the back of the RAV and to the driver's side. As he reached for the handle, his watch beeped. A text message.

HW WS BRKFST?

Stacy never let any vowels into her texts. He wasn't sure what they'd ever done to her, but she had no tolerance for the way they took up space.

He pulled his cell from his pocket and shot back a quick response—with vowels.

GOOD. BUT GONNA NEED TO TALK ABOUT...THINGS. HE'S ASKING QUESTIONS.

He dropped the phone back in his pocket and climbed behind the wheel.

"What were you doing?" Joseph asked.

"Mom texted me. Wanted to know how breakfast went."

"And?"

"And I told her you got us thrown out."

He smiled.

"Alright," Jack said, running a hand through his hair. He caught his own reflection in the rearview and leaned forward, examining himself. "We *are* getting shaggy, aren't we?" He turned and looked at Joseph, who was running a hand through his own hair.

"I like it," he said.

"You like it, or you like that Mom doesn't like it?"

Joseph grinned. "Both." Then he looked at his dad. "You think my hair will turn black like yours?"

"I doubt it. Might get darker as you get older, but I don't think you'll ever be black."

He frowned. "Guess I could dye it."

"How 'bout you concentrate on growing your beard first." He raked his fingers through his own. "Then you can talk about dying your hair."

"Okay."

Jack put the RAV in reverse and backed out of the parking spot. "T-minus three hours. You sure you don't have to use the bathroom?"

"And give you a head start on the poop trench? No way."

"Suit yourself, but we ain't stopping."

"Roger that."

Jack pulled out of the parking lot and headed back to 295.

"Dad?"

"Yeah?"

"What made you choose this campsite?"

"What do you mean?"

"Why not north, in New Jersey? The Trail goes through the top of our state."

He thought about it. Camping in northern Jersey had never even crossed his mind. "I don't know, I guess I'm more familiar with these roads since I grew up in Philly. This way I get to drive through all the places I used to go."

"Like where?"

"Well, we're going to pass Newtown, Fairless Hills, and Core Creek Park, and Sesame Place, and then Feasterville, Willow Grove, and King of Prussia—not that you're going to be able to see much from the turnpike, but I know what's out there. Used to have friends all throughout the area."

"Like a trip down memory lane, then."

"I hadn't really thought about it, but yeah, maybe. My grandmom used to drive me all over. She took me to Sesame Place every summer."

"Not your mom and dad?"

Jack's eyes darted to the mirror. "I don't remember too much of my parents."

"Did they die?"

Jack couldn't believe they were having this conversation. That they'd never had it before—apparently. "I never told you about them?"

He saw Joseph shake his head.

"They died when I was six."

"How?"

"Car accident." And he could see in his son's eyes that he was applying that knowledge to all manner of filters, his perspective recalibrating on the spot.

"That sucks."

Jack studied the lines in the road as they flew past. "Yeah. It sure did."

They drove in silence for a few minutes, and then Joseph said, "I miss Grandma."

The car could have easily went off the road at that point, but Jack managed to keep it between the lines. He swallowed. Felt the heat begin to rise in his face. "I wasn't sure you remembered your grandmother."

"I remember a little bit." He was staring out the window. "What was her name?"

"Viktoriya."

"How did she die?"

Your mother's ex-husband threw a steak knife into her eye. "She… was old." He quickly tried to turn the conversation elsewhere. "She loved you though. Loved you to death."

"We don't have any pictures of her."

Jack blinked. "Sure we do."

"Not on the walls or anything."

That's because she was a KGB agent… "We have some in photo albums."

"Can I see them?"

"Of course." He propped his elbow against the door and leaned his head against his fist. He looked up into the mirror again and studied his son. He wondered how long he'd been thinking about this stuff. Why he'd never said anything before. He looked at the scar across his neck and knew it was only a matter of time before that became the biggest question of all. Someday (and sooner rather than later, it seemed), he was going to start adding things up. And what answers were his parents going to have waiting for him when he wanted to cross-check his answer?

Or, *What if he actually remembers everything? What if he never forgot any of it?*

He needed to get them out of the past and into the present before another question could come. "Hey, if you'd rather go to Sesame Place instead of the campsite, I totally understand."

"Yeah, right."

"You sure? You could get your picture with Elmo..."

"Very funny."

"Okay, okay. Just putting it out there since we'll be passing it."

Joseph leaned forward. "You sure the real reason you picked this campsite isn't because it's only half a mile from the nicest shelter on the whole Trail?"

He laughed. "Man, you are definitely your mother's son."

"Well?"

"It may have influenced the decision a little." He held his forefinger and thumb up, half an inch separating them.

"You're not planning on ditching the campsite, are you?"

"What? No! It's just that...if something goes wrong, we'd have a nice place we could stay at. A lot of the other shelters along the Trail are basically small pavilions. First come, first serve. This place has cabins."

"But you're not planning on going there."

"Nope."

"Okay..."

But Joseph didn't ask the question that was suddenly so glaringly obvious to Jack. Why camp near the Trail at all? There were plenty of other campsites closer. He supposed it was Jerry who had really picked someplace so close to the wilderness. That part of him that wondered what it would be like if they'd ever needed to escape the cities and survive in the woods. If they could do it.

His watch beeped again. Stacey had responded to his text with an emoji that looked a little worried, a little puzzled.

Tell me about it.

He followed the signs for the PA Turnpike and entered the CASH ONLY booth. He reached out the window and took the ticket, and as he headed for the on-ramp, he checked his mirrors to make sure there were no black SUVs following them. He figured that anyone who had been tossed off a cruise ship in the middle of the night by masked men would still do the same.

5

STACEY GREEN POURED ANOTHER cup of coffee from the fresh pot she'd made. She didn't know what had gone wrong with the brew Jack had conjured. She took the mug to the front porch and sat on the rocking chair that faced the Delaware River on the other side of the street.

She rocked back and forth absentmindedly, two hands wrapped around what was in effect Jack's porcelain *Tremors* movie poster. It was a cool morning, not as humid as most, though the forecast said it would be eighty-eight by three. She couldn't believe she'd actually let them go. She didn't think she would ever let them out of her sight again. But things seemed to have settled down, and she didn't think there was a present danger to any of them now. She'd told Jack that she hadn't spotted any activity in years. That was true. From a certain point of view.

She sipped the coffee, her gaze captured by the moving water rushing along the bank a hundred and fifty yards away. Sunlight sparkled in its reflection, and birds darted in and out of the light show.

The text from Jack had her concerned, but she told herself not to worry about it until she had more information. Jack could be paranoid—*no thanks to me*—and it was possible that he was just overreacting to what had been an innocent question. But she knew better. Yeah, Jack could be paranoid, but he wouldn't bring all that stuff up unless he had to. His pretending that the events of eight years ago never happened had been his coping mechanism. Which had worked out well for her, as it kept him from digging too deep and asking too many questions. It had also eased the mind of the Agency, which had begun to see Jack as a liability.

She often wondered what was really going through his head though, what psychological damage had been done. No one could go through what he'd endured without accumulating scars. From believing she had cancer and then finding out that it was all a deception meant to get him onto a boat so that he could be tossed overboard in the middle of the night... From the torment of trying to find Viktoriya and Joseph afterward... Their son having his throat slit right in front of him, which alone would be enough to render most people unstable... Learning about her and Vadim and the question she was sure he still asked himself in the middle of the night: was Joseph really *his* flesh and blood? Their house burned to the ground... Killing a person with his bare hands... And of course, the cherry on top of it all, that October 17 night... The event in Trenton.

Jack still played the good husband, the loving father, but she knew there were demons in there somewhere. There had to be. Lots of them.

She sat there for another twenty minutes until her coffee was gone, thinking about her life. Where she'd started, what she'd done. The guilt came, as it always did, but the "end justifies the means" philosophy she adhered to came through on cue and exonerated her once again. Jack didn't share in that belief, which was one of the reasons she'd had to keep so much from him. He wouldn't understand.

She then thought about what they'd lost, that empty room upstairs. And then more guilt came...for the way she'd used her pregnancy to manipulate Jack into staying quiet. No, she hadn't planned the pregnancy for that reason. Or maybe she had. It always got fuzzy here, the pain of what actually happened blurring her original intent. If she did, she argued, then this time it would've been as a countermeasure to save Jack's life. To save their family.

She stood. Waved to the neighbor next door.

She needed to exercise, to hit the bag. Needed to beat these feelings out of her. *Is this what it's going to be like all week?* she wondered. *Alone in the quiet, with nothing to distract me from the past?*

She'd work out, take another shower, and then head into town. It was almost ten o'clock now. She didn't have to be at work until one, and she didn't want to spend the day sitting around waiting to leave. Maybe she'd go shopping, visit the bookstore. Hell, maybe she'd call out of work and catch one of the movies Jack would never go see with her. *There's a thought...*

As she reached for the door handle, she turned and quickly surveyed the front of their property. Everything looked to be in order. But just as she was about to turn her head, a cardinal landed in the driveway, its bright red feathers like a flash of fire on the asphalt next to her black Ford Edge. It captured her attention instantly. She stepped back from the door and walked to the railing. The bird flew away.

But there was something else in the driveway.

She stepped off the porch, her eyes darting left and right. She walked beside the Edge and stopped when she got to where Jack's RAV had been. She crouched down. Picked the thing up.

Then she went back inside to get her phone.

JACK DROVE ONTO THE gravel lot and pulled up against a row of pine trees. He turned the car off and stretched while letting out a big yawn. Here they were. He killed the music, which they had started blasting around the hundred-mile mark, and turned in his seat.

"Ready for this?" he asked Joseph.

"I was born ready." He opened the door and hopped out.

Jack opened his own door and stepped down onto the stones. He looked around and spotted a dirt path that cut through the grass and disappeared into the woods. A sign at the end of the lot where the path started said CAMPSITE and had an arrow that was pointing toward the mountains. There were no other cars parked on the lot, though he supposed there could be other lots scattered around the area.

Joseph came walking around the back of the Toyota with his backpack already on and ready to go. "C'mon, Dad. We gotta make camp before sunset."

"Sunset?" He looked at his watch, recalling the alarm he'd set to remind him of that very thing. "It's not even noon yet." He noticed that he'd gotten another text from Stacey. He must have missed it while they were rocking out down I-76.

"I'm not sure how long it's going to take us."

And by "us" he clearly meant "you." Jack shook his head. "We'll be set up in time for lunch. You just wait and see."

Joseph looked at his own watch. "Yeah, right."

"Unbelievable. You and your mother..." He started pulling the gear out of the car.

When he had everything in a pile and ready to start loading it on his person, he stopped and went back to the car. Began looking on the seats. Under the seats.

"What are you looking for?" Joseph asked.

"The hotspot. It was right on the passenger seat."

Joseph came over and helped him search the entire car. When they didn't find it, he asked, "Are you sure you didn't pack it in one of the bags?"

"Yeah, I kept it on the passenger seat next to me all week. I remember seeing it last night when I was loading the car."

He pulled out his cell and read the text from Stacey.

U FRGT SMTHNG. CLL ME.

"Crap." He checked the signal. It was weak, but it was there. He dialed. As he waited for her to answer, he asked Joseph, "Hey, Mom ever say anything about vowels to you?"

Joseph looked at him the way anyone would after being asked such a question.

"It's just that she never uses them when she texts. Except she used a *U* and an *E* in *me*, because how else would you—" He held up a hand, letting Joseph know that she'd answered. "Hi. Where?" He sighed and leaned against the car. "Must've knocked it out with the stuff I put on the seat. No, it's fine. Probably don't need it anyway. If there's no signal at the campsite, we can always walk back here. Got a couple bars." He shot Joseph a thumbs-up. "Nope, we're good. Have some competitions lined up you don't want to know about—"

Joseph smiled and adjusted his pack.

"Okay. Yup. Love you. Be careful. I don't know, just…be good. I will. Okay, here he is." He held the phone out to Joseph. "Mom wants to talk to you."

Joseph took the phone. "Hey, Mom."

Jack put on his belt pouch with the knife and other essentials and locked up the RAV. Then he lifted the pack and slipped his shoulders through the straps. "Okay, I will. Love you too," he heard Joseph say.

"Here." He handed the phone back.

Jack slipped it into his pocket. "Alright, here we go." They picked up the rest of the stuff and headed for the path.

"How far away do you think it is?"

"Shouldn't be too far," Jack said.

They stepped off the gravel and into the grass. Trees surrounded them on either side and grew denser as they went.

"Is it a big deal?" Joseph asked.

"What's that?"

"The hotspot."

"Nah. It's a satellite hotspot, so we would've had Wi-Fi whether there was a cellular network in range or not. I could make a phone call, send texts, maybe look stuff up, send out an SOS. But looks like we have cell service—at least in the parking lot—so we should be just fine."

"You know, the settlers and Native Americans didn't have phones."

"They didn't have cars either. Did you want to walk here?"

"Just sayin'."

"Yeah, I hear you sayin' it too."

"I'll tell you what," Joseph said, skipping along. "If I see a Sasquatch, I'll grab your phone and run as fast as I can to the car and call 911."

"If we don't have a signal at the campsite."

"Right."

Jack looked down at him and grinned. "Or you planning on leaving me to the Bigfoot and making a run for it yourself?"

He shrugged. "You lived your life."

Jack laughed and ruffled his hair. "C'mon. We only have about nine hours until sunset."

JOSEPH LOOKED LIKE HE was walking through undiscovered territory. Like he was an explorer who had just landed on a foreign planet. His eyes never looked so big, not even when meeting Snuffleupagus at Sesame Place for the first time. He was in a constant state of wonder, unable to take his eyes from all the trees and flowers that surrounded them. Jack couldn't tell if he was legitimately in awe of the scenery or if he was hoping to catch a glimpse of Bigfoot. But if he was this excited to be at a campsite, then some of the sights on the Appalachian Trail would knock his socks off. He decided they would go in the next couple of days. Maybe not to Maryland, but they'd spend a good portion of the day hiking what they could. He'd read that the Trail through Pennsylvania had a bad reputation among thru-hikers because of how rocky it was and how many rattlesnakes there were. He didn't want any part of snakes. *Yet here I am.* Snakes, Sasquatch, and bears...oh my.

They let the packs slide off their backs and stretched.

"What do you think?" Jack asked.

Joseph gave a thumbs-up.

"Hey, do you know what the five Ws are when picking a place to camp?" Jack asked.

A breeze carried a strand of his hair into his eyes, and he brushed it away. His blue eyes sparkled. "Water."

"That's one."

"Wood."

"That's two."

Joseph looked around and tried to imagine what other considerations they would have made had they not been given a campsite already prepared. He couldn't think of anything else that started with a *W*. "I give up."

"You got water. Water should be close, and it should be moving water." He peered through the trees. "We'll have to find it." He knelt to tie his boot. "Is there enough wood nearby to last the whole trip? And what kind of wood is it? Apparently, there's cooking fire wood and heating firewood. Though to be honest, I couldn't tell you which of these trees are cedars and which are oaks."

"Most of these are oaks," Joseph said.

Jack squinted. "What, do you keep a stack of *Ranger Rick* magazines under your bed or something?" Though he could think of worse things.

"Who's Ranger Rick? Sounds like a perv."

Jack laughed. "He's a raccoon. Never mind. The other Ws are wind, widowmakers, and wildlife."

A picnic table stood in the little clearing that was the campsite, and Jack transported some of the equipment to it. Started laying it out across its peeling surface. "Want to make sure the wind isn't gonna blow smoke in your face all night or start a raging fire." He looked at Joseph. "You do know who Smokey the Bear is?"

"No." He set some more stuff onto the table.

Jack dropped what he was holding and put both hands over his heart. "My son doesn't know who Smokey is..."

"What's the widowmaker?"

"Dead trees that could fall in a strong wind."

Joseph looked up at the trees around them. "Guessing wildlife means not setting up camp in a bear's den or under a hornet's nest."

"I guess. I didn't read that part." He checked his watch. "Do you want to gather some stuff for a fire?"

"Sure."

"Okay, stay close where I can see you. Try to find hardwood. They say that's best for cooking."

"Why?"

"They say it doesn't have the resins and oils that soft wood has."

"Hardwood. Got it."

"Like oak or hickory or something."

"Or something."

"And watch out for rattlesnakes."

"And Sasquatch."

"That goes without saying."

Joseph headed for the woods, and Jack watched after him, wondering what he'd bring back. Once Joseph was out of the clearing and concentrating on the ground in front of him, Jack reached into his pack and pulled out his book. He flipped it open to the chapter on setting up camp and quickly went over his notes. Then, before Joseph could turn around and spot him, he shoved the book back into the pack.

"Okay... Let's get this done," he whispered to himself. Birds sang their songs around him, cheering him on.

AFTER SETTING UP THE tent, collecting enough firewood for the night, and Joseph getting a head start on their wager, they'd gone in search of the water they knew must be nearby. They found it by following a small footpath a hundred and fifty yards west of them (Jack keeping a careful eye on his watch's pedometer and compass the whole time). It had led through the woods and between some underbrush that was dense enough to block the sight of the river running past it on the other side. By then it was close to one o'clock, and they were hot and thirsty. So they walked all the way back to the car, grabbed the cooler, and carried it back to the camp.

And now here they were. Sitting on a pair of big rocks, the sun beating down on them, their feet in the water, and ice-cold sodas in their hands.

"You ever wonder what it was like before we got here?" Joseph asked. The moving water seemed to have him in a trance.

Jack stopped scanning the riverside for slithering serpents and thought about it. "Like a couple hours ago, or—"

"Like before Christopher Columbus. When the Native Americans lived here."

"I think they lived here a little after Columbus too."

"You know what I mean."

The roiling and churning and bubbling of the water was symphonic. Like the crashing surf on a secluded beach. Across from them, about a hundred feet away on the opposite bank, trees spread their branches and bent over the water, dipping their green fingers into the liquid dance.

"Yeah," Jack answered. "But I usually have that thought when I'm standing in a Walmart parking lot." He took a sip of the soda, wishing he had some of the other Jack to add to it. "Then I think before then. Like the dinosaurs."

Joseph nodded. "Like *The Time Machine* book we read in school! What if we got in a time machine right now, set the calendar to a thousand years ago, and arrived at this exact spot?"

"I don't know. You'd have to be careful what time of the year you choose. Could be we appear right in the middle of a Sasquatch spring break."

He laughed and took a sip of soda himself. "Does Mom know you brought these?"

"The soda? Of course. We don't keep stuff from each other." He thought he saw his nose grow a foot longer in the shadow he was casting onto the water, or maybe it was a cigarette extending from his mouth. But no, it was just a stick that happened to float by his phantom self at that exact moment.

"Thought this stuff was poison," he said, holding it up and examining the can.

"It is. Except when you're camping."

"Can we go fishing?"

"Sure. I have some string and hooks. We'll find sticks and make some rods. You want to get up early and catch some trout for breakfast?"

"Yeah!"

They wiggled their toes in the water and sipped their sodas.

"Oh," Jack said, thinking of something. "Don't ever drink the water without boiling it first. Even though its flowing pretty good, you don't want to take the chance of getting some brain-eating amoeba."

"Yeah. Or fish piss."

"Or fish piss."

"Cheers, Dad," Joseph said, holding the can out.

"Cheers, dude."

They clinked cans, drank, and then burped.

7

JACK PUT HIS HANDS on his hips and looked down at their work. "Looks pretty good to me," he said.

Joseph nodded in agreement.

They'd followed the instructions in Jack's book on how to make a Dakota firepit. The book said that these types of fires got really hot and would be good for pit forging. He hadn't planned on any forging, but he thought it might be a fun project.

They had dug two nine-inch holes two feet apart from each other and connected them with an underground tunnel. They'd sloped the side of the intake hole toward the breeze in order to boost airflow and then set a big rock on the ground between the two holes.

Jack looked at his watch. "Guess we'll start on the fire lay. Thinking about going teepee. What do you think?"

"Sounds good."

"You wanna work on the bird's nest?"

"Yeah."

"All right. It says that the materials for a bird's nest are best if they're a little green or a little damp. Says grass is okay to mix in with bark. About this size." He cupped his hands. "Like a softball."

"On it!" He ran to the edge of the clearing.

Jack went to look for a branch he could use as a crane over the pit and found one he thought would do just fine. Now he needed a stick that forked into a Y. That was a bit harder to find, but he found one eventually. He carried them back to the firepit and got the axe off the picnic table. He removed the mask and used the butt end to hammer the Y stick into the ground about six inches from the downwind hole. He set the branch onto it, testing its length. It looked good. He took the axe back to the table, masked it, and spotted Joseph nearby. He was bent over, picking stuff up off the forest floor. Jack stood and watched him for a minute, and a sense of paternal awe began swelling inside him, first as a subtlety and then as a flood. *Flesh of my flesh*, he thought. He didn't know it was possible to love this much, this hard. It was a different love though than other loves, this love between a man and his son, a parent and his or her child. The roots of it were deep, thick and intertwined way down into the soul.

These moments of realization didn't come often, but he thought that maybe they should. Work, school, everything scribbled on the calendar... Life just got too busy sometimes, and you forgot what you had, who you were with. How special it all was. He again thought of the day they'd almost lost him and wondered how they would ever have gotten past it if they had. He was pretty certain, with everything being what it was, that "they" wouldn't have made it. Not by a long shot.

And then out of nowhere, to steal the wonder of this bond he was feeling, came an equal and opposite sense of pain and loss. It came with a vision, as it sometimes did. An image as clear in his mind as if he were seeing it with his eyes—Joseph scavenging in the underbrush with his little sister right there alongside him, helping out and giggling at something unseen. And then she turns and looks back over her shoulder at him—at her dad—and smiles. And in that instant, the love that he has for Joseph is multiplied and swells to encompass this little blond-haired girl that looks so much like her mother. And as their eyes meet, a connection is formed. A bond so strong, so unique, so—

But then she's gone, and all that's left is the emptiness. The outline of what should have been. Of what maybe was going to be. Or, in some other way that he can't even begin to comprehend, even is.

The day they'd lost Baby Bethany (Beth-Beth, as Joseph had called her during the two short months they'd had together) was the worst day of his life. He'd had other bad days for sure, days that would haunt him for the rest of his life. But that day...

Joseph turned around. "Look," he said, running over and holding out the bird's nest he'd created. "What do you think?"

"Wow." Jack took it from him and examined it. "You sure you never did this before?"

"Make bird nests? Yeah, I'm sure."

"I don't know. By the looks of this, I'd have to assume you've got a secret stash of bird nests somewhere." He handed it back. "So where you keeping them? C'mon, jig's up. Spill it. Where you putting all your bird nests?"

Joseph sighed. "I don't keep them. I sell them."

"Sell them? To who?"

"To the birds in the neighborhood. The blue jays mostly. Saves them the trouble of having to steal someone else's."

Jack frowned. "I thought blue jays were in Toronto."

"Immigrants, I guess."

"Immigrants shouldn't be stealing other bird's nests."

"They're not, they're buying them from me."

He gave him that one. "So how much does one of those nests go for on the market?"

Joseph shrugged. "A robin's egg."

Jack scratched at his beard. "And where do they get a robin's egg from?"

"They steal them."

"And you accept these eggs, knowing they're stolen?"

"Why not? The robin isn't going to take it back, so it would just be a waste not to."

"But aren't you just perpetuating this kind of criminal activity by creating a demand for it?"

He thought about it.

"What do you do with the eggs, anyway?" Jack asked, curious to see where this would end up.

"I eat them."

"You eat the stolen babies?"

"Only the malted ones. The other ones I give to Mom and she hatches them in her secret lab. Sells them to the cats in the neighborhood."

Jack stared at him. "You are diabolical."

They walked back to the firepit.

"Okay, so we have the bird's nest to get the teepee going," Jack said. "Next time, do you want to try using a twig bundle or a feather stick?"

"Why can't we just use another nest?"

"What? Are you kidding me? We're here for a week, son. We're gonna try everything we can. We're gonna make feather sticks and keyhole fires and long fires, and we're gonna get good at making notches and chopping wood and splitting logs, you name it. I got a whole book of stuff we're gonna try. That is, if you're up for it."

Joseph's blue eyes sparkled with delight.

Jack smiled. "Okay, well, right now I'm going to carve the end of this branch so I can stick it into the ground, and then I'm going to make a log cabin notch at the end of it so we can hang a pot from it." He pointed toward their tent. "Can you go grab me that log and bring it over? I want something to sit on."

He ran over and carried it back. Dropped it on the ground next to the pit. "Guess someone left it here," he said.

"Looks that way," Jack responded. "Unless it was—"

"Sasquatch, I know!" He rolled his eyes.

"Should we call your future employer? Maybe we should see if there's any clumps of hair stuck to it first..."

"Is this going to be an all-week joke?"

"Probably."

"Wonderful."

Jack pulled out a pair of leather gloves from his back pocket before sitting on the stump. Then he slipped his belt knife out of its sheath. "You should wear gloves when carving with the tip of the knife if you have to choke up on the blade. You don't want to cut yourself out here. Take every precaution you can think of. It's always better to be looking at your fingers than for them."

"Ha-ha."

"You hold the knife in a safety grip, like this." He gripped it in his fist. "And you avoid the triangle of death. That's the space between your upper legs. You get cut there, you could hit your femoral artery, and you'd pretty much be a goner. Or you'd be wearing a tourniquet so long you'd probably lose your leg. Be hard to catch Sasquatch on one leg."

Joseph just shook his head, but his eyes were locked on the blade.

"If you're not alone, you have to check your blood circle."

"What the heck is that?"

"It's the area around you at arm's length. You shouldn't use a knife if anyone is closer than that. Unless you're trying to kill them, of course."

"Of course."

"Now, for carving the point, I'm going to use a knee lever." He got off the log and knelt. Then he held his knife hand against his opposite leg, pressing it against the inside of his knee. "You want to have as much control over the knife as possible and have it do most of the work for you. So I'm not going to move the blade, I'm going to move the stick." He drew the stick across the knife, shaving a long sliver of wood that curled on itself as he went. He did it a few more times, turning the stick each time. "You want to try?"

The way he nodded, you would have thought he was being handed the keys to a Lamborghini.

"Then here." He reached into his back pocket and pulled out another knife, this one a pocket knife, the blade folded into the handle. "Try it with your own."

The Lamborghini is yours, kid.

Joseph took the knife, and before Jack could even tell him how to work it, he had the blade snapped open. Christmas in June.

THEY HAD WALKED AROUND the woods to get a greater sense of their surroundings. They found a deer path, another campsite (which was unoccupied), and had followed the river to a bridge they would fish from in the morning. They hadn't seen another person, and the sense of being alone was beginning to sit on Jack's shoulders. He thought it was a little eerie, but Joseph seemed to love it all the more. *We're just two hours away from Lincoln Financial Field,* he kept reminding himself.

Now, two hours later, they were getting ready to start the fire and cook up some dinner.

"You sure you want to try this?" Jack asked. "I have a lighter."

"No, I want to do it all natural."

"Okay."

The bird's nest was between his feet, the teepee in the pit and ready to take it in. They'd carried large tree branches over and set them down nearby. They'd chop them up into fuel once the teepee was going.

"Here we go," Joseph said, and he began working the bow drill they'd made.

"Slow at first," Jack said. "If you go too fast out the gate, you'll create heat but nothing to light. Gotta get those shavings out of the board. That's gonna be your coal for the bird's nest."

The boy's arms were the small arms of a twelve-year-old, but they were strong. Jack could see the muscles flexing beneath his skin as he worked the bow, moving it back and forth, pushing it all the way through to the end of the string, and then all the way back, getting the most revolutions out of the spindle with each stroke.

Jack would be shocked if Joseph was able to get a coal going on his first try. He wasn't sure if the bearing block they'd chosen would work. The book was very specific about it needing to be a harder, denser wood than the board and spindle or else there would be too much friction at the block and not enough at the board where you needed it to be. But they weren't even using wood. They were using a rock, since Joseph's book said a rock was fine as long as it had a notch in it for the top of the spindle to rest in. Otherwise, the spindle would spin out from under the rock.

Joseph worked the bow back and forth, one of Jack's boot laces wrapped around the spindle and drilling it into the hearth board. Slowly, the board began to spit dust into the notch.

"Lock your block hand against your shin and use your leg to help put pressure on the spindle," Jack said. He was beginning to think this might just work. He got a big leaf and stuck it under the notch in the board to collect the coal. "Okay, now faster. Get heat to the dust."

He worked it faster, and they could smell the wood starting to smolder. Sweat dripped down Joseph's face. Then there was smoke.

"Oh, yeah! C'mon, Joe!"

Joseph gritted his teeth, the sweat getting into his eyes, the veins showing in his forearms. A spark appeared, and then a flame.

"You got it!" Jack yelled, laughing. "Grab the nest!" He pulled the leaf out from under the board. The coal resting on it was glowing hot.

Joseph held the bird's nest up, and Jack tipped the coal off the leaf. It landed right in the middle of the nest.

"Blow on it, nice and soft," Jack said.

Joseph did, and the nest began to burn.

Jack clapped his hands. "Okay, quick, put it in the teepee!"

Joseph got on his knees and bent over the pit. He carefully lowered the nest down and slowly set it inside. Then he grabbed a handful of sticks off the ground next to him and boarded the nest in.

"Let's see if this works," Jack said. He was getting excited now. "The air should flow down that hole and pass through the tunnel, providing a steady stream of oxygen to the coal. The teepee is designed to use the updraft—"

"The heat rises into the sticks, I know."

And sure enough, the teepee lit.

They jumped up and down, hollering like lunatics. Jack gave his best Tom Hanks impression, telling the sky that he had made fire.

"*I* made fire," Joseph protested.

"*He*"—Jack held his hands out toward Joseph—"has made fire!"

They high-fived each other and danced.

"Okay, okay, okay," Jack said, calming down. "We're not done yet. We got a fire going, but now we need to give it fuel to keep it going. But the books say not to add it until the flames are above the wood. Otherwise it won't have enough oxygen or something." He ran over to the picnic table and grabbed the axe. As he ran back with it, he said, "Don't ever run with an axe in your hand." Then he grabbed one of the tree branches and rolled it away from the rest. "Let's say we chop us some fuel."

"Yeah!"

"They say never use your knife when you can use your axe. So we're not using a knife. Then"—he got on his knees—"they say to swing from your knees if you can."

"So you don't miss and chop your shin."

"Yeah, that'd suck. I'd need you to pull it out, and that would probably hurt even more." Then he paused. "Actually, this is overkill." He placed the axe on the ground and stood. "Don't ever place an axe on the ground. Always lean it against a tree or something." And he grabbed the stick and set it against the log they'd sat on earlier. Then he brought his laced boot down on its center, and the stick cracked. "C'mon! Help me kung fu these things."

They kicked a dozen of them into twenty-four.

"Okay, the flames are shooting out the top now. Start putting the branches in." Jack let Joseph do that, and he enjoyed watching him do it. He was beginning to second-guess his initial feelings of this whole camping thing. Maybe there was something to it after all. "Now we need to get some green sticks to put across the hole."

Joseph hopped to his feet and took off for the woods. "Got it," he called back.

Jack went to get the bush pot and skillet and the stainless steel water bottles they'd filled up at the river earlier.

Ten minutes later, they were frying eggs and bacon and boiling chicken noodle soup and hot chocolate.

"This a mighty fine dinner, Pa," Joseph said, his mouth full.

"You mind yer manners now, ya hear?" Jack answered back. "No talkin' wit yer mouth full, or I'll have to whip yer hide some."

"Aww, Pa, don't talk about yer whippin's now," he said.

Jack leaned forward. "Yer still doin' it, boy! Talk wit yer mouth full one more time and you'll not be able to sit on that scrawny little crack of yers for a month!"

Joseph swallowed. "Sorry, Pa. I just meant to say that I sure love hot chocolate and soup for supper. Goes together like nothin' else in life, wouldn't ya say?"

"Aye, matey, that it does."

Joseph laughed so hard he farted and fell backward off the stump. "How are you a pirate again?"

"I'm a pioneer pirate, escapin' from Port Royal to the colonies. I got a wooden leg and a hook for a hand, what of it, lad? Are ye gonna make fun of me now too? 'Cause that's what had me in the noose the first time, I tell ya. Man started callin' my stump some unkind names, and I put my hook in where the sun don't shine, I sure did."

Joseph was rolling around, holding his stomach.

"Now I'm just tryin' to find the railroad. I heard it comes through this way, does it not?"

But he was laughing too hard to answer.

"What? Speak up, lad, I can't hear ya. I only got half a good ear, and I lost me hearing horn."

"What happened to them?" he managed to ask.

"What's that you say? What happened to me ears? Well, I'll tell ya, sonny. After I hooked the miserable wretch who called me wooden limb somethin' yer little ears should never hear, his wife come up from behind and grabbed both me Dumbos and yanked 'em straight off me head. Though she only got most of the one. I asked for them back nice and polite, thought maybe I could get 'em sewn back on, but she wasn't havin' it. She was screamin' about somethin', but I couldn't hear her 'cause she had me ears in her hands. I told her to stop spattin' in my face and to talk into me ears. So she did! She held me ears up and started yellin' in them. Didn't help none; I still couldn't hear nothin'."

Joseph climbed back onto the stump. "Sounds to me, mister, that you must've escaped the loony bin down yonder. The way yer talkin', you think yer a pirate one second and a settler the next. Yer sayin' things like 'Dumbo' and talkin' about the railroad and Port Royal, and I think they call that a case of the split personality. What's yer pirate name, sir?"

"Darko. Capt'in Darko."

"And what's yer other name?"

"Capt'in Darko only has one name. Unless yer referrin' to the stump, which ye better not be."

"Who's lookin' for the railroad?"

"That would be me, boy," he said in his cowboy.

"Who's me?"

"Wyatt."

They went on like that for another hour, until Jack's watch sounded at 7 p.m.

8

SHE DID END UP calling out of work, but she hadn't gone to a movie. Instead, she found herself in a coffee shop that overlooked the river, where she sipped iced tea and read. She'd only meant to sit there for an hour or so but ended up spending most of the day engrossed in her novel. It felt wonderful to relax, to not have to worry about making dinner or wonder what Joseph was doing. She was completely her own. No employer, no husband, no child, no mother, no country. Just her. Right now. All that other stuff would come back sure enough, and she would welcome them. But she would enjoy this moment of freedom while it lasted. Because she knew it wouldn't. The haunting silence at the house was waiting for her, and all the ghosts of the past—and present—with it.

She climbed behind the wheel of the Edge and set the book on the passenger seat beside her. She wondered what Jack and Joseph were doing right now, if Jack was losing his mind, or if the two of them were doing a fire dance and howling at the moon with painted faces, having the time of their lives.

She started the engine and looked at the dashboard clock. Almost seven. She drummed her fingers against the wheel, wondering what to do next. She thought about calling Jack, but settled on a text. And then thought better even of that. She shouldn't disturb them. This was their time.

And this is my time.

She knew what she would do. She drove out of the lot and headed for the cemetery.

SHE SAT DOWN IN the grass, Indian style, and stared at the marble slab. In seven years, she'd only come here twice. She wasn't exactly sure why. Or maybe she was, and it was her presence here now that she wasn't sure about.

Bethany Rose Green, the engraving said.

Rose was Jack's grandmother's name. Bethany was just a name she loved. She knew Jack liked it too. Around the time Jack had started going to churches, she'd picked up his Bible one day and found a passage about Bethany underlined. Jack had made a note in the margin next to it, saying that Bethany was the only place on earth where Jesus was always accepted. She didn't really know what that meant to Jack, whether the note was personal or educational. She'd never asked. In fact, she'd never asked him about any of it. The churches, the Bible reading, what he was thinking, feeling... She wondered if she should have. At the time, she figured she would just frustrate him, end up arguing or something. Thought it was best to give him his space. But now she wasn't so sure.

She looked up and moved her eyes back and forth over the smooth surface of her daughter's tombstone. The sun was lowering over the treetops to the west, and the cemetery looked like a picture beneath the red-orange sky. The clouds were dark with the coming night, purple even.

There were crosses everywhere, and she wondered about that. She imagined that it signified hope. Hope in something more than a hole in the ground. She wondered what it would be like to have that hope. To believe that her little Bethany wasn't really six feet under her right now, confined to a box until the elements consumed her and she was no more. To believe—no, to *know*—that there was more than all this. *What would it be like?* she thought. What if she'd been raised by someone like Jack's grandmother? *Is that what it all comes down to, who raises you?* But that couldn't be the whole story, could it? After all, here she was the daughter of KGB agents now a CIA operative working against her homeland.

She closed her eyes and reached out, her finger tracing the lines that gave expression to her daughter's existence. She went back to the memories of those days and found that they were a bit...less than the last time she'd visited them. That scared her, and tears suddenly burst forth. But she clung to what was there. The nights rocking her to sleep. The way her eyes shone when they focused on hers. The laugh. The little fingers wrapped tight around her thumb.

She'd loved every second of those moments. But she'd also been terrified of them, because beneath it all was that question of the future. Of what Beth would do if she ever found out what her mother had done. Even from day one, when handed her little girl for the first time, she'd known that her past was a ticking time bomb set to one day blow her and her little baby apart from each other. She'd seen it play out, everything between that moment and the impending detonation, all the memories, all the life spent together, suddenly ruined by revulsion, by mistrust and betrayal...

As it turned out, however, worrying about the future had all been wasted energy. Her daughter hadn't been given one.

Stacey opened her eyes and watched the sky burn in reds, yellows, purples, and oranges. She recalled Jack's position on beauty and wondered if it really could be a signature. And at that moment, she felt some kind of ethereal link between death and life, the above and the below, her daughter and the setting sun. She had no words for it, couldn't call it anything more than a sense of something great, something...there.

It took another ten minutes before she could move again. Then, once she could, she shifted her gaze to the right.

"Hello, Mother," she said. "I hope you two are behaving yourselves."

She'd meant to spend some time in front of her mother's stone too, but that would have to be for another time. She was emotionally spent now, and she just wanted to go home and cry herself to sleep. She stood, kissed her fingers, and then pressed them against her daughter's name.

She walked past Viktoriya's grave, running her hand over the top of its curved surface as she went. "I'll come back," she whispered.

After she got back in the car, she dialed Jack's cell. She needed to hear his voice, to know that they were okay. She wouldn't be able to talk to them tomorrow.

Tomorrow.

The thought of what she had to do the next day was another dagger into her guilt-ridden soul. Jack didn't deserve such deception, but it was the price she had to pay. It had been their only way out.

9

THEY WERE LYING ON their backs and staring upward. It was spectacular. The stars twinkled with silver fire, exploding across the night sky. The contrast was so brilliant that it seemed to be in 3D.

Jack looked over at Joseph and saw that his son's eyes were locked on the display, his mind fully engaged. He thought this could either be the God moment or the alien moment, he wasn't sure which. He didn't feel ready for either conversation, though talking about little green men would probably be safer. He didn't care whether Joseph would be the next UFO hunter or one of the Roswell weather balloon crowd. But would he care if he thought this was all a grand hoax? That life and beauty and justice and love all came from nowhere, out of nothing, and for no reason? He wasn't ready to go there, not when he was still wrestling with it all himself.

But that wasn't what was on Joseph's mind. At least not directly.

"Dad?"

"Yeah?"

"Do you miss her?"

Her. He wasn't sure whom he meant. There were a few possibilities. His mother? His grandmother? Viktoriya? "Miss who?"

Joseph turned his head and looked at him. "Bethany."

And all the stars in the heavens started falling from their places. "Yeah. Of course." He guessed that Joseph had overheard some of his conversation with Stacey when she'd called earlier. She'd gone to visit their daughter's grave and had called him to tell him about it on her way home. The reception was spotty, so the conversation was short, but Joseph must have heard him say her name.

"I don't really remember her." There was a sadness in his voice now.

"You were only five. And to be honest, there isn't much to remember. She was still sleeping a lot, and it wasn't like you two were running around together."

"I know. But I do remember holding her."

"You do?"

He saw the shape of his head move a little and knew he was nodding. "I used to call her Beth-Beth."

A fault line in Jack's heart began to tremble. "I had no idea you remembered that," he whispered.

"Is that why we don't talk about her?"

He blinked and looked back into the sky. "I don't know. I guess it's hard to talk about. And..." He trailed off, not knowing what to say.

"Do you think about her a lot?"

"Not as much as I should, I think. But it's strange when someone that young dies. You miss who she was, all the experiences you shared with her. But then you find yourself missing who you think she would have been too. And you have this fictitious character that never existed standing in as your seven-year-old daughter. But is that really what she would have been like? Who knows?"

There was silence for a while, just the crackling of the fire still going in the firepit.

"I think she would've been fun," Joseph said.

A tear escaped the corner of Jack's eye. "Yeah, I think so, too."

"Do you think she's up there somewhere?"

Another tear, and suddenly the heavens seemed to dance. "Yes."

They stared into the lighted map of eternity for another ten minutes before Jack sat up and looked at his watch. "If you want to get up early and go fishing, we should try to get some sleep." He stood and helped Joseph to his feet.

They walked to the tent. It was just a twenty-foot journey, but it was significantly darker since most of the firelight was concealed underground.

"Tomorrow night, let's try a long fire," Jack said. "We could just sleep out here under the sky."

"Sounds good—" He stopped.

"What is it?" Jack asked, stopping too.

"Thought I heard something."

"Like what?" Jack turned and followed Joseph's gaze into the surrounding darkness.

"I don't know. Like something walking."

"Like a bear?"

Joseph shrugged. "I don't think so. Maybe a fox or a rabbit or something."

"Or—"

"Don't even say it."

Jack laughed. "C'mon. Let's go to sleep." They started walking again.

"I heard you tell Mom that you wanted to put string with bells around the campsite."

"Yeah, I saw it in a cowboy movie. That way if something comes walking into camp"—he motioned toward the noise Joseph said he'd heard—"it'll wake us up."

"What did she say?"

"That I was paranoid."

They crawled into the canvas tent, and Jack turned on the LED lantern. The space was small, but Jack figured they didn't need that much space to sleep. The book said as long as they got a good four-hour sleep, they should be okay. Guess they'd find out.

"Get your sleeping socks," Jack said.

They took their socks off and exchanged them for the socks they would only be using while sleeping (this one was in both their books). Then they got positioned on the exercise mats (they were supposedly more versatile and easier to transport than ground pads), and pulled the wool blanket over themselves.

"Why didn't we just bring our sleeping bags?" Joseph asked.

"They say they get saturated with sweat and start to get funky. This here though"—he grabbed the top of the blanket with both hands and lifted it—"is one hundred percent handwoven virgin wool. Water resistant, flame retardant, and warm."

"You sound like a commercial."

"Well, we'll see how it goes. I have sleeping bags and an actual tent in the car. Thought you'd want to rough it though, wilderness style."

"This tent looks like it's from the Civil War." He yawned. "What if it rains?"

"I have the tarp." He started pushing buttons on his watch. "What time should we wake up?"

"I don't know. Six?"

"Six it is." Then he took out his phone and plugged it into the solar charger. "Pretty good day, huh?"

"Yeah it was. Thanks, Dad." He was holding his new knife in his hands, staring at the blade while he twirled it. "Maybe I'll name it Hugh," he said.

"Hugh? As in Hugh Hefner?"

"I don't know who that is."

"Was. And good."

"No, Hugh Jackman."

"Ah. Wolverine."

"Exactly."

"Because Wolverine would be too obvious."

He nodded.

"I like it." Then he said, "Actually, I think I might like this whole camping thing."

Joseph chuckled. "We'll see."

"Yeah, yeah. You and your mom. Hey, don't sleep with the knife, okay? Don't want you to roll onto it or anything."

He folded the blade and clipped it to the inside of his waistband.

Jack turned on his side and stared at him. It had been a good day. A great day. Their relationship had reached another level, and he'd learned things about his son that he hadn't known before. He felt guilty for not having known them, but now was better than never. He couldn't believe that Joseph remembered holding Bethany, or that he'd called her Beth-Beth. That wasn't too far removed from when he'd had his throat slit, and now he knew he'd have to find out what else he remembered. Whether he liked it or not, and whether he and Stacey were ready or not, he'd try to learn it this week. The thought of him carrying around that memory for the last eight years, unbeknown to them, was unfathomable.

He leaned over and kissed him on the head. "I love you," he whispered.

"Love you too, Dad."

Jack turned the lantern off, and they fell asleep to the sounds of the night.

10

THE KNIFE IN Vadim's hand—it stands still, paused. Sunlight from the window reflects off its edge and dances throughout the room. The knife. Pressed against Joseph's little neck. That enormous hand holding it. Could cut straight through. Was *going* to cut straight through. The knife pauses. A drop of blood seeps out of Joseph's skin and rolls onto the blade. The sun hits it, and the room goes red. Then the knife is in Viktoriya's eye. There's screaming. Vadim has his wife bent over the counter. Flames engulf their house. The ocean. It's vast and empty and terrifying in the night. And he's under the water, sinking. He can't breathe. He calls out for Donny, but he's not there. Where is he? There's a bomb. The countdown has begun. Someone is singing. Five. Four. Three. Two. One. *Beep. Beep. Beep. Beep.*

Jack opened his eyes and turned off the alarm on his watch. Then he returned his hands back to his sides and closed his eyes again. The dream was gone, but he was still left with the lingering panic of it. He took a deep breath, allowing the present to gradually replace the past.

He was surprised that he'd slept so soundly. He had no recollection of waking up at any point throughout the night, and if it weren't for the alarm, he might have slept for another hour or so. He yawned and stretched on the mat. There was a twinge of soreness in his back, but it wasn't anything a little stretching wouldn't take care of.

He looked over at Joseph, expecting to find him still sound asleep, but he wasn't there.

Jack sat up and rubbed his eyes. "Joseph?"

No answer.

He guessed his son was probably getting a head start on filling in his trench. Though he had told him not to leave the tent without first waking him up and letting him know. Or maybe Joseph had, and he'd responded with a thumbs-up in his sleep. Wouldn't be the first time he'd agreed to something while still in the throes of a dream.

He threw the blanket off and crawled out of the tent. He stood and stretched while sweeping his eyes back and forth. The surrounding woods were half hidden in mist, and the many trunks looked like shadowed pillars weaved in and out of some ethereal realm. The ground was wet with dew, and patches of cobwebs lit up like crystal in the early light. He looked down at his socks. He'd have to dry them out now.

"Joseph?" he called. He looked toward the tree line over where they'd dug their poop trenches. He expected to see him there squatting with a big grin on his face and two thumbs-up. But he wasn't there.

Jack walked forward a few feet and then turned back toward the tent. He'd made footprints in the dew that he could only see at a certain angle, when the light hit it just right. He looked for other footprints but didn't see any.

"Joe," he called, louder this time. Maybe he'd gone to the river to get water—which he knew he'd get in trouble for, well intentioned or not.

He ran a hand through his hair as a little flame sprouted to life in his gut. He went back into the tent to change his socks and to get his boots on. The speed at which he did this told him all he needed to know about the situation he faced, whether his brain had fully accepted it or not. Before leaving the tent again, he reached for his phone.

It was gone.

He blinked.

The solar charger was there, but the other end of the USB cord was empty. He tossed the blankets and flipped over the mats. Went through their packs as fast as he could.

Nothing.

Had Joseph taken his phone? Maybe Stacey had called and he'd answered it, left the tent so that he didn't wake him, searching for a stronger signal. A few scenarios like that flashed through his mind, but they did nothing to extinguish the fire that was now smoldering in the bird's nest that was his stomach.

He exited the tent, grabbing his belt pouch and fastening it around his waist as he jogged across the campsite. Then he stopped. Went back to the tent.

Joseph's boots were still there, so wherever he went, he'd gone in his sleeping socks. And his feet would be soaking wet.

Sleepwalking?

But Joseph didn't have a history of that. What if a bear had taken him? Dragged him out of the tent by his feet while he slept? And just like that, the scenarios that were popping into his head were no longer that innocent, and the flames in his belly were rising higher.

This time when he emerged from the tent, he sprinted past the firepit and straight into the mist.

He reached the river and went to its edge. Looked up and down its banks. Looked across. "Joseph!" he yelled. His voice echoed off the water. He stood still, listening for any kind of response.

Just the sound of the water moving past him.

He chased after the current, heading for the bridge they were planning to fish from. But it was empty. He ran halfway across it before stopping to look upriver, then downriver. He called out again, and again his voice echoed.

He ran back to camp.

"Joseph?" he said, running to the tent. But the tent was still empty. *The car*, he thought. It was the only place left that he could think of. Instinctively, he patted his pockets, looking for his keys. They weren't there. He thought back to the night before. Had he taken them out before going to sleep? He didn't think so. If he did, he would've put them in one of his boots. But they weren't in his boots, and he hadn't come across them while going through the tent looking for his cell phone just—he looked at his watch—seven minutes ago.

Seven minutes.

He was losing time. He ran for the car.

HE TOOK THE MIST-COVERED path, sprinting all the way back to the gravel parking lot. When he got there, he bent over, hands on knees, to catch his breath. He looked left and right, but his RAV was the only thing in the parking lot. He called for Joseph again, and again got no response.

He went to the car and tried the handle. Locked. He cupped his hands to his face and peered through the windows. No one was in there.

He took a step back.

His phone was gone. His keys were gone. His son was gone.

What the hell is happening?

Then he noticed the front tire. It was completely flat. He ran his hand over it and quickly discovered what appeared to be a railroad spike protruding from between the tread.

The fire in his gut reached a propane tank and exploded into a bonfire. His mind raced.

The shelter. It was truly the only thing left. That or the Trail, but there wasn't any way in the world Joseph would have gone to hike the Trail alone and in his socks. But maybe someone had found him and taken him to the shelter? It would be a waste of time if that turned out not to be the case, but he wasn't about to sit still at the campsite and wait for him to come back on his own.

He recalled the map in his mind, of where the shelter was in relation to their campsite. Then he ran through the lot and turned onto the street. It was less than a mile to the shelter. He checked his watch. 6:14. He'd make it to the shelter by 6:20.

It took him five minutes. The physical shape he was in, fueled by adrenaline and panic, had his feet moving so fast that he seemed to be gliding on the balls of his feet. Which was quite an accomplishment given the hiking boots he was wearing.

The shelter was nothing like he had been expecting, and he wondered if he'd confused this shelter with some other place that had come back in his online search. He'd expected cabins that he could rent, but these were just—shelters. Granted, they were bigger and cleaner than all the other pictures of shelters he'd seen along the Trail, but this was still a far cry from a room with a door and electricity. His backup plan, as it turned out, had been no plan at all.

He ran through the grounds, looking into the enclosed spaces. They were all empty. He thought he'd be able to find a manager or a groundskeeper or someone who ran the place, but there was no one here.

"Joseph!" he shouted.

No answer.

He ran back to camp, a little slower this time and with a trail of terrible questions chasing after him.

11

STACEY ROLLED OVER AND hit the alarm that was buzzing on the nightstand. She turned onto her back and stretched, forming a human X. Then she clasped her hands over her head and pointed her toes as if trying to gain one more inch toward the empty corners of the bed.

The empty bed.

She looked over at the pillow beside her and realized that this was the first time she'd slept alone in a long time. Of course, there was the time after Trenton when Jack had slept on the couch for a week while trying to wrap his head around what she'd done. Not that he ever really knew. But she'd been able to get him back into bed easily enough. And she supposed there were a handful of other times since then when duty had called her away.

Duty.

She threw back the covers and swung her feet onto the floor. Then she stood and went to the bathroom, pulling her clothes off along the way. The tile was cold against her bare feet, and it helped to awaken her senses. She reached into the shower stall and turned the knobs. Water fell from the showerhead. When the mirror began to fog, she stepped into the stream.

The water splashed against her skin, its warmth relaxing, soothing. She leaned against the wall and closed her eyes. Thoughts of the day began knocking on her mind, but she didn't want to let them in yet. She just wanted to enjoy the hot water massaging her body, to fall asleep standing there.

But she couldn't. It was a big day, and she needed to start getting her mind right for it.

Duty.

She forced her eyes open and pushed herself off the wall. She turned her back to the spray and reversed into it so that the water was striking her head. She ran her hands through her hair, pulling it off her shoulders and letting it hang down her back, between her shoulder blades. Then she let the doors spring open and all the thoughts come rushing in.

Five minutes later, she shut the water off and reached for a towel. Five minutes after that, she was dressed and doing her hair. It was 6:13.

When she was finally ready to go, she stood in front of the mirror and looked herself in the eyes. This was the first time she'd been alone in a very long time, so it was the perfect opportunity for her and her employer to catch up. They'd been in contact throughout the last eight years, and she'd played a small role in a few ops that had taken her out of her own bed and put her in another. But it had been over a year since the last one, so she figured she was probably due for an assignment.

She held her hands out to see if they were steady. They were steady enough, though there was a slight tremor that didn't used to be there. She was getting old. Or soft. Probably both.

When she was a little girl, her father used to tell her stories of Lyudmila Mikhailovna Pavlichenko, the Soviet Union's female sniper who racked up 309 confirmed kills during the fight against the Germans in WWII. They called her Lady Death, and Stacey—*Anna*—had wanted nothing more than to follow in her footsteps. Her father, a KGB agent himself (though she certainly didn't know it at the time), would often tell her to hold out her hands, proclaiming, "Look at that, she has the steadiness of Lyudmila Pavlichenko!"

She smiled at the memory and then wondered what her father would have said about the Russian sniper's relationship with Eleanor Roosevelt, something she'd learned much later after moving to the States. She often wondered if her hero's friendship with the First Lady had been what set her on the path toward an unnamed star carved into a marble wall at Langley. She'd been an easy recruit when the Agency finally came around. They, of course, knew about her parents, so it wasn't even a question as to whether or not they would come for her. There was no way they couldn't. And her first assignment was the trip back to Russia. Which was when she'd met Vadim and Fedyenka and her life as a double agent had begun.

At least that part of what she'd told Jack was true—that she'd met those guys in Russia her sophomore year—though most everything else he believed was a carefully constructed lie. Even after Trenton and Agent Johnson had called into that conspiracy show, she was still able to keep him in the dark as to just how deep her involvement really went. It didn't hurt either that, deep down, he didn't want to know.

The story she gave him and the story her mother had given him had been convoluted by the simple fact that Viktoriya hadn't been aware that Stacey knew she was an agent when in fact she had known for a very long time. And Viktoriya certainly hadn't known about her daughter's recruitment by the CIA and then the SVR. So even though her mother thought she was telling Jack the truth, it was the furthest thing from it. And that gave her the ability to change her mother's story and work in her own, both versions twisting together and forming an impenetrable fiction.

The life of a double agent, she thought. So many lies to try to keep straight. She was tired of it all. But she owed it to the Agency to stick around after they'd gotten her off the hook with the SVR. She knew they had been an inch away from needing new identities. But with whatever deal the Agency made, they had felt that such measures were unnecessary. The last eight years seemed to have proved them right.

She left her room, stopping briefly to look at the closed door at the end of the hall, and then went downstairs. She grabbed her keys off the counter top, noting Jack's hotspot still sitting there, and headed out the door.

After a quick trip through a Starbucks' drive-through, she was headed for I-95 south, which she would be on for about the next three hours. She texted Jack, letting him know that she had a busy day at work and probably wouldn't be able to talk until tonight.

She hated herself for doing it. But this was what she'd signed up for.

She looked at the dashboard clock. It was 6:31 on Tuesday morning.

12

JACK GOT BACK TO the campsite and sat on the stump beside the firepit. His heart pounded in his chest, and sweat ran down his face. He didn't know what to do. Where to go. And every moment he stayed here doing nothing was another moment closer to Joseph maybe being gone forever. Yet, if he went off looking in the wrong direction, he'd only be compounding those moments. So did he stay, or did he go?

A trio of squirrels raced through the underbrush, the sound of their claws on the trees as they scurried up and down them loud in the morning calm. The mist was breaking, and the woods were marching back into view, but still they brought with them no sign of Joseph. He checked his watch. 6:31. In thirty-one minutes he had eliminated the campsite, the creek, the shelter, the car and parking lot, and the immediate areas that led to those places. And that was all.

He stood, about to run—his whole being screamed at him to run, to go! But all he could do was look this way and that while the pressure of needing to be somewhere else continued to build and build and build.

Ticktock, Jack... What're you gonna do?

He put his head back and vented the pressure in one long frustrated yell that echoed off the mountains. The veins in his neck and arms stood out, pulsing. Panic was beginning to take over, but he couldn't let it. He had to think. Had to come up with a plan. He had no keys and no phone, and the shelter was empty, so it was all up to him. He could walk back to the road and head for 233, hope to flag someone down and have them call the police. But how long would that take? And what would they actually do? He recalled how much help the law was in helping track down Joseph and Stacey eight years ago. If it hadn't been for Agent Johnson pulling strings, he might never have found them. But that would be a better plan than sitting here doing nothing, right? One person looking for his son over the next two hours might not be as efficient as thirty men looking for his son starting two hours from now. Unless he was hanging on to a ledge somewhere, his grip weakening and hoping for his dad to show up at the last second to save him.

Ticktock.

He started to move, thinking he would work his way out in a spiral formation, circling the campsite in clockwise rings, each ring further out than the last. And he would do it as fast as he could, as far as he could.

He ran into the woods and broke right. He called out Joseph's name every ten seconds or so as he went, and the sound of snapping twigs, crunching pine needles, and crackling leaves underfoot only seemed to add to his sense of urgency and pushed him faster.

But before he could even complete one ring, a bang echoed from somewhere in the distance. He stopped, suddenly frozen, and looked up at the sky, toward where he thought the sound had come from. Against the backdrop of the distant mountains, he saw a flock of birds suddenly take flight, fleeing western treetops.

He abandoned his strategy and ran as fast as he could in the direction of what he knew had been the blast of a rifle.

JACK RAN BACK TO the creek and, without slowing, skipped across the scattered rocks, making it to the other side without getting his feet wet. The grassy bank quickly gave way to a steep fifteen-foot incline, and he grabbed at protruding roots and half-buried rocks to help him scale it. At the top was a trail that stretched left and right. It followed the creek on the west side and a sheer cliff wall on the north, large sections of rock poking through the side of it. It was so high and close to the trail that it almost seemed to loom over him, and he couldn't see what was on top of it. But he was sure the shot had come from somewhere up there.

He looked down at the creek. Moved his gaze up and down its banks. Nothing but grass and rocks and some moss-covered trees that had fallen ages ago, their branched arms collecting debris from the current. The water was shallow and crystal clear, and he could see straight to the bottom. No sign of Joseph.

Another shot.

It was much closer this time, and the sound of it raced past him before bouncing back and echoing past him again. It had definitely come from above. *Hunters*, he thought. And he knew he had to find a way up there. He started jogging along the path, running through clouds of buzzing insects. They chased after him, attacking his eyes, drawn to his sweat. He swatted at them, but it was no use. They were too small and too many. Their tiny wings whined in his ears with a maddening, supersonic pitch. Then bigger insects joined in the chase, flies getting in his hair and biting the back of his neck. He followed the path around a large boulder, too busy waving his hands about his head to see the large network of roots that suddenly crossed his path.

He went down hard, landing on his chest and forearms. The bugs didn't care, only seemed to call in more reinforcements. He quickly got back to his feet. There was no time for tripping. He had to find a way to get to the hunter. He called out, shouting up to the top of the cliff as he ran, but didn't get a response.

He ran until he saw a way up. Below him to the right, a footbridge crossed the creek, and then wooden stairs led from the creek up and across the path he was on, continuing on up the side of the cliff (which had become more like a steep incline now). There was even a handrail to assist with the ascent. He took the first half-dozen steps two at a time but had to slow down when his legs started to burn, and he felt a cramp trying to sneak up on him.

He didn't count the steps as he went, but it felt like there were a hundred of them. When he got to the top, he bent over to catch his breath and turned to look back down the way he'd come. The creek looked far away, a silver snake slithering up against the bottom of the cliff.

The area in front of him was level, but the woods were thick and seemed to go on forever. Another footpath stretched out from beneath his feet and continued straight on into the woods, but then it disappeared after a quick turn behind some thick underbrush.

"Hey there, mister," a voice said.

Startled, Jack snapped his head toward the sound. A man was walking toward him. He was wearing a bright orange vest over camouflage and had a rifle slung over his shoulder. Jack stood up and ran to him, thankful that he'd happened across the hunter right away. More time spared. "Have you seen a young boy out here?" he blurted.

The man tilted his head a little and studied him from beneath the brim of an old baseball hat. He took his time doing it too, his jaw working slowly against whatever was in his mouth. "Lost someone, did ya?"

Jack didn't have time for this. "Yeah, I can't find my son. Have you seen anyone out here?"

The man nodded slowly, his beady eyes still locked on Jack's. He had a long goatee and big sideburns. He was maybe in his mid-thirties. "Sure did."

Jack straightened. "Really? Where?" He couldn't keep the desperation out of his voice.

The guy grinned and walked over to the stairs. He raised his hand and pointed down at the creek, further upstream. "Saw some little rascal runnin' along the creek and chasin' a butterfly or some such thing."

Jack blinked. "A butterfly?" He couldn't imagine Joseph chasing a butterfly ever, let alone wandering off into the mountains on his own to do so. Maybe a four-year-old girl would go chasing colorful wings (he recalled such an episode of *Little House On The Prairie*), but a twelve-year-old boy?

He shrugged. "Suppose it coulda been somethin' else. I was way up here so couldn't really make it out." He turned, raised his hand higher, and pointed further upstream. "Last I saw, he was headin' that way. C'mon, I'll show ya." He followed the edge of the cliff.

Jack went after him, not knowing what else to do. He couldn't wrap his mind around what the guy had said, that he'd seen Joseph running along the bank of the creek. But unless there was another boy out here on his own, who else could it be? "How long ago did you see him?"

The man looked back over his shoulder. "Oh, I'd say 'bout ten or fifteen minutes ago or so."

If that were the case, Joseph should have been able to hear him calling for him from the campsite. They were just about perpendicular to it now. Though maybe the creek was too loud. "Did you hear me calling?"

"That was you, was it?"

Jack blinked again. Who the hell else would it be? He wanted to ask the guy where he was from, because his accent was definitely not from around here. But he really couldn't care less where the guy was from right now. Instead, he yelled at the top of his lungs for Joseph, his voice echoing off the rock.

The guy stopped walking and turned to face him. "Yer gonna scare the game away, mister."

There was something in the guy's voice that Jack didn't like. He had a whiny voice that he found about as annoying as the gnats in his ears, but he also had a sort of bored confidence that was starting to creep him out a little. And those eyes. They belonged to a rat. "Are you serious?" he managed to ask.

The hunter stared at him, dead serious. Then a grin opened his face. "Naw, yer fine. Yell all ya want. We need to find your son."

And that was when Jack realized the guy was high. Or crazy. Maybe both.

The man started walking again. "Anyhow, I can always come on back some other day if all the animals go off'n hide."

This time Jack did ask. "Where you from?"

"Say, how'd you lose your boy, anyway? Yous have a disagreement?"

It was a not so subtle avoidance, and Jack knew something was wrong here just as sure as he knew his son would never go off chasing butterflies. He didn't know what was going on, what this guy was playing at, but his Jerry brain was on fire now. As subtly as he could, he reached down and unbuttoned the safety strap to his knife. "No. I woke up and he was gone."

"Guess you'll be whoopin' his ass when you gets him back then, huh? Ass whoo-pin'!" He laughed.

It was a disturbing laugh, an unstable laugh. The laugh of a guy who had gotten sexual pleasure from pulling the legs off insects when he was a kid.

"I don't think that's funny," Jack said.

The guy stopped and turned around again, his face suddenly sad. He took his hat off, holding the bent rim, and put it against his chest. He had a mullet, and Jack knew for certain he wasn't a 76ers fan.

"Gee, I'm sorry, mister. Didn't mean no offense." Then he smiled and resumed walking.

"I asked you where you're from," Jack said. He couldn't take his eyes off the rifle but didn't think he was in any immediate danger as long as it was positioned on his shoulder with the barrel pointing skyward. He'd be on the guy before he could get it in his hands if he felt the situation called for it. And he had his knife. He wondered if the guy was out here alone, and a bunch of *Deliverance* scenarios suddenly began playing through his mind. What if the guy was leading him back to his camp where a bunch of degenerates were waiting to—

"Name's Theodore. But you can call me Theo if ya want."

Jack was debating on whether to hang back and slip away from the guy when "Theo" suddenly came to a stop. "There," he said. "There's where your boy was headin'. Right there. Fact, I think I can see him now."

Jack came up alongside him, joining him at the edge of the cliff. It looked to be a sixty- or seventy-foot-drop straight down onto a stretch of huge rocks. He took a step back.

"What's your boy's name? Joseph?"

"Yeah."

"Like the kid in the Good Book that had the coat?"

Jack frowned. "Sure." He tried to see where the guy was looking. "I don't see anything."

"No?" He pointed. "Right there by that tree."

That tree? There were hundreds of trees.

Theodore put his left hand to the side of his mouth and hollered down, "JooooSeeee—"

And right about then, in mid-yell, he placed his right hand against Jack's back and shoved him as hard as he could.

If Jack had not been on guard, had he not been expecting something (though certainly not this), and if the guy had had more leverage to work with, he would have certainly gone over. Be that as it may, things were still moving in that direction. Theodore had pushed against his left shoulder, sending his momentum forward but twisting. Maybe it was all the work he'd done with Stacey on the mats in the basement or all the martial arts classes he'd taken down the street from their house or all the tuck and rolling on the artificial turf when diving for a ball in the flag football league. Whatever it was, he had worked at it hard enough for it to become instinct, and instead of panicking and flailing his arms all the way down to the rocks, he let his body roll with the push. He bent over at the waist, absorbing the impact with his upper half in order to keep his feet under him. But just bending over wouldn't be enough. He could already feel the weight of his head and shoulders pulling his lower body with them. It might only result in a single step forward, but there was no step forward. Only air. So he kicked both his feet out behind him and brought his hands down to his sides. For a split second, he was suspended in the air, half of him parallel to the ground and the other half staring straight down the side of the cliff. If he managed to land on his stomach with his hands firmly planted beside him, he would be able to pull himself back and twist himself into a sitting position.

And that was just what he did. The entire thing lasted only a second, and Jack was back on his feet before Theodore could do anything about it. In fact, the guy's brain seemed to be overloading, unable to process what he'd just seen.

Jack didn't wait for him to recover. He had to keep him from getting the gun off his shoulder, and that meant getting him on his back as fast as possible.

Dumbly, Theodore began to ask, "You some kind of ninj—"

Jack went for a double leg takedown. He launched himself low, wrapping his arms behind Theodore's knees and pulling upward as hard as he could while pushing him backward with his shoulder. Theodore landed hard on his back, the impact chasing all the air from his lungs.

Jack knew from his classes that once people went to the ground in a street fight, the fight was over and a beating ensued. He quickly moved in to apply a bar choke, his left knee on the ground next to Theo's waist, his right leg extended all the way back for leverage. He put his forearm against the guy's skinny throat and leaned into it, applying as much pressure against the windpipe as he dared. He didn't want to kill the guy or take his voice away, not before he knew what the hell was going on.

Theodore started kicking his feet, trying to push himself out from under him. But Jack grabbed his collar with his left hand and pulled him down into the choke while driving his knee into the ground to keep himself from sliding. Still, this wasn't an ideal position if he didn't want to kill the guy. Should he grab the rifle off his shoulder, throw it aside, and then jump up and grab it? But he already had the guy on the ground where he wanted him. If he held the rifle on him only to learn that it wasn't loaded, they'd be back to square one. Only this time, maybe the guy would take off and he'd have to chase him. Or maybe he would put up a better fight the second time around. Or maybe he had another weapon on him.

No, he couldn't let the guy back to his feet. Unless...

He let go of the guy's collar and pulled his knife from its sheath. Then, leaning close enough so that their noses were almost touching, he stared into those bulging rodent eyes. The guy was throwing panicked punches into his back and side, but he ignored them. He felt the guy's body shaking and flailing beneath him, and he remembered the guy in his garage. Remembered pouring kerosene down his throat before shooting him in the head. But that had been a different Jack. A Jack who hadn't been anything more than a salesman with conspiracy theories. But the last eight years had changed him, and this time around, being on top of another guy who had just tried to kill him was proving to be a totally different experience.

"You're going to tell me what's going on here," Jack said, watching Theodore's face go from red to purple. Then he very deliberately pushed five inches of the knife's carbon steel into Theo's left buttock.

Theodore tried to moan or scream or something, but of course he couldn't. His light blows fell away as he tried getting to the knife in his rear end. Jack pulled it out and away from his reach. He slipped it back into its sheath, freeing that hand and using it to slip the rifle off the guy's shoulder. He yanked it down past his elbow and then tossed it aside. Then he took the knife back out.

Theodore was on the brink of passing out, so Jack lifted his arm off his neck and allowed him to gulp for air while he grabbed his shoulders and rolled him onto his chest. Jack threw himself onto Theo's back, pinning him down with his body weight. He felt the unmistakable form of a pistol tucked into the back of his pants and yanked it out. A revolver. He tossed it behind him. Knocked the baseball hat away and grabbed the back of his mullet. Climbed up his back and planted a knee between his shoulder blades. Yanked his head back. He thought he could snap the guy's neck easily enough, but he didn't want to do that either. Instead, he brought the knife around and held the blade against his throat. The guy gagged as he tried to swallow, his Adam's apple unable to rise above the blade.

Jack smelled something and knew the guy had crapped himself. Good. It meant he was taking this seriously.

"I'm going to ask you some questions, and you're going to answer me. You understand?" He loosened his grip on Theo's hair and moved the knife off his throat so that he could swallow. He felt him try to nod as he gasped for air. "And just so you know I'm serious about not wasting time..." He slid the blade down the guy's cheek, carving a deep gash into his face all the way down to his jaw. Jack was surprised how easily the Scandinavian grind cut through the flesh. Like butter.

Theo screamed, and the sound went down the cliff and traveled over the water. But then Jack yanked his head back, and the scream was cut short by a gurgle.

"Shhh... You're gonna scare the game away." Blood ran down the blade, spilling over the handle and getting onto his fingers. "Where is my son?"

"They have him—"

Jack shoved Theo's head forward, smashing his face into the ground. He held it there while he slashed the backs of his legs.

Theodore screamed into the dirt.

Jack quickly checked Theo's waist, making sure he had no other weapons tucked down his pants, and then got to his feet. He let Theo turn over onto his side, and then he kicked him full in the face. They say not to kick because there's a dozen things your opponent can do to you if they catch your leg. But this guy wasn't catching anything.

Blood flowed, and something white glistened at the bridge of his nose.

Jack grabbed him by the jacket and dragged him to a nearby tree. The guy kicked and screamed and cried all the way, grabbing at his face, at the backs of his legs. Once Jack had him leaning against the tree, he threw a punch right at the slash in his face. Thought he caught a flash of cheekbone. "Better start getting specific." He looked at his watch. "You have thirty seconds until I cut you again. And I'll keep cutting you every thirty seconds until I know everything you do."

He spit blood out of his mouth. "Yer gonna k-kill me anyway."

"Time is more important to me than anything else right now, so if you keep wasting it, I'll kill you just to save more of it. But if you tell me what I need to know quickly, I promise I'll leave you here to die on your own or crawl to wherever you want to crawl to." He held up his watch. "Ticktock, Theo."

"Okay, ok-k-kay." Blood sprayed when he talked. He pressed his hand against his face, trying to hold it together.

Jack knew there wasn't much time left before Theo either passed out or bled to death, so he needed to prioritize his questions. He'd start with the four Ws. Not the four Ws he'd gone over with Joseph, but four *other* Ws—who, where, why, and when. He figured he could piece together most of what was going on with the answers to those questions. "How many guys?" It wasn't one of the Ws, but Theo had already defined the who as "they." He'd come back to specifics in a bit, but first he wanted to know what he was up against.

Theo seemed to think about it.

Jack took a step toward him. "You don't have time to think."

"Eight!" he shouted. "Eight others!"

One against eight. There have been better odds. "Why?"

"A job."

"From who?"

"I don't know..."

"Not good enough." He took another step.

"I don't! Our boss said it was through a middleman. Said it was somethin' different than we usually do."

"What do you usually do?"

He started to pout.

"That's thirty seconds." He stabbed him in the shoulder.

Theodore cried harder, his whiny voice begging, blood pooling in his lap. "Please... P-please..."

"What do they want with him?" Jack hollered. He was beginning to feel himself come undone. He needed to finish this quick, while he still had control.

"I don't know. None of us does, but...I think maybe some little-kid sex thing..."

Jack took a step back. Things were starting to slip out of his grasp quicker now. "You're traffickers?"

"No, we ain't traffickers! That's what I'm talkin' about. It ain't what we normally do. But we was just gonna hold him for 'em."

He was up against eight people who had been hired by an unknown party for some kind of business transaction. Now he needed to know where they were and where they were heading. "Hold him where? 'Til when?"

"A cabin in the mountains."

He tapped the blade of the knife against his palm. "Specifics, Theo."

"They call it Hollow Mountain. I ain't gotta clue where it is though. Somewhere maybe in the Cranberries. I don't know nothin' more than that, I swear! It's the other guys that's with us. It's their cabin. They're the ones that know."

"How long are they planning on holding him there?"

"Till Saturday."

"What happens on Saturday?"

"We deliver him to who hired us, I guess."

"How are they getting him to the cabin?"

He put a finger in his mouth, and a tooth fell out. He swore. "Quads."

"Is that how you got here?"

He nodded.

"Through the mountains?"

"Usin' the fire and logging trails, the state game sites..."

"From where? With that accent, you ain't local."

"West Virginia?" He said it like a question, fearing that naming the state might not be specific enough.

Jack frowned. "You took quads from West Virginia?"

"No. We drove trucks to the border. Took the quads into Pennsylvania."

"This morning?"

"Yesterday. Made camp about half a mile from here." He lifted a finger and pointed west.

"And that's where they're taking my son right now? Back to this camp?"

His head was starting to dip, and his mouth was like a waterfall of blood, continuously flowing, filling the red pool in his lap. "For the quads."

"And take him back to the trucks. How do you know where you're going? You have maps?"

"GPS..."

"Give it to me."

"Don't have it. Other guys have 'em."

"When did you take him?"

He was fading, and Jack thought maybe he'd lost him. Then he answered, "Five, or around thereabouts..."

Jack swore.

"...drugged you..."

"Took my phone too. And put the spike in my tire."

His eyes closed. "...real s-sorry, mister..."

"So how you supposed to communicate? How do you check in and let them know you did your part?" He saw Theo's eyes open, and it was like his eyelids were bench-pressing three hundred pounds. His eyes went to something behind him. Jack turned and saw a radio on the ground. It must have fallen off Theo when he tackled him. He walked over and picked it up. Then he walked over to the revolver. Picked that up too. "Fully loaded," he said after spinning the cylinder and seeing none of the chambers empty. He pulled the hammer back and aimed it at the bleeding mess on the ground in front of him. But it was all he could do to keep the gun steady. He tossed the radio to him. "Tell them you did it, that I'm dead on the rocks. Ask them where they are." Then he took a shooter's position. "And make it an Oscar-worthy performance, or I'll shoot you dead and then shoot all of them when they come back for you."

"...kay..." He put his head back and swallowed blood. Then he raised the radio to his mouth and pressed the transmit button. "James, ya there? This is Theo. Over."

Jack was impressed. There was hardly any indication that his face was falling apart while he talked.

A crackle and then: *"Yeah, we're here. You take care of him?"*

"Yeah. Pushed him over right like we planned. He's down on the rocks, all broken up."

"He fell while he was lookin' for his kid, right?"

"Right. That's all it'll look like. Where y'all at?"

"Did that first thing we had to do. Almost back to the wheels now. We'll be there before you, and we ain't gonna wait too long, so try to catch up."

"How's the kid?"

"Drugged. Why you askin'?"

"No reason."

"Alright. See you in a bit. Be careful."

"Copy that. Over...and out." He dropped the radio to his side and closed his eyes again.

"What's the first thing?" Jack took the radio back. "What's he talking about?"

"...told us to put your phone by the road..."

"What the hell for?"

"...don't know...part of...deal..."

It didn't make sense, but Jack didn't have time to try to figure it all out right now.

"You said your boss got the job from a middleman. Who's your boss?"

"...Ham..."

"Ham? As in Porky the Pig?"

"...sure..." His face widened into a red yawn, and Jack realized he was laughing. "Though don't let him hear ya say that..."

"Where's he at?"

"...at his cabin, I reckon..."

"West Virginia?"

He nodded the best he could, about to pass out. But then he opened his eyes and began looking around with a renewed sense of energy, his gaze darting through the surrounding woods.

While Jack was turning to see what he might be looking for, it clicked. The voice on the radio. It had said "y'all." As in "you all." Or, "All of you." Meaning more than one.

Theodore wasn't alone. Which made sense if there were eight others. Why would they entrust this drugged-out bum to complete such an important part of their plan? Unless they were all like him. But if they were all like him, who would hire them for a job like this? He turned and faced Theodore. "How many are still here?"

"One other guy. Went to see that there wasn't no one around could hear you yellin'."

"He just left you to deal with me on your own?"

"...supposed to wait..."

Jack swore again. No doubt the guy had heard the shots. Maybe had his own rifle and was lining him up right now. It wouldn't look like the accident they had planned for, but...they obviously hadn't planned on Theo here messing everything up. He had to get out of there now. He went over and pressed the barrel of the pistol against Theo's temple. "They said they weren't waiting for you. So if you don't have a GPS, then how are you supposed to catch up?"

"...other guy...Cullin. Real psycho that one..."

"He's one of the ones who knows where the cabin is?"

He did his best at nodding again. "The Baker brothers. Sons of bitches sure as shit," he slurred. "...to Bakerville..."

"Bakerville?"

"...they run the place. Just ask around... You'll know you're there if you ask 'round..." He coughed up more blood.

Jack clipped the radio to his belt and picked the rifle up off the ground. Slung it over his shoulder.

"Good luck," Theo mumbled.

"I'll be needing the key."

"Left it in the—"

"If you don't give it to me, then I'm going to search you to make sure you're not lying. And if you are lying, then there's no sense in either one of us keeping our word, is there?"

"...Cullin'll kill me..."

"I'll kill you."

He managed to pat his pocket, but it was clear he wasn't going to be getting anything out of it no matter how bad he wanted to.

Jack reached inside the pocket himself and pulled out the key and a handful of loose bullets. He checked the other pocket and found an extra magazine for the rifle. He shoved them into his own pockets and then went as fast as he could back to the wooden stairs. Theodore's voice rambled on behind him. Something about God's judgment on him for agreeing to get involved with a kid.

Jack nearly fell down the staircase twice but managed to get back to the trail in one piece. He sprinted for the tent, expecting the other guy to start shooting at any moment. Halfway back, he stopped and threw up.

13

JACK'S MIND RACED THROUGH an obstacle course of scattered clues, but he couldn't make his way out of it. Kept falling on his face halfway across the rings—the next one just too far away to reach. It just didn't make sense. If they had traveled from out of state with plans to take Joseph, then they had to know that they were going to be here. Had to. The whole thing had been thought out and planned ahead of time. They were using GPS devices! They could have killed him in his sleep, but they wanted him to have an "accident" that no one would later question. He fell off a cliff while looking for his son. But how would they know they would be here? Only three possibilities came to mind. Either these people had access to the reservations for the campsite and did this all the time, or someone else who knew tipped them off, or they had been watching them.

He couldn't think of any other way this could have gone down. He wrote off the first possibility right away. No one would keep abducting kids from the same campsite and continue to get away with it. Not unless they had people at the top helping them. Which... No, he didn't think that was it. Could they have access to all the registrations for all the campsites all along the Appalachian Trail and target the ones with two campers and no neighbors? But that was ridiculous. How would they know one of the two campers was a kid? Besides, the guy had said they'd never done anything like this before. And the other guy was out making sure there were no witnesses in the area.

They were hired hands, but hired by whom?

Could it be that someone had been watching them, spying on them? Wanting to kidnap Joseph and just waiting for the right opportunity? Who? The CIA? For what purpose?

Or was it possible that some sex trafficker had marked Joseph at the mall one day or at the bus stop? Took his picture and shopped it around to all the perverts in high society until one came back with a huge offer? But wouldn't Stacey have noticed if—

Stacey.

The ring moved toward him, suddenly in grabbing distance.

He felt guilty for even considering it, yet he'd been here before, hadn't he? Could this be Mission: Get Rid of Jack Part Two? No, of course not. Not after all they'd been through over the last eight years. It wouldn't make sense for her to put in all the time training him if she was just going to have someone take him out. And how could she do that to Joseph?

The rings were spreading apart again.

But the hotspot... Could she have taken it out of the car?

He grabbed the next ring and went forward on that line of thought. And swung right into a wall. Nothing made sense, and every scenario led nowhere, so he gave it up for now. He needed to focus on getting Joseph back regardless of who was behind it. Though if Stacey did have something to do with it, then he was sure Joseph would be quite alright. And he could even relax a little knowing that was the case, his own life be damned. But it just didn't make sense. So he'd get Joseph back, and then he'd find out who had hired these people from West Virginia.

He got the bedroll back together as fast as he could. Then he went to the cooler and tossed a couple of handfuls of prepackaged food into his pack. Grabbed his axe.

A shot rang out. It echoed down from the hill, same place he'd heard it before, and he knew the other guy had finally caught up with Theo. He guessed Theo was right about the Cullin guy killing him after all. And now he was out of time.

He went back into the tent and grabbed Joseph's backpack, turning it upside down and dumping its contents on the ground. He grabbed his book and quickly flipped through it, hoping that—

There. A map of the Appalachian Trail spread across two pages. He stuffed the book in his own pack and then finished tossing the tent. If someone wandered by, he wanted them to know something had gone wrong. He slashed a long line into its side with his knife.

Then he went for the woods, stopping only one last time to grab the bottle and the pot from next to the firepit he and Joseph had made. And he wondered if that might turn out to be the last thing they ever did together. *Hell no*, Jack said to himself.

He ran. He needed to get to the ATVs before the other guy.

THE PACK, BELT POUCH with the axe, rifle, and revolver were like another person sitting on his shoulders while he ran. His legs were burning. He kept looking at his watch, using the compass to make sure he was heading in the general direction Theo had said they'd made camp. If they really had only parked half a mile away, then he should be getting pretty close.

He ran through the trees, taking the most direct route and not wasting time by following a winding path. But the undergrowth got thick in parts, and he had to fight against thistles and thorns that pulled at his pants. And then, finally, the trees spread out, taking the undergrowth with them, and he was able to use the open ground to make up some time.

The radio crackled.

"This is Cullin. You there?"

The voice was deep and hollow, and an image of a lazy bear popped into Jack's head. It was the psycho Theodore said had stayed behind with him. One of the Bakers. From Bakerville.

"It's Seth. What's happenin'?"

"That idiot of theirs didn't wait for me and took the father on himself."

"And?"

"And looks like the guy tore him up with a knife."

Jack held the radio by his head as he ran.

"He dead?"

"Theodore? Yeah, that little rat is dead. I shot him in what was left of his mouth."

There was silence over the frequency until the voice that had spoken to Theodore earlier finally came across—James, Theo had called him.

"*You're gonna have to answer for that, Cullin.*"

"*Whatever you say. He was dead anyways, just thought I'd help him along is all.*"

Another gap of silence.

"*Listen,*" Cullin said. "*He has Theo's radio, and I don't know how much that turd told him. Could be he's goin' to the police right now.*"

More silence. Jack jumped over a rotting tree limb.

"*Is that what you're doin', Daddy? You goin' for the law?*"

It was Seth again.

Jack almost answered but managed to get a hold of himself in time. He wasn't going to show them his hand just yet.

He heard motors turning over up ahead of him.

"*If you're listenin', Papa, then know this: if we see any sign of the law, and I mean even so much as a park ranger, we'll cut your boy's head off and count our losses.*"

That came from a new voice, but it was a lot like Cullin's. Dry, humorless, and dead.

The motors were being revved, the sound shooting through the woods around him and sending birds into the sky. Then, just as quickly, the noise was fading as they drove off for the waiting trucks near the state border.

The threat to cut Joseph's head off hit a little too close to home, and Jack wondered if it had just been the first thing to come to the guy's mind or if he'd noticed the scar.

Two minutes later, Jack came up on the two remaining ATVs. They were both four-wheelers that looked pretty similar to the ones he'd once ridden with Donny. That was about ten years ago though, and he hoped he could remember how to start them. He took out Theo's key and hopped on the first one he came to. He was relieved to find that his eyes were going to all the appropriate places, and he flipped the switch to the ON position. Then he put the key into the ignition. It fit, and he turned it. Then he hit the thumb tab on the left handle to open the choke. He squeezed the break lever and hit the starter. The engine came to life.

But he couldn't just go right after them. Not with this Cullin guy coming after him. So he hopped off the quad and removed the axe from its mask. Walked over to Cullin's vehicle. He swung the axe hard, chopping huge gashes into all four tires. Then he put the blade to all the stuff beneath the seat, trying to destroy fuel lines, brake lines, pipes, and anything else that might keep the thing from running. Then he went to the front and swung at the handles, severing wires there too.

Satisfied that Cullin would now have to come after him on foot, he got back on Theo's quad and went after his son.

14

THEY PARKED THE ATVS in a circle facing each other. They were in a field of tall grass and about to head down a ridge and across a creek, but James wanted to check on the kid first. "How's the kid?" he asked. The boy was lying on a wooden bed that had been fitted to the back of Seth Baker's vehicle.

Seth turned and lifted the blanket that was covering him. "Still asleep."

The seven of them sat there as wind rustled the grass.

Then John Tyler leaned over and whispered something to Michael.

Michael listened and nodded, his eyes locked on the two Baker boys.

"Is there a problem?" Lee, the oldest of the three Baker brothers, asked them.

They looked at him. Took in his ice-cold eyes and the parts of his weathered face that could be seen around the big beard. They watched him blink in that all-confident, slow-motion and unimpressed manner.

"Yeah, there's a problem," John Tyler replied. "Your brother just killed our friend."

Lee looked up at the sky and seemed to watch the clouds. "That's not what I heard. I heard that boy's son killed your friend. Stabbed him."

"You know—" John Tyler started.

Lee cut him off. "How is it, do you suppose, that your friend managed to get himself stabbed in the first place?"

"That's beside the point," Michael growled.

"You think my brother was gonna take the time to nurse him back to health? Sure, he didn't like your friend, so maybe he did enjoy ripping a hole through his head, but that don't change the outcome none."

Michael adjusted his hat. "We'll be having words with Cullin, is all we're sayin'."

"No you won't," James interjected. "We're here to do a job, and we're gonna do it. We don't have time for this now."

"Like hell—"

The radio came to life.

"Seth, you copy?"

They fell silent as Seth brought the radio to his mouth. "I copy."

"Daddy took Theodore's ride. Slashed my tires and cut the fuel line. Broke it up good. You're gonna have to send someone back for me."

"He's comin' after us," Colt said.

James leaned forward on the seat and looked around, squinting in the morning light. "We need to change frequencies. Could be he's listening."

Seth spit. "Oh, he's listenin' alright." Then he said into the radio, "Our father's birthday."

Lawrence waved his hand at a fly that had landed on his scalp. "The hell does that mean?"

Lee and Seth both changed the frequency on their radios.

"You there?" Cullin's deep voice came through the speaker, answering Lawrence's question.

"We're here," Lee said.

"I gotta get rid of this body. Just carried the stinkin' thing half a mile."

"You do that," Lee said. "Then go after the father." He looked at James. "Which one of your boys you wanna send back?" As James thought about it, Lee leaned back and folded his arms across his belly. "When yer makin' up your mind, might want to consider someone a little more...*capable* than the last guy you paired up with one of my kin."

James twirled the toothpick between his teeth. No way would he send his brother out there to team up with that psychopath. He'd love to send John Tyler, but he was likely to lose control and get himself killed too, which would lead to the very altercation with the Bakers that he was hoping to avoid. So it came down to Colt or Lawrence. Colt wanted to go, was practically raising his hand. Hell, he was the obvious choice, but James wanted him here with him just in case things went sideways with Lee and Seth. "Lawrence, head back and see if you can't cut the father off. Try to make it look natural, but if you can't—"

"I'll make him disappear."

"If you get to the guy first," Seth said, "then meet up with Cullin after. You can catch up when we make camp. He's got the waypoint."

Lawrence nodded, but no one missed the look in his eye.

"Lawrence," James said loud enough for everyone to hear, "you drop this thing with Theo, ya here? Maybe one day there'll be a time and a place to sort that out, but it sure as hell ain't today or tomorrow. You got it?"

Lawrence looked away. "Yeah, James. I got it." Then he looked at Cullin's twin brother. "So what's your daddy's birthday?"

"Thirteenth," Seth said.

"Of course it is," Lawrence mumbled. He changed the frequency.

"Cullin," Lee called over the radio.

"I'm here." He sounded out of breath, like he was digging.

"Lawrence here is gonna head back and try to cut the father off. When that part's all done, you make sure Lawrence makes it back to camp."

"I understand."

Lee hooked the radio back to his belt. "Alright, let's get a move on. I want to reach the waypoint by nightfall—" He was interrupted by the radio.

"Daddy's got Theodore's rifle, by the way."

They'd all figured as much.

"Cullin," James said, "did Theo have a pistol on him?"

"He sure didn't."

"Then he's got his pistol too."

"Thought this was just supposed to be some city guy," John Tyler said. "Just whose boy did we steal?"

"Don't matter none," Michael said. "He sure ain't no Rambo, and that's about what it would take out here."

Lee brought his ATV to life. "Let's get moving, then," he said.

The rest of them started their vehicles, and the sound of the engines echoed off the tree lines that boxed the field.

Before Lawrence pulled away from them, James leaned over and told him to watch himself.

"You don't gotta tell me," Lawrence said.

Then James said, "If something happens with that psycho, don't come back. Figure out a way to get back to Ham on your own, ya hear?"

"Yeah," Lawrence said, and drove back the way they'd come, crossing the field and disappearing into the woods.

15

IT WAS 9 A.M. already. Three hours since he'd woken up and found Joseph missing. At least Joseph had spent that time sleeping—according to the voice on the other end of the radio. Still dreaming, completely unaware of the danger he was in. That was good. Better than thinking he'd been awake and terrified, begging for his dad to come and save him.

Jack had followed the sounds of the departing ATVs to a trail that was crisscrossed with tire tracks. He was being careful to stay back a little. He didn't want to get too close, though he realized that if they were to depart the trail at some point, he'd lose them. The odds of a path connecting the campsite to the border were pretty slim, so he had to assume they'd be veering off the path eventually, which meant he had to stay close enough.

The radio sounded.

"Seth, you copy?"

He brought the ATV to a stop and listened.

"I copy."

"Daddy took Theodore's ride. Slashed my tires and cut the fuel line. Broke it up good. You're gonna have to send someone back for me."

There was a moment of silence and then the response: *"Our father's birthday."*

Then nothing. Jack swore. He assumed they had just switched frequencies to whatever their father's birthday was. Well, if that was the case, then there were only thirty-one options. Unless they were referring to the year of their father's birthday. So channels 1 through 31 if it was the day, and he guessed somewhere between 45 and 60 if it was the year. And only if it really was their father they were referring to and not just a code for something else. He looked at the radio and saw that the channels only went to 22. Day of the month it was, then.

He took a sip of water from his bottle and wiped the sweat from his brow with his forearm. *So they know I'm on Theo's ATV, and they're sending someone back to pick up Cullin.* No doubt they'd figured he was chasing after them. And now, if he stayed on this trail, he'd ride straight into whoever was coming back for Cullin. They couldn't afford to leave him riding around in the woods. Not after all the trouble they'd gone through trying to make his death look like an accident.

He ran through his options and weighed the pros and cons for each. He could hide off the path and try to ambush them when they passed, maybe get the GPS off Cullin. If he could do that, then he wouldn't need to follow anyone. It would just be a race to the trucks. He wondered how far away they were parked. Theo had said they'd left them at the Pennsylvania border, but he hadn't said whether it was the Maryland or West Virginia side of the border. Could be twenty miles. Could be one hundred and twenty miles. If it was the Maryland border, then they'd probably head straight there. But if it was West Virginia, then maybe they'd need to make camp for the night, which could give him time to catch up.

He thought about the GPS devices. Theo hadn't said how many devices they had, but he'd said that the "other" guys had "them." Cullin being one of the "other" guys. He'd also said that only the Baker brothers knew where the cabin was. So could he assume that there might only be two GPS units and that they were both with the Bakers? In the short exchange between Cullin and the voice that had identified itself as Seth, Seth had said "*our* father," which made Seth and Cullin brothers. Were there more? He didn't know, but whoever they were sending back would most likely not be one of the Bakers or have a GPS. So if he wanted to get his hands on one, he'd need to get it from Cullin. Then he'd know how far away the truck was.

But he figured he should play it safe. Getting himself killed trying to take on two of them wouldn't help Joseph any. He would head southwest and then turn northwest, circling around whoever was coming back. When they figured out what he'd done, he knew they'd just turn around and come after him, but he'd have to work that part out later.

He set the channel to 1 on the two-way radio and listened. He'd work his way up through the twenty-two channels and hope he stumbled across them talking at some point. He turned to channel 2.

Another thought. He was still pretty close to the Appalachian Trail, and he could try searching out some hikers. Maybe use a cell phone to call... Who? The police? So they could tell him to stand down, or send the FBI to storm the Bakers' cabin on Hollow Mountain? He couldn't let that happen. Once these guys knew the police were involved and that delivering Joseph was no longer an option, Joseph would not only lose all value to them, but become a liability. They'd just as soon bury him somewhere and "cut their losses," as they'd said. But even if they didn't, even if they held him hostage, there was no way they were going to be taken alive. Not these guys. And that meant Joseph would most likely go down with them.

No police or FBI. Not yet.

Stacey, then?

He thought about that. If she was behind this, then what good would it do to let her know that he was still alive? And if she wasn't, what could she do about it?

The sun broke through a hole in the canopy, and a ray of light struck the ground in front of him. He took it as his signal to get a move on and motored off the trail, heading southwest into the surrounding woods, navigating around rocks and saplings, going up and then down tiny ravines, through runs and over scattered underbrush.

After he'd gone about a mile (comparing his average MPH to his watch), he turned northwest. If someone did come back for him, then they should have already passed him by now, putting that person and Cullin behind him.

He switched the radio channel, waited a minute, and then went to the next. He ducked as he sped beneath a low-hanging branch.

16

IF THE FATHER REALLY was coming after them, then Lawrence should have come across him by now. Maybe he wasn't. Maybe he was trying to get help or get to a phone. Maybe he hadn't followed their tracks over the access roads but instead headed back to one of the main roads. Lawrence didn't know anything about the roads around here, how far away they were or what they led to. Had never been in Pennsylvania before. Lee and Cullin had the GPS devices, and everyone had been following them.

He twirled the tip of his mustache as he weighed his options. It was possible the guy was looking for his son but, unable to identify the fire trail they'd used, was just driving around in the woods, lost somewhere. If that was the case, he might never find the guy. He thought about turning around and catching back up with the others so that he didn't need to depend on Cullin to get him to the trucks. The last thing in the world he wanted was to have one of the Baker boys sitting behind him while he was operating an ATV. He wouldn't put it past the freak to go sticking a knife in the back of his neck just for fun. You didn't turn your back on the Baker brothers. Ever.

But if he didn't pick him up, he'd hear about it from Ham, and though he didn't think he'd really follow through on his threat to have the next guy who screwed up chainsawed, he sure didn't want to put that belief to the test.

He ran a hand over his razor-shaved head and looked around one more time before bringing the radio to his mouth. "James, you copy?"

"*Yeah.*"

"I don't think he's usin' the access road. I shoulda run into him by now."

"Just get Cullin. You can try trackin' him from there."

Lawrence swore. So he and Cullin were going to play trackers like a pair of Indians now? Well, that was fine. But if he felt for an instant that Cullin might be thinking of doing to him what he'd done to Theodore, then it would be Cullin who was going to be having the accident. What his twin brother, Seth, and his older brother, Lee, would have to say about that, well, they'd just have to cross that bridge if and when they got there, wouldn't they?

"Theodore has been put to rest," Cullin's voice announced through the speaker.

"I bet he has," Lawrence muttered. Then he pressed the transmit button. "I'll be there soon."

He hit the accelerator and continued backtracking through the woods.

17

JACK WORKED THE ATV over thickly wooded hills and down through rocky ravines. The terrain was getting increasingly wild, and he'd come very close to smashing his leg against a boulder and had almost flipped the quad when trying to get up a steep ridge. A broken leg or a broken back would put an abrupt end to his pursuit, and his only option would then be to try crawling back to the Trail, lay himself across it, and hope someone with a radio or phone stumbled upon him before he died of internal bleeding or exposure or dehydration. And that was even if he'd be able to crawl.

He turned sharp left to avoid some deadwood, and then another quick left to keep from ending up in a long row of thorn bushes. The trees were getting too close together and the underbrush too dense. Soon he'd be spending more time searching for ways to get the vehicle around obstacles than it would take him to just walk straightaway on foot. He checked the compass on his watch and corrected his course again.

With all the bouncing, Theo's rifle had slipped beneath his pack, and the bolt handle was jamming into his kidney. He took a hand off the handlebars and reached behind him, trying to pull the rifle out from beneath the backpack. Just as his fingers grazed the stock, he hit a bump and nearly flew off the seat. He swore and slowed to a stop.

There were two V-shaped grips screwed to the utility rack in front of the ATV's handlebars. He swung the rifle off his shoulder and pressed it down into the grips so that it was fixed securely across the front of the vehicle. Then he readjusted his pack. He could probably strap it to the ATV, but he didn't want to take the time figuring it out.

He checked his watch. 9:17. He wondered how far ahead they could have gotten while he was taking his detour. If they'd started out half a mile ahead (seemed as good a guess as any), and he'd matched their speed until turning southwest off the access road for what he guessed was a mile and then northwest at five to ten miles per hour through the draws, slopes, rocks and undergrowth, then they could be ten miles ahead of him by now. Maybe more if they were able to open it up to twenty, thirty, or even forty miles per hour on the access road.

He was beginning to feel that nervous weight in his gut, that maybe he'd screwed up and had already lost them. That the small window he'd had just slammed shut. If they'd turned off the path, then he'd never be able to find them. He changed the channel on the radio. He was up to channel 15. Still nothing.

He came into a hollow and hit the accelerator.

18

LAWRENCE SPOTTED Cullin walking toward him on the fire path about twenty yards off, and he had the sudden urge to hit the gas and run him over. He looked like a serial killer from one of those Dirty Harry movies with his big square jaw and his dumb-ass hairdo. It was something between a mullet and a bowl cut, though it parted off-center and swept across his brow like a drape tied to one side. But instead of striking him down, he slowed to a stop. He parked a little sooner than he needed to, and he enjoyed making Cullin walk the extra few yards. "Where's Theo?"

Cullin looked up from underneath that hair and stopped. Turned and looked behind him. "Somewhere back there."

"You bury him?"

He squinted. The sun was still behind him in the east, but it was reflecting off the side-view mirror of Lawrence's ATV in front of him. "More or less."

They stared at each other. Lawrence with fire in his eyes and Cullin with a soulless, zombie-like gaze that didn't give a damn about anyone or anything. It made Lawrence shiver.

"Did you see the father?" Cullin finally asked.

"Yeah." Lawrence turned his head and spit. "Fact, we had ourselves some moonshine and played a game of cards. He won, so I let him go."

Cullin grinned and walked to the ATV, slinging his rifle over his shoulder. "You are a funny man."

Lawrence looked away. He didn't like that grin. Reminded him of a shark. He didn't like that rifle either. Some kind of WWII-era Nazi semi-automatic. Lawrence had no idea where he'd gotten it, whether his granddaddy had smuggled it back as a keepsake or if his granddaddy was the Nazi trooper who'd used it. Lawrence didn't like Nazis. He recognized his own prejudices and figured he could blame most of them on ignorance, but the Third Reich and all that bullshit was just fucked up. There was just no other way to put it. Cullin and an SS uniform seemed like a match made in hell for sure.

"If you didn't see him, then I reckon he left the path at some point."

Lawrence almost remarked on the obviousness of that fact but managed to hold his tongue. One wrong word and Cullin might have that hunting knife he kept at the small of his back out and across his neck before he even knew what was happening. And if things were going to end up that way, it would be Lawrence doing the surprising. "Unless he never took the path to start with."

"Meh." He gave a little shrug. "Let's go see." He climbed onto the back of the ATV.

Lawrence cringed at the sudden closeness of his body and immediately began thinking of ways he could dump him along the way. Maybe hit a hill too fast, or swerve real sudden like.

Cullin reached his arms around his waist.

Lawrence turned. "Get your damn hands off me." And he was about to end it all right then. He'd launch himself into Cullin and send them both to the ground. See which one of them could get to their knife or pistol first.

Cullin smiled and let go of him. Held up his hands, palms out. "Did not know a man's touch would bother you so much."

"Touch me again and you'll find out just how much it bothers me." He turned the ATV around and headed back the way he'd come, looking for signs of where another ATV might have veered off the path. As he drove, he spoke into the radio and reported he had Cullin and that they were now looking for the father. He clipped the radio onto the handlebars.

19

JACK DROVE THROUGH SCRUB brush and then down a ridge into another run and then back up the other side. Went through more scrub and between two big oaks he barely fit through. Then he was on the edge of a large field. Knee-high grass. The sound of insects. He checked his heading. Turned to the next channel on the radio. Had he missed the access road? Driven straight across it? Or could it have come to an end further east? *Of course it could have.*

He started across the field. He'd give it another ten or twenty minutes before getting panicked.

The clearing was the size of a half-dozen football fields. The tree line was distant, and beyond that he couldn't tell if he was seeing clouds or mountains. There was a single dead-looking tree in the middle of the field.

As he reached the tree, he caught movement to his right. He looked over in time to see something dart through the grass and out of sight. Too big to be a cat, it was also smaller than your average dog. Probably a fox. And just like that, he was taken back to the first time he'd ever seen one of the red animals with the bushy tails. He had been playing left field, with Gandma and Grandpa in the stands, cheering him on. The ball field was off Roosevelt Boulevard, right next to the infamous mental hospital that had just closed a couple of years earlier. From where he was standing in the outfield, he could see the building through the trees. Fascinated by the mystery of it, he took the opportunity between batters to imagine what might have gone on in there. The rumors were plenty. Grandmom had just been talking to a friend about it over the phone, reading stuff out of the newspaper.

That was when, as the next batter was stepping into the box and taking a few warm-up swings, he saw the fox. It had been standing there, between two trees, staring right at him, its little triangular ears raised. It licked its lips. Flicked its tail. Took a step back, then looked to its right. Took a nervous step forward. Jack had been so fascinated by the sudden appearance of the fairy tale character that went about hunting down gingerbread men that the sound of the aluminum bat connecting with a pitch didn't register until the ball struck him in the thigh. He'd howled, and the fox disappeared. But it hadn't vanished from his imagination, and when it came time to choose the topic of his next school report, he had chosen the fox. That was how he knew there were two types of foxes in Pennsylvania, Maryland, and West Virginia. The red fox and the gray fox. He had yet to see a gray fox.

He had completely forgotten about that day. In fact, he'd completely forgotten about that whole part of his life. Grandpa had died early on, so memories of him were scant. But this was one a darting fox in a field had managed to resurrect. They'd gone for ice cream after that game. He remembered pulling up his pant leg and showing them the purple bruise. He could see in his mind's eye his grandpa's large hand engulfing the sugar cone as he passed it to him.

It was strange the things that could unlock a memory, and he wondered if the fear and stress of being kidnapped might serve as a trigger to some of Joseph's own memories. *That's the least of my worries*, he thought. Making sure that his son was around to remember anything at all was all that mattered right now.

He found a deer path in the field and followed it through the adjacent tree line. After five minutes of bushes and twisted vines, he found the access road. Or at least *an* access road. At this point he had no choice but to hope it was the same one. It was wide and pretty flat, and he was able to open it up a little. The trees on either side of him smeared into blurs, the wind in his hair.

LAWRENCE STOPPED THE ATV when Cullin tapped his shoulder and pointed to a section of brush that was bent and broken alongside the path.

Cullin climbed out of the seat and walked to the edge of the trail. He bent down and pushed the hair out of his eyes, examining the crushed foliage. His fingers danced over long blades of grass that seemed to have been snapped halfway up. He stood and stared into the woods, trying to pick out the path the stolen ATV could have carved through the undergrowth. "He's smart," he said.

Lawrence looked up and down the access road. There was only one reason that he could think of that would make the guy suddenly veer off the path. "He heard you ask to be picked up over the radio, knew he had to get off the path."

Cullin rubbed the tip of his nose with his thumb. "He skirted 'round you."

That answered the question as to whether or not he was coming after his son himself or going for help. "Do we follow him through there?"

Cullin shook his head. "No. He'll eventually wanna get back on the path we're takin'. He'll turn back. Sure he will. And if we continue on down the trail, we might just drive up his ass."

Lawrence figured he was right. He radioed James and let him know.

JACK'S STOMACH GROWLED. IT was past ten, and he hadn't eaten anything yet. Who cares, he thought. Missing breakfast and lunch wouldn't kill him. He'd eat once he had Joseph back.

As he switched the channel on the radio, he wondered how long this path might go on for, and if maybe they'd already left it. It was his third time cycling through the frequencies, and he thought he might be out of range or that the mountains were blocking the signal. He didn't know what the range on these radios were, but knew from his reading that not many boasted of distances over a few miles. Some advertised up to twenty, and HT ham radios could reach forty, but he was sure the mountains would have something to say about that. Unless there was a repeater they were able to use, in which case they might be able to communicate over hundreds of miles. If the repeater connected to the internet, then they might be able to contact people all over the world. Of course, he recognized that the chances of stumbling upon the correct frequency just as they were transmitting were—

"—n see him."

He slowed the ATV and brought the radio to his ear. Hope blossomed in his chest. Was it them, or had he stumbled upon some random hunters? He waited.

"*He just stopped. Hold on.*"

"*Copy.*"

Jack recognized the voices. The first was Cullin, and the second was his brother Seth. But who were they talking about? He turned in his seat and looked behind him.

And there they were, about two hundred yards away and coming fast.

Jack's heart stopped. He turned back around and hit the gas.

"—saw us—comin'—you."

He could only make out a little of what they were saying over the sound of the engine and the way his body bounced every time he hit a bump.

"—send—at 'em—pinch him—nowhere to go."

"—JT—to help—"

He didn't need to get all of that to understand what they'd just said. Cullin was asking the people ahead to send another person back to meet him head-on, and they'd responded by saying someone named JT would be coming back to help. Now he'd have to do the same thing he did last time and skirt around them. But first he'd have to lose his tail. At least long enough to get around the bend up ahead and disappear into the forest. He knew he was far better with a gun than with an ATV, so he hit the brake, swinging the quad sideways, and skidded to a stop.

By the time the dust cloud cleared, he was kneeling behind the ATV and propping Theo's rifle against the seat, lining up the speeding ATV in its sights.

They were only a hundred and twenty yards away now, but that was too far for him. With them bouncing up and down over the path, it'd be a miracle shot. Yet if he didn't shoot soon, he wouldn't have enough time to make it down the road and out of sight.

He settled for simply trying to force them off the path.

He worked the bolt and made sure there was a round in the chamber. Then he fired, trying to account for distance while anticipating the dip they were coming up on. And damn if he didn't hit one of them.

The blast echoed up and down the trail as one of the bodies jerked. He couldn't tell whether it was the person on the front or the back, only that arms shot out and a head went back, and now the ATV was swerving into the woods. He hoped it would crash into a tree or a rock or something debilitating, but he didn't hear any crash.

He climbed back onto the seat, jammed the rifle into the grips, and hit the accelerator. He took the four-wheeler to 60 mph, every little bump like a bucking bronco trying to toss him.

But he had no choice. He had to clear their line of sight before more reinforcements showed up ahead.

"Lawrence—shot—cover in the—that motherf—"

He went another two hundred yards before the path made a slight turn, and he knew they'd lost sight of him. He left the path and headed south back into the forest.

IT WASN'T LONG BEFORE he knew his plan would not work. The forest had become wild and thick very fast, and there was little room to fit the four-wheeler through the trees with all the dense vines and shrubs filling the space between them. The land kept falling away into shallow ravines too, a lot of them leading to much larger drop-offs. He couldn't see any way south that wouldn't require him trying to motor down a steep, rocky hillside. He didn't trust his handling of the ATV, and even if he could manage to get to the bottom without toppling the thing, he wasn't sure there'd be a way out. Maybe it ended at a river. Then what? Or maybe the slopes turned to walls of rock further on. No, he couldn't risk ending up at the bottom of the hill without knowing where it would lead. If the others found him, he'd be a fish in a barrel.

His mind raced.

He could send the quad over the side, leave the engine running, and crawl beneath it. Play possum. The sound of the engine would bring them to him, and they'd think he'd flipped the ATV and landed with the vehicle on top of him. When they came down to make sure he was dead, he'd raise the pistol and shoot them in the face. Assuming they didn't just shoot him before coming down. After all, this wasn't one of those movies where the bad guy walked over to the pretending hero and kicked his foot to make sure he was really dead instead of spending one more bullet just to make sure. Or maybe they'd want to crush his head with a rock to make it look like an accident, in which case they would have to come even closer. But still, who was to say all the angles and distances would be right for shooting them before either one of them could retaliate? Or what if one of them stayed at the top of the hill, covering the other and pinning him down until more reinforcements arrived?

He'd have to ditch the ATV and go on foot. It was the only option he could see. It meant he'd most certainly lose their trail. Or maybe he could find a way to get the GPS off Cullin after all. It was Cullin's voice he'd heard over the radio saying something about Lawrence being shot, so it would be Cullin coming for him from behind and JT from up ahead.

He looked around, his heart pounding in his chest, and tried to think.

22

LAWRENCE CLUTCHED HIS SHOULDER, and blood oozed between his fingers. He couldn't believe the guy had hit him from that distance and while they were moving that fast. With Theo's rifle and without a scope no less. *Lucky shot*, he thought. Unless this guy *was* more than they'd suspected. What if he *was* some ex-army Rambo type like Colt? What if he was a Navy SEAL or Green Beret or something?

He stumbled out of the woods and back onto the fire trail. He could just make out Cullin disappearing around a bend on his ATV. Right now, he cared less about killing the boy's father than he did about cutting off Cullin's head and beating his brothers to death with it.

After driving the quad into the woods for cover, Cullin had tossed him off the vehicle and left him behind.

There was no other way this thing could end now. Not as far as Lawrence was concerned. This wasn't just about completing a job for Ham anymore. The Baker boys had declared war.

He reached for his radio, but it wasn't there. He looked behind him, back where he'd been hit, thinking maybe it had fallen off him when he'd thrown his hands in the air. He didn't see anything. He jogged back into the trees and searched around in the undergrowth. Nothing. Then he remembered that he'd clipped it to the handlebars. He didn't have his rifle either.

He yelled in frustration, then got back on the path and started running. John Tyler was on his way, intending to pinch the boy's father between them. Since Cullin had the GPS, then catching up with JT would be his only hope of not getting left behind. Even if he could find his way back to the road they'd left the trucks on, it'd take him too long to walk the hundred miles to get there, and they wouldn't be waiting around for him once Cullin told them he'd been shot and killed by the boy's father. Then he'd have to find his way into a nearby town and try to catch a bus or something. With a bleeding shoulder.

He wondered why Cullin hadn't shot him like he'd shot Theo, and figured it was probably just because he hadn't wanted to take the time. Well, if that was the case, then Cullin had made a mistake, and Lawrence was damn well going to make him regret it.

23

JACK TOOK THE SPARE container of gas off the back of the ATV and unscrewed the cap. Then he emptied it onto the vehicle. He took a lighter from his pack and touched the flame to the gas. Fire burst over the surface of the four-wheeler, and he took a step back, feeling the surge of heat blast up against his body.

He had the ATV in neutral and positioned at the edge of the slope with a rock wedged under its front wheel to keep it from rolling down into the ravine. Now that the flames were dancing back and forth over it, he picked up a fallen tree branch and used it to push the rock away. Then he went around to the back of the vehicle and used the branch to push it down the slope.

It picked up speed as it went, bouncing wildly over outcroppings and over roots, the rushing air turning it into a streaking comet. But it didn't overturn until its left wheels rode up over a large rounded rock more than halfway down. Then it landed on its side, flipped, and rolled the rest of the way, coming to a stop upside down in the ravine. The flames were not doused by the rolling, rather they seemed energized by the increased flow of oxygen. Smoke began rising from the blaze, heading upward toward the forest ceiling.

To his right, about halfway down the hill, there was an old fallen tree lying on its side. It was wedged against another healthy tree that had prevented it from slipping further down the slope. From the tree, he would have a clear line of sight to the ATV below. He started working his way there. Assuming Cullin saw the smoke, he would have to leave the ATV at the top of the hill and work his way down on foot if he was going to get visual confirmation that he was dead. He'd be an easy target. And even if Cullin waited for JT to arrive, there would be enough cover for Jack to get off a second shot before JT could locate where the first had originated. At least that was his plan. Because now, he needed the GPS device.

HE WAS LYING ON his stomach, the radio turned down to a whisper, his body hidden from view by the tree and the foliage that had grown up around it. The tree was large—about four feet wide—and there was a space beneath its center where it had landed on some smaller rocks. There was about two feet of space between the ground around the rocks and the bottom of the tree that he was able to slide the rifle through, the ATV continuing to burn downrange. He'd gotten lucky with the terrain. The ground sloped away from the fallen tree without any bumps or rises between his position and the bottom of the ravine. Clear line of sight.

The rifle didn't have a bipod, but he had the barrel resting in a patch of grass, which freed his left hand from having to hold it steady. Instead, he had his arm bent in front of him and his hand holding the top of the stock tight against his shoulder like he'd seen snipers do in the movies and like Stacey had taught him. He wished he had more time to look over the acquired rifle, but other than making sure it was loaded and ready to fire, he hadn't had the chance. But it had already proved itself reliable, so he wasn't too concerned. The ATV was only about forty yards away.

He heard the unmistakable sound of a small engine approaching. It got louder and then stopped. He moved his eyes to the top of the hill where he'd set the ATV on fire, and saw that another quad had taken its place.

The sound of breaking branches and rustling leaves drew his attention away from the vehicle and to the slope stretching down beneath it. Passing behind trees and partially hidden by the underbrush, he spotted a man working his way down into the ravine. He had an odd-looking rifle in one hand, the other reaching out to steady himself against passing trees. The guy had a haircut from the '70s or something, and it was flopping around as he bounced from tree to tree.

He saw no signs of another person, so it had to be Cullin or JT. He hoped it was Cullin with his GPS, because he might only get one chance at this.

Jack watched as the guy approached the inferno with his rifle at the ready. He crouched beside it, trying to see if Jack was pinned beneath. After finding no one tangled in the wreckage, he looked up and began sweeping his gaze through the forest. He unclipped the radio and raised it to his lips.

"The boy's father went off the trail."

Jack heard what the guy said over the radio on his belt.

"There's a fire," the guy added.

"A fire? What're ya talkin' about? Lawrence, are ya there?"

"Lawrence can't answer ya right now," the man in the ravine answered.

Jack lined him up. He was standing behind the quad, everything above his belt an open target through the hot, shimmering air.

Another voice came over the radio that Jack didn't yet have a name for. *"Where is Lawrence, Cullin?"*

"I told you. He got shot and fell off. Didn't think to take his radio with him."

It was Cullin. Jack put the sights over his heart, ignored the gnats buzzing in his ear, and pulled the trigger.

THE SOUND OF THE blast ricocheted down the ravine, and any birds that hadn't already taken flight were making their getaway now.

Cullin dropped from sight.

Jack waited, keeping his aim laser-focused on the burning vehicle, looking for any sign of movement through the dancing flames.

Nothing.

But he couldn't wait any longer, not with JT on his way. He stood, keeping the rifle trained on the quad, and moved around the tree. Careful not to slip on the loose leaves, he worked his way across the slope. He didn't want to go down into the ravine without first being able to see Cullin.

As the gasoline burnt off and the flames lessened, Jack worked his way parallel to the overturned vehicle. And saw a foot sticking past it on the other side. He began to sidestep, moving laterally, rifle trained on the foot. The foot led to a leg, then to another foot attached to another leg, bent at the knee. Cullin was lying on his stomach, left arm bent down at the elbow, right arm bent up at the elbow. He was in a classic chalk-outline pose. There were no weapons in his hands, and the rifle he'd been carrying was lying a few feet away from him.

Jack adjusted his pack and began descending the rest of the hill, expecting Cullin to be lying on top of a pistol and to roll onto his back and raise it at any moment. But he wasn't moving. Jack thought about shooting him again, just to make sure he was dead, but he didn't know how far away the other guy was and didn't want to give away his location. Plus he was going to need every shot he could get for when he got to the trucks.

He saw the radio next to the rifle and picked it up. Clipped it onto his belt next to the other one. Now he'd have a backup if the battery died on Theo's. He set the rifle down and pulled out the revolver. He pressed it against the back of Cullin's head, the barrel sinking into the mop that was his hair. He patted him down, looking for the GPS, but he only found a hunting knife and a pistol. He tossed them aside and rolled him over onto his back. Cullin's face appeared, his eyes closed under a swathe of hair. The guy really did look like he could be a villain in some bad eighties movie. He searched the front of him and didn't find the device there either.

Jack stood straight and stepped away from the body, pistol still ready. He noticed blood on his hand from patting Cullin down and saw where he'd shot him. He'd aimed for his heart, but the blood was above that, soaking through the shirt at his shoulder. The shot had been about seven inches high and to the right. Maybe Jack could blame it on the heat shimmer. Maybe the last shot had just been luck.

But was he dead?

No. His chest was rising and falling, so he was still breathing. The force of the blast must have sent him to the ground. Maybe he hit his head on a rock or something. He didn't know. But he was going to—

"This is JT. Where are you? I see the smoke."

Damn. If he could see the smoke, then he was just moments from appearing at the top of the ridge. There was no more time. He picked up Theo's rifle and slung it over his shoulder. Then he ran over to where he'd tossed Cullin's knife and pistol. Maybe he should take them, or maybe they'd just slow him down. *No time,* the voice in his head cried. And he chucked them into the fire. Then he grabbed the rifle. Thought about taking that too—it had a scope—but so far he was two for two with the one on his back, even if the last shot had been a little off. He tossed it in the fire with the others.

He looked at Cullin one last time, again debating on whether to kill him. He could slit his throat easily enough. Or maybe it would work to his advantage to keep him alive. Maybe he'd slow down JT, or maybe the two of them would kill each other.

He was out of time. He turned and ran up the hill as fast as he could, grabbing at roots and rocks and any handholds he could find that would help get him to the top faster.

When he reached the top of the hill, he went to the quad and looked it over.

There it was.

A yellow handheld GPS device, clipped to the handlebars. It was next to another radio.

He wished he could just hop on the quad and ride away, but with JT about to show up, there was no way Jack could stay out of sight while motoring away on a quad. He grabbed the key out of the ignition and shoved it in his pocket. Then he grabbed the GPS and the radio and ran.

Above the sound of the birds and the insects came the approaching sound of a vehicle working its way toward him through the trees. Jack ducked behind some undergrowth and waited until JT passed. He tried to get a good look at him as he went by, but he was a good fifty yards away and weaving in and out of trees. Still, he could tell that he had short hair, a beard, and a big mustache. He wasn't skinny like Theodore either. This guy, even from so quick a passing and at such a distance, struck Jack as the typical drunk who liked to run his mouth and pick fights with smaller people. But maybe he was wrong, maybe he was an intellectual who just helped the local trash kidnap kids over summer break.

Jack clipped the GPS and the radio onto his belt, and as soon as JT's back was to him, he sprang to his feet and continued running. Thorns pulled at his clothes, but he pushed through them. He scampered across the dead leaves and scattered rocks and eventually found himself back at the path. But he didn't stop to catch his breath or take in his surroundings. He ran straight across the path and through the tree line on the other side of it. They wouldn't think to come after him north of where they'd originally started, and he wanted to put some distance between him and the ATV before he started heading for the trucks.

He assumed that JT had found Cullin by now and that he'd radioed the others to let them know. Jack still had Theo's radio turned down to a whisper, and he wouldn't have heard it over his labored breathing and pounding feet. The weight of the pack was pressing down on him, and his legs were burning. The axe handle was knocking against his thigh.

24

JACK CHECKED HIS PROGRESS on the digital display of the GPS device. The device itself looked like a walkie-talkie with a few extra buttons on either side, except that it had a screen with a topographical map instead of a speaker. Inserted in the middle of the map, between lined waves representing the elevation of the current terrain, he saw himself as a red arrow pointing west. He was halfway through a swatch of forest that joined the mountains he and Joseph had been camping in and what looked to be state game lands that stretched into the Allegheny Mountains. There was a trail of hash marks dissecting the map, and he knew from his limited research into GPS devices that these were referred to as breadcrumbs. It marked the path that the device had traveled. There were only two waypoints showing, one at the campsite they had abducted Joe at and another all the way at the Pennsylvania-West Virginia border. Both waypoints were connected by breadcrumbs, showing the route Cullin had taken from the trucks to where Jack was right now. So they had come over the West Virginia border, which meant they would most likely make camp somewhere tonight. That gave him a chance.

He worked the buttons on the side to move the map to the left and right so that he could see the first waypoint and his destination, but he didn't dare do anything else. For all he knew, this map had been uploaded to the device, and if he hit the wrong button, he might delete it or maybe reset the trail and erase the breadcrumbs or remove the waypoints.

He was a little north of the breadcrumbs Cullin had left the day before, and the two dotted paths were traveling parallel to each other. From his position now, assuming the legend showing on the screen was correct, he was, "as the crow flies," about eighty miles from their starting waypoint.

He hadn't heard anything over the radio in a while and wasn't sure if that meant the mountains were interfering or if he was out of range. Had JT already passed him, heading back to meet up with the others, or was he out there looking for him? Had he killed Cullin? He didn't know. But if the rest of them were going to make camp somewhere along the route they'd taken yesterday, then maybe he could catch up and grab Joseph while they slept.

He adjusted his heading southwest so that his course merged with Cullin's. He crossed over a stream, skipping across slick, algae-covered rocks, and saw an access road through the underbrush up ahead. Tire marks ran through the dirt.

He started to jog, the afternoon sun breaching windows in the canopy and blinding his eyes. Sweat ran down his back.

25

IT WAS NEARLY FIVE o'clock when Stacey left Langley, and she was starving. She stopped at a diner somewhere around Baltimore and had breakfast for dinner. She sat there for almost an hour, staring into space and sipping at her coffee.

The meeting had gone fine, though what they wanted her to do now was going to be tricky. It wasn't that it was dangerous (though it was), but rather how she would pull it off without Jack knowing. Which meant more lies.

She checked her cell phone to see if she'd gotten any missed calls or texts from Jack. Nothing. She thought that was strange but figured they were just out of cell range. And without the hotspot...

She'd have to come up with a reason to go to New Orleans in October. One that Jack would buy. And Jack didn't really buy anything. The other ops she'd been assigned had all been within driving distance, and she'd arranged for them to correspond with other, more plausible reasons for traveling. This time it would require a flight.

When she finally left the diner, she resolved to spend the rest of the three-hour drive home trying to forget this half of her double life.

26

THE ALARM SOUNDED ON his watch. It was 7 p.m. Time to think about getting settled before dark. If only he could settle. He was exhausted. After jogging on and off for hours, he was more than ready to collapse. Or at least ditch the pack. Did he really need it anyway? He might if he managed to get Joseph back. Depending on where they'd made camp, they could find themselves fifty miles from anything. Then he'd want to have the stuff in the pack.

He moved his foot forward again, once more thinking it had to be the last step he'd take before falling over. But then he took three more. Ten more. Twenty.

The sun was dipping, and the light in the trees had begun to change. It was getting darker, the light no longer coming straight down through the gaps in the leafy canopy, but at a lower angle, casting shadows everywhere.

Joseph. *I'm coming.*

The access road had ended miles ago, and without knowing how accurate the breadcrumbs were in relation to the little triangle that was his current location on the GPS, he figured there could be a hundred yards separating where he was actually standing from the actual route Cullin had taken. So he was trying to follow a path that a group of quads could have navigated, but it didn't look to him like any kind of vehicles had come through here. Not that he had tracking experience of any kind. But he figured it didn't matter as far as getting to the trucks was concerned. He was confident he'd be able to find them. But if there was leeway between the breadcrumbs and his current position, then finding their camp could be a problem. He could wander right past it in the dark.

He'd covered almost twenty more miles since shooting Cullin, which meant he had about sixty miles to go before reaching the waypoint. Too far. He could only hope they made camp nearer to his location than the waypoint. Otherwise, he might not reach the camp in time.

He knew that some GPS devices could link to others of the same model. If this particular device had the capability, then he could maybe ping the other device and see where it was on the map. Or was that something that had to be preset when they were together? There was nothing on the screen that gave any indication that was an option, and as he'd already determined, he wasn't about to go pushing buttons he was unsure of, messing with settings. There was an envelope icon in the top corner of the screen, but again, he didn't dare do anything that might lose the waypoint. Some devices could be used anywhere in the world due to their use of satellite networks like Iridium, and could not only track you and send an SOS to the system's monitoring center but could also be used to send text messages or emails to any phone number or email address in the world.

Could he send a text to Stacey? He was so tempted to play around with it, but again, too afraid to lose the map and waypoints. Especially right now, when his brain was on its way down a greased sliding board and into a pool of exhausted delirium.

Things were making less sense, and suddenly Ws came to mind, but he wasn't sure why. "W, w, w, w, w..." he whispered to himself, trying to capture the meaning of the letter. "Water," he said. "And wood." But he couldn't remember the other Ws or how many more there were. He was so thirsty. Despite sweating through his clothes, he'd managed to only drink half his bottle of water. But he knew he'd need to drink the rest soon or risk getting cramps or fainting. The wood was for...fire. Then there were the other Ws, right? Who, where, why, and...was it when? But did he even have the answers to any of them yet?

He looked around. Trees and rocks grew out of brown leaves. Sapling, vines, and dead wood all entangled in some chaotic rave. Then he stumbled over to a large boulder, quickly scanned the area for snakes, and finally slipped the gun and backpack off his shoulders.

He thought his boots must've come off the ground a little when the weight on his shoulders suddenly vanished. Until, finally standing still, cramps came shooting up his legs.

"Shit," he screamed, and he went down, clutching at his quads, trying to get them to relax. It felt like his muscles had turned into balls of knots and were going to explode like grenades if he couldn't get them to stop contracting right now. He forced his legs straight and lay on his back. The knots disappeared. He breathed heavily, trying to recover from the sudden and intense pain. He needed water. He shifted to reach for the pack, and his quad exploded again. He screamed and began breathing like a woman in labor. "Whooo-whooo-hee. Whooo-whooo-hee." He stared at his leg and thought that his jeans might rip apart. Was this what Bruce Banner felt every time he turned into the Hulk? "Whooo-whooo-heee..."

Thirty seconds went by before the muscle relaxed, but he had the bottle in his hand. He swallowed, feeling the liquid travel down his throat and fill his stomach. He kept drinking. And drinking. He drank the rest of it. He lay on his back and tried not to move. This was not good. He decided he'd give himself twenty minutes before trying to move again. Let the water do its thing.

The cool evening air whispered through the trees, and he felt his eyes suddenly grow heavy. He couldn't fall asleep. Not now. He had to catch up.

He thought about the GPS. Wondered how long the batteries lasted. Once he could move again, he'd take out Joseph's book and do his best to copy the breadcrumbs from the GPS onto the map in the book just in case the batteries did die before he could get there.

His stomach growled. He would eat a protein bar from his pack.

But he fell asleep before he could even reach for it.

27

STACEY TOSSED HER KEYS onto the counter next to Jack's hotspot and kicked off her shoes. It was about ten o'clock now, and she just wanted to go to sleep. Though she was sure the six cups of coffee she'd had would have something to say about that.

She checked her phone again. Still nothing from Jack. She was about to call him when the phone started ringing in her hand. Jack's picture appeared on the screen. *Finally*, she thought. And then the guilt hit her full in the gut when she realize she was going to have to fabricate her entire day when he asked about it. That was what she should have been thinking about on the drive home, not what the CIA wanted her to do next.

She accepted the call and brought the phone to her ear. "Hey, babe. I was start—"

"Mrs. Green."

Her heart froze. In the time it took for just those two words to be spoken, her mind had already pieced together enough information to trigger panic. It wasn't that it was someone other than Jack calling her from his phone. That could be explained a dozen different ways. It was the synthesized voice generator that spoke the two words that had immediately indicated what was happening. Maybe it was all the movies she'd seen, or maybe it was her intelligence background, but she anticipated the next four words even as the emotionless computer-generated voice spoke them.

"We have your son."

The floor seemed to fall out from beneath her, and she leaned forward onto the counter to keep from collapsing. Everything was spinning. She couldn't breathe.

"If you do not wish for him to be harmed, you will do exactly as we say."

She sat on the floor. Pulled her knees to her face.

"If Douglas T. Newell is still alive Saturday morning, your son will not be. We will call you with more details. Do not attempt to contact anyone. We are watching you. And you will never find us."

The phone went dead.

Stacey sat there with the phone pressed against her ear for another thirty seconds, her hands shaking as her mind tried to come to terms with what she'd just heard. She put the phone down, stood, gripped the edge of the counter until the veins surfaced in her arms, and screamed.

—Joseph was kidnapped—

—they have Jack's phone—

—didn't mention him; why wouldn't they mention him?—

—who are "they"?—

—why Douglas Newell?—

—how would they want her to—

—no, she wouldn't—

—she would, she knew she would—

—no, I'll find another way; I'll get help—

—then Joseph will die just like Jack, and you'll be alone—

—we'll all be dead; they won't let me live—

Slowly, she forced herself to calm. She had to get it together. She had to figure this out, to be smarter than them. There was no time to waste trying to compute how suddenly her life had just turned upside down. No practical purpose sitting there paralyzed by the news. No, she would overcome the hurricane of emotion with swift and sound reason. She would find the floor beneath her and restore her balance. It was time to do what she did best. To work. To find out who *they* were. That was the only thing that mattered right now.

Jack's dead. You know he's dead...

She pushed the thought away. Couldn't afford to go there right now. She couldn't save him, but she could still save their son. She wiped her eyes with the back of her hand while sweeping her eyes back and forth through her home, searching the walls, the lights, the air vents. The voice had said they were watching her. Were there cameras in her house? She didn't think so. The Agency would've known. She started to think about how she could get a trace on Jack's phone, though she knew they wouldn't use it again. That had just been their way of proving Jack was dead and that they had her son. Now that that had been established, the next call, which would no doubt be longer, would come over a secure line. In the meantime, while she waited for the next call, she divorced herself from all emotion and focused instead on the person they wanted dead.

Douglas T. Newell, the senator from Vermont who would be running for President of the United States in the upcoming primary election.

28

HAM CHECKED THE TIME. It was after ten. Usually he'd be asleep by now, but not being in communication with James for so long had him on edge. Pacing back and forth, staring at the map, pouring another drink—that had become the day's routine.

He looked at the map again, wondering where they might have made camp for the night. He wouldn't be able to get them until they were back on the road, when James could call him on the burner phone he'd given him. Once they were at the top of Hollow Mountain, he'd be in constant communication with them. It was just this initial part of getting the boy back to the trucks and then getting up the mountain that he'd be in the dark.

He wasn't exactly sure where Hollow Mountain was, just that it was somewhere in the Cranberry Wilderness or close to it. The mountain was somewhat of a mystery to those who didn't live in its shadow. From what he was able to gather, the mountain was forbidden, whether legally or by reputation alone, he wasn't certain. Though he wasn't so sure the Bakers themselves hadn't been the ones spreading such information as a way to keep people away from whatever they might have stashed on it—like the cabin. He sure didn't like his guys being dependent on the Baker boys to get them to their destination though. He understood why it was that way. Hell, he would've done the same. But not knowing what was going on was just driving him insane. He couldn't stop his mind from conjuring up every conceivable thing that could be going wrong. And that was just to get the boy to the cabin. His gang holing up with Lee and company until Saturday was almost unthinkable. He prayed they would keep their differences under wraps, at least until after the boy was delivered. Ham had a sneaking suspicion that if anything went wrong, and they couldn't get the boy where he needed to be on time, there would be hell to pay.

He ran a big hand through his short sweaty hair, and the glass almost slipped from his hand when he went to pick it back up.

He wasn't exactly sure who was supposed to be paying him, though the middleman who'd delivered the job had left him with a bad feeling. Like spiders down the nape of the neck. Which Ham only got when talking about one entity.

He'd implied to the others that the boy was wanted for some sex-trafficking thing, that the people who hired them were going to sell the kid off to some billionaire or some kind of boy brothel in New Jersey or something. And he'd half-believed it when he said it, but that feeling just wouldn't go away. And in fact, it was getting stronger, the spiders growing, their legs now hairy tarantula legs. But what did it matter? If the spiders were right, then he couldn't say no to the job anyway. You didn't say no to these people without pitting yourself against them, which was about the same as digging your own grave and waiting for them to push you in it. The job was to hold the boy at the cabin until Saturday and then drop him off at a gas station in town. That was it. Simple. Nothing to get worked up over.

Except that it wasn't so simple. Because whoever it was, they'd also brought the Bakers into it. Was it just coincidence that they didn't get along, or was there something else to all this? Something that maybe the Bakers were in on? After all, there was no reason to even involve Ham, was there? There was enough help in Bakerville to get the job done, so why include him and his crew? The employer had provided the Bakers with two preprogrammed GPS devices but hadn't given anything to him. Which for all intents and purposes put Lee Baker in charge. Maybe the Bakers had requested Ham's help? He took his glasses off and rubbed his eyes. He didn't trust any of this for a New York minute.

He took another sip, put his glasses back on, and looked out the window and into the darkness. He wondered how they would come for him if it all went sour. How many would they send? He'd be as ready as he could be, that was for damn sure.

But how do you defend yourself against a ghost story? About things heard around campfires and at the town potlucks?

He drained what was left in his glass. He would go visit Carl, the person who brought him the job. See if he could find out just who it was that hired them. See if it really had been the boogeyman. He'd wait until James called him on the cell, and then he'd go looking for answers.

He took his pistol and a cigarette into the bedroom.

29

STACEY WAS STILL SITTING at the kitchen table at 2 a.m. As she'd expected, the kidnappers had called her back on a secure line half an hour later and told her how she was supposed to assassinate the senator and when she was supposed to do it.

Tomorrow night. With a bomb.

And just like that, the course of her life had been forever altered. A life, she was pretty certain, that would not see the weekend if she were to do what they wanted. Not that she believed they would let Joseph go after completing the job. If they'd already killed Jack and were planning on blowing up a building full of people, then they wouldn't have any qualms about burying a twelve-year-old kid in the woods. Yet she couldn't come up with a scenario that would give him better odds.

After she'd used the thirty minutes between calls that they'd given her to settle down and accept her situation, she had logged in to the account she used to track Jack's phone activity. She knew the Agency was still tracking him too, but she'd wanted to be able to keep her own eye on him as well. Now she was glad she'd been installing the tracking apps on his phone over the years, because going to the Agency for help with this was out of the question. She just couldn't risk it.

The tracking app would show his location as long as his phone had a signal, which it didn't right now because they'd most certainly destroyed it after calling her. But the app stored the cell towers that were used when making calls from his phone, so she could see which tower was nearest to the last call.

And that location had been Marlinton, West Virginia.

She looked it up. Saw that it was in the mountains. Though West Virginia was the only state considered to be entirely part of Appalachia, so it didn't necessarily mean anything. The kidnappers could have pulled over to make the call on their way to Mexico.

But who the hell were they? How did they know she was CIA? Because they obviously chose her for that reason. No way in the world this was a random kidnapping. They hadn't just been sitting around in the woods for the last week, hoping that some guy and his kid would show up before Thursday so they could kidnap him, counting on the mother having connections they could exploit in order to—

It wasn't even worth expending the brain power on. She'd been selected by someone a long time ago, and that person had been waiting for the chance to use her. And Jack's trip with Joseph had been the perfect opportunity.

So who knew she was CIA? Obviously, the CIA knew she was CIA. Or at least certain members within it. Could this be them getting rid of Jack like they'd always wanted to while at the same time "retiring" her with one last op? Were they finally tying off all Trenton's loose ends?

But why would the CIA want the senator dead? Was he opposed to an operation they were drafting like Kennedy had been opposed to the Joint Chiefs' Northwoods operation? Or was it just your classic case of problem-reaction-solution, and they were setting up whatever enemy they wanted to justify going to war against? Maybe both?

She stood up to stretch her legs and to get her blood moving. A tear escaped, and she wiped it away, continuing to push back the storm. She was tired now, all the caffeine having worn off in the adrenaline rush prompted by the phone call. Now she was crashing. But there was something nagging in the back of her mind that she wasn't ready to abandon just yet, something she was trying to tease into the light. Something just on the tip of her brain.

She went back to the laptop and closed out all the articles she had brought up on the senator. She hadn't found anything the CIA would be opposed to yet, but she tried a new keyword search. His name paired with the words "foreign policy."

Suddenly, she was reading remarks that could have been taken straight from the 2016 presidential race. Stuff about Russia. It was just a remix of the classic Red Scare song, the beat behind the new lyrics the same war drums. But that would be something the CIA would like, wouldn't it? Or had things changed that much? And wouldn't that be ironic, if they used the person they had first tasked with trying to start a war with Russia to now take out the person who would actually have the power to finally get it done? One day you were a hero, the next a liability. Guess it all depended on the day's agenda. It was a bad business.

She thought about why they would call her to Langley for another mission if they were the ones behind this. Misdirection? Or a case of the left hand not knowing what the right was doing? Was it just a coincidence that the Agency had called her back at the same time someone else was setting her up as a political assassin?

She closed the laptop and looked out the window in the living room, saw the moonlight reflecting off the river.

There was another possibility. And it was this possibility that proved to be the right bait, summoning the illusive thought off the tip of her tongue and into the spotlight.

Appalachia.

30

JACK WOKE UP TO a sound that he couldn't immediately interpret. As it penetrated the different levels of consciousness, slowly pulling him out of sleep, his mind tried to match the sound with images. The first few images were nonsensical and could only be understood within the context of whatever dream he was having. But then the dream faded, and the images became clear.

A wind chime.

No...it was a cabasa.

Or was it a baby's rattle?

Rattle.

His eyes snapped open as the sound finally registered a match. And sure enough, about six feet away from him and coiled in a patch of sunlight was a snake, its tail in the air and shaking so fast that it was just a blur above its triangular head.

He stood, instantly awake. There was a boulder behind him, and he quickly pulled himself up on top of it, expecting to feel fangs sink into his calf as he scrambled atop it. He grabbed a decaying branch that was leaning against the boulder and threw it at the serpent. The branch shattered when it hit the ground, and the reptile slithered out of the sunlight and into the shaded grass. *Sitting on a boulder and watching a rattler.* Must be Southern Pennsylvania.

He looked at his watch. 6:26. He swore. He must've slept through the six o'clock alarm. Which meant he'd been asleep for nearly twelve hours. He had woken up around ten and then again around three, but he'd thought using a flashlight to navigate the woods at night would not be a good idea when there were people out there looking to kill him. He'd figured rest was his best option so that he could cover as much ground as quickly as possible in the daylight hours. But now he was really behind schedule. He looked at the GPS. There were still nearly sixty miles between his current location and the waypoint. Now he had to hope that they'd made camp somewhere close *and* that they hadn't set out yet.

He looked down at himself and noticed that he was covered in burs. He began picking them off and flicking them onto the ground. Then he stretched, the early light coming through a gap in the canopy and warming the rock. His body ached, and his feet were a little sore, but he hadn't developed any blisters yet. The legs, the seat of his jeans, and his back were wet from lying on the ground all night, but he knew they'd be dry in an hour or so.

He slid off the boulder and landed next to his pack. His mouth was dry, his throat tight. He'd have to find a water source soon.

He knelt and dug through the backpack until he found the plastic-wrapped jerky. He didn't want to spend the time making breakfast, so the EMRs would have to wait. He'd eat the jerky and protein bars first. He could worry about his diet later. For now, he just needed to maintain an adequate energy level.

As he chewed the dried meat, he felt something crawling on the back of his neck. He reached back and pinched it, knowing immediately what it was. He brought it up to his eyes just to confirm. A tick. He flicked it away as a series of shivers racked his flesh.

Then he became aware of something moving across his stomach. He lifted his shirt and found more ticks. Seven of them. All on their way up his torso and toward his head. He picked them off one at a time, which he was surprised took an incredible amount of self-control. It was all he could do to keep from trying to swipe them all away at once, but he wanted to make sure he got every single one of them. He did not need to accidentally brush one down the front of his pants.

He wanted to take his clothes off, and to put on the clean clothes that were in his bedroll. But he didn't have time for that now. Whatever ticks were still on him—in his socks, burrowing into his legs, slipping beneath his underwear—he would have to deal with later.

He checked the radio. It was still powered on and broadcasting silence. As he chewed the jerky, he walked over to a nearby tree and relieved himself. The sunlight caught the stream, and it glistened a darker shade of gold. It wasn't orange, but it was on its way there. He knew that meant he was already dehydrated. It smelled strong too. He didn't know how long it would take for his kidneys to shut down from dehydration—if that was something that could happen in a single day or if it would take a few—but he knew it did mean Charlie's horses were still in the area.

He thought of Joseph, figuring that he was probably awake by now. Unless they really were sex traffickers and they already had him on a steady dose of heroine. He shoved the thought aside. He couldn't go there. Couldn't put himself in his son's shoes. Couldn't imagine what Joseph was thinking, what he was feeling. Couldn't think about what they might be doing to him or what might happen to him if he didn't reach him in time. Not if he wanted to save him. If he started concentrating on those things, if he let those feelings in, then they would immobilize him. Shut him down. Turn him into one of the slobbering psych ward patients that had lived next to his old baseball field. He couldn't afford to let that happen. So he fortified his mind from all those thoughts, from all those memories made eight years ago.

Think, he told himself. *Think*.

He grabbed his pack and climbed back on top of the boulder, not wanting to have to worry about snakes slithering up his pant leg while trying to figure things out. He bit off another piece of jerky and pulled Joseph's book out of the pack. He sat down atop the rock and opened it to the map of the Appalachian Trail. He put the GPS next to it, noting that the battery icon was on the wrong side of half. He didn't think it would last the rest of the day, so he did his best to compare Joseph's map with the map on the GPS display.

Though the map in the book was mostly showing the Appalachian Trail, a portion of the border between Pennsylvania and West Virginia did make the cut. The two waypoints showing on the GPS were separated by 116 miles, so he took a pencil from his belt pouch and drew a line from the shelter to the West Virginia-Pennsylvania border and wrote "116." Then he used the book's legend to count out roughly sixty miles from the border and marked that spot across the line. Now he knew where he was in the book and where he had to go (at least in approximation) for when the GPS died.

But that still wasn't good enough, because once he got to the border, then what? So he toggled the map on the GPS to the waypoint and opened to a blank page in the book. Then, as detailed as he could make it, he copied the map from the screen into the book, marking the breadcrumbs, the roads, and the legend. At least that way he had a general idea of where the trucks were once he reached the border. Would they still be there by then? And if not, then what?

He'd worry about that then. He tore out the pages he'd just modified, folded them, and stuck them in his pocket. Then he shoved the book back into the pack along with the two other confiscated radios and took another bite of his breakfast.

As he worked his jaw, sucking the juices and savoring the taste, he reached down for Theo's rifle. He set it across his lap and looked it over. It looked like a standard hunting rifle to him. Minus a scope. It had a wooden stock, whether actual wood or synthetic, he wasn't sure, but it felt real to him. The magazine held four rounds, and since there were two left after shooting Lawrence and Cullin, Theo must have just loaded in a fresh one before Jack had run into him. With the extra magazine now in his pack, he had a total of six rounds left. He was two for two with the gun thus far, so he wasn't too concerned with its accuracy (even if the last shot had been four inches high and to the right). But would six shots be enough? Maybe he *should* have taken Cullin's rifle.

He laid the rifle aside and took the revolver out of his pants. It was about eleven inches long and had a six-round cylinder. It had a gold circle at the top of the handle that said Colt. It looked like something from WWI. The cylinder was full, and he had six more bullets in his bag. So twelve shots with the revolver. Eighteen altogether. Could be enough for eight combatants. Or bears or anything else he stumbled across out here in the mountains. If he didn't miss.

He got to his feet and stuck the pistol into his belt, pulling his shirt down over top of it. Then he pulled the pack over his shoulders and picked up the rifle. He hopped off the boulder, took a heading, and began marching southwest, continuing to retrace Cullin's trail.

As he walked, he tried again to come up with theories of who could be behind this. Who could've known where they'd be. Why they needed his cell phone. And the more he thought about it, the less convinced he was that it could be Stacey. Even if he did believe that she could do this to him, he couldn't imagine her putting Joseph through it. There would have been much easier ways to get rid of him without Joseph's involvement. Hell, just tamper with his brakes, and a car accident on his way to work would've taken care of things.

He looked at his watch again. It was Wednesday. 6:50 a.m. He had three days before Joseph was to be handed off. If he let that happen, then he'd never see his son again. He'd have to go to the FBI and then endure all the coming years of them coming up empty-handed.

The GPS made a noise, and he looked at it. The envelope icon on the screen now had a number 2 next to it. He was getting messages from someone. Lee? The people behind this whole thing? He wanted to open the texts, but again was too afraid that he'd lose the map and wouldn't be able to get it back. What if they knew he had the GPS and the text was some kind of virus that would erase all its contents? Was that even possible? How the hell would he know? It was something he thought would seem reasonable in a movie. Though he did have a general sense of where he was going handwritten on Joseph's map, so would it even be a great loss if he were to lose the GPS? Maybe not. But in a situation where every minute mattered, the breadcrumbs to the waypoint gave him his best chance at getting to the trucks in time. If he missed the trucks or the device was about to die, then he'd try to look at the texts. But right now, salvaging every spare second was what mattered most. Besides, he figured the messages were just wondering where the hell Cullin was and why he wasn't responding. Which would not help him get his son back or find out who was behind it.

He clipped the device to his belt and double-timed it through the mountains.

31

JAMES STARED AT THE mountains, watching the mist that blanketed them begin to stretch apart and break loose. He took a drink from his canteen.

"This all's gone to hell, hasn't it?" Colt asked behind him.

James turned his head and looked at him. He was dry shaving with his hunting knife, shirtless, all his tattoos on display.

"You should put a shirt on. You'll scare the kid," James said.

The knife paused mid-streak, and Colt squinted. "Are you serious?"

James looked back to the mountaintops and nodded.

Colt ran a hand through his black hair. "We kidnap him, drug him, drag him out here, kill his daddy, gonna hand him over to people that're gonna sell him for sex, and yer suddenly worried my tats'll scare him?"

"Is he awake?"

"I don't know."

"Go check on him. Take him some breakfast. I want to be on the move in half an hour."

Colt nodded. "Oh, I get it. We're supposed to deliver him in tip-top shape, right? For the pictures? I mean, no one's gonna wanna bugger a boy who looks like he was just pulled from a POW camp, right?"

"Just go check on him."

"Okay, boss."

"Don't call me that."

Colt laughed. "Not yet, ya mean." He turned and went off toward the campfire.

James watched him go. Watched the crossed M16s squirm on his back as his arms swayed and his shoulders moved back and forth while he walked. Watched as he reached out and grabbed a shirt off the handlebars of an ATV.

Michael got up from the fire and walked over to his brother. "Everything okay?" he asked.

James nodded.

Michael looked off into the distance, tucking his hands into the front pockets of his coat. "What are we gonna do 'bout Lawrence?"

"We'll figure that part out once we take care of the father."

"I don't like that we haven't heard from JT or Cullin yet."

"They're just out of range is all. Still looking for the father. They know they can't come back without taking care of him first."

Michael shook his head. "This is gettin' messy."

"Just need to get the boy to the cabin."

But Michael shook his head. "That wasn't the only part of it. You think Ham won't mind we only done half of what he said?"

"It ain't Ham I'm worried about."

Michael looked back at the fire. "The Bakers?"

"For starters."

"The father?"

"And whoever the hell hired us."

Michael looked down at his boots. "What're you thinkin'?"

"I'll let ya know when I know."

"We'll be in Baker territory soon."

"I know." He watched Colt take a plate into the boy's tent. "Keep an eye on Lee."

"What do ya mean?"

"Just watch him. But keep your cool, brother. We don't need another one of your episodes. Not yet anyway."

32

JACK WAS GLAD HE'D spent the last few months breaking in his hiking boots. He'd gone on an hour-long walk around the neighborhood after first purchasing them, and he'd gotten so many blisters on his feet, he thought he could wear the blisters themselves as shoes. But he'd upgraded his socks and shortened his walks, and the boots had broken in nicely. All the books he'd read in preparation for the trip said that when it came to hiking and camping, your feet would be the biggest factor in determining how miserable you were. Thankfully, his feet to this point hadn't been an issue, though he realized he still had a long way to go. He'd wanted to take his socks off before falling asleep, like he and Joseph had done the night before, but of course that had been the furthest thing from his mind at the time.

The woods in this area were emerald green. The dense undergrowth he'd worked his way through had given way to open ground, and he was walking easily among tall maples and what he thought Joseph had said were oaks. The sun was coming through the canopy in an almost mystical fashion, rays of light highlighting endless shades of green as the leaves swayed easily in the morning breeze. Or maybe it was more than a morning breeze. Jack could make out darker clouds coming at him from the west whenever the trees spread apart and there was a break in the forest's ceiling. If rain was on its way, then he'd be finding out about his feet sooner than he'd like. He hadn't seen the pale underside of the maple leaves yet, which he was always told signified rain. Whether or not that was true or how accurate it was, he wasn't sure. There were certainly times he remembered rain showing up after seeing the leaves of trees blowing upside down, but there were also times when he'd anticipated a storm that never came.

A noise to his left.

He dropped to a knee and brought the rifle to his shoulder in one fluid motion that surprised even him. Stacey's training had apparently transitioned to instinct. He swung the rifle in the direction he'd heard the sound.

He waited to hear it again, his heart hammering in his chest, his finger on the trigger.

There it was again—a rustling through dry leaves. About ten yards away. Was it JT? A bear?

Then he caught sight of the little gray culprit as it leapt across the forest floor and darted up a tree, its fluffy tail its identification card. It was the fifth time this morning that a squirrel had nearly given him a heart attack. But he'd take squirrels over snakes any day. He stood, took a deep breath, and resumed his jogging.

He jogged for another five minutes before he came to another stop. There was something up ahead that was glistening through the trees. He squinted, trying to make sense of it. It seemed like a string of diamonds hanging from the trees like a necklace, catching the light. Then he realized it was water.

He'd come to a river.

HE WALKED OUT OF the woods and stepped onto the bank of a wide, lazy river. It was running north to south. He saw it on the GPS and wasn't sure why he hadn't noticed it before. Cullin's trail went right over it, a little to the northwest of his current position. Either they'd all driven across a low spot, or there was a bridge up that way. He wondered if there was a town or a highway nearby and turned to look to his right, upriver.

He saw smoke floating off the bank and over the water.

Quickly, he jumped back through the tree line and dropped to a knee.

The wind was carrying the smoke northeast and away from him, so he hadn't noticed it through the trees. He peered through the branches and could see the remains of what looked to be a recent campfire.

Movement caught his attention. About thirty yards ahead of him and walking through the woods toward the riverbank. It was a person. He could make that much out through the flashes of clothing between the foliage. Unless Bigfoot was wearing jeans these days.

The person stepped out of the forest and walked to the water.

It was Lawrence.

Jack knew from the color of his clothes, the bald head, and the bloodstain on his shirt.

Jack studied him from inside the tree line, settling down behind some brush, being as still as possible.

The man was a bull, his neck like a concrete footing, barely visible between his head and muscled shoulders. Jack could only guess how many noses had been smashed by that wrecking ball of a head. The handlebar mustache made him look like one of those old circus strongmen—striped red and white single-shoulder singlet and holding a barbell loaded with 100-pound balls over his head. Yeah, that was exactly what Jack thought he looked like. As if he'd stepped right out of a vintage circus photograph. Except for the gun sticking from the back of his pants.

The bloodstain was on the front and back of his shoulder, which meant the bullet had passed straight through. Or that he'd somehow managed to dig it out through his back. The rest of the shirt was dirty and streaked with a night's worth of hobbling through the forest. He didn't look too good. Didn't look like he had any supplies other than the gun in his pants and the jean jacket he was now trying to delicately pull on. He must've walked all night to get here before him. Bleeding and with no food or water... Jack figured that he had to be more exhausted than he was. Maybe well into a game of Russian roulette with the Grim Reaper by the time he'd been able to get the fire going.

Jack thought about shooting him again. To finish him off once and for all. He could easily step out of the woods and unload the revolver into his back before he could draw his gun.

But then Lawrence began walking upriver, retracing what were the breadcrumbs on the GPS display. He was headed for the bridge, Jack was sure of it. He squinted, looking for a radio on him. Didn't see one. Jack had three of them on him. Theo's, Cullin's, and he guessed it was Lawrence's that had been on the quad next to the GPS. Which meant the others couldn't know that he was still alive and heading for the waypoint. He could give Lawrence Cullin's radio and make him check in with the others, tell them he was on the way and to wait for him. If they were in range, of course.

And then it hit him. He could use the GPS to text Lee, pretend he was Cullin, and tell him to wait. Why hadn't he thought of that before? Of course, JT was still out there with a radio, and he'd be letting them know that Cullin was dead or at least without the GPS device as soon as he was within range. And that would ruin any chance of him taking them by surprise. But without the GPS, would JT even know how to get back within range? Well, apparently Lawrence did, so he couldn't rule it out. He'd follow Lawrence and decide what to do along the way.

Lawrence was taking tired, sickly strides. Like every step was a chore. If Jack wanted him to radio in, then they'd have to quicken their pace in order to get within range. But it didn't look like Lawrence was capable of quickening anything. Except maybe dying. Or maybe he knew where they'd made camp. Maybe he knew where Hollow Mountain was. Maybe he knew other things.

After a hundred yards, the river curved around a bend, and he waited for Lawrence to follow it out of sight before leaving his cover. He went to the fire and discovered a large bowl-like hole beside it. It was filled with small rocks.

Jack knew what it was. He'd read about it in his books.

Without a pot or a bottle, Lawrence had dug a hole in the ground and smoothed its edges with clay that he must've gotten along the bank. Then he filled it with river water and put the rocks he'd heated in the fire into the water. The rocks then brought the water to a boil, sanitizing it for drinking.

He placed his hands over the rocks and could still feel their heat. Jack had no idea how Lawrence was able to build a fire, find rocks, construct a hole, and somehow fill it with water from the river after he'd spent hours walking through the forest with a hole in his body. This guy was no Theodore.

He slung the pack off his shoulder and took out the bottle and an iodine tablet. Then he walked to the river, filled the bottle, and dropped the tablet into it. It would be twenty to thirty minutes before he could drink it, so he walked back to return it to the pack. Before he did so, he unscrewed the cap a little bit and held the bottle upside down, letting some of the iodine leak out over the bottle's mouth.

He zipped the pack, hefted it back onto his shoulders, and grabbed the rifle. By the time he rounded the river's edge, Lawrence was a good quarter mile away, still hobbling alongside the river's edge. Jack looked at the GPS, trying to see how close the arrow that marked his location was to where the trail crossed the river. Pretty close. He shielded his eyes with his hand and tried to squint through the reflection of the eastern sun off the water. He thought he could see something spanning the river but couldn't be sure if it was a bridge, a tree, or an optical illusion.

He ducked back into the trees and hustled to get closer.

33

STACEY SAT IN HER car and watched another train pull up to the platform. It was the third one that had come to empty some passengers and pick up others while she'd sat there lost in her thoughts.

She was supposed to pick up the bomb at an address in Trenton, which she thought to be rather ironic. It also made her wonder about that other possibility she'd come up with last night, of who else besides the Agency could be behind this.

She tapped her fingers against the steering wheel and watched the train pull away. She knew she would have to get out of the car and board the next one in—she looked at the dashboard clock—twenty-three minutes. She sighed and ran a hand through her hair. Chewed the inside of her cheek. As crazy as this all seemed, it wasn't so far-fetched, was it? In a way, she had been preparing for something like this ever since she'd accepted her first black op. She'd known, way in the back of her mind, that it would all end like this. Whether she'd be ordered by her country into a mission she had zero chance of walking away from, or some enemy slapped a bomb under her car while she slept, there was really only one way this could all end. She knew that. Had maybe forgotten at times, actually getting lost in the role of wife and mother while the Agency seemingly lost interest in her, but the foreboding had always been there under the surface of that so-called normalcy.

Jack was dead. He had to be if they had his phone. *Or maybe he isn't.* Maybe they had him chained up, torturing him for information he couldn't possibly know. If it was the CIA, they could be trying to find out if she'd told him anything. If it was the other possibility, then perhaps they thought he was in on everything. Either way, they wouldn't let him live when they were done with him. Wouldn't let Joseph live either. No, her whole family would be gone by the weekend. Just like that.

Unless she figured something out. Though try as she may, she couldn't think of a damn thing. The only thing her mind kept coming back to was that FBI agent, Johnson, who had helped Jack eight years ago. But what he could do to help, she had no idea. Didn't know where to find him or if he would even be willing to help. Why would he after everything that had happened? He probably knew enough to piece together Donny's death with her involvement in the Trenton operation and was just as likely to shoot her on the spot as he was to help her find Jack and her son.

The show in Philadelphia she had booked online started at three o'clock, so she had to get on the next train. It was the last one that would go to Philadelphia in time. Of course, she wasn't actually going to Philly, just needed to create a digital footprint as an alibi. Purchasing tickets to a show and a train ticket to and from Philly should be enough to let her slip into Trenton without anyone knowing where she'd been. She wasn't supposed to pick up the package until tomorrow morning, but she wanted to scope out the pickup site ahead of time. Besides, what else was she going to do all day? She had to keep moving, to get her mind working. She wasn't going to solve this sitting on her front porch and staring at the Delaware.

She slipped her sunglasses on and pulled a black baseball cap down over her forehead. She opened the door and stepped into the parking lot. Walked to the platform.

As she stood there in the small crowd, she made sure that her body was positioned away from the surveillance cameras.

34

IT WAS AN OLD and faded footbridge that time seemed to have forgotten, probably part of an old trail. It crossed a narrow point of the river, and it was just wide enough for a convoy of ATVs to cross single file.

Jack watched Lawrence hobble across it, leaning against the splintered rail for support as he went. The clouds that were passing overhead drew his attention. They were definitely getting darker, coming from behind the distant mountains and bringing rain.

He waited until Lawrence was across and had disappeared into the woods on the other side before crossing after him. He felt vulnerable out over the water with no cover. All Lawrence had to do was look back over his shoulder and he'd see him coming. He ducked low, trying to stay beneath the railing, and quickened his pace. But not too much—he didn't want to rattle the bridge as he went. He ignored the wasps that were hovering around a large paper nest hanging from beneath the railing.

When he got to the other side without being shot, he figured he hadn't been detected. He stepped off the bridge and saw that it had indeed been part of a trail. There was a footpath carved into the terrain, though now overgrown, running alongside a rotting four-by-four post still sticking out of the ground. Jack was sure there was once a colored arrow attached to it. He followed the path, tracking his progress on the GPS. He was right on top of Cullin's breadcrumbs. But then all signs of the path suddenly disappeared, and he found himself descending a ridge and entering a run. He stopped and looked around. He didn't think the path would be in a run, because the run would flood whenever it rained. Maybe the trail crossed it? He climbed up the ridge and looked at the GPS again. He was still on the red hashes. He looked around for Lawrence, listening for any sign of movement through the woods.

Birds and insects were all he heard.

And then a loud *click.*

There was no second-guessing what that sound was. He slowly turned.

"You the boy's father?" Lawrence asked, leaning against a tree and pointing his pistol at him.

Jack tried to think of a response, something sarcastic or a question of his own, but he could just stand there and stare until the only thing that mattered slipped through his lips. He hated himself for it, thought it made him sound weak. "Are you gonna kill me?"

Lawrence turned his head and spit. "You shot me."

Jack didn't say anything.

"Pretty good shot. You trained for that sort of thing?"

"Not really."

"Just lucky, then?"

"Sure."

"Not so lucky crossing that bridge though."

Dammit. He had seen him.

Lawrence waved the gun at him. "You got water?"

He nodded. "Iodine tablet. Hasn't been twenty minutes though."

"Put the revolver and the rifle on the ground."

Jack obeyed.

"Now the pack and your belt."

Jack slid the pack off his shoulder and lowered it to the ground. The GPS was in his front pocket, concealed by his shirt. He dropped the belt pouch that held his knife, axe, and Theo's radio.

"Now step back," Lawrence said. He walked forward until the equipment was at his feet and Jack's back was against a tree. He got to a knee and used his injured arm to unzip the pack, grimacing as he did so. He found the bottle of water and unscrewed the cap.

Jack watched him drink, thinking that if he went bottoms up, he could maybe make a lunge at him. Who knew, maybe the shock of it would make him choke on the water. But Lawrence kept the bottle level, drinking slowly, gun and gaze steady.

"You could use a doctor," Jack said. Lawrence's face was ashen, but there was enough spark in his eyes to let Jack know he was still capable.

"Yeah," Lawrence said.

Jack's mind was racing, thinking of ways he could turn the situation. He knew he had a little bit of time, that Lawrence wouldn't shoot him here. Not when it would mean he'd have to get rid of his body—which he was in no condition to do. No, he'd have him dig his own grave first or walk him to a cliff again.

"You planning on making it to the trucks in time?" Jack asked.

"Don't think there's much of a chance of that happenin'."

"You going to the cabin, then?"

He looked at him, wondering how much he knew. "Theo sang like a lark, then, did he?"

"Said it was on Hollow Mountain and that the Bakers knew where it was."

"That what he told you?"

"So you don't know where it is?"

Lawrence screwed the cap back on the water. Then he took one of the radios out of the pack. "You got three radios."

"Yup." Jack tilted his head. "So did I shoot you off the quad, or did Cullin push you off?"

Lawrence squinted. Twirled the end of his mustache.

"Theo said I'd know Bakerville when I got there."

"The Baker gang pretty much runs things up that way. Probably meant you'd know you were there as soon as ya started asking questions."

"Because I'd find myself being tossed into a wood chipper or something?"

"Or somethin'." He waved the gun again. "Sit on your hands."

Jack did so.

"What else did Theo tell you?"

"He told me you were hired by sex traffickers. That you were kidnapping my son and holding him until Saturday."

"It's just business."

"Just business..." Anger flashed in Jack's eyes, and he felt a flicker of rage stirring in his gut. "Well, why didn't you just say so? I would've just handed my son over and jumped off the cliff myself." He clenched his fist. "Just business. When I left him, Theo was begging God to forgive him."

Lawrence finally broke eye contact, glancing quickly to the left. It was quick, barely noticeable, but it was enough to let Jack know that Lawrence wasn't happy about the job either.

"Not what you typically do, then?" Jack asked.

"No."

"Money must be pretty good."

"Must be."

Jack looked up at the sky, saw the clouds passing through the holes in the canopy. "It's gonna rain."

"So you're a weatherman, then?" He pulled a protein bar out of the pack and removed the wrapper.

Jack realized that Lawrence was stalling too, trying to figure out how to use the situation to his advantage. He probably knew he wasn't going to be able to get to wherever he wanted to go on his own.

"You know this isn't about child sex trafficking," Jack said. "Maybe Theo thought it was, but you don't."

He took a bite and chewed.

"You knew where I would be and when I would be there. That means someone has been watching me for a long time, waiting for the right opportunity. Whatever they have planned, I'm obviously not part of it since you were told to kill me."

"Guess your boy made an impression on someone."

"That's what you think, huh? That some trafficker happened to be driving by a playground in New Jersey a couple years ago and decided my boy could maybe make him a lot of money some day? Enough money that it would be worth putting resources into spying on my family? And then when they finally see this opportunity, they reach out to your boss in West Virginia to go pick him up in southern Pennsylvania?"

Lawrence didn't say anything.

But talking out loud was actually helping Jack process his thoughts. "Why take my phone? Theo said someone was picking it up? Who?"

More chewing.

"And why?"

Lawrence swallowed. "Don't really care. If it ain't for sex, then even better."

"They needed to prove I was out of the picture. They're not selling my son to perverts," he said, realizing it even as his lips formed the words, "they're using you to hold him hostage."

"For what?"

"Oh my god," Jack said, revelation dawning. "He's leverage."

"Leverage?"

Jack looked back at him. "They're going to make my wife do something for them."

"Them?"

He stared into Lawrence's eyes. "Only two options that I can think of. And neither one ends with you and your gang making it out of this alive."

"What the hell you talkin' 'bout?"

Jack's mind reeled. *That's it. Has to be. It's the only thing that makes sense.* But what would they want her to do? If they called her on his phone, then she probably thought he was dead. His heart sank, and he felt a wave of guilt sweep over him for thinking that she could have had anything to do with this.

A faint rumble of thunder rolled over the mountains in the distance.

Lawrence looked at the radio. "Who'd you get the radios from? What'd they look like?"

"If you're wondering if one of those is Cullin's, the answer is yes."

He looked up.

"I shot him too."

Lawrence squeezed his eyes shut and clenched his jaw while he ran a hand over his bald head. "You shot Cullin?"

He nodded. "Set Theo's ATV on fire and pushed it down a hill. When he went to check it out, I shot him from beneath a fallen tree."

"He dead?"

"He was still breathing when I left him. JT was on his way, and I didn't have time to finish the job. Plus, I sort of hoped they'd kill each other."

Cullin studied him for a minute. Then he said, "Give it to me." He held out his hand.

"Give you what?"

"The GPS device Cullin had. Give it to me now."

"I didn't—"

"I can always shoot you and take it from you myself."

Jack thought of throwing it into the woods. All he would need was for Lawrence to turn his head for a second so that he could slip behind the tree and make a run for it. He'd just have to hope that the trees would cover him until he got far enough away. But the way Lawrence was staring at him told him that he was ready for anything.

"How else would you have gotten here?" he asked. "C'mon."

Jack sighed and pulled the handheld from his pocket and tossed it to him.

Lawrence caught it and stared at the display. Then he moved his fingers over it. "Son of a bitch," he said. Then he stuck it in his own pocket and tried to get James on the radio.

"*Lawrence?*" a voice responded.

But it wasn't James, it was John Tyler.

"Yeah, it's me. Where are you?"

"*Almost to the bridge. I'm with Cullin. You okay?*"

"I'm fine. Caught up with the father and got Theo's radio back."

"*You're with him now?*"

"No, he got away." He looked at Jack. "But I shot him good. He won't be makin' it too far."

"*Where are you?*" JT asked.

"Not too far past the bridge."

"*Copy that. We'll be right there.*"

Lawrence let the radio fall in his lap, and he closed his eyes for a second. He took another bite of the protein bar.

Jack leaned forward. "James didn't answer."

"Out of range."

"I don't understand. What the hell are you doing?"

He smiled as the sky growled again. "You're gonna help me kill Cullin."

35

JAMES TOLD EVERYONE TO pull over, and he turned the ATV off the path. He parked it and hopped off, checked on the kid, and then walked over to Lee. "How much further?"

Lee looked at the GPS. "'Bout ten miles."

"What do you wanna do?"

Lee scratched at the stubble on his neck, his hand disappearing behind the beard. "Not really keen on the idea of leavin' my brother behind."

James nodded. "So we wait."

"For a bit."

"What about the father? What if they can't find him?"

"Then I think we have three options." He looked up at the sky and seemed to study the passing clouds with his dark, beady eyes.

James reached into his pocket and took out a box of toothpicks. Slipped one onto his tongue. "Yeah?"

Lee lowered his gaze and locked eyes with him. "Either we do find him, or we lie and say we did and hope to god he expires out there."

"And the third option?"

"We kill the sons of bitches before they can kill us." He blinked. "Which we might have to do anyway."

James studied him, wondering if this was some kind of test. But Lee's eyes were balls of ice, and he looked dead serious. "Who you talkin' about?"

"Whoever it is we're workin' for."

"The sex traffickers?"

Lee's brow furrowed. "What?"

"It's what Ham suggested."

He spit on the ground. "Then Ham's as stupid as he is fat."

James looked back at the boy and watched him eat a sandwich. "What then?"

"Can't say for sure, but I'm pretty certain they won't be all that tolerable of loose ends."

"And we're loose ends," James said.

"We could be. But the father most certainly is, and there will no doubt be consequences for that."

James studied him, trying to get a read on the game he was playing. He nodded toward the GPS. "They went to you for the job, didn't they? How is it that we got involved, exactly?"

"Ham didn't tell you?"

"No, he didn't."

"Hmm. Well, how about that."

James used his tongue to move the toothpick to the other side of his mouth. "What does that mean?"

Lee shrugged his big shoulders.

James decided to stop following Lee down this head trip of his. "It's possible Theo told him about the cabin. If he gets to a phone, he could have the FBI out here lookin' for the kid."

Something flashed in Lee's eye at the mention of the FBI, something that told James that Lee would love nothing more than such a confrontation with the Feds.

"If the FBI shows up," James warned, "the deal will be off, we won't get the money, and we'll be the ones stuck holdin' the kid when the music stops."

Lee rolled his shoulders and cocked his neck, cracking it. Then he closed his eyes and tilted his head back, letting the sunlight settle on his face. He let out a deep moan and stood there like a statue, as if he were absorbing energy from the sun through his face.

James looked around, shuffled his feet. Was the oldest Baker brother thinking or simply enjoying the warmth on his face? He'd heard stories of Lee, people suggesting that his was a seat on the crazy side of the class. Bonkers Baker, he'd heard someone say once. Of course, no one ever dared suggest it above a whisper. But looking at him now, James wondered if it just might be so. They all knew he was crazy in a violent way, and Lee himself wouldn't deny that. But this was a different crazy. This was a straightjacket-at-the-silly-farm type crazy. Bonkers.

Lee started humming.

"Lee?" James interrupted.

His eyes snapped open, and he leveled his gaze again. Rolled up his sleeves, revealing tattoos all down his forearms. Then he flashed a wicked smile that unnerved James. "We'll get the Yank, I think. And who knows, maybe we just won't be loose ends after all."

James took the toothpick out of his mouth.

Lee looked over at the kid. "We'll get to the trucks and give 'em an hour or two. If we get nothin' over the radio by then—"

"Then what?"

"Then we get the kid to the cabin and then worry about it. Like you said, the F-B-I could soon be snoopin' 'round, and we should not be on the highway when they are."

"So you'll leave Cullin behind?"

"Cullin can take care of himself. Can your guys?"

James didn't know what state Lawrence was in or what had happened when JT caught up with Cullin. Could be they were all dead. He walked back to the quad and made a hand motion, signaling everyone back onto the trail.

36

STACEY WALKED DOWN THE sidewalk, holding her cell phone against her left ear and pretending to talk on it. She was recording a video of where the pickup was to take place. As she approached an alley on her left, she moved her head this way and that, feigning an animated conversation while making sure her camera got the tops of the buildings. She was walking behind a restaurant and guessed that the drop would be in or behind the dumpster in the alley, placed there by a worker in the employ of whoever was behind the plot.

She wondered if she would be shot during the pickup. Set up by the CIA or FBI to make it look like a foiled terrorist plot. But she didn't think so. Not here, not in an alley. It wasn't a tactical location, not for a shoot-out.

But maybe down the street, after I pick it up?

Maybe, but she didn't think that was what this was.

Appalachia... The word had tickled something in the back of her head that she couldn't at first place. But then after reading about the senator's foreign policy, it had tumbled into position.

The Illegals. Directorate S. The Thirteenth Department. DRG...

She recalled that the KGB had sabotage and intelligence groups (DRGs) along the Delaware River and in Big Spring Park near Harrisburg, that they'd been planning to sabotage the power supply for all of Pennsylvania before disappearing into the Appalachian Mountains. Could there be some Cold War remnant still hiding out in the mountains? Maybe leftovers from the massive Illegals program just out there living the mountain life and no longer waiting on orders from the KGB but now from the SVR? As far as she was concerned, there were only two suspects in this thing, and the fact that the KGB had a history in Appalachia was too much of a coincidence for her to ignore.

Although Greenbrier was also located in the foothills of the Blue Ridge Mountains...

The Greenbrier resort. Built in 1778 and home to Eisenhower's Project Greek Island, where a Walmart-sized concrete bunker was secretly added to the resort, meant for the House and the Senate in the event of nuclear war. Eleven hundred beds, many bathrooms, an airstrip the locals never really understood, a communications center, a sophisticated air-filtration system, a hospital, a room that would serve as the House floor, Senate chamber, and joint sessions of Congress... She recalled that government agents doubled as hotel employees who, for thirty years, kept the bunker ready for operational use. That AT&T serviced both the resort and the bunker and that all calls from the bunker went through the hotel's switchboard so that it appeared the calls were originating from the resort. But the bunker had been decommissioned in the 1990s when the *Washington Post* exposed it. Last she'd heard, part of it was still used as a secure data storage facility, and tours were being offered to the public.

She didn't think that black ops were now being run out of Greenbrier, but she did wonder how many other facilities were out there that hadn't been exposed by the press. Was it possible that there was a CIA black site in the Appalachian Mountains? If there was, she didn't know about it. But she was pretty sure that this was not her current employer wanting to send her out with a bang.

This was Russia. Her former employer. They must've been watching for years, waiting for an opportunity to step in. When they found out that Jack was taking Joseph to a campsite right beside the Appalachian Trail, they must've activated those old Cold War leftovers.

She walked to the end of the block and paced back and forth, looking at her feet while pretending to still talk on the phone. Then she turned and headed back the way she'd come, this time scanning the other side of the street with the camera.

37

THEY HEARD THE SOUND of the ATV coming from across the river, and they both walked to a spot from where they could see the bridge through the trees.

"Sounds like just one," Lawrence said.

Jack patted his pocket. "Yeah, I have the keys to yours."

Lawrence pointed his gun at him. "Go hide in the woods."

"What?"

"Not too far. I'll shoot ya if you run. But you and I gonna talk more 'bout this thing yer sayin'. Could be I need your help. And just maybe you could get your kid back." He spit. "If yer not making it up."

Jack knew that he was just saying that to get him to stay put, though he didn't need to. Where would he run off to without a weapon or food and water or the GPS? "I'm not going anywhere. But can I at least take the belt? In case something goes wrong?"

Lawrence glared at him for a second and then nodded while holding the gun up to his head. "I'll shoot ya if you run, Yank."

Jack didn't doubt it for a second. He bent over and picked up the belt, fastened it around his waist. Made sure the axe head was secure in its mask and the knife was snapped tight. At least if things went sideways with whatever the hell Lawrence was planning to do, he'd have those to work with. "Can I get my bottle?"

Lawrence stared at him while he unscrewed the cap and emptied the rest down his throat. Empty, he tossed it to him.

Jack caught it and clipped it to his belt.

"Now git on over there a ways," Lawrence ordered.

Just before he started off in that direction, Jack saw the ATV come out of the woods and motor along the shore. It was coming fast for the bridge.

The radio in Lawrence's hand squawked. *"Lawrence, we're crossin' the bridge. Where you at?"*

As Jack headed for a tree-studded rise, he heard Lawrence give directions to his location. These people were crazy, and Jack didn't want to be anywhere near what was about to go down. He hurried as fast as he could, feeling lighter without the pack on his back. He climbed up the embankment, grabbing roots and saplings for assistance. When he reached the top (what he estimated to be about twenty feet), he turned back to face the spot he'd come from. Lawrence was standing there looking at him, but he turned away when he saw him duck into place. Jack was about a hundred feet away, looking down through the labyrinth of branches that surrounded Lawrence's position, breaks in the clouds letting in momentary rays of sunlight.

He watched Lawrence make sure the rifle was loaded and lean it against a tree, out of sight from where Cullin and John Tyler would be approaching. Then he checked the pistol again and stuck it in his waistband at the small of his back. Put Theo's revolver alongside it.

Jack's heart started pounding harder and harder the louder the ATV got. If Lawrence did manage to kill Cullin, then he'd be at his mercy along with John Tyler's. But maybe he was starting to get somewhere with him, making him double think this whole thing. Not that they cared at all about him or his son, but if he could convince them that they weren't going to get out of this alive, that he knew more than they did about what was coming, then who knew? At least there would be possibilities. But if this didn't go well and Cullin somehow came out on top, then he would have no choice but to run. There would be no reasoning with him.

He peered from behind the wide trunk and gripped the rough bark to keep his hands from shaking. The motor cut off, and silence came over the forest. Then came the sound of snapping twigs and rustling leaves as Cullin and John Tyler walked from the path to the spot Lawrence had picked for them.

"Lawrence!" one of them shouted.

"Over here," Lawrence answered.

They appeared, slowly at first, just random slashes of color flashing through the maze of twisted vines and low-hanging branches, and then there they were, stepping into full view.

John Tyler appeared first, Cullin a step behind.

Jack knew from his recent Bible reading and from his grandmother that people judged other people by their appearances whereas God looked at each person's heart. But damn. There was no way this guy was not a psycho. Back ramrod straight, chin up, hands still at his sides. He moved like an evil machine, like under that ghoulish complexion and demented haircut was either a metal exoskeleton or reptilian eyes and a forked tongue. He seemed to have recovered quite well from the gunshot, and now Jack wished he had taken the time to kill him.

"What happened?" John Tyler asked, spotting Jack's pack and then looking around.

Jack had to force himself not to move, ignoring the instinct to duck his head completely out of view lest the movement itself attract eyes. Sweat beaded across his forehead.

"He—"

It wasn't clear whether the "he" was intended to be Jack or Cullin, whether he was about to tell him a story about how Jack got away or how Cullin had pushed him off the four-wheeler and left him for dead. But before he could get the next word out, Cullin pulled a pistol from his own waistband and raised it to John Tyler's head.

The blast rocked the forest and rolled away into the distance before rebounding and coming back again over the river.

And then a lot of things happened all at once.

The other side of John Tyler's head exploding, blood, brain, and bone flying through the air and splashing against a nearby tree. Birds fleeing the canopy in a loud exodus. Lawrence pulling the pistol from his pants and bringing it around. Cullin swinging his gun away from John Tyler's body and toward Lawrence. More bangs, simultaneous. John Tyler's body still standing, eyes unfocused, confused. Lawrence moving. Cullin moving. More shots. Bark flying. John Tyler collapsing to his knees. Lawrence spinning and falling, a bloody mist in the air around him. John Tyler landing on his face. Cullin racing toward Lawrence, flames dancing out of the barrel of his gun.

Jack turned and ran.

But in his haste to escape, he knew he'd made too much noise. He looked back over his shoulder, down the hill, and saw Cullin running past Lawrence and looking right at him. His entire face seemed to be one twisted smirk. He raised the gun, and Jack braced for the impact, praying that the hammer would fall on an empty chamber.

A loud explosion, and Jack flinched. But it was Cullin who did the dance. Like he'd been mule-kicked in the back. Cullin stumbled forward. Then spun around, turning the gun on something behind him. Jack heard the shot but didn't see its result, though it wasn't hard to imagine.

He ran as hard as he could, hoping that Lawrence's added bullet might prove enough to slow the psychopath down.

38

THEY REACHED THE TWO box trucks at exactly noon. They were parked off the road in an old gravel lot that was overgrown with weeds and far away from any human activity. If anyone happened to see them parked there, they'd assume they had been used to transport ATVs. Which was true.

It took them ten minutes to load the vehicles into the trucks and get situated. Only three people would fit across the bench seat, which meant the others would have had to make do on the ATVs or folding chairs in the oven that was the back of the truck during summer. They had a battery-powered fan and plenty of water, which would help a little. But as of right now, there were only six of them here.

"It's gotta be a hundred degrees in here," Michael said, climbing up into the open box.

Seth stuck his head in. "More like a hundred and twenty."

"JT and Cullin can sit back there for makin' us wait," Michael said.

"How long to the mountain?" Colt asked.

Seth answered, "Drive should be less than three hours."

"Should we put the kid in the back?" Michael asked. "What if someone sees him sittin' between them"—he motioned at Seth and Lee—"and gets suspicious?"

"He'd cook like a weenie," Colt said.

Michael pulled on the brim of his hat. "You sure?"

"Only takes about an hour for a small kid to die in a hot car," Colt explained. "I seen it myself."

"Yeah?" Seth asked, raising his eyebrows in mock excitement. "You lock a bunch of raghead kiddies in your Humvee or something?"

Colt just stared at him.

Lee walked over and leaned against the bumper of the open truck. He looked at his watch. "One hour."

"One hour," James repeated. He looked over at the kid. He was sitting on the ground, leaning against a tree. He was awake, but he was still out of it from the drugs they'd given him. He'd be coming around soon enough.

39

STACEY STARED OUT THE window of the train, watching the scenery flash by. She'd paid cash for the ticket and knew that if anyone were to scrutinize her day, they would find inconsistencies sure enough. Like the fact that her car would be leaving the parking lot earlier than her returning train. Or that she never made it to the theater she'd bought a ticket for, her seat empty throughout the entire show. In fact, they wouldn't be able to find her in Philadelphia at all. But she wasn't willing to spend the rest of the day cementing her digital itinerary. She had too much to think about, too much to prepare for.

The train passed a playground, and she saw a group of kids playing basketball, saw one of them sink a three-pointer. Then the playground was gone, and there were broken-down buildings, graffiti, boarded windows, homeless people watching the train go by with lifeless eyes. Then there were cop cars and a man sitting on the curb with his hands behind his back. Thirty seconds later, there were suddenly nice houses with expensive cars in the driveway. The contrast, within such a short distance, was glaring, and she couldn't help thinking about Joseph's future. Which world he would end up in. Until she realized that, unless she could figure a way out of this mess, his future was likely going to be buried in quicklime at the bottom of some old mine shaft in the mountains.

Her hands trembled at the thought, and she squeezed her knees to steady them.

Think, she kept telling herself. There had to be a way out, had to be something she could do.

She went through it all one more time, and again stopped when she came to the senator.

She asked herself again why they would want him dead. Because they didn't want a war with America? Or maybe because they did. Maybe taking him out would galvanize public support for a military retaliation. But if that were so, then it would need to be obvious that it had been Russia behind the attack.

She swallowed the lump that suddenly rose in her throat. Was that it? Was Russia setting her up as a triple agent? Was that why they were using her? Not only because she had access, but because her parents were KGB agents, herself having worked for the FSB?

She swore under her breath. She couldn't let that happen. She couldn't go down as a Russian operative who took out the presidential candidate who everyone knew was looking to play hardball with Russia... My god, she thought, if the media went nuts over Russia's alleged election interference, what would they do when they found out there was a double agent in the CIA who just blew up—

She stopped. But why a bomb? Why not just shoot him or poison him?

Because the CIA does want to start a war.

Maybe.

Or they want mass casualties to divert attention away from who was really responsible, arranging things so that another enemy, new or old, could take the fall. But if they wanted to blame some Islamic terrorist group, they'd have to spin a reason why terrorists wouldn't want a Russia-U.S. conflict. Because to the public, that would be the indication. If jihadists wanted a war between the two superpowers, then certainly they would want the senator to win the election and simply proceed on fulfilling his word. The spin doctors wouldn't write a script the public couldn't follow, so if they were looking to blame terrorists, then they would have to come up with a reason as to why they had targeted the senator.

No, she thought. That just wasn't feasible. If it was her own government behind this, then they had to be setting up Russia. It was the only fall guy that would stand up to inspection. The whole "They hate us because we're free" narrative just didn't hold up anymore.

She massaged her temples, knowing that there was yet another possibility. That the senator was not the real target. Or maybe not the target the public would assume.

She had to find out who else was going to be at the event, and she had to do it fast.

She was running out of time.

40

JACK STOPPED RUNNING. HE felt as if he couldn't take another step. He'd run up and up and up the side of a ravine before sprinting across level ground, weaving in and out of trees, avoiding the low-hanging vines and thicker brush scattered across the forest floor, the axe hanging from his belt pouch knocking against his legs the whole time. He didn't know how long he'd run. Maybe ten minutes, though it had felt more like thirty. However long it had been, he hadn't paid any particular attention to the direction he'd run, just followed the natural course the terrain had presented as best his mind could detect it while in motion. A bare strip of dirt that resembled a path here, a break in the trees there. And now he was bent over, hands on his knees, panting, sweat dripping into his eyes.

Thunder rumbled.

He tried to think, but all he could hear in his head was the pounding of his heart. He tried to break the catch twenty-two that his short and shallow breaths were creating—his heart beating faster to compensate for the lack of oxygen while his short breaths deprived him of oxygen and made his heart beat faster. He forced himself to take a long, slow breath. To exhale it nice and slow.

His mind began to clear, and he wiped the sweat from his brow. A minute later, he stood straight. Put his hands on his hips.

What the hell is going on? John Tyler's head blowing apart replayed in his mind, the suddenness of it and the cold indifference on Cullin's face when he'd pulled the trigger—as if he'd just struck a match or turned on a television—was disturbing.

These were the people who had his son.

He started walking again, knowing he had to keep moving to keep Cullin from catching up to him. But keep moving toward where?

He reached into his pocket and took out the pages he'd torn from Joseph's book. Theo had said he thought Hollow Mountain was somewhere in the Cranberries, which he guessed was the Cranberry Wilderness. At least that was marked on the map. The problem was, he wasn't exactly sure where he was now, or how far from the breadcrumbs he'd gotten. He couldn't be too far if he'd only been running for ten minutes. He could try retracing his steps, to get back to the bridge, where he could reorient himself with the map. Maybe see if his pack was still there. Or the GPS device. But he didn't have time for backtracking. *Don't have time to wander in the wrong direction either.*

So he could take his best guess at where he was in relation to the breadcrumbs on the map and continue on toward the trucks, knowing he would never reach them in time unless they waited until the last possible moment before leaving without Cullin, Lawrence, and JT.

Or he could just head south toward the Cranberry Wilderness and look for someone along the way who'd be able to tell him where Hollow Mountain was.

It was Wednesday afternoon. But even if he traveled through the mountains at four miles per hour over the next sixty or so hours, that would take him how far? Two hundred and forty miles? Would that even be far enough? Could his body hold up for sixty hours without food or rest? Not at a four-mile-per-hour pace, that was for damn sure. And that was assuming he'd even be heading in the right direction.

He shoved the pages back into his pocket. He would go back to the bridge, see what was still there, and use JT's quad to catch up. He turned and—

The *crack* of a rifle shot rocketed past his ears, and the tree beside him exploded.

He dropped to his stomach and quickly scrambled for cover behind a large piece of deadwood.

The deadwood blew apart as another blast echoed back and forth between the mountains, and a piece of it struck his face.

It felt like his right eyeball had exploded, and he recoiled into a fetal position, holding his face. Had he just been shot in the eye?

He looked up, trying to open it. He thought he succeeded in that part, but he couldn't see anything out of it. Squinting with his left eye, he could make out a small depression about ten feet away. He went for it, army-crawling to its edge and slipping down beneath the horizon. He touched his face and felt blood on his fingertips. But he didn't think it was his eyeball, just scratches on his face from the wooden shrapnel. It must've been a chunk of wood that struck his eye, and it still felt like it had exploded in its socket. But at least now there was a sliver of light in the bottom left-hand corner of his vision. No time to worry about it now, though.

He crawled to his left, following the ravine. He scurried until he came to a rock that was positioned at the top of the ridge, and then worked his way up behind it, peering over its top and scanning the woods.

Movement caught his good eye, and he ducked just as another bullet ricocheted off the rock.

Jack slid back down the slope and raced through the draw, looking for cover. He hardly noticed the sky growing darker or the raindrops that had started to pitter-patter off the leaves above him.

41

JAMES LEANED FORWARD OVER the steering wheel and looked up at the sky as rain splashed against the windshield. It'd been raining for about half an hour, and it was just about the time Lee said they'd be leaving. Still no sign of Cullin or Lawrence or JT. He looked across Michael and Colt, who were sitting beside him, and out the side window to the other truck. To Lee sitting behind the wheel, the boy between him and his brother. Were they just as concerned about Cullin as they were about Lawrence and JT, or did they know something they didn't? He had a feeling they knew a lot more. He'd been watching Lee play with the GPS device for the last fifteen minutes, his thumbs moving over the keys like he was playing a game. Or writing a message. Was it possible that he could be communicating with Cullin or even the people who hired them over the GPS device? James didn't know that much about the things, but he thought he should find out. He patted his pocket and felt the burner phone resting tight against his thigh. Once they got on the road and he got a signal, he'd call Ham and fill him in on the shit show.

The radio he'd set on the dashboard came to life.

"...*there? Do you read me?*"

James watched out the window as Lee brought his own radio to his mouth. "*Cullin?*"

"*Yeah.*"

"*What the hell's going on? Where are you?*" Lee asked.

Michael and Colt both turned to their right and joined James in watching the Bakers in the other truck.

"Lawrence is dead. John Tyler is dead. Boy's father killed 'em both. I'm on his trail now. Best not wait for me. Daddy's got some spunk. Could take me a while."

Michael punched the dashboard.

James tapped the horn. "Roll down the window," he said to Colt.

Colt worked the lever, and rain blew into the cabin.

James waved to Lee, and Lee rolled down his window. "If Cullin's within range and close to the father..." He saw the boy's face through the rain, sitting there between the two brothers, still and scared and confused. But there was no missing on his face his understanding of what they were talking about.

Lee rolled the window back up, ignoring him. Then he spoke into the radio again. *"Catch the son of a bitch already. Then get your ass back to the cabin. We're leavin.'"*

"See ya later."

Lee looked back into their truck and said over the radio, *"Let's get the hell out of here."*

As James backed the truck out of the gravel lot, Colt asked, "You really think the boy's father just killed half our gang?"

James put the truck in drive and turned onto the road. "No," he said. He took the phone from his pocket and propped it up in the cup holder. "Keep an eye on the signal and let me know as soon as there's a bar," he said to Michael.

As he followed the truck in front of them, he replayed in his head the way Lee had answered the radio. The calm, almost expectant way he'd raised it to his mouth, void of any urgency whatsoever. As if everything was going according to plan.

Bonkers Baker.

Or was it something else?

IT HAD BEEN A two-and-a-half-hour drive to the foot of Hollow Mountain through the storm. James had gotten a signal on the cell phone ten minutes into the trip, and he'd pulled back far enough so that Lee couldn't see him talking on it in his side-view. The call lasted just five minutes, because that was as long as it took to let Ham know that Theo, Lawrence, and JT were dead and that the father was still out there somewhere.

Ham was not happy, obviously. But he agreed with James in that he thought there was something else going on that the Bakers knew about and weren't sharing. He said they should be careful and that he would see what he could find out on his end and call them back.

James looked up at Hollow Mountain, though he couldn't see anything but its ghostly form in the stormy skies. This wasn't going to be a pleasant trip up to the cabin.

"Stay close to us," Seth yelled over the rain. "The whole mountain's like a honeycomb of caverns and caves and old mine shafts that no one's bothered to mark. We're the only ones who knows where they are! If you drive over one, you better hope you die sudden. Be a slow death otherwise."

"Can we just get on with it already?" Colt hollered.

Lee had given the boy another injection for the trip and had him sitting, back-to-back, against Seth, a rope pinning his arms to his sides and securing him to Seth's body. He walked away from the boy and climbed onto his own ATV. "Ready?" he called back over the pounding rain.

James revved the engine and gave a thumbs-up. Then he turned and looked at Michael and Colt.

"How long is it going to take?" Michael asked.

"'Bout an hour in these conditions. Maybe more. Watch out for mudslides and flooded streams. We're gonna have to take a longer, less elevated route. Straightaway"—he made a ninety-degree motion with his hand—"the tires will just spin in the mud."

"Why can't we just stay with the trucks until this passes?" Colt yelled up.

"Because people are on their way to get them back to where they came from before anyone notices they're missing."

"They're not your trucks?"

"Of course not." He faced forward and started moving.

James motored after Seth, and the boy's body faced him, his sleeping face bobbing left and right in rhythm with the terrain. James found his eyes focusing on the kid's feet. On his socks. They'd taken him without even his shoes. He didn't like it, and part of him couldn't help sympathizing with the boy's father. But it was too late to do anything about it now. He had Michael to look after, and he'd kill the kid himself if it meant keeping his little brother safe.

Which led him to wonder what the Bakers were willing to do for each other.

LIGHTNING FLASHED SIDEWAYS, REACHING out and forking across the sky in a dozen branches. It reminded Jack of the Nile Delta, which Joseph had learned about last year—Mesopotamia, Moses, Masada, Marcus Aurelius, Memphis, Mary, mummies...

"All things that start with *M*..." He spoke the words aloud, rainwater spraying from his lips as they formed them. "Not related..."

Everything is related in time. Ever hear of the butterfly effect?

He ignored himself and continued to mumble, "Tom Cruise, Peter O'Toole, Christian Bale, Billy Zane..."

You're losing it...

But it helped reel his mind in a little, assigning actors to the random *M*s.

The thunder that followed the lightning shook the whole mountain, and it seemed like the clouds must be dropping bombs along with the rain.

After he'd come out of the draw, he'd stumbled upon a deer path and had taken it as far as it went, running and running, the whole time hoping that Cullin wasn't right behind him. He'd never bothered to check his compass, and he had no idea where he was.

The rain and wind had picked up considerably, and the trees were all performing some spastic dance at their behest.

The rain was freezing cold, and he couldn't keep his teeth from chattering. The wind was driving the rain and other debris into his face, and he was using his arm to shield his eyes. Visibility wasn't great, and it varied depending on the density of the forest, but his right eye was still throbbing, so he didn't know what he'd be able to see anyway.

The rain had come so hard and so fast that he was sure there was flooding in the ravines, little rivers now rushing down the slopes. The sound of it was deafening. He could be standing ten feet from a waterfall and he wouldn't be able to hear it. Not to mention a psychopath with a gun.

The thought of Cullin sneaking up behind him made him reach for his knife, but then walking with a blade in these conditions wasn't such a great idea, so he decided to leave it in its sheath. The last thing he needed was to slip and stab himself. Even still, he kept turning around, expecting to see that face peeking through the curtains of rain. It had been a while since he saw Cullin, though he had no idea exactly how long because he hadn't looked at his watch since Cullin had shot at him. Maybe he'd lost him. Or maybe Cullin had gone for shelter.

Jack's feet stopped moving, and he had to look down to see why. But he couldn't see his feet. He wiped the water from his eyes and peered down, squinting to see what could have happened to them. He closed his bad eye to see if that would help.

"Where the hell are my feet?"

Where could they have gone? How would he get Joseph back without feet?

It's mud, you idiot, he told himself. *It's only mud.* He was exhausted, thirsty, and freezing, and his mind was slipping. Would Cullin kill him? Or a bolt of lightning, a falling tree, or pneumonia? It seemed like a toss-up.

He lifted his foot as hard as he could, and the ground finally released his boot with a sucking noise he could hear over the rain. But when he went to lift the other foot, the one he'd just liberated sank back into the mud again.

He looked around for more secure footing, but could only see a white blur. He dropped to his hands and knees and started crawling, distributing his weight more evenly and working his way through the mud until his outstretched hands found a root. He followed it to a trunk and sat against it, pulling his knees to his chest and wrapping his arms around his legs. As he sat there, he wondered how long the storm would last. Did it matter anymore? He couldn't remember what day it was. And, damn, his eyeball felt like it was being squeezed in a vise.

He closed his eyes.

MK-Ultra, MK-Delta, Mekong Valley, Minute Men, Muffin Man, Mac & Me, Mac N' Cheese, Mom...

43

HAM SAT DOWN AT the table and leaned forward onto his elbows. He put his head in his hands and swore. This was not good. Not good at all.

Theo. That little turd. He should've seen it coming. Or maybe he had and just hadn't cared enough to do anything about it at the time. He'd always been the weak link in the group. Even with Cullin sent to help him, the bastard had still managed to screw everything up. But even so, Cullin shooting him was unacceptable. Ham knew the rest of his crew was probably aching to cut the Bakers to pieces for that, and he would certainly allow it. But not yet. Not until the kid was where he was supposed to be and the father was dead.

Rain pelted the windows.

He stood back up, cursing himself for even sitting down in the first place, and went for the nearest bottle. He didn't bother getting a glass, just took the bottle to the window and leaned against the frame. He watched the rain fall over the mountains as he took a long drag on a cigarette, and thought of all the more things that could go wrong trying to get to the cabin in this weather. If something happened to the kid, then...

Then what?

Then they'd all be in deep shit.

Unless he could get Carl to do some singing tomorrow. Then maybe he'd have options.

He blew smoke into the air and brought the bottle to his lips as thunder rattled the window.

Three of his men dead. Supposedly at the hands of the boy's father, if they were to believe Cullin. Which, of course, he didn't.

His gang was growing smaller, and his idea that there was something else going on here was beginning to take on substance.

His eyes went to the cell phone on the table.

Could the Bakers have been hired to not only facilitate the kidnapping of the boy, but also execute the cleanup afterward? Maybe that was something they had even suggested themselves, hoping to expand their enterprise into a new territory. One with a sudden vacuum.

He felt as if he was being lured to his own demise. But by whom?

He'd see what Carl could tell him.

Carl, Carl, Carl. Poor ol' Carl...

He drank.

44

THE LATE AFTERNOON SUN was shining through the window, and Stacey closed the blinds. She'd been walking back and forth through the living room since she got back, going over it again and again in her head. The light had started as a golden beam that cut diagonally across the floor and up the side of the bookshelf, but with each lap of the room, the beam had gotten wider and wider until finally the sun had declined to just above the window and was now blinding her eyes.

She was absolutely convinced that it was Russia. But whether they meant it to stop a war, start a war, or as a false flag to get America in a war with someone else, she didn't know. She still needed to find out who else was going to be at the event. She'd spent time on the train ride back searching the internet on her phone for clues, but she hadn't been able to find anything about an event involving the senator on Friday night.

Leaving the living room, she wondered if it was a sanctioned operation or an SVR black op. Or maybe a rogue agent walking in Fedyenka's footsteps. If it was the latter, maybe she could contact Moscow and let them know what was happening in the hopes that they would put a stop to it themselves. What did she have to lose at this point?

Joseph, of course.

No matter what idea she came up with, she couldn't envision a scenario in which Joseph was likely to make it out alive. The best chance she had was to go through with their demands and hope they would keep their word.

She went up the steps, passing framed pictures and doing her best not to look at them.

But her best wasn't good enough, and her eyes locked on a picture of her and Jack holding each other on the riverbank a few years ago, fall leaves being carried by the current behind them.

It sent a tremor through her resolve, and a crack raced across the dam she'd erected to hold back the building emotion. Its contents began spraying through, and she fell forward, collapsing onto the last few steps. Tears ran down her face, and she screamed. But no sound came out of her. She threw her hands against the floor, pounding it until sound finally did escape her throat—a high-pitched wail that morphed into low, guttural groans. Suddenly exhausted, she pulled the rest of herself up onto the hallway floor and continued to sob.

Then with her face in the carpet, she caught a glimpse of the door at the end of the hall. She wiped her eyes and got to her feet. Slowly, she walked the length of the hall and, when she reached it, opened the door to her daughter's room.

The rocking chair in the corner of the room had been sitting there empty and unused for years. Since the night before Bethany died, she realized. She sat in it now, further remembering that day to have also been a Wednesday, and the song that she'd sung as her beautiful baby smiled at her before closing her eyes and drifting off to sleep for the last time.

Even though it burned like hell going down, she closed her eyes and savored the memory.

45

THEY MADE IT TO the cabin without any major incident, though at one point the rain had been so heavy that James had lost sight of Seth, and they had to pull over and wait for him and Lee to come back for them. A couple of times one of the ATVs got stuck, and they needed to push it out of the mud, but they still managed to make the trip in under two hours. James could certainly see how someone could get lost up here. Without knowing exactly which ridge to climb and what hill to look for, you could easily find yourself lost in what was a vast wilderness. Or, according to the Bakers, fall into a cavern.

They'd parked the ATVs in an old horse barn that sat at the back of the cabin and then got the kid situated in a room with boarded windows and a locked door. They'd given him a warm blanket and let him undress, hanging the clothes he left at the door over the fireplace to dry. The rest of them all stripped down to their own undergarments as their clothes dried alongside the kid's.

James looked out the window and could barely make out the outline of the distant hills. They looked like rolling waves beneath the dark skies. "Where's Colt?" he asked Michael.

"Think he's runnin' a bath."

James turned and walked out of the room, his bare feet soundless on the wooden boards. Michael followed him.

They passed in front of the tiny kitchen, where Seth was getting a fire going in the woodstove. He had a short glass in his hands, and he raised it to them in salute as they went by.

"You watch him good," James whispered back to Michael. A few steps later, they were in front of what passed as the bathroom. He knocked on the door and pushed it open. Colt was standing naked beside an old porcelain tub and aiming a gun at his face.

"What's the point in knocking if you ain't gonna wait for an answer?" he asked, lowering the pistol.

"Just checking on ya, is all."

Colt lifted a leg and stepped into the steaming water. "Well, I'm just peachy. Now you mind gettin' the hell outta here? Startin' to get a little weird with my dick all out and you two standing there in your skivvies, starin' at me." Then he turned his back to them and sat in the water, clouds of steam, like smoke, rolling over the M16s on his back. He still had the pistol in his hand.

James turned when he heard sobs coming from the other side of the locked door behind them.

"Shut up, kid," Michael shouted.

James closed the bathroom door and walked back to the fireplace. He shivered as a cool breeze infiltrated a hidden crack somewhere in the cabin. His stomach growled, and he hoped Seth would have dinner ready soon. The kid was probably starving too.

He looked around for Lee, but didn't see him anywhere.

46

SOMETHING STRUCK HIM, AND suddenly he was moving. He opened his eyes but saw nothing. An impact against his side. Pain in his knee. In his shoulder.

He was moving fast, tumbling end over end. He didn't know what was happening, where he was. He didn't know which way was up or down. He couldn't breathe.

A flash of light and then back to darkness. His fingers grazed something. He couldn't hear anything but the blood rushing in his head. Like he was under—

His head exploded back into the light with the realization that he'd been underwater. And once he understood that, he was able to find the ground beneath his feet and free himself from the sense of vertigo that had almost drowned him.

He kept his head above the flowing water and tried to look around. Everything was moving fast, and he could barely make out the trees in the rain as they flew past. Then he was under again, his hands trying frantically for a handhold.

He struck something that brought a sudden and painful stop to his momentum. He was no longer moving, but there was a wall of pressure at his back that was pinning him against whatever he'd slammed into.

His hands worked over it, and his brain signaled that it was a tree that had fallen across the water. It was thick, too thick to get his arms around. Branches were protruding all over, and for a moment, he thought he might have been impaled by one.

Needing to get his head above water, he reached for the branches. He felt no resistance in his midsection and concluded that he'd somehow avoided being skewered. The force of the rushing water made it hard to move, and he had to pull on the branches with all his strength just to move an inch.

He stuck his arm up between two branches, and his hand broke the surface of the water. He tried pulling himself up through the branches, but they were too close together, and his chest wouldn't fit.

He needed air.

Instead of pulling, he tried to push against the wooden appendages, to drop beneath them. If he could get beneath the tree, then perhaps the current would carry him past it. He pulled himself deeper and deeper, feeling like a fly in a wooden web, searching, searching... What if the branches didn't spread apart? Or what if there wasn't enough room beneath—

The current flung him forward, and his head hit the bottom of the tree so hard as he passed it that he nearly blacked out. But something caught in the branches, and he was dangling in the current like a bobber on a string.

His axe.

Bright spots were beginning to flash in his head, and he knew he only had a few more seconds before he either passed out or inhaled a lungful of water. He swung his hand at the axe handle, hoping that he didn't have to lose it. It didn't budge. He tried again, but still nothing. He had no choice. He unbuttoned the mask and pulled the axe head from it. And he was away.

His head exploded out of the water, and he took one of the biggest breaths he'd ever taken in his life. The vision in his left eye returned, his right still clouded from the earlier trauma. He rotated in the current, turning in time to see the mammoth tree that had almost drowned him. The top half of it, with all its branches and leaves, had indeed crashed into the rushing water. It was so big that its leafy green appendages were like a green sun rising or setting into the river and blocking from view anything beyond it. He had no idea how he'd managed to slip through its arms.

Everything was moving so fast that he had a hard time making sense of his surroundings. He looked ahead, peering through the rain with his good eye, and for a split second thought it odd that there appeared to be nothing but stormy sky in front of him. He thought it must be an optical illusion, his eyes playing tricks on him. And then realization struck. But before he could do anything about it, he was flying through the sky, legs and arms bicycling in cartoon fashion as he hopelessly fought against gravity.

He was falling off the side of a mountain.

THE FALL TOOK ONLY a handful of seconds, but it seemed like an eternity as Jack waited to discover what was at its end. A white flash burst in his head, and for a nanosecond he wasn't sure if he'd landed on rocks, the brightness the proverbial light at the end of the tunnel traveling at warp speed, or if it was just his brain being jolted from its moorings as he struck the surface of more water.

It was water, which he understood half a second later when he realized he was still alive. The force of the waterfall, however, was pushing him down into the water's depths, tumbling and rolling him in the dark, its pressure pinning him to the bottom. He knew not to fight it and tried to relax. Then he was free, his head breaking the surface and gulping air.

He looked up behind him and could just make out the top of the cliff he'd been jettisoned from. The floodwater was shooting over its side and dumping into the creek he was in now.

The trees along the banks continued to fly past him at a dizzying speed. He was turning in circles, doing his best to keep his head above water. The creek was deep, no doubt swollen from the storm, and he couldn't touch the bottom. Sticks, branches, and other debris flowed along beside him. He tried to grab something that would help him float, but everything remained just out of reach.

Finally, he came across a derelict tree limb that he was able to hook his arms over, and he let it carry him off toward wherever it was going.

He had no idea how much time passed while he hugged that branch, because he'd been too exhausted to look at his watch and was afraid that even the slightest movement would threaten his grip on the limb. But then the branch struck a pile of debris that had gotten caught up in some large rocks, and he was flung from his lifeline.

He tried to swim to the flooded bank, to make his way to the trees that were protruding out from the water, but he couldn't fight the current, and it continued to carry him away.

STACEY WOKE UP TO the sound of rain pitter-pattering against the windowpane beside her. She leaned forward in the rocking chair and looked around the strange room. It was Bethany's room. Why was she in Bethany's room? And for the tiniest instant, she thought that Bethany must be asleep in the crib. That she had drifted off after feeding her and laying her down for her nap. She almost stood up to catch a glimpse of that gold hair above the top of the crib.

Almost.

But just as quickly as it came, it was gone, replaced by the here and now and its terrible truth.

The raindrops sliding down the window cast eerie shadows across the carpeted floor, and she watched the dark lines wiggle and dart and merge with ethereal randomness.

How long have I been asleep? It hadn't been raining before. She turned her head, looked out the window, and watched the rain fall over the river. She didn't want to see the framed picture of Bethany that was resting on the dresser next to her. Not now. She couldn't handle seeing those bright eyes after such a strong notion of her still being there.

Her cell rang outside the room.

She jumped, startled, and the shock of it brought everything back all at once.

Jack, Joseph, the senator, what she was supposed to do...

She ran out of the room, closing the door behind her, and went for her cell.

"Hello?" she answered when she'd finally gotten to it.

"There has been a change in plans," the synthesized voice stated.

Stacey's heart froze. "What change?"

"The location for the pickup has been altered. As has the time of the event."

"What? Where? When?"

"We will call you with the location when it is time to pick it up."

"Wha—"

The voice cut her off. *"You're son is still alive. This is your only option to keep him that way."*

The line went dead.

She stood there in the living room for a minute and stared at the floor, her mind turning it over. Did they know she'd scoped out the location? Was that why they were changing it? And when was the new time? Earlier or later on Friday or a different day altogether?

Her eyes went to the framed images on the wall, and she found herself staring at a picture of their first Christmas in the new house. She remembered that Christmas. It was when Jack had put the events of Trenton together. When he'd heard the FBI guy call in to that conspiracy station.

Johnson.

She went back up the stairs and into their bedroom. She stood before Jack's dresser and once again pushed his fate out of her head. There would be plenty of time to cry for him later. Or none at all if she wasn't able to find a way out of blowing herself up. She took a breath and opened the top drawer. She'd seen it in here before, but that had been years ago. She shuffled through his socks and underwear and found a picture of herself posing in some sexy contraption. Garter belt, leggings, and all. She smiled. She remembered the night. But the smile quickly faded when she remembered that she'd worn the same outfit for Vadim a week later.

She pushed the picture back beneath the socks, fighting the urge to tear it to pieces. So much guilt. So many secrets. But that was what service to her country had required, and she never hesitated to do her duty. Even in Trenton.

Her fingers grazed something at the back of the drawer. It was standing up on its end, wedged in the crack where the back of the drawer met the bottom. It felt right. She forced it out with her fingernails and held it up.

Bingo.

Agent Johnson's card that he'd given to Jack eight years ago. It had the FBI crest on the front. She flipped it over, and in faded handwritten ink was a phone number.

She closed the drawer and sat on the edge of their bed, the card in her hands, her brain wondering at the possibility...

48

JACK OPENED HIS EYES and blinked. Tried to make sense of what he was seeing. His right eye still throbbed, and he thought it might be distorting his vision. The sound was off too, like only one speaker was working. But not really working, because it was just spitting static.

He tried to move but couldn't. His arms were stuck. Or missing.

Damn.

He'd already lost his feet, and now that he didn't have arms either, how would he ever get to...

Joseph.

He blinked again. Wiggled his toes.

No, his feet were still there. Why had he thought they weren't?

Mud.

They were stuck in the mud.

But still, even with feet, running around the forest with no arms wasn't going to help him get Joseph back. How would he eat or drink? Shoot a gun? Hold Stacey again? And then the image of himself running around the woods like the black knight from *Monty Python And The Holy Grail* struck him as hysterical, and he started laughing. Couldn't stop laughing.

Until he began to choke on water, and his laughing turned to coughing.

He moved his head, and the left speaker suddenly came to life, and there was surround sound again. He realized that what he thought had been static was in fact flowing water and rain.

He moved his head a little further, and the whole world shifted sideways with it. Or rather it seemed to level out. And then something bumped his head and snapped him out of his delirium.

The side of his face had been submerged in water, which was why half his vision and hearing had been distorted. He was on rocks and could see the bank just on the other side of them. He fought to use his arms, which he could now tell were still attached to his body. He managed to get them under his shoulders, into a push-up position, but felt the weight of something across his back. He pushed, trying to lift it. It didn't budge. Turning his head, he saw more branches. He was under another damn tree.

Instead of trying to bench-press the tree (which wouldn't do him any good unless he was able to roll the thing off to the side once his elbows were extended), he maneuvered his body between the rocks he was lying on and tried to sink lower, to get beneath the tree more. It had worked the last time, and worming his way between the rocks, he again was able to push himself out from under it. And once again, the water tried to sweep him away. But this time he was able to grab a branch and work his way along the tree until his feet touched the ground. He climbed up the rocks and collapsed onto his back. But the rain pelted his face with such ferocity, it felt as if he were being waterboarded. He rolled to his side, coughing.

He must've blacked out, because the last thing he remembered was trying to swim to shore. He looked around. Trees everywhere. He flexed his arms and legs. Nothing appeared to be broken. Sore, but not broken. His belt pouch and axe mask were still with him, but no longer the axe. Hopefully the knife would make do. He'd also lost his water bottle.

Thunder exploded.

He took a couple more minutes to recover, and when he finally stood, a blinding flash filled the sky, followed by a bang so loud that it seemed the entire mountain had exploded. He skipped across the rocks and up onto the bank as fast as he could, knowing that the lightning bolt had shattered a nearby tree but unable to tell which one or how close it was.

It landed, in flames, parallel to his frantic route, striking the ground just ten yards away and shaking the earth. He threw his arm over his face to shield it from the exploding debris and the other broken branches that were now raining down from the shattered canopy above.

The tree was so big that with the rain and his bad eye, he couldn't see the end of it.

He could hear another tree falling somewhere close by.

He kept going, stumbling half-blind through the wilderness, no idea where he was.

49

JAMES SAT IN A wooden chair, leaning back on its legs, his feet propped up on the windowsill. He was back in his clothes again and chewing another toothpick while watching the lightning tear through the sky over the mountaintops in the west. The wind was driving the rain so hard that he thought the window might break. More than once, he'd lifted his gaze to the wooden rafters, thinking the whole roof was coming off.

The boy was at the table, eating the supper Seth had made. Everyone else was standing around watching him. The kid was tough. Hadn't thought so in the beginning with all the sniveling whenever he was even half-lucid, but he'd seemed to come to grips with the situation in the last hour or so. James felt sorry for him, knowing what he'd be used for. Made him sick thinking about it. If it were his boy who was to be raped a dozen times a day over the next six years, then he wouldn't sleep until he'd gotten to see the degenerate shits choke to death on their own cocks.

Which, of course, was the irony, wasn't it? He thought there was a legal term for it. Dissociative behavior, or some such thing. Whatever. Downright hypocrisy was what it was. He looked over at the kid. "How old are ya, son?"

"I'm not your son," he answered without looking up from his food.

Yeah, he'd toughened up all right. James smiled. "Where'd ya get that scar on your neck?"

The boy stopped eating and looked up, his eyes full of... It wasn't hate, not exactly. Not yet. Right now it was just anger.

"None of your business."

Michael laughed. "Kid's grown a pair, eh?"

Lee, having rejoined them a little bit ago, stroked his long beard, watching the kid with interest but not saying anything.

"Where did you get it?" Seth pushed. He stepped up to the other side of the table, leaning forward against it, and dropped his head for a closer look. "Looks like someone tried to bleed ya like an animal."

The boy didn't respond. Just lifted the spoon to his mouth.

James wondered if it was whatever past the kid had been through that had hardened him like this. If so, then maybe there was a chance he would survive all this. Come out the other end someday with a future still to be had. Maybe. More likely he'd die of an overdose once he was too old for the appetites of degenerate men.

Colt walked over and leaned against the wall beside the window and stared out into the storm with James. "So we gonna do somethin' before Cullin gets back?" he whispered.

"We'll see," James answered without moving his lips. He caught another glimpse of the white line across the kid's neck and wondered again who it was they were messing with. Was it possible that the boy's father was still out there, coming for them like he himself would be? Or would it be Cullin coming through the door with four scalps hanging from his belt? He hoped the storm would kill them both.

He looked at Lee, but trying to read him was like trying to read a snake. He could only hope that there would be a rattle before the bite.

50

JACK STUMBLED DOWN THE side of a steep decline, careful to keep his feet under him. The rain was still falling though it was no longer being driven sideways by the wind. Once he reached the bottom, he pushed his way through a thicket and eventually found himself in a hollow. He made his way to its grassy center and looked up into the sky, running his hands through his hair.

He needed to get warm. He looked at his watch and knew that the sun was beginning to set behind the clouds. It was already much darker than usual because of the storm, which meant he had little daylight left. He could make a shelter pretty much anywhere, but how was he supposed to start a fire when the whole world was soaking wet? A cave would be nice, but what were the odds of finding one? His teeth chattered as he stood there in the rain, the thunder sounding further and further east, the storm passing.

He checked his compass and headed south. He didn't know what else to do.

AN HOUR LATER, THE rain was still falling. Jack was about to start constructing one of the shelters he'd read about in his book when he tripped over something and fell onto his hands and knees.

He turned his head and looked behind him, blinking rainwater out of his eyes. Whatever he tripped over didn't feel like a root or a rock. It felt more like...

Rail.

He looked closer, peering through his good eye. It was definitely a metal rail, and it was running northeast and southwest. There were no wooden ties though. He figured they must be buried or had rotted away long ago. But why would there be tracks out here in the middle of nowhere? Or maybe this hadn't been nowhere a hundred years ago. Did it lead to the nearest town, or was it part of a project that had been abandoned before completion? Had the start of World War II shelved the idea, as it had so many others like it? He had no idea where it might lead, if anywhere at all. But regardless of its original destination, it had to have started from somewhere. And since Joseph was most definitely not northeast, he followed the old tracks south.

IT WAS 6:30 ACCORDING to the time displayed at the bottom of the screen. Stacey was only half-watching the evening news. The weatherman was pointing to a very colorful radar, where a large green blob was growing out of Texas and heading across the country toward Vermont in an animated time-lapse. Storms were coming, and there would be rain until tomorrow evening.

She watched the area over West Virginia, where the cell tower had pinged Jack's phone. Throughout the day, the area went from light green to dark green to yellow with spots of red. She wondered if Jack was still out there, in the storm. Again, she didn't *know* he was dead. Hell, he'd been thrown off a cruise ship in the middle of the ocean and had survived. He'd gotten into a fight with a hired assassin and had emerged victorious. Had fought Vadim...

No. She wouldn't allow herself to hope. Couldn't.

She stood up, walked into the kitchen, and took a bottle of vodka out of the freezer. She didn't trouble herself with a glass. She unscrewed the lid and dropped it on the counter. She watched the rainfall through the window over the sink as she sipped from the frozen bottle. She reached into her pocket and extracted the business card she'd taken from Jack's drawer. She stared at it. Sipped. Stared at it. Sipped.

Then she dropped it in the trash can.

There was no way out of this. Besides, even if she could track down the former FBI agent, she figured he would be just as likely to shoot her as he would be to help her.

She leaned her head back and gulped.

THE TRACKS DISAPPEARED BENEATH thick undergrowth at times, and he had to skirt around it and pick them up on the other side. But they just kept going. And going. He felt like he'd been following them for hours, though it had only been one. The rain was miserable, and most of his body was numb. His feet certainly were.

It was getting darker, and the alarm he'd set on his watch to remind him of when he should start preparing for nightfall would be going off soon. When had he set that? He tried to think how many days he'd been out here in the woods.

He looked at his watch. It said it was Wednesday.

That would mean...

But his exhausted brain couldn't recall what day they'd gotten here, that they drove up and built the firepit and talked and laughed... It seemed like another lifetime ago.

Monday, he realized. They'd gotten here on Monday. And Joseph had been taken Tuesday morning.

So this was only day two out here in the wilderness. It didn't seem possible.

He moved one foot in front of the other and continued to watch the old ties pass beneath him, wondering if the rain would ever stop. He was starting to get thirsty, too. But he didn't have his bottle anymore. So he sipped rainwater off random leaves as he passed them.

RATHER THAN THE RAIN stopping, it was instead picking up again. Lightning was dancing in the sky, and the thunderclaps that accompanied the show seemed to indicate another approaching storm.

Jack stopped walking, his numb feet paused between the two rusted rails. He began looking for a spot that would make for a good shelter. He was done walking in the rain.

He stepped off the tracks and made his way through some underbrush. There was a pine tree with low-hanging branches that he thought would serve him well.

He removed the knife from its sheath but could barely feel it in his hands. When he got to the tree, he began cutting at the needled branches. After collecting a pile he could use, he returned the knife to its sheath. He looked around for a tree he thought would be unlikely to fall on him as he slept.

Over there. It was the fattest one he could see, at least six feet wide, even bigger than the one that had almost crushed him. It was atop a little rise, which would also keep him from being swept away in a runoff again. With a branch in each hand, he began dragging them up the incline toward the tree.

When he reached the tree, he found that the ground on the other side of it quickly descended into a hundred-foot slope. He was on the top of a ridge. He tried to shield his eyes from the lashing rain to make out the scene below, but the rain was too thick, the clouds too dark. Still, it seemed that there was some kind of opening down in the trees. A field or a hollow or something.

Then a flash of lightning ripped open the sky to his right, drawing his eyes. And it was like a giant silver finger pointing out a secret.

Jack forgot about the branches and his plans for a shelter and instead started working his way down the slope. It was so steep that he found himself leaning back and sliding down the hill, using the trees that dotted the hillside to keep from picking up too much momentum.

He was nearly thirty feet into his descent when his feet finally did go out from under him. He landed on his back, but the hill was so steep that when his feet hit a rock that was protruding out of the ground, it catapulted him forward head over heels. He went tumbling down the hill, flying through underbrush, bouncing off trees, and grazing rocks. He waved his arms, frantically trying to grab hold of something. He waited for the *crack* of his head striking rock and for all this madness to come to an end.

But it wasn't a crack that ended his plummet. It was another splash, and he was back in the water.

It wasn't deep, just a couple of feet, and he figured he was in a flooded stream. He stood and started to make his way to the other side, toward whatever it was he thought he saw in the flash of lightning. When he got to the other side, freezing and out of breath, he looked back up at the hill he'd tumbled down. Miraculously, he'd somehow managed to navigate all the rocks and trees.

Minutes later, he was through the woods and standing in a clearing, thanking God.

53

THE OLD TWO-STORY BUILDING stood before him in the pouring rain and waning light. To anyone else, it would look like something out of a horror movie and the last place someone would want to get near on a stormy day. But all he saw was shelter.

Two big barn doors faced him. The one on the right was hanging down at an angle, the metal track it used to slide back and forth on bent away from the frame. The door on the left still seemed intact.

He walked toward them.

Something caught his foot as he neared the entrance, and he stumbled forward. He looked down to see what he'd tripped over and noticed that the ground was littered with rusted metal. There were corroded cylindrical shapes sticking out of the mud all around. They looked like old cans. Then he noticed other, larger pieces of things that he couldn't identify. Farm equipment, he guessed.

He reached out and touched the doors, trying to determine if they'd recently been used. The door that was hanging off the track was buried twelve inches into the ground, so it was clear no one had moved it in a long time. The left door still looked intact, but he didn't see any footprints other than his own. Which didn't mean there wasn't another way in.

The handle on the left door was gone, so he pushed against its side, trying to slide it along the track. It moved a foot and then stopped. He leaned into it with his shoulder, and it moved another foot before his boots started slipping in the mud. But two feet was enough.

He took out his small waterproof flashlight from the belt pouch and clicked it on. A silver circle appeared, and he was surprised that it had survived the day. He put the flashlight in his mouth and drew the knife. Then he squeezed through and entered the darkness.

A MUSTY STILLNESS IMMEDIATELY replaced the wind and rain, but it was nearly pitch black inside. The flashlight revealed missing sections of the second floor and holes in the roof with water leaking through and forming large puddles along the floor. In fact, the entire center of the floor looked like a giant lake.

He aimed the flashlight at the back of the building, but the beam couldn't reach the end of it. Large sections of wood paneling were missing from the walls. Either the wood had rotted away from the nails, or the nails had rusted and snapped.

A pile of lumber was positioned near the wall to his left, and he walked over to it. He picked a piece off the top and found it to be wet and slimy. He used the toe of his boot to poke the pile, hoping snakes or bees hadn't made a home of it. Wooden planks spilled toward him but nothing else. He stepped over them, looking for a piece that he could use.

He found one that seemed dry enough, and he snapped it in half over his leg. He kept snapping it, breaking it down into more and more pieces, finally tossing them onto a dry spot of the floor. He found another piece. And another.

Once he had a good pile of wood to work with, he took out his knife and, with trembling hands, began carving. It was hard to do. His entire body was shaking, his teeth chattering. He made sure, like he'd taught Joseph the other night, to move the knife away from his body so that if it slipped, he wouldn't cut a finger or slice his femoral artery. The three to five torturous minutes it took him to create a pile of wood shavings that he could use as tinder felt a lot longer. But he looked at his watch and saw it was only 8:47.

He took the lighter from his pouch and started looking for something that would be able to catch fire right away.

Something he could lay the shavings on top of. He swept the flashlight back and forth.

The light caught an old rusted machine against the right wall. There were wheels attached to it, and he was sure that once upon a time large belts used to turn them. Maybe it was a saw and this had been a sawmill. He was certain it had been some kind of mill. It was what he had hoped for when he'd seen the distant shape of it in the lightning, what he suspected after discovering the nearby stream. He continued moving the light around, picking out other remnants of a bygone era that were scattered across the floor. Rotting cabinets hung from the walls.

There was a pile of leaves against one of the walls that he figured had been blown there over the years by wind rushing through the holes in the walls. He walked to it. They were dry and brittle. Perfect.

He grabbed an armful and walked them back to the wood. Then he began rubbing handfuls of them between his palms, reducing them to powder form. He put some full leaves on top of a board and then poured the powder on top of them. Put the wood chips on top of that.

He thumbed the lighter and held the flame against the leaves. They caught, and a crooked red-yellow laser began consuming them, leaving a small cloud of smoke in its wake. He quickly cupped his hands around the tiny fire and urged the laser line to the tinder with soft blows.

Little fingers of flames appeared among the shavings, and he set a few six-inch lengths of board across them. He waited anxiously for the bigger pieces to ignite, silently encouraging the little flames onward as he sat there dripping and shivering. If he put too much fuel on the fire at once, he could suffocate it, and while he'd love to pour the contents of the lighter onto it, it was a butane lighter, and the fuel was only kept in liquid form by pressure. If he cracked it open, the liquid would just turn to gas and disappear. He told himself that he'd carry a lighter that used actual fluid next time. As if there would ever be a next time.

Finally, the boards caught, and flames began swimming up and down their undersides. He added more pieces until the fire was big enough to handle the larger sections of wood. He started placing two-foot sections in a teepee configuration around the fire, and soon it was ablaze. Blessed heat warmed his face, and he held out his hands. He sat there for five minutes, until he could feel his hands again, and then removed his socks and shoes.

It felt wonderful.

Once his feet were dry, he stripped down to his underwear. Then he thought of heating up rocks that he could dry his clothes on, but remembered wet rocks could explode when heated. Instead, he just laid his shirt, pants, socks, and boots on the ground beside the fire.

As he sat there staring at the flame, his right eye throbbing but unable to look away, he felt sleep calling to him. But before he allowed himself to drift off, he needed to get some water. He pulled his boots back on so that he wouldn't cut himself on the rusted metal scattered across the floor and walked over to where a steady stream was dripping down through the roof. Typically, he wouldn't trust rainwater coming off an old ceiling. Who knew what kind of paint was in the wood and so forth? But this place had to be from the 1800s or early 1900s, and he thought that any chemicals used then would be long gone by now. At least that was what he hoped. Besides, he probably had a gallon of floodwater in his belly already, so maybe any old chemicals would kill the brain-eating amoebas. He stepped beneath the fountain and opened his mouth.

Once his thirst was quenched, he went back to the fire and took off his underwear. Then he got as close to the fire as he could stand and lay on his side.

Naked by a fire in an abandoned building in the middle of nowhere. He thought of when he had run naked around the cruise ship, looking for Stacey.

But she hadn't been on the ship anymore.

No, she had been...hiding.

With the...

He couldn't remember.

Russians? No, the other ones.

They thought he'd killed her.

...she'd tried to kill him...

For Joseph?

Or...or...

He fell asleep to the sound of a crackling fire and the pounding rain.

54

IT WAS NINE O'CLOCK, and Stacey still had not received a call about the new pickup location. She looked at the bottle of vodka sitting on the table beside her. It was half empty. She wouldn't be going anywhere tonight. Though maybe driving into a tree wouldn't be so bad. Spending the next week or so unconscious in the hospital would get her off the hook, wouldn't it? But would they just let Joseph go? No harm, no foul, we'll try someone else? Or would they kill him and come for her anyway?

No harm, no foul? They'd killed Jack.

She looked up at the framed verse Jack had hung over the television when they first moved in. *Love believes all things, hopes all things, endures all things...* She'd let him hang it without protest. She'd figured it was the least she could do after her role in Ivan's death—not that Jack had known about that at the time, but she'd been feeling bad about it anyway. Jack still didn't know the extent of the role she'd played in that, and she hoped he never would. *The ends justify the means*, she'd told herself. And she believed it. It was how she was able to do the things she'd done.

She read the verse again.

Love.

She brought the bottle back to her lips. She couldn't stand the waiting and wondering, and she held up the business card she'd pulled out of the trash can an hour ago. She couldn't stop looking at the handwritten phone number on the back of it, even as the numbers began to blur and dance in front of her.

55

THE KID WAS ASLEEP. Or at least he was pretending to be. James wouldn't put it past the boy to try to make a run for it. He'd been getting bolder and bolder as the night went on, and James could tell he was smart. That was why he'd told Colt to check on him every half hour. The window in the room was boarded, but still... There was something in the kid's eyes that had him feeling cautious.

But James was more concerned with Lee and Seth right now. They said they hadn't heard anything from Cullin yet, so all assumed he was still a hundred miles north, either trying to catch up to them, still trying to find the boy's father, or dead. But James suspected they were lying. That Lee and Cullin were still in contact with each other and maybe always had been. Again, he wasn't sure how. If they had a satellite phone he didn't know about or if the GPS devices really could communicate with each other. The way Lee kept sneaking off...

It was dark now, and there was nothing to see out the window but the occasional flash of lightning. All of them were tired and trying to stay awake, neither clan trusting the other to not cut their throats while they slept.

James slipped the cell phone out of his pocket and checked the display again. The storm was interfering with the signal, a line through the satellite image on the screen still indicating that he had no service through which to contact Ham. Or Ham to contact him. He put it back in his pocket before anyone could notice.

He drank more coffee out of the old tin cup as he tried to figure out just what the Baker brothers were up to.

56

IT WAS A DREAM about his parents, and he rarely had them. So it was special. Which was why when the dream started to fade, his barely conscious mind protested. Memories were both the fuel and framework of the current fantasy, and the feelings they invoked were like precious flakes of gold slipping through the pinched neck of an hourglass. He didn't want it to end. He missed his parents, and these visits they paid him were too few and far between to let them go without a fight.

He blinked. Something wet ran down the side of his face. His vision was blurred.

Don't go.

But they were gone, leaving him with just a few more seconds of their lingering scent, the impression of their visit.

He heard something that seemed unrelated to the dream, and the noise kicked open the door to the here and now.

A bright, shifting light. Heat.

A fire.

His eyes snapped wide as he remembered where he was, the dream shattering into a million pieces and sucked away by the vacuum of his current situation. He was lying on his side, still naked.

"Ah, wakey-wakey," a deep voice announced.

Jack squinted through the dancing flames and thought he could make out the form of a person on the other side of them. Unless it was his damaged eye. He lifted his head.

"Thought ya might sleep 'til kingdom come, so I took the liberty of growing your fire some."

Jack tried to prop himself up on an elbow and realized that his wrists were bound. "What the hell..." He blinked, trying to get his eyes to focus as he maneuvered to a sitting position.

"Found it upstairs," the voice said. "Hemp. Very strong."

Jack's eyes focused on the thick rope that bound his hands together. He followed its slithering form across the floor and into the shadows where it disappeared. "Who are you?" he asked.

Then the form on the other side of the fire stood, and its flickering silhouette stepped closer to the flames, his face materializing and framed by hell.

Cullin.

"Hello, Jack." He smiled, the fire dancing in his teeth. He reached a hand up and grabbed a rope that was hanging from the ceiling on his side of the fire. "Let's begin, shall we?"

"Begin wh—?"

Cullin reached up with both hands and pulled down on the rope.

Jack watched the big braided rope straighten across the floor and then rise into the air as tension suddenly bit into his wrists.

Then, with the rope taut, Cullin jerked hard, and Jack's arms flew into the air above his head.

Jack looked up and saw that the rope was going through the ceiling above him before coming back down again by Cullin. He realized that the rope must be over a beam or something—

The next jerk pulled him to his feet and had him stumbling toward the fire. Jack pulled against the rope, pitting him against Cullin in a game of tug-of-war, the fire itself the line between them. But though he was strong, his muscles bulging all over his body, he wasn't very heavy, and his bare feet found no traction in the dust that covered the old wooden floor.

Cullin pulled him closer to the heat.

Closer.

Jack reached up and grabbed the rope with his hands, trying for better leverage. But it was no use.

Except that he made the only move he thought might give him a chance, and instead of pulling against the rope, he used the two remaining steps he had left to propel himself up into the air and over the fire, playing into the slack and hoping to tackle Cullin on the other side.

But it didn't work at all.

Cullin had been standing too far away, and he'd been pulling on the rope so hard that when the line went slack, he went flying backward onto the ground. And maybe it would have worked had Cullin lost his grip in the fall, but he hadn't, and all Jack managed to do was surrender four more feet of rope to the wrong side of the beam. And now, instead of his feet landing on the other side of the fire, he found himself swaying in the air.

The flames reached up to his thighs, and he screamed.

Cullin had been able to get back to his feet without giving up any more slack, and now he was continuing to pull the rope hand over hand, raising Jack higher and higher until his feet were up and out of the fire. Then, once he was hanging about four feet above the open flame, Cullin tied the rope off on something Jack couldn't see.

Shit. He was really in a situation now. With only a couple of feet of rope between his arms and the small hole in the ceiling, he'd have little room to work with, either to swing himself past the fire or to pull himself up onto the next floor. The only thing he could hope to do was fall, naked, straight into the fire and then get out as fast as possible.

Double shit.

He hung, arms above his head, suspended like a roasting pig, turning slowly like a rotisserie ham. How long could he hang like this before his shoulders popped out of joint? Or his feet blistered and seared? He tried to keep his knees bent and his feet away from the heat.

Cullin bent over and picked up a rifle. It wasn't the same strange gun Jack had tossed into the fire the other day, so he figured it had to be JT's.

"I couldn't decide whether to hang you from your feet or your hands," Cullin said. "So I flipped a coin. Guess I shoulda gone with the feet. Ya almost got me."

"You flipped a coin?"

"I did."

"Okay, *No Country For Old Men.* What do you have there, a bolt gun?"

Cullin cocked his head, obviously not getting the reference. "What are these words yer sayin'?" He held up the rifle in the firelight. "This is not a bolt gun. And actually, the rifle that you threw into the fire..." He shook his head. "That was a family heirloom."

Jack was starting to twirl away from him, and he couldn't help repeating Chris Hemsworth's line when Thor found himself in a similar situation in the beginning of the third Thor movie. "Hold on a sec," he said. "I'll be right back around." He started to laugh.

An air pocket exploded, and a shower of sparks flew upward, engulfing his body. He howled, but then resumed laughing. When he'd completed the turn and was facing Cullin again, he found that Cullin was clapping, the rifle in the crook of his arm.

"I saw that movie. Very good, Jack."

Jack stopped laughing. "You have movies where you come from?" But it wasn't funny anymore.

"I wonder," Cullin continued. "Did you see it with your son? Did you and little Joey watch it together? Maybe with some popcorn? Some...Coca-Cola?"

In fact, they had.

"What do you want?" Jack asked. The heat was getting unbearable. He was sure the bottom of his feet were turning black.

"I want to kill you."

"Then why didn't you just shoot me while I was sleeping?"

A sudden impatience came over his dark eyes. "Are you kiddin' me?"

"I don't think so."

"After how hard you've made this, you thought that when I finally caught up to you, I'd just shoot you in your sleep?"

"I'd shrug if I could, but—"

"If I'd put the barrel of this rifle"—he held it up for him to see—"to the back of your ear and blew your head apart while you were dreaming, you'd never know that I found you. That I killed you."

"So it's personal, then, is it?"

"No, Jack, it's not personal. But after one goes through so much to obtain somethin', there is a certain level of satisfaction one then expects to draw out of obtainin' it."

"So you enjoy this?"

"I do. Now, I couldn't decide whether to watch your testicles melt as your shoulders and elbows dislocated, or whether to have all the blood in your body drain into your head and watch your face drip off."

"So you flipped a coin."

A smile lit up his face. "I flipped a coin."

"I get it. Heads or tails." And he started laughing again.

Cullin laughed with him.

Jack pulled himself up on the rope and swung his feet up toward the ceiling, trying to get as far away from the heat as he could. He held that position until his biceps began to tremble and his abs felt like they were going to cramp.

Cullin clapped again. "Monkey-boy!"

Once he was vertical again, Jack looked up at the ceiling, at the hole the rope was coming through. There were a few missing floorboards, maybe two or three wide. Too narrow to fit his shoulders through. But maybe if he could find a way to make the hole bigger...

He began to swing back and forth as much as he could, just trying to spend a little more time out of the fire's direct line of heat.

Cullin chuckled, deep and maniacal, like something stolen from a horror movie. "Gooood. Fan those flames, monkey-boy." He ran a hand through his hair. "And to answer your other question, yes, we do have movies where I come from. But isn't this so much more entertainin'? I really should have popcorn."

As Jack's body grew more and more fatigued and sweat poured off him, his momentary delirium ran out of steam and his laughter came to a stop. He pulled himself up so that his hands were against his face, and he closed his eyes. "What are you going to do with my son?"

"Yes! Now we are gettin' somewhere, Jack! No more playin' around! What about your son? You wanna know what his fate'll be before you meet yours, as any father would."

A tear escaped Jack's eye. The veins in his shoulders and arms bulged.

"Well, as you pass from this world, let me assure you that little Joey will suffer every day for the rest of what will certainly be a short life." He shrugged. "Or maybe not. Maybe he'll actually enjoy himself. I don't know which way he swings, ya know what I mean?"

Jack clenched his teeth.

"But that's not all I want ya to know." He reached into his pocket and pulled out a wallet. And from that wallet he removed a piece of plastic. Held it up even as he tossed the wallet itself into the fire. "I'm guessing there is a wife? That she is back home, wondering why you haven't answered your phone or called?"

But now Jack did find it in him to laugh again.

"You think it's funny that I'm gonna go to the address on your license and rape your wife and then cut her in half? And when I say 'in half,' I don't mean across the stomach from side to side." He motioned across his own stomach. "What I mean is..." He placed two fingers between his legs at his crotch and moved them up over his stomach, chest, neck, and all the way to the top of his head.

"Please..."

"Don't beg. There's no point."

"No, I *am* begging you. I'm begging you to go. *Please* go." He started yelling. "Go, you psycho asshole! Go to my house and see what my wife does to you! I *beg* you to go! She'll rip you to pieces, you hillbilly fuck!" He couldn't stop laughing. "Go get her, tiger! She's all yours!"

Cullin cocked his head. This was not the response he'd expected. His hand involuntarily went to the bloodstain on his shoulder.

"She'll turn you inside out and upside down. Why don't you take this backwoods act you got going on into the city and see how far you get against a professional killer? That's right. You want to know who my wife is? She's an assassin, and she'll see you coming a mile away! In fact, she might be on her way to your cabin already!" He began to twirl away from him, but he kept going. "Oh, I forgot, you don't even know what 'all this' is, because you're just a hired gun. Disposable, expendable, a little cog in a big machine." More laughter. "You don't even know you're already dead! These people who want my son, they're not traffickers, they're terrorists! And if you think they'll leave you and your friends around as loose ends, you're dumber than the goats you bang on Friday nights!"

When he came around again, Cullin wasn't wearing the same happy face.

"That's right. You have no idea what you've stepped in. And that's what I'll take with me as I go—the pleasure of knowing what it is they're going to do to you. And let me tell you, it ain't gonna be roasting chestnuts. You have any idea what Russians do to their enemies?"

Cullin blinked, his mind suddenly working through something Jack had said. And then he was pulling out the GPS device Jack had taken from him before.

"Put it down," a new voice said from behind Jack.

JACK LOOKED BACK OVER his shoulder and saw Lawrence step out of the shadows and into the firelight. His bald head was oozing blood down his face, and it looked like he'd been shot multiple times. Once in the leg, judging by the way he was hobbling. His shirt was ripped, and a piece of it missing, exposing half of his chest and his left shoulder. He was covered in blood and mud, and it seemed almost impossible that he would've been able to get here at all. The most important thing, however, was Theo's rifle he had trained on Cullin.

"I said put it down," Lawrence repeated.

Cullin dropped the device.

"Now drop the rifle."

Cullin bent over like he was going to set the gun on the ground, but at the last second, he swung the barrel back up and

—

Lawrence shot him.

The explosion rocked the old mill, and Cullin went down, holding his knee.

"Thought my hand wasn't steady no more, huh?" Lawrence limped toward the fire. "I still got a smidgen of time, don't you worry."

Jack's shoulders were burning, and he could feel the tension pulling at his joints. He didn't have much strength left. He pulled on the rope while flipping upside down and pulling his legs to his chest. Then he thrust his feet at the ceiling, kicking at the broken floorboards. Pieces of them snapped away and fell down into the fire. He lowered himself back down, hanging like a pinata between Lawrence and Cullin.

Cullin was writing on the floor, his knee shattered. He reached for something that was tucked into the back of his pants.

"He's got a pistol," Jack said.

Lawrence shot him again, this time in his shoulder. And then again in the other shoulder. Then he walked around Jack and around the fire until he was standing over Cullin. He kicked the rifle away and pulled the pistol from his pants, tossing it across the room.

"I'm gonna kill you," Lawrence said, and then blew apart his other kneecap.

Cullin howled.

Lawrence placed the barrel of the rifle against Cullin's right elbow and fired. But no blast came, just the click of the hammer against metal. "Out of bullets," he said, and dropped the gun. Then he grabbed a handful of Cullin's hair and began dragging him across the floor, toward the big doors. Cullin couldn't kick his legs or flail his arms, he could only lie there limp and be dragged away by his hair. And, of course, scream.

Jack was about to make his move, to turn himself upside down and try to pull himself up through the hole feetfirst when Lawrence reached over on his way out and unwrapped the rope from whatever Cullin had attached it to.

Jack fell on top of the fire, sparks exploding as he crushed the charred wood with his weight. He threw himself out of the flames as quickly as possible, rolling along the dirty floor and into one of the puddles. The cool water was a relief, and he thought he could have lain submerged there for a long time. But there was no time. He got to his knees and tugged on the rope, pulling it end over end until it was free from the beam and its tail fell down into the fire.

Lawrence stopped dragging Cullin for a second and looked back to Jack. He held up a knife and then dropped it on the floor. "I'm gonna need that rope," he said. Then he resumed pulling Cullin to the doors.

Jack ran to the knife, hoping not to step on anything that would hurt his feet worse than they already were, the shifting shadows and the floaters in his right eye making it nearly impossible to see the ground ahead of him.

Lawrence reached the barn doors and kicked the broken one so hard that it pulled the rest of the track out of the frame. The big door fell forward, its weight and momentum freeing its bottom corner from the mud. It fell flat with a splash, and Lawrence walked over it, dragging Cullin out of the building and out of sight.

Jack cut the rope off his wrists and went to pick up Cullin's rifle and pistol. Then he went for his clothes. He used his flannel shirt to pat himself dry before pulling on his underwear and jeans. They were nice and warm from the fire, and after the quick ice bath, they too felt good. It brought to mind whenever Joseph would put on clothes right out of the dryer, closing his eyes, wrapping his arms around his chest, and sighing with exaggerated satisfaction. The memory made Jack smile. And then he winced when he pulled the socks over his seared and blackened feet.

Once he had his boots laced, he stood up and pulled the T-shirt on. Then his flannel shirt, not bothering to button it. He looked around, found that Cullin had left a water bottle behind along with what he guessed was JT's radio. But there was no sign of the GPS device. Lawrence must've picked it up.

Jack jogged to the bottle, every step a painful one, and had half of it swallowed before Lawrence stumbled back in.

The guy who had helped kidnap his son didn't look at him, didn't say a word. He just grabbed the end of the rope that was closest to him and turned, pulling it back outside with him.

Jack watched the rope slither after him and wondered what the hell Lawrence was planning to do with it. He quickly got his belt pouch fastened around his waist, hooked the bottle to it, and then picked up the radio. He slung the rifle over his shoulder and went to the doors. He held the pistol out in front of him, and when he reached them, he peered outside and into the night air.

Only it wasn't night. It was dawn. And it had stopped raining.

The sky was a deep blue, but there was a serrated red-orange stripe across the distant treetops in the east. Mist weaved in and out of the trees surrounding the old building, and as he stepped outside, he saw that it was in fact an old sawmill. The river he'd crossed seemed to run right up alongside its stone foundation, and he could see some kind of concrete wall beneath the water where he guessed a water wheel used to be.

The river flowed away from him and eventually disappeared into the mist. Looking around, he saw other buildings, all in various stages of collapse and scattered across the clearing.

He moved quietly, sweeping the pistol back and forth, using the techniques Stacey had taught him. He looked back to the mill and saw the drag marks in the mud from Cullin's calves and ankles. They swung to his left, away from the river and into the fog's cold fingers.

He followed them.

HE HEARD SOMETHING. GRUNTS and groans, it sounded like. He kept going, eyes darting back and forth, unable to see more than a few feet in any direction, trees slowly materializing like giants as he neared them.

A sound to his right.

He swung the revolver around, trigger finger already applying pressure.

There was something there, just behind the veil. A shape...

He stepped forward, and the mist began to thin.

Another step. And another.

The form came into focus, and Jack stopped. Lowered the gun.

"Please..." Cullin spat.

He was tied to a tree, the big hemp rope wrapped around him from his ankles to his neck, like it was a python getting ready to swallow him whole.

Jack looked around for Lawrence, but there was no sign of him. Which, in this fog, didn't mean much. He could be two feet behind him, and he wouldn't know it until there was a knife buried between his shoulder blades.

"Don't leave me like this," Cullin said. Blood bubbled between shattered teeth.

"Oh, how the mighty have fallen," Jack said. "Looks like he did quite a job on you."

"Yeah..." His bloodshot eyes went to something on the ground by Jack's feet. "But I got him before he was done."

Jack thought he saw a tooth fall out of his mouth as he talked. He looked down to where Cullin's eyes had drifted and saw a bloody knife lying in the grass.

"So he tied you to this tree and left you to die."

"But you're not going to," he gagged. "'Cause I'll get out and kill your boy if you do."

Jack smiled. "You're shot to hell. Couldn't drag yourself three feet."

"You wanna take that chance?"

"I'm thinking I know what Lawrence was hoping for here. That before you could bleed out or die of exposure, some hungry bear would wander on by." He looked around. "Sounds kind of like hanging someone over a fire and watching their face melt off."

"You better shoot me, Jack. Or I swear you'll regret it."

Jack stared into his eyes. "I'm not a killer."

"I can tell you where the cabin is."

Jack stopped. "And why would I think for a second you'd tell me the truth?"

Cullin managed to chuckle. "'Cause when you get there, my brothers'll kill you and what's left of Ham's gang."

"Fine. Where is it?"

"Outside the Cranberry Wilderness. On Hollow Mountain. But you won't get there in time." He laughed. "If you get there at all."

"Well, I appreciate your concern." He patted him on the shoulder where Lawrence had shot him. "But I already knew all that. Now if you had the GPS and could mark the cabin on that, then maybe we'd have something to talk about. But you'd probably just mark a pit of punji sticks, wouldn't you?"

Cullin smiled. "That sure would be a good one."

"Guessing mama bear will be around with her kids soon, and that's not really something I want to see. In the meantime, though, you may want to think about your eternity. That fire you put me over was pretty hot. Can't imagine what it's gonna be like where you're heading." He slipped his hand inside Cullin's pocket and retrieved his driver's license. Then he turned and walked back the way he'd come.

By the time he got back to the mill, the sun was breaching the horizon. He looked around, wondering which way Lawrence could have gone. Should he go look for him? See if he could get the GPS back? Or was it even worth getting if the cabin wasn't marked on it? Hell yeah, it was worth it. Because he didn't have a clue what state he was in, let alone which direction to head. At least the GPS would tell him where he was.

He looked at his watch.

58

STACEY POPPED TWO MORE ibuprofen in her mouth and swallowed them along with half a glass of water. Then she put the glass in the sink and ran her hands through her hair, pulling at the roots to get some relief from the headache. Rain pelted the window in front of her and blurred the world outside, which was a perfect representation of how she felt. Blurred, distorted, disoriented...hungover from both alcohol and tragedy.

After she had woken up and rolled over to stare at the glowing numbers on the bedside clock (their meaning eventually breaking through the hangover), she'd managed to throw herself out of bed, falling onto the floor and scrambling on her hands and knees to her phone. She'd wrestled it out of her jeans, sure that she'd missed their call. But she hadn't. The display showed no missed calls.

Now she was beginning to see Joseph everywhere she looked. When her eyes went to the living room, she saw him sitting curled up on his favorite couch cushion, reading a book. When they looked out back, he was swinging from the monkey bars. Right now he was sitting at the kitchen table and eating cereal.

The phone rang.

She picked it up off the counter so fast that she almost lost her grip on it and sent it across the room. She stared at the number. It wasn't the blocked number she was expecting, but for some reason she recognized it. Why did it look so familiar?

She answered it.

"Stacey Green?" a man's voice asked from the other end.

She didn't recognize the voice, and she hesitated.

"I'm sorry. Did I wake you?" he asked.

"Who is this?"

"It's Johnson."

Her mind spun through the haze, searching for a handle. "Johnson?"

"Yeah," he said, light impatience in his voice. "You did call me last night, right?"

"*Agent* Johnson?"

"So you didn't call me?"

She could see him about to hang up and dart from wherever he was, looking over his shoulder for a hit team. "No, I mean...I could have."

"You have ten seconds. Did you call and leave a message at this number or not?"

"Hold on." She began tapping the screen on her phone and pulled up her call log. And sure enough, a call went from her phone to the number currently displayed at 1:42 a.m. She put the cell back to her ear. "I had a lot to drink..."

He sighed. "Why are you calling me? Where's Jack?"

"Look, I know it's been a long time and that you don't trust me—"

"Ha!"

She squeezed her eyes shut. "I wouldn't have called... Probably shouldn't have called."

"Well, you did, so you might as well tell me what the hell is going on. Unless you think I'm one of your loose ends, in which case I'll save us both the time—"

"Jack is dead."

Silence.

She continued. "At least, I'm almost positive he's dead." And for some reason, saying it out loud managed to hammer it home in her brain. Her eyes instantly stung, and her vision became as blurred as the windowpane. She blinked, and hot tears splashed onto the counter. "Joseph's been taken. They want me to—"

A beep on the other line.

"That's them, they're calling. I have to go."

Johnson blurted out, "Who's calling? What do they want you to do? Stacey, what—"

She switched over. "Hello?" She wiped her eyes.

"*It is time,*" said the synthesized voice. "*Get dressed. Pack a dress. You will not be coming back.*"

59

HE WAS PARKED ALONG the road, across the street. When the sun cleared the treetops, Ham flipped the visor down to keep it out of his eyes. A song was playing over the radio, though it was hardly discernible through the static. He drummed his fingers on the steering wheel while he watched two kids with fishing poles go into the gas station. They came out two minutes later with a paper bag, walked past the LIVE BAIT sign that was leaning against the door, and went around the back of the station and into the woods, where they would follow a path to the local fishing hole.

The fishing hole was one of the only two reasons anyone ever frequented this old dump. The ancient pumps hadn't had anything to do but rust over the past decade, and no one was coming for the burnt coffee.

Five minutes later, someone else went into the store and came out with a bag. This guy, however, was not interested in the watering hole. He was here for the other reason. And he tossed that reason into the glove compartment of his station wagon and drove off the gravel lot.

Thirty seconds after that, the station owner walked out the door, flipping a sign in the window that read WILL BE BACK IN 5. He went around the back of the building, same as the kids had.

Ham opened the door of the pickup and wrestled himself out from behind the wheel. God, he hated being fat. Nothing he could really do about it now, though. The only exercise he got was whenever he used ol' Joanna. And he wasn't even sure his heart could put up with that much longer. His late wife's suggestion that maybe he should give up the booze and maybe try some Tae Bo was one of the reasons she'd had to go. But maybe she'd had a point.

He crossed the street and walked onto the gravel lot, passing between the two antique pumps. His heavy footsteps crunched out the announcement of his arrival, but Carl hadn't been able to hear it from behind the building. Ham found him lighting a cigarette—clearly not the only one of his products he was using.

"Hey, Carlos," Ham said.

"Dammit!" The guy jumped and turned away from him, clutching his chest with his hand.

"Did I...spook you?"

"Yeah, ya sure did, you fat f—" Then he saw who it was he was talking to and bit his tongue. "Ham, what the hell?"

"On a smoke break?"

"Yeah, ya need somethin'?" He took a drag on the cigarette. "I'll be in in a minute."

"I'll wait 'til you're done," Ham said, leaning against the wall beside him.

"Why you always gotta call me Carlos? Do I look Hispanish to you? It's Carl. No os."

"Potato, patata."

The guy blew smoke out of his nostrils and peered at him through the cloud. "You need some—"

"Information," Ham cut him off.

Carl blinked. "That ain't the sort of stuff I'm into, Ham. You know that."

Ham nodded and scratched at his beard. "Today it is."

"This isn't about the job, is it?"

"It actually is."

"You know I'm only the messenger. I don't know—"

Ham drew his pistol. "What do you say you and I get some breakfast? I'm starving."

60

LAWRENCE WATCHED WITH SATISFACTION as the bear walked up to Cullin and began sniffing him. Cullin turned his head to the side as the bear licked his face. Then it nibbled his ear. Then it ripped it off.

Cullin yelled, swearing at the six-hundred-pound beast as blood flowed from the hole in the side of his head.

The bear took a step back and cocked its head. Then it stood on its hind legs, blocking the sun and casting Cullin into its shadow.

Cullin looked up. He stopped swearing.

The bear swatted him with its paw, its claws raking through his shirt and tearing open his flesh.

Cullin screamed some more.

The bear had clawed through a section of the rope, and Cullin's left arm fell free. He held it out in front of him, trying in vain to push the creature away.

The bear clamped its giant teeth on his bicep and tore his arm from his body.

As Cullin shook his head back and forth and howled, his hair flopping, the bear lay down in front of him and began to pull the skin off his severed arm. It chewed, the bones crunching, blood getting on its snout.

Lawrence smiled from his position among the rocks. How perfect was this? He was about forty yards away, upwind. He'd never in all his life seen a black bear do this to a man. He thought Cullin would just bleed to death. But maybe God or Mother Nature or the Great Spirit or the Universe or whatever thought bleeding to death would just be too merciful an end for a demon like him.

Cullin was shaking himself back and forth like he was on fire, and Lawrence wasn't sure if it was pain or if he was trying to get free. But the rope was getting looser, and now Cullin was trying to slip his remaining hand out from under it.

The bear got back to its feet and returned to him. It eyed his hand for a moment as he wriggled his wrist around. Then the bear chomped it right off.

Cullin's voice echoed off the mountains.

The bear, after the hand flopped out of its mouth and landed on the ground like a dead crab, began to lick the blood pouring out of his shoulder. It licked and licked, trying to work its tongue further into the wound, between the bone and the tendons. Not satisfied with the results, the bear then began using its teeth to try to get at whatever it was digging for. Or trying to rip out. Cullin was jerked sideways by the tugging, which enabled him to finally slip his other arm out of the rope. He started striking the bear with his bloody stump.

The bear pulled back, then roared. It wasn't the roar of a grizzly, but it was still enough to make you shit your pants.

Cullin used the moment to try to work the rest of the rope off him, and it began to fall down around his legs, to pile at his feet.

Where did he think he would go even if he did get free, Lawrence wondered. With inch-deep gashes across his chest, a missing arm and a missing hand (not to mention all the bullets in him), he was already dead.

But before Cullin could step out of the rope and away from the tree, the bear had come back. It turned its head sideways and opened wide, then planted its face into Cullin's midsection, clamping its teeth into the flesh of his sides and stomach. When it pulled its head back, it took half of his stomach with it, slippery eels tumbling out of him and piling up on his boots. Again the beast backed up, and that was when three cubs appeared.

They walked over to him, stepping on his guts and squashing them like rotten bananas. They dipped their little noses in it and began licking and chewing and pulling.

Lawrence was sure the bear was a male. It was too big for a female. So he wasn't sure what the story was with the cubs.

Maybe Cullin had killed the bear's wife yesterday, and this was its revenge.

The bear stood on its hind legs and leaned its two arms against the tree above Cullin's head. Then it leaned in close and licked his face. Cullin turned his head.

And that was when he spotted Lawrence watching him from the rocks just forty yards away.

Lawrence smiled and waved.

"I'll see you in hell," Cullin screamed. Then the bear opened its mouth and ripped his face off.

Lawrence watched for a few more minutes before turning his attention to the sun. It was climbing a day he knew he wouldn't see it set on. He lay on his back and started hitting buttons on the GPS. He scrolled through the texts Cullin and Lee had been sending back and forth to each other, and it was plain as day what they were planning. Though it didn't seem like they knew who exactly had brought them into their employ.

He selected the conversation and forwarded it to another number. To the cell phone Ham had given James.

Then, with the life he had left, he started writing his own message.

JACK WAS ABOUT TO head south with the assumption he was still north of Mount Hollow. Whether he was now east or west of it, he wasn't sure. But he didn't think he could've gotten that far south in just two days, half of which he'd spent heading in no particular direction.

And then he heard Cullin's screams echo off the mountains. The sound sent a series of shivers up his spine. Had Lawrence gone back to finish him off real slow, or had a bear actually claimed him as its breakfast?

The screams continued to reverberate, turning the morning calm into a sort of freak show. He tried to think, but he couldn't. He thought he should be happy to hear Cullin in such torment, but he wasn't. Maybe because it was such a horrible sound, and he wished he'd just shut up and die in silence. Let the birds get back to their morning songs again.

And then he thought he heard Cullin shout something. He couldn't make it out in the echo, but what was left of the inflection and tone that had made it through the mix gave him the impression that Cullin had just yelled at someone. Or something. He could just be cursing the bear that was eating him. Or he could be yelling at Lawrence. Who had the GPS device.

He had to be sure. He ran toward the sound of slaughter, hoping there weren't bears with AK-47s waiting for him.

JAMES COULD TELL THAT Lee was on edge about something. Since waking, he'd been steeling sideways glances out the windows and to the door, looking at his watch, and absentmindedly tapping his fingers on the radio. He'd paced back and forth until he must've noticed he was doing it, and then went outside.

Now all five of them were outside, James, Michael, and Colt sitting in old chairs and watching the morning mist dissipate over the surrounding mountaintops while Lee and Seth stood further off. The boy was sleeping. Or pretending to sleep. James didn't care which as long as he was in the room and being quiet.

"Two more days of this?" Michael said under his breath.

James sipped his coffee. "Yup."

Colt leaned over and pointed at the two Baker boys. "Somethin' ain't right with them," he said, keeping his voice low and his eyes ahead. "They were up to somethin', and now that somethin' is nothin', and so they're trying to figure out their next move."

James crossed his leg over the other and squinted at the sun. "That's about how I'm reading it."

"I don't think he's heard from Cullin, and it's botherin' him," said Michael.

Colt lit a cigarette. "Could be he's just worried about him."

"That's part of it for sure," James agreed. Then he waved at the smoke that just drifted across his face. "Do you mind?" He coughed.

Colt shook his head. "Nope." He took a long drag and blew it into the crisp mountain air.

"When you're finished givin' us all cancer, why don't you go get the kid some breakfast," James said. Then he stood and splashed the rest of his coffee into the grass. He slid a fresh toothpick in his mouth. "I'm gonna go have myself a chat with our compadres."

MICHAEL CAME BACK TO the cabin instead of Colt. He took off his hat and hung it on the back of a chair. Scratched at the short blond hair that covered his scalp while looking around. Everything was quiet now after the storm. He didn't like it.

He walked back to the stove, the sound of his boots like gunshots in the silence, and scrambled some eggs in a pan. He could see the four of them out the kitchen window. James was standing beside Lee, both of them far off and attempting a civil conversation. Seth and Colt were sitting thirty feet away on opposite sides of the meeting, each watching for any sign of hostility from the other.

It was going to be an interesting day for sure.

Michael dumped the eggs onto a plate and took it to the kid's room. He knocked on the door.

No answer.

"C'mon, kid. Breakfast time."

Still no sign of movement from the other side.

Michael sighed. "I'm just gonna eat it myself if you don't open the damn door."

Still nothing.

"Comin' in." He pushed the door open, but it stopped right away, blocked by something that was up against it. He pushed harder, and whatever was in the way scratched the wooden floor as it moved.

The bed. The kid had moved the bed up against the door.

"Real cute, kid." Michael pushed himself all the way inside and looked around. The room was empty. His eyes went to the window. "Damn," he whispered. He set the eggs on the bed and went to it. The window had been nailed into the frame and then boarded over. But now the boards were missing.

Broken glass crunched under his feet, and when he looked down, he saw he was standing in a puddle. He swore and ran out of the room.

JAMES STOOD NEAR LEE, both of them at the top of the hill overlooking the valley. The sun was beginning to burn through the mist, revealing that the prior day's storms had not completely flooded the world below, as one might have assumed. Trees began to poke through the wisps of cotton, and their pointed tops seemed to stretch on forever.

"Cullin killed Theo," James said. He didn't bother adding JT and Lawrence to the equation, though he was sure that was exactly what had happened to them too. "So what I want to know is, what are you gonna do about it?" He put the toothpick back between his lips and twirled it with his fingers as he waited for Lee to formulate an answer.

Lee crossed his arms over his belly. It wasn't much of a belly, but there was enough to rest his big forearms on. "You see all this?" he asked, bringing one arm up so he could stroke his long beard. "My family's been in these parts since before the War. People 'round here know us. Know to stay away or, if they're desperate enough, to seek our services." He turned and fixed his lifeless eyes on James. "But this, I can assure you, is a first."

"Kidnapping?"

Lee choked on a laugh. "No, of course not. But the way this was done... Ain't never seen it before. Except maybe in the movies."

"Me neither."

"Don't make a lick of sense."

James realized that Lee had changed the subject, and though a subject worth exploring, it wasn't why he'd walked over here. But before he could refocus the conversation on the obvious issue, the phone in his pocket vibrated. He looked at Lee, wondering if he'd heard it.

"You gonna check that?" Lee asked.

He had good ears, apparently.

James looked at him.

"You don't think I know you got a cell phone from Ham on ya?"

James pulled the phone out of his pocket and gestured toward Lee's pocket. "What about you?" With the storm gone, the phone was showing plenty of signal.

"What about me?"

"You—" He stopped when he looked down at the screen and saw the messages. They'd come from a number he didn't know, but it wasn't hard to put it together. He began scrolling through the forwarded conversation.

He could feel Lee's eyes on him as his face grew red with anger. It was all here in the texts, laid out between the two numbers.

He quickly sent a text off to one of the numbers and, sure enough, two seconds later, as Lee went to reach for the GPS, his suspicion was confirmed. Lee and Cullin had been conversing over the devices. But Cullin didn't have this number, which meant...

A new text.

ITS LARNC HAV GPS CULLN KLLD JT

James looked up, watched Lee read the text he'd sent before getting the new one.

Another text. The letters were all over the place, Lawrence's fingers and brain apparently having a hard time cooperating.

I KLLD CLLNN BBUT I NT CMN BAK GOTT METO

James's hand began to shake. He sent off a quick response asking where he was.

DNT MATTR GOOT MINTS LFTTT JUST WATHINNNNNNNN SUN RSS ANRETHIKINGGG LLLLLLLIIIIFE

James could see him lying there, bleeding out, hanging on just long enough to relay this information to his friends. He struggled to find something to tell him.

BUT HVE TO TLLLL U THISSS

James waited.

"Did you send this?" Lee asked beside him, raising the GPS.

"Send what?" James asked, stalling. He took a step back.

Another text.

THHHE BOYYSS MOMM S ASPYY RUSSIANNS DBLLE AGENT WRRKS FR CIA

James heart began to beat faster, and he ignored whatever Lee was saying.

RUSSNS AR USSING BOY HOSTGE TO GET HERRRR TO DO SMTNGGGG FAHTER SAYS THY WNT LET ANY OFFFF US LIVVVE

James sent off another text: THE RUSSIANS HIRED US?

Lawrence: YESSS

Lee reached a hand out towards James's shoulder, and James shrugged it off, stepping further away from him.

James: YOU SAW THE FATHER?

Lawrence: YES HES COMMINGGGGG

James: DO THE BAKERS KNOW?

Lawrence: ODONTHKSOOOOOO

The Os went on for a few lines, and James knew Lawrence's time was up. He shot off one last text. It was all he could think to say. SEE YOU ON THE OTHER SIDE. Then he started to read Lee's own conversation with Cullin back to him

Colt and Seth stood behind them, and they were able to pick up pieces of what was being said. They slowly began walking, Colt with his rifle up now, Seth trying to decide if he was fast enough to get his gun out or not, Lee's own hand hovering over the pistol in his waistband.

James read on.

63

JACK FOUND WHAT WAS left of Cullin scattered around the bloodstained tree. From the carnage and the large paw prints in the mud, it was plain as day what had happened. Jack had never seen anything like it before, and he turned and vomited the little food that was still in his stomach.

He could almost hear his grandmom shaking her head and quoting, "You reap what you sow." Or maybe, "The wages of sin is death."

Jack turned his back to the gore, a little leery that the bear might still be around, and began looking for signs of Lawrence. He put his hands on his hips and stared into the green world. The sunlight was cutting wide swathes through the—

There.

A pile of rocks to his right.

He squinted, trying to make out what it was that was stretched out on them. He began walking toward it, and after ten yards, he could tell that it was indeed a person. He led with the pistol, waiting for the body to bolt upright and start shooting.

But the body never moved.

When Jack got to the rocks, he saw that Cullin, just as he'd said, had been able to deliver a mortal blow before being served as breakfast.

Lawrence lay there on the rocks, eyes open and fixed on the sky, one hand over the wound in his stomach, the other clutching the GPS device.

Jack bent over and, without really knowing why, closed Lawrence's eyes. He didn't know what to think about the man.

He hated him for being involved in the kidnapping of his son, yet the man had saved his life.

But there was no time to waste trying to make sense of his feelings right now. He looked around, making sure the bear wasn't coming back for seconds, and then took the GPS away from the dead.

64

EVEN BEFORE JAMES WAS done reading the incriminating messages detailing what the Baker brothers had planned to do them once the job was done, Lee pulled his gun. He was bringing it up when James kicked him between the legs. Lee's knees buckled, and James grabbed his gun hand. Kicked him again. Harder.

Colt started to run, continuing to aim his rifle at Seth, screaming for him to get down on the ground.

Lee was on his knees, and James kicked him again, this time able to wrench the pistol from his grasp. He stuck it in his belt and grabbed Lee's beard. Pulled his face up and punched him between the eyes. He pulled on the beard again, punched again.

Lee leaned forward and wrapped his arms around James's waist, trying to get him in a bear hug and to lift him off his feet. But his belly was too big and his arms too short, and he couldn't reach his own wrist with his other hand to lock James in.

James could feel his feet come off the ground, but knew Lee wouldn't be able to get him in a bear hug. Still, he didn't like his feet coming off the ground, so he took the toothpick out of his mouth and jammed it into Lee's eyelid, just above the eyeball. It pierced the thin skin and slid into the socket. James was about to use his fist to pound it all the way in when Lee let go of him, stumbling back, one hand reaching for his face, the other for something in his pocket.

There was a *snap*, and suddenly Lee was waving a switchblade back and forth. He pulled the toothpick out of his eye.

James drew his pistol.

Colt came up beside him, his rifle still trained on Seth and hoping he was about to make a move.

Then there was a sound from the cabin, and they all turned their heads.

It was Michael. He was running toward them, holding his hat down on his head to keep it from blowing off.

"He's gone!" he was yelling. "The kid is gone!"

65

JACK WAS WADING THROUGH a waist-high field of yellow flowers that glowed like gold in the morning light. The field was immense, bordered by tree lines a thousand yards away. He put his hands out and moved his fingers over the petals and thought of that classic seen in *Gladiator*. He wondered if this could be Valhalla. Was he dead? Had Cullin actually shot him in his sleep and everything since was some sort of dream meant to carry him into the afterlife? He remembered questioning his reality before, after surviving the fall off the cruise ship, and he wasn't particularly interested in revisiting all the furniture that had been behind that door.

Birds flew overhead. He shielded his eyes against the sun and watched them for a few seconds. He looked down at the GPS, amazed that it hadn't yet depleted its power source. He'd read through the messages Cullin and Lee had written back and forth, and it was pretty clear that they had planned to wipe out Ham's gang once Joseph was handed over. Apparently, they were offered extra money by the employer to do so. But there was nothing in the messages that indicated they'd known who had hired them. Which explained the look in Cullin's eyes when he'd told him this morning, just before Lawrence showed up.

He also saw the texts that Lawrence had sent, along with their replies. He didn't know if they'd been sent to another device or a cell phone or a satellite phone or what, just that it was a different number than the one Lee had been writing from. So now Ham's guys knew that the Bakers were planning to kill them all. Lawrence had kicked the hornet's nest on his way out. Good for him. Except what did that mean for Joseph? Was there a civil war now raging on Mount Hollow with Joseph in the crossfire? If so, maybe that would give him a chance to slip away. Though, mountain-man wannabe or not, a twelve-year-old kid lost in the Allegheny mountains might not be a much better situation.

Then again, he could be underestimating his son...whose favorite books were *Hatchet, Robinson Crusoe,* and *The Mysterious Island.* Maybe he'd be all right out there after all. Maybe.

But Lawrence had also told them that he was coming, and he couldn't be sure what they would do about that. Not that Jack was even sure how he'd get there, but they didn't know that. He figured that he had at least lost the element of surprise, though maybe they were so concerned with each other that they didn't even care about him anymore.

He thought of pretending to be Lawrence and sending another text to see if he could find out what was going on. In fact, he already had the text typed out, even scrambling the letters in an attempt to mimic Lawrence's dying hands. He wanted to know how Joseph was. To make sure he was even still there. Still alive.

He would never have seen all this had Lawrence not had it open. At first, when he saw the open text thread, he was afraid that the map was gone, which was his original fear and why he hadn't tried to explore the GPS to see if he might be able to contact anyone with it. But closing the threads revealed the map and the waypoints still in place. The new breadcrumbs Cullin had created in his pursuit of Jack were all over, and Jack couldn't believe how far they'd come over such a short amount of time. The breadcrumbs showed that Lawrence had come over the West Virginia line and traveled south, which surprised Jack. He thought for sure he'd crossed over the Maryland border. Though, moving the map around, there appeared to be a lot more farmland between his current location and Maryland, and he hadn't been traveling over flatlands, that was for sure.

Then the red hashmarks followed a river southeast, and Jack supposed that it was the same river he'd been swept into. And if Cullin had been following his footsteps, he'd apparently traveled a lot further in the rushing waters than he even thought possible, because the breadcrumbs followed it for miles and miles.

So where was he now? According to the GPS, it looked like he was in West Virginia, which he guessed was good. But he was still more than forty miles north of the Cranberry Wilderness, with nothing but wilderness between them. He wondered if he shouldn't head southeast, toward the AT and the towns alongside it. It was further, but once he got there, he could find a way to call Stacey, acquire a vehicle, and maybe get some more information on the Bakers and their cabin on Hollow Mountain. It was Thursday, so he still had time.

His stomach growled.

There would be no eating in the mountains.

He turned east, lined up the nearest town, and took a heading with his compass. Then, after he started walking, he went back to the text messages. He would hit send on the one he had ready to go, and then he would try to get a message to Stacey.

Just as his thumb began to press the key, however, the device shut off.

"You gotta be kidding me," he muttered, the battery finally dying. Well, at least he'd been able to see where he was and got a heading for where he was going.

He started walking, and for the first time since waking up Tuesday morning, he had no one following him.

66

JAMES PULLED ANOTHER TOOTHPICK from his shirt pocket and slipped it between his lips. He looked over at Michael, who was standing ten feet to his left and peering intently through the trees around them. Then he looked to his right, toward where he'd seen the Baker Boys head off to. He didn't know where Colt went, but he had a pretty good idea that he wasn't going after the boy.

"You sure you know what yer doin'?" Michael asked.

James nodded. "We need them to help cover more ground. We'll straighten out our differences after if we need to."

"You know they ain't gonna let that stand, you beating on Lee and all."

"I know. But if we don't get the kid back, none of us will be gettin' out of this."

"If you say so."

"Just keep an eye out. I don't know that they'll try anything now that we know what they were planning, but they're also insane, so..."

"Damn straight."

They were a hundred yards from the cabin, making their way alongside the mountain and looking for any sign of the kid. The ground was muddy from all the rain, but they hadn't been able to find any footprints yet.

James shook his head, but he wasn't really thinking about the kid. He was thinking about what Lawrence had texted over the GPS. It hadn't surprised him that the Bakers had plans to get rid of them, but the stuff about the boy's mother... About Russians, and about *none* of them getting out of this alive...

He raised the cell phone and tried calling Ham. It rang, but no one picked up on the other end, so he sent him a text.

"What're you doing?" Michael asked, running up to him. "You ain't tellin' Ham, are ya?"

James held up a hand. "We'll tell him it was the Bakers' doing. They killed our guys and are plannin' to kill the rest of us. They let the boy escape to get us out here looking for him so they can split us up and take us one at a time."

Michael frowned.

James sighed. "It'll probably be Colt that kills them and not the other way 'round, but I need to tell Ham what Lawrence said about the mother and see if the fat fool knows anything about it."

Michael took off his hat and scratched at his scalp. "What did Lawrence say 'bout the mother?"

"Nothing good."

67

HAM WASHED THE BLOOD off his hands, disappointed. Carl wasn't a direct messenger, but a messenger once removed. He hadn't known the first thing about who was behind the job, only that another person offered him a hundred bucks to deliver the message for him. Smart move. Otherwise it'd be that guy who'd fallen into a wood chipper. People were so careless these days. Probably was on one of those smartphones, not paying attention to anything around him and just fell right in.

Carl had started talking right away, before Ham even got the chipper running. But he had to make certain he was telling him everything, so he'd dipped his foot in first. After Carl had watched his foot come out the other end in red rain, he passed out.

Ham then had a decision to make. If he let Carl live, then he'd be missing a foot. But he could always do the wooden-peg thing. Ham knew someone who could turn him into a pirate for a small fee. Carl would then live in fear of Ham for the rest of his life, willing to do anything and everything to keep him happy. It could be the start of something new, expanding borders and such.

But in the end, Ham just didn't feel like dealing with it right now. So he put all of Carl in, head first, and that was that. He'd have the boys clean up the mess when they got back. He'd probably have a heart attack if he tried. Just getting the guy's skinny body into the churning blades had his ticker racing at a troubling rate.

He closed the barn doors and walked back to the cabin. He needed a drink. And then he needed to go find this other guy.

This Ron Pearlman Carl had talked about.

When he got back to the kitchen and after he washed his hands in the sink, he saw that he had a missed call on the cell phone. He picked it up. It had been James. He didn't leave a voicemail, but there was a text message. He read it. And then needed to sit.

After a long sixty seconds, he managed to respond with a text of his own. Then he was up and walking back to his truck.

He never did get that drink.

JACK SAW ELECTRICAL WIRES between the trees ahead, and his heart jumped. He was close. Or at least closer than he thought. Now he just had to follow them to a pole, and then the poles into town.

When he reached the first telephone pole, he put his hand on it to make sure it was really there. It was, and he laughed. He recalled Joseph asking about them a couple of years ago. "They're telephone poles," Jack had said. "What are telephone poles?" Joseph had responded. And that was when Jack realized that he wasn't quite sure what all the wires were that still stretched along the wooden crosses. It certainly wasn't all telephone wire, and at that point he'd had to explain the concept of landlines to Joseph, how house phones worked, and Alexander Graham Bell, and any other piece of telephonic information he could dig out of the ancient past. Joseph had followed the big black wires with his eyes, trying to imagine a world where people didn't carry phones in their pockets everywhere they went. A world that Jack realized wasn't really that ancient at all. Hell, he was practically in college when cell phones became the norm, and now kids had smartphones, tablets, PS5s, social media accounts out the wazoo... At this rate, he figured his grandkids would be living most of their lives within some type of AI computer simulation. Life experienced through avatars...

Jack shook the vision of a sci-fi future away, realizing he wouldn't have any grandkids if he didn't get a move on. He followed the black wires southeast.

HAM PULLED OFF THE gravel road and parked with the truck's right tires up on the grass. He sat there for a second, watching the double-wide from fifty yards down the road. It was supported by cinder blocks, the surrounding foliage edging closer and closer so that soon the trailer would be swallowed completely. There was a dirt bike leaning against thè side of it and an old Ford Mustang in the driveway. Ham didn't recognize either one of them.

He waited for any sign of movement and was rewarded after just sixty seconds when a shadow passed by one of the windows. He shut the engine off and reached for Joanna.

The cell phone on the seat beside him chirped. He flipped it onto its back so he could see the screen. A new text from James. He said they were still looking for the kid. Thought Colt might be going after the Bakers. Then he asked if he'd found anything out about the Russians yet.

He texted back that he was about to.

Damn Russians.

He couldn't believe it, though it was what he'd suspected. The stories of some Cold War leftovers hiding out in the mountains, the unexplained and rather gruesome deaths over the years that no one had taken credit for... There was a boogieman after all, and he wore a cossack ushanka, drank vodka, and carried an AK-47. But where were they in the mountains?

Ham couldn't believe he was caught up in some spy vs spy shit involving a CIA agent, and just thinking about it had him feeling like someone was squeezing his heart with a pair of pliers.

He left the cell phone on the seat and stepped out of the truck. As he crossed the road, he let the axe head drag on the ground behind him. It carved a line through the gravel, like a spark on its way to dynamite.

He trudged his heavy boots across the wild grass, eying the dirt bike as he approached the front door. He took the two steps that compensated for the dwelling being set up on blocks, and rapped his hand against the door.

There was no peephole.

Amateur.

He heard movement inside, some glass bottles rattling against each other. Guy was drinking already. Good for both of them, maybe. Might make this go a little quicker if Ron had a loose tongue. As the chain lock sounded from the other side (seemed to take the person a couple of tries), Ham wondered if this guy had been hired to pass along the job because he was a reliable and faithful employee or if he was expendable and couldn't be traced back. How things were about to go largely depended on that answer.

The door swung wide open, and the brazen carelessness so shocked Ham that he almost froze and missed his window of opportunity. The guy was older, his white hair victim of some do-it-yourself Flobee crew cut. He was tall and stocky, his face distinct and oddly familiar. Maybe the guy was on the Russians' payroll and someone to be taken seriously, but right now he was standing there in the doorway, legs spread, one hand holding a bottle, the other gripping the door.

"What in—"

Ham thrust Joanna's four-pound head into Ron's stomach, doubling him over. Then he stepped into the trailer, took one disappointing look around while he got in position, and swung the axe at his head, using the flat side of it to knock him down. His head bounced off the floor, and he flopped onto his back, the beer bottle he'd been holding leaking all over and foaming on the stained carpet.

Ham stood over him. He used Joanna to move his head from side to side, trying to figure out why he looked so familiar. He was also trying to determine if he'd accidentally fractured his skull. He'd be up the creek if he had.

But a moan slipped through Ron's lips, and he tried to bring a hand to the side of his head. He missed twice before his fingers touched where the axe had struck him. He opened his eyes.

"What the hell," he stammered.

"Hi, Ron," Ham said. He unzipped his pants.

Ron blinked and tried to lift his head. "Who are you?"

Ham set the axe on its head right between Ron's legs and started to relieve himself right then and there. He shot a jet stream of dark yellow urine straight into Ron's face and mouth.

Ron turned his head, spitting, and raised a hand to block the gold river. He tried to squirm away, to roll onto his stomach and get to his hands and knees, but Ham lifted the axe up and dropped it down on the side of his knee.

Ron screamed, both hands going to his leg, the piss in his face again.

The stench was strong, and Ham frowned at the color of it. Were his kidneys going? His liver? He could hear Lilly laughing at him from the great beyond. He slammed the head down on Ron's other knee. When he finished, he zipped his pants back up and stepped back away from Ron, letting him sit up and hold his knees. "Why do you look so familiar?" he asked him.

Ron lifted his eyes and looked at him. "Ron Pearlman, you asshole!"

Ham shook his head. "That supposed to mean somethin'?" Usually the whole pissing-in-the guy's-face thing broke a person's spirit right away. This guy was holding on to some self-worth. Meant it might take a little longer than he'd hoped.

"The actor! I look like the actor!"

Ham wiped a line of sweat from his brow. "You look like an actor?" And then it clicked. "Yeah, I see it now. Can't for the life of me remember which movie, but yeah, that's it." He swung the axe up onto his shoulder. "What's the actor's name?"

Ron turned his head and spit. "Are you serious?"

Ham looked around and spotted the forty-three-inch rear-projection television over in the corner of the room. He started walking toward it. "Well, Ron, we don't all have the luxury of cable TV." He swung the axe into the Sony, the head lodging itself in the glass.

"It's Ron Perlman, you fat piece of shit!"

"Wait." Ham turned, yanking the axe out of the TV. "You're tellin' me that your name is the same as this actor you look like?"

Ron nodded.

"Well, damn. That's kinda weird, isn't it?"

Ron turned his head and vomited on the floor. Then he said, "Thought it would discredit anyone might try reportin' me to the law. The cops would say, what's this fella's name, and they'd say Ron Perlman. Then: what'd he look like. And they'd say, like Ron Perlman."

Ham ran a hand through his beard. "That work?"

"I don't know."

Ham was beginning to feel some tightening in his chest. It was time to move this thing along. "Okay, Mr. Pearlman. Let's talk about Russians."

As if it were possible, with urine dripping down his face and vomit hanging from his chin, Ron's face dropped even further.

JACK STUMBLED OUT OF the woods and onto a road. An *actual* road, and he thought he could cry tears of joy at the sight of it—the *feel* of it beneath his feet. He picked up his pace over the even asphalt, and before he even got a hundred yards, a car was coming up behind him and honking as it passed. Then it pulled over.

Jack stopped. Was this a friendly neighborhood carpool, or had he been found by whoever had been sent back to kill him? He approached the car with caution, ready to pull out the pistol if need be.

"Howdy," a bearded old face said when Jack came alongside the open passenger window.

He peered in. "Good morning."

"You headin' anywhere in particular, son?"

Jack wasn't entirely sure how to play this. He was aware that the rifle on his back was in plain sight, as was his missing pack. "Town, I guess."

"Hungry, huh?"

"Yeah."

"How long since you had a proper meal?"

Jack thought about it. "Monday, I guess."

"Damn, son, hop in. I'll take you to the best breakfast spot in town. On me."

Jack eyed him suspiciously.

"You ain't from around here," the man stated, reading the skepticism in his eyes. "Let me guess, you're from a big city or somewheres thereabout."

Jack nodded.

"That's what I thought. City folk don't trust hospitality when it's offered to them. C'mon, get in. I ain't gonna eat you or bugger you or whatever else nonsense is runnin' through that mind of yours. Just do me a favor and put that rifle of yours in the back seat. The knife too, if you don't mind. Not that I don't trust you, but..." He smiled and shrugged.

Jack did as he said, removing the belt pouch and putting it in the back with the rifle. He kept the pistol in his waistband, making sure that his shirt was pulled down over it.

"Buckle up, please," the man said, putting the car in gear.

Jack obeyed.

"What happened to your eye?" the man asked.

"Got hit with a branch."

They pulled back onto the empty road. "Ouch. Where'd you start?"

"What do you mean?"

"On the Trail. You're a thru-hiker, ain't you? So you start in Maine?"

Jack wondered if the guy really thought he'd come off the Trail or if he was testing him. The Trail was further east and not close enough to draw such a conclusion. He forced a smile. "Nah. I started in Pennsylvania. Not quite ready for the whole twenty-two hundred or so miles just yet."

"Ah, gettin' your feet wet, then. Good plan." He glanced in the rearview. "Got lost though, did ya?"

Jack played along. "Yeah, a little while ago. Started following the telephone lines. How far did I stray?"

"A ways. But you ain't the first person I've picked up wandering around after a storm." Then the guy looked at him closer. "You find shelter of some kind? You're pretty dry for someone the skies wept over all night."

"Yeah, found an old mill." He wondered if that was a wise thing to disclose, if it might place him at a soon-to-be crime scene. Or if it would contradict the guy's assumption that he'd been hiking the Appalachian Trail—which he was half-convinced the guy didn't really believe anyway.

"That's some mighty good fortune. I ain't familiar with any old mills around here."

"Looked like maybe a sawmill. Found some old train tracks that led me there."

The guy started nodding. "I've heard stories of an old rail line in these parts. Never saw it myself though. Don't think it was ever finished. Smallpox or some such thing came in and brought the world to a standstill. By the time it cleared, the people it left behind had forgotten what they'd been doing. Maybe the same thing with the mill you're talking about."

"Maybe," Jack said.

"Either way, you got yourself mighty lost. Good thing you found the electrical lines. You could've been out there forever." Then he glanced down. "I see you got one of those fancy watches though. So you would've gotten somewhere eventually. Unless of course you fell off a cliff or drowned in a river, or got bit by a rattler, or had a run-in with a bear or a mountain lion." He laughed.

"Mountain lion? I thought they were extinct in these parts?"

"Depends who you talk to. If you talk to the state, they'll say they declared it extinct 'bout ten years ago. Others'll say there hasn't been a confirmed sighting since the late eighties." He leaned toward Jack and added, "the *eighteen* eighties." Then he shrugged. "But there's been reports lately, and now they're setting up infrared doohickeys along the Trail to see if they might just catch one." He laughed. "Maybe find one chewing on your leg if you hadn't spotted the wires."

"Yeah. I was mostly worried about Sasquatch."

"Nah. My momma was the only Sasquatch 'round here, and she's passed on." He laughed again and hit the steering wheel with his palm.

Jack raised his eyebrows.

"I'm Charlie, by the way," the old guy said.

Jack hesitated.

"I get it. You're thinking, do I give this guy my real name or my Trail name? I always like hearing the Trail names, not that I understand them all."

"Haven't got one yet."

"Is that a fact?" He looked him over. "Not sure I have the authority to give you one or not, seeing as I'm no hiker and we ain't currently on the Trail, but if I did have the power to so name you, I think I'd call you..." He trailed off, turning his attention back to the road. "Well, I'll have to keep thinking on it, I suppose."

Jack smiled. For the first time since waking up Tuesday morning, he smiled.

"Where's your pack?" Charlie finally asked.

Jack had been waiting for it. "Lost it in the storm. I set it down, and it got swept over the side of a cliff. Landed in a river."

"Well, that's unfortunate."

He made a right onto another road and after a mile or two made another right. He talked about the storm and the one time he'd visited New York City, talked about Time Square and the Naked Cowboy. He talked about Appalachia and its economic history and the stereotype he knew they were to the rest of the country. Jack did very little talking, which was fine with him. He found that he actually enjoyed listening to the ramblings of this old coonhound.

"Here we are," Charlie said, and he turned the car into a small parking lot. "The Henhouse."

The smell of bacon hit Jack immediately, and his stomach responded with a churning he couldn't suppress.

Charlie looked at him with a big toothy smile. "Oh, son, your starvin' bones are gonna love this." He threw open the driver's side door and hopped out with an energy and grace Jack didn't see coming.

"Pretty spry for an old guy..." He got out and walked up behind him, and the scene and its smell took him back to that backwoods joint in the Poconos. What had it been called? He couldn't remember. But he remembered the guy he'd conversed with. The guy had talked about stuff that Jack hadn't thought about in a long, long time. Without Donny around to feed him all the conspiratorial news, and with his promise to Stacey to stay off all the independent sites, he was out of touch with that world. And since he didn't trust a single thing that came from the corporate-owned mainstream media, Left or Right, he was getting very little "news" at all these days. But if truth be told, his days were a lot more peaceful without worrying about the New World Order coming to take his family to some Orwellian joy camp for their microchip. Ignorance is bliss. Until, he guessed, you found yourself wearing a star or an armband and standing in a long line for the next train.

Charlie opened the door for him and then called out, "Hey, Bernadette, where you at, woman?" He slapped his hand down on the counter next to the register.

A tall thin woman with gray hair appeared through the kitchen doors behind the counter, wiping her hands on her apron. "Charlie, I swear, if you call me woman one more time, I'm gonna put more than grits in your grits."

Charlie winked. "You promise?"

She smiled and then set her eyes on Jack. "What've we got here?"

"A hiker," Charlie said. "Got lost. I just picked him up. Said he hasn't eaten since Monday."

"Oh, you poor thing," she said. "I assume Charlie will be taking care of the tab, so what'll be your pleasure, dear?"

"Whoa," Charlie said, and turned to Jack. "That ain't what it sounded like, son." Then he turned back to Bernadette. "Bern, this kid's from the city. You can't be talkin' to him like that. He's got smog brain. He can't help it, mind you, it's just the habitat, but he sure's gotta be thinkin' you're suggestin' something different than what it is you're suggestin'."

Bernadette leaned forward onto the counter, her bosoms peeking out from over her neckline. "And how would you know what I ain't suggestin'?"

Charlie almost choked on his dentures.

Bernadette laughed and then turned, waving them after her. "C'mon." She walked them past the two other occupied tables and to a spot nearer the back, by a window that looked out to the parking lot. "Have a seat." She looked at Jack once he got settled in the chair. "Coffee?"

"Yes, please."

"You look like a man who takes it black."

"I do. Thanks."

Charlie looked up. "And I'll have—"

"I know what you'll have, and you won't be gettin' it from me, that's for damn sure." She turned and walked away.

Jack watched Charlie's eyes go with her. "Listen, Charlie, I can't let you pay for my food."

Charlie's eyes returned. "Oh, you got a lot of cash on you?"

Jack hesitated again. "As a matter of fact, my wallet was in my pack."

"Doesn't matter. See, I figure it's my Christian duty—no..." He stopped himself and waved a dismissive hand. "No, it's my *privilege* to help my neighbor."

"Well, I sure can't thank you enough."

Then Bernadette was back and setting the coffee in front of Jack. She put a mug in front of Charlie too, but the steaming liquid in his cup was a caramel color. "See that," she said to Charlie, nodding at Jack's cup. "A real man." She put a hand on Jack's shoulder. "I've got just the thing for you, honey." And then she walked away. Again, Charlie's eyes went with her.

"So what's the story there?" Jack asked.

Charlie's eyes rebounded again. "With Bern? Oh, she's my ex."

Jack was in mid-sip and almost spit the coffee across the table and into Charlie's face. Instead, he managed to swallow it, burning his throat and coughing instead.

"Yeah," Charlie said, "she's great."

"So what happened?"

"Oh..." He sipped his coffee. "Things I regret every day." Then he winked. "Now we date."

"You date your ex-wife?"

"Yup."

When the ex came back, she slid a plate full of pancakes, eggs, bacon, sausage, and fruit in front of Jack.

Jack's eyes must've grown into saucers because both Bernadette and Charlie laughed.

Jack tried not to think of Joseph as he ate. He couldn't afford to get upset right now. He had to play this just right, so he said a silent prayer for his son as he forked pancakes into his mouth.

AFTER BERNADETTE CLEARED THE plates, Jack looked at his watch. It was almost eleven. "Do you know anything about the Cranberry Wilderness?" he asked Charlie.

Charlie took a sip of his coffee. "Sure. I been there once. The Rainbow Gathering back in eighty." He crossed his arms on the table and leaned forward. "That would be *nineteen* eighty, in case you was confused." He smiled. "It's where I met Bernadette, actually."

"Really?" What were the odds?

"Yeah." His eyes went out of focus as they looked into the past. "Two girls were killed while hitchhiking to get there. Found shot to death. Cops thought maybe it was someone from the Gathering that did it. They questioned me and Bern." He took another sip. "Strange time, it was. Anyway, guy from around those parts made a film about it. You should see it. Lots of mystery and intrigue."

"I'll add it to my watch list."

"They say the Wilderness is one of the most remote places." He chuckled. "It's also a black bear sanctuary, so if you ever visit, be careful not to leave your food out."

A black bear sanctuary. Wonderful.

"How'd it get its name?"

"From Cranberry River and Cranberry Mountain, I suppose. Though don't ask me how they got their names."

"You ever hear of Hollow Mountain?"

He nodded. "Yeah, I heard of it."

"Was walking with a guy for a bit and he mentioned it. Said he'd hiked through the Cranberry Wilderness without seeing another soul. He was trying to get to Hollow Mountain but decided against it when he saw more than a couple bears." Jack smiled and hoped Charlie didn't recognize his story as being a regurgitation of his own words—Keyser Soze style.

"Well, I'm not sure why anyone would want to go up that mountain. Lots of bad stories about it."

"Maybe that's why he was going."

"Sounds pretty stupid if you ask me."

"What kind of stories?" Jack asked.

Charlie shrugged. "Well, they say it's called Hollow Mountain because the mountain is hollow. Lots of caves. The Confederates used them to store equipment; the Indians used them for traps and smoke pits. Stuff like that. Then you have your ghost stories and legends and all."

Jack nodded. "Is there a town nearby?"

Charlie seemed to think about it. "I'm not too familiar with the area, but I'd think it'd be Durbin. At least that's where me and Bern ended up talking to the police back in the day."

"How far away is that from here?"

"Oh, geez, I dunno. Seventy miles or so."

Jack swore in his head. Still so far away.

Charlie scratched at his beard. "You ain't thinking of goin' there yourself, are ya?"

Jack shrugged. "Maybe someday."

"For why?"

"Adventure, I guess."

He laughed and clapped his hands. "Look it here, we got us a middle-aged Huck Finn! So what about today? What's your plan?"

"Well, I'm thinking I'm gonna have to replace my pack before getting back on the Trail. Is there a store around?" Maybe he could get batteries for the GPS.

"Yeah, just down the road some. Thought you didn't have any lucre."

"I don't. Guess I'll be testing my bartering skills."

Charlie thought about it. "Hmm... You trade in that rifle of yours and you just might be able to get yourself back on track."

"Is it hard to get back to the Trail from here?"

"Nah. You should be able to find someone to give you a lift. Just put out your thumb."

"I won't get arrested?"

Charlie laughed. "Not 'round here you won't." Then he reached his hand out across the table. "It was nice to meet you, Mitch."

Jack shook his hand. "Mitch? That my Trail name?"

"As I so christen you. You know the film *City Slickers*?"

He smiled. "Billy Crystal."

He flashed that toothy smile. There was a speck of pepper between his teeth. "Now if you don't mind, I'm gonna invite my lady to take your spot. Car's open, so you can just grab your stuff. Store's just down the road some. I reckon you can get there okay?"

"Of course," Jack said. He appreciated the old man's bluntness. Not many people had the tact to say it was time to leave in such a polite manner. He'd picked him up, fed him, and gave him the information he needed to continue on, and now it was time for the guy to resume his day. "I can't thank you enough. Really." He stood. "And good luck." He nodded toward Bernadette.

"Thanks. I could stand to get lucky today." He winked.

Jack smiled, though it was not a picture he wanted to dwell on, and he headed for the door. He thanked Bernadette when he passed the register, and then he was crossing the parking lot toward Charlie's car.

He had his belt pouch on and the rifle slung over his shoulder when Bernadette appeared in the doorway, calling for him to come back.

He met her at the door, where she handed him a water bottle.

"Thank you so much," he said.

Then she stuffed a brown paper bag into his hands. "Lunch."

He couldn't help himself. He leaned forward and gave her a hug.

71

JACK WENT TO THE store down the street, but they didn't have any batteries. He could've maybe bartered for another pack and some more supplies, but he wasn't willing to part with what he had for them. If things went the way he hoped, he wouldn't need them anyway. But he'd really wanted batteries for the GPS so that he could contact Stacey. Not only let her know what was going on down here but to find out whatever it was that she knew. Because if he was right about them using Joshua as leverage, then by now she would have a much better understanding of what was going on than he did.

He'd look for another way to contact her.

He continued to walk down the street, and as the guy had suggested, he kept his thumb out whenever a car passed. After just ten minutes, a faded blue pickup was slowing to a crawl beside him. The driver asked where he was heading.

"Durbin," Jack answered. "Or as close as I can get to it."

The guy stopped the truck and seemed to think about it for a second. He adjusted his fraying trucker cap and stared ahead. Then he looked back. "I'm just going down toward Harrisonburg. I can drop you off along the way if you don't mind riding in the back."

Jack assumed that Harrisonburg was closer to Durbin than he was right now; otherwise why would the guy even offer? "How far from Durbin is that?" he asked.

The guy shrugged. "You'd have to take 33 over the line and through the forest. Hour and a half drive, maybe."

"Okay. I appreciate it." He didn't know what other option he had at this point.

"Hop in." The guy motioned with his thumb over his shoulder.

Jack climbed in and made himself comfortable.

The guy pressed on the accelerator, and the old truck continued on its way down the road. He never asked Jack for his name or offered him his. Never mentioned the rifle or his bloodshot eye, or asked where he came from or why he wanted to go to Durbin. It was a different world than Jack was used to down here.

When he got to this Harrisonburg, he'd try to find a phone to use. Then he'd try to find a way to Durbin. If he had to steal a car to get there, that was what he'd do.

It wouldn't be the first time.

The guy pulled a cigarette out of a pack and lit it. After taking a long draw and shooting smoke out his nostrils like a dragon, he held the pack up to the rearview mirror. "Want a smoke?"

Boy, did he ever. "No, thanks."

72

JOSEPH HAD WATCHED THE men running back and forth, in and out of the woods. That was about an hour ago according to his watch. Though it sure hadn't felt like just one hour. Time seemed to stand still down here.

He didn't know what was happening or how he got here. He didn't know where his dad was or if he was coming for him or if he was even okay. He thought he heard some of the men talking about his dad, but he wasn't sure.

He looked to his left and stared at the mountains. Should he make a run for it? They looked really vast. Was there a town on the other side or just more mountains? Would he be able to survive without any equipment? He didn't even have a pair of shoes, though he did still have his knife. It was tucked inside his pants.

He rolled onto his back and reached for it. He was pretty lucky he'd put it there before falling asleep the other night, and even more lucky they hadn't felt the need to search him.

The decision on whether to stay or go was like a building pressure in his chest, causing his heart to race. Stay or go, live or die? Which was which? Would it be worse to get caught by these men again than to get lost in the wilderness? He found his fingers tracing the scar on his neck, and thought of the kid in one of his favorite books. Would he have the strength and guts to survive out there like Brian Robeson had? They were about the same age, though he didn't have a hatchet to rely on like Brian had. He looked at the knife and wondered if it would be a good enough substitute. Maybe he could steal some food. *Or the radio.* If he could get his hands on one of their radios, maybe he could call for help.

He held the knife in folded hands, resting them on his chest, and stared at the boards above him. Then he closed his eyes. He was exhausted. Other than drifting off five minutes here and there, he hadn't slept at all last night.

He fell asleep.

73

STACEY STOOD IN FRONT of the bed and stared into the full-length mirror, noting the way the red dress accented her more rounded features. She was sure that was the point. In this tight Ferrari-red dress that had no back and barely a front, there wouldn't be a person at the event who wouldn't notice her. Smart move on their part. Whatever their endgame was, they were setting her up like a billboard in the middle of it all. She wished she knew what they were planning, what would become of her reputation.

No, that wasn't true. She didn't give a damn about what they wanted or what the history books would say about her. She only wanted to know that Joseph was safe.

She tucked a strand of hair behind her ear. She looked like a hooker. An expensive, world-class hooker, but a hooker.

A hooker with a bomb.

She still didn't know where she was supposed to get it. They'd told her to leave her phone at home, so the next set of instructions must be coming some other way. Or maybe the bomb was already in place, and they'd managed to plant evidence that connected her to it. If that were the case, then she wouldn't be the one detonating it. Which meant she would have no idea when it was coming. That was not a pleasant thought, and it made her sit down.

Sitting on the hotel bed, she turned and looked out the window beside her. She could see the streets below. Could see all those people walking around, not a single one of them having a clue about what was going to happen. Though that was always the case, wasn't it? And in her profession, she'd needed to rely on that fact often.

What should I do? she thought. She was running out of time. *There has to be a way...* She thought of Johnson again. But, really, what would he be able to do? Maybe get the event canceled? He could call in a bomb threat. That would really stir things up. But then what would happen to Joseph?

She couldn't risk it. Her entire career, she had been willing to sacrifice others for the greater good, so she didn't really have a problem with collateral damage. Right now, her greater good was her son. Whatever it took. *Whoever* it took. Even herself. The hypocrisy of it didn't even bother her. But then again, it never had.

A knock on the door.

Stacey whipped her head around, startled, and reached for a gun that wasn't there. She stood and walked across the carpet in her bare feet. The stilettos would not go on until the last possible second.

As she approached the peephole, she kept her eyes on the crack beneath the door, searching for a moving shadow.

Nothing.

She stood to the side of the door. "Yes?"

No response.

"Who is it?"

Still no response.

She stepped in front of the door, but kept her body to the side of it. Then she lifted her hand to the peephole. If whoever was out there was waiting for her to be standing in front of the door and peering through the peephole before putting a bullet through her eye, then the shot would only pierce her hand.

No shot from a suppressed pistol came.

She turned the handle, leaving the chain latched, and stole a glance into the hallway. There was no one there.

Only a Gucci bag.

74

COLT HAD SPENT MOST of his enlisted time in the desert, but he had been born and raised in the mountains. He'd spent more time hunting animals in the forest than just about anything else. And it wasn't so different, tracking a man or an animal. He'd done both in different environments, but he'd learned quickly that it was a simple thing to do, applying the one to the other. And now he was hunting Seth Baker, keeping his distance and careful to remain undetected. Seth had started out with Lee, but just as Colt had hoped, the two of them eventually split up and went separate ways.

He had to wait for the perfect moment. Underestimating his prey would be fatal. A silent wraith, he moved through the trees while the sun reached its zenith and continued to dry the forest around him. He had to get close enough to use his knife, which meant he had to be patient. Navigating the moist ground was like walking on pillows, and he knew it was just a matter of time before he got close enough to overtake Seth from behind. Maybe when he stopped to take a piss or stretch or look through his scope. Besides, a gunshot would alert Lee and send him slipping away for reinforcements. There was no telling how many guys in these parts he had tucked in his back pocket. In fact, was it possible that he'd already put in a call for backup? Was there a convoy of pickups on their way up the mountain right now?

He pulled his own radio off his belt and brought it to his mouth. He whispered into it, instructing James and Michael to keep a lookout. James then asked if there was any sign of the boy. But Colt didn't care about the boy anymore. Otherwise, he'd tell them where the kid was hiding. But letting everyone think the boy had run into the woods was what had allowed this very scenario—Seth and Lee separated in the mountains.

"No sign of the boy," he lied.

75

SO IT WAS THE Russians who had hired him.

Dammit to hell, he thought. The boy's father was right, there was no way the Russians would let them live. They had it all nice and planned out with the Bakers, didn't they? Or maybe the Russians would just kill the Bakers once they were done tying off all the other loose ends. Either way, there was only one thing left to do about it now.

Ham looked down at what was left of the Ron Perlman impostor. The trailer was a mess. Blood all over the walls, the ceiling, soaked into the carpet. He was sitting in the kitchen area, a glass of water in his hand. It shook as he lifted it to his mouth. He swallowed and wiped the sweat from his brow with the back of his hand. Set the glass down.

The person who was now a pile of limbs and guts on the floor had known he was working for some Cold War KGB operatives. Not that they ever disclosed that to him, but he'd eventually figured it out. The problem was that he only knew where one of the guys lived, and had no idea where that guy fit into the rank and file of this backwoods Soviet empire. Which meant he'd have to go pay this new guy a visit and try to get him to talk too. Three sessions in one day. He didn't know if his heart could take another interrogation. But time was running out, wasn't it? No, this had to be done today. Tonight.

He sat there for ten more minutes until his heart stopped pounding, and then he got up, grabbed Joanna, and walked back to his truck.

As soon as he got behind the wheel, the cell phone on the seat began to ring. He answered it.

"You find anything out?" James asked right away.

"Yeah. It's the Russians. The boy's father was right."

"What do we do?"

"I got an address. I'm gonna take a little drive and see if I can't get some more information."

"Do you want us to come back?"

"No. Stay there and try to find the boy. If we run out of time, he may be the only chance we got."

"What about Lee and Seth? Colt thinks they may have called up reinforcements."

Ham swore. "Do you know where you are? Can you give me coordinates?"

James told him just where they were on Hollow Mountain, but warned about the pitfalls.

"Okay, I'll send a few more boys up there just in case. But as for the Bakers…if you get the chance, kill 'em."

"Got it."

"And be ready to get the hell outta there. With or without the boy, when I find out where these bastards are, I'm gonna need ya there right away. We need to do this tonight if we can."

"Got it."

"I'll call you back soon." Ham hung up just as a dizzy spell came over him. He gripped the steering wheel with his free hand until it passed. He slipped his glasses on and fumbled with lighting a cigarette. Then he started up the truck and pulled onto the road. It was going to take him more than an hour to get to where he was going.

STACEY SET THE BAG down on the bed and opened it. It was empty except for a white envelope resting on the bottom. She reached in and pulled it out. Her name was on the front of it, handwritten in gold calligraphy. She opened it, knowing exactly what it was. A stationery letter formally inviting her to a dinner in honor of Douglas T. Newell. Tonight at 7 pm. In Connecticut.

She looked at her watch. Noon. It'd take about three hours to get to Connecticut. So why was she wearing the damn dress now? She wasn't about to spend the next seven hours in it.

She took it off.

The phone on the bedside table rang.

The dress now a red puddle on the floor, she walked over and answered it. "Hello?"

The garbled voice answered, *"The dress looks stunning on you."*

She turned toward the window, crossing an arm over her bare breasts. "Are you watching me?"

"Of course. We are always watching you. In fifteen minutes, you will get in your car and drive to the address that is written on the back of the invitation." A pause. *"Remember your son. He will be let go Saturday morning if you do everything we have told you."*

"And what if something goes wrong?"

"Like what?"

"How the hell should I know? I'll be in a billion pieces by then!"

"If you do your part, we will do ours."

"And I'm just supposed to take your word for it?"

"You don't have a choice."

The line went dead.

She hung the phone up and walked back to the invitation. Turned it over. There, written in pen, was a note.

Doll, let's meet before dinner, okay? Come to this address at 4. Can't wait to get into foreign affairs with you.

It was signed Doug.

Stacey looked up. "What the hell?"

77

JACK HOPPED OUT OF the truck and adjusted the rifle on his shoulder with one hand and the belt pack with the other. Then he reached back into the bed and grabbed the food from Bernadette. He walked up to the passenger window. "This Harrisonburg?"

"Nope. Said I was goin' *toward* Harrisonburg. Harrisonburg's probably more like what you're accustomed to, coming from whatever Yankee city you're from."

Jack thought he must have "Mitch" tattooed on his forehead. He looked around. Wherever he was, it had been here for a long time, carved into the foothills. "Any idea where I can find a phone?" he asked.

The guy looked ahead and pointed.

Jack followed his finger and saw a phone booth across the street. Maybe he shouldn't have been surprised, but it had been so long since he'd seen one that his reaction to a Stanley Kubrick monolith might not have been much different.

"Yeah, there's still a few left around these parts," the guy said, taking note of his reaction. He lifted a finger off the wheel and waved it at the windshield while dipping his head to see beneath the visor. "The mountains tend to make cellular service a little tricky." He reached down and took a coin from the cup holder and flipped it through the open window.

Jack snatched it out of the air.

"Good luck."

Jack opened his hand and saw a quarter sitting on his palm. When he looked back up to thank the guy, the truck had already begun to pull away. The guy drove down the street, made a left at an intersection, and vanished.

Jack looked at the quarter. 1973. He flipped it, caught it, and slapped it on the back of his hand. Tails. Of course it was tails. He crossed the street, feeling sort of like John Rambo at the beginning of *First Blood*. He kept his eyes peeled for the local sheriff. *Your kind ain't welcome here.*

But all that faded when he reached the phone. His heart was beating hard, his hands beginning to shake. At best, he would have to tell Stacey that he'd lost their son. At worst, it would be the people behind all this who answered the phone.

He stepped into the old box and couldn't help but think of it as a glass coffin. He left the door open. He didn't see a Bell Atlantic or Verizon logo, even though James Earl Jones's voice began promoting both of them in his head. There didn't seem to be a slot for a card, which he thought most pay phones had near the end of their reign. He remembered using a phone card or a calling card (he couldn't actually remember what they'd been called) with the one he used on Temple's campus. He remembered reading an article or seeing a news piece about new pay phones in New York being free, having Wi-Fi, a USB charging station, and even access to the internet. This was definitely not one of those.

As he lifted the phone from the cradle, the mountains drew his gaze. They seemed vast, and he thought of Joseph an hour and a half beyond them. How was he going to find him in all that? It seemed impossible. But he'd faced impossible before, hadn't he?

He put the phone to his ear and actually heard a dial tone. He slipped the quarter into the slot, wondering if twenty-five cents would be enough. He thought calls had been at least thirty-five cents when he last used one, and he had no idea how this old technology interfaced with the new and what determined the price.

He listened to the sound of the quarter going in, making sure he didn't hear it fall into the change slot, and then punched in Stacey's cell phone number.

Voicemail.

Damn. He didn't know what to do. He wanted to hang up and try again, but wasn't sure he'd get the quarter back. It felt like it had been months since he last heard her voice, and the recording almost brought him to tears.

He left a message.

Now he needed to find someone heading toward Hollow Mountain. Or find a car he could borrow. But stepping out of the booth, he didn't see a soul anywhere.

78

JAMES LOOKED UP AT Michael, and the two of them stared at each other without speaking. A slight breeze blew in from the west, and wind chimes sounded from the cabin's porch behind them. The trees in the distance waved their leaves. The sun warmed their faces. Neither one said what they were thinking, but they didn't need to. It was in their eyes. *This could be it, brother.*

Colt's warning to keep their eyes peeled for any reinforcements Lee might have already called in had them making their way back to the cabin, scanning the hills and tree lines the whole way. They knew it was more than a possibility. It was *likely*. And up here, in these mountains, they were square in the middle of Bakerville. A hundred guys could show up at any moment, and then what?

But perhaps even more disturbing than that was what Ham had said over the phone. About the boy's father. About his wife. About who was behind this whole job. The stories they'd grown up hearing about the KGB being in Appalachia since the Cold War, a secret Communist government operating behind the scenes. It was all true. And here they were, little puppets on their strings, doing their dances, singing their songs, forwarding their agendas.

James and Michael were a lot of things, but Commie errand boys were not among them.

"Always had a feeling it was true," Michael said, keeping pace beside his brother.

James squinted at the rolling hills, not saying anything.

Michael took his hat off and ran a hand over his hair. "What are we gonna do?"

James didn't know. If he could talk Lee into somehow helping them, use his people to fight the Russians, then maybe they'd stand a chance. But he didn't think that was where Lee's head was at. It certainly wasn't where Colt's was. He looked at his brother. "I figure we have two options. We find the boy and use him as an insurance policy. If the Russians want him that bad, they can't kill us if we're the only ones who know where he is."

"What if no one knows where he is?"

"If it comes to that, then they can't know we're lying."

"They'll torture us."

"If they catch us, absolutely."

"But we won't be able to tell them what we don't know."

James moved the toothpick to the other side of his mouth and stepped over a branch that had fallen in the storm. "No, it'll just buy us a little time."

"What's the other option?"

"Ham finds out where they are, and we get them before they can get us."

They reached the cabin and went in for some more firepower.

79

JOSEPH WASN'T SURE HOW long he'd been asleep before the noises woke him up. He rolled back onto his elbows, the mud he was in beginning to dry, and stared out between the porch steps. He could see the sun between them, and he was almost certain that the ball of fire was on its way back down to the earth. Which meant it was past noon, right? Was the sun's highest point at noon? He figured that was why they called it "high noon." He looked at his watch, and it confirmed his estimate. Which meant he'd had a good little nap, but nothing more.

He was hungry. The dinner they'd made him last night wasn't that bad, but he hadn't eaten anything since. He wondered if he could sneak back into the cabin to look for some food. Then maybe he could make a run for it. But making a run for it now would be dumb. They were out there looking for him, and he'd only have half a day's worth of light to work with. No, if he was going to escape, he'd do it first thing in the morning, before the sun even cleared the mountains. Though the thought of spending the rest of the day and all night in this same spot was almost enough to make him take his chances.

He would be freezing tonight, just like he had been last night. Maybe even get pneumonia or something, like Mom always suggested whenever he went out of the house in the winter without a coat or hat on. Maybe he could dig a hole and cover himself with dirt. Or crawl beneath where the fireplace was. Heat rises, he knew, but maybe there would be enough of it in the floor to make even the smallest difference.

His stomach growled, and he set the knife aside. He rolled onto his stomach and scanned the tree line in the distance, again thinking of climbing back into the cabin. He didn't see any of the men around, but if he left footprints, they'd find him pretty quick. No, it was safer to stay here and look for another source of food. All the characters in his favorite books had to do it, so why not him?

He spotted a worm and picked it up between his fingers. It squirmed in his grasp, coiling spasmodically. The body seemed to pulsate.

Joseph took a deep breath, opened his mouth, and lowered the slimy, dancing thing in. *I'm a survivor*, he told himself. He chewed twice and then threw up.

He spit and wiped his mouth. *Great*, he thought. *Now I'm gonna have to lie here with the taste of worm in my mouth all day.*

Then he heard someone coming and looked back to the tree line. Two of the men were coming. They were talking to each other loudly.

Even though he was pretty sure they couldn't see him, Joseph ducked his head down.

They crossed the grass and climbed the stairs. He could have reached out and grabbed their feet they were so close.

He wondered how long it would take them to figure out what he'd done. That the window had just been a misdirection. If they got suspicious and started looking around, they'd soon find the loose floorboard beneath where he'd slid the bed. Hopefully not before tomorrow morning.

He listened to their feet walking back and forth in the cabin above him, and once again closed his eyes.

80

JACK WALKED DOWN THE empty street, wondering where everyone was this Thursday afternoon. He thought they must be working. Maybe there was a factory nearby, and most of the town was parked over there. But then the road turned right and brought into view some signs of life.

An old grocery store stood a hundred yards away on the right side of the road. Maybe it used to be a Pathmark or something. He could see where there used to be big letters across the top of the building, the paint slightly less faded, but they were long gone, and he couldn't make out what the title might have been. There were about a dozen cars parked in its parking lot. Across the street from that was a movie theater and a bank. He counted eight cars at the theater and two at the bank. Beyond that, mountains.

He headed for the theater.

The big sign said there were two movies playing. He knew one of them had come out over a year ago. He checked his watch. Assuming the movies were about an hour and a half long, he had about an hour before the people who arrived in the eight cars came out looking for them.

As he made his way to the theater, he kept looking over at the grocery store, expecting to see someone staring at him and his gun. But so far as he could tell, there were no eyes coming from that direction.

He passed beneath the sign and made his way to the first car. It was a warm day, getting hotter, and he hoped that one of these older cars might not have a functioning AC. And, indeed, three of the first four cars he saw had their windows down.

He went to the first one, a blue 2000 or 2001 Dodge Neon he guessed, and reached through the window to flip down the visor. Nothing. He opened the door and checked beneath the floor mat and then in the cup holders, the center console, and the glove compartment. No dice.

He moved on to the next one. And the one after that.

He was getting nervous. His heart was pounding, and sweat was dripping down his face. He kept looking back over his shoulder, expecting to see that sheriff pull in to the parking lot.

What're ya doin', son?

I'm waiting for the next show.

With a rifle?

What rifle? Oh, you mean this rifle...

Finally, he found a set of keys in a gray Chevy Caprice. It was the same car his grandfather had owned, and when he sat behind the wheel, he couldn't help but turn and take in the whole of its interior. He told himself he was checking to make sure there was no baby in the back seat, but it was just pure nostalgia that had him taking it all in. The smell was different, of course. There were rips in the seats and bubbles in the upholstery where the cloth had separated from the ceiling, but it was still the same make and model and enough to transport him back in time. The old theater and a few of the other cars around him only added to the sensation that he was five years old again.

He shook his head and put his childhood back into the history section of his brain, replacing it with Now. With Joseph.

He inserted the key into the ignition and started the engine. He took one last look around, making sure no one was running to a phone booth to dial 9-1-1, and then put the car in drive.

He rolled out of the parking lot and made a left toward the mountains, toward Durbin and where he hoped was Hollow Mountain. *You'd have to take 33 over the line and through the forest,* the guy had said. *Hour and a half drive, maybe.*

As Jack drove down the street, he thought about the message he'd left Stacey. Wondered when she'd hear it and how she would react. Then, while keeping his eyes peeled for a road sign, he reached into the bag Bernadette had given him and took out a sandwich. He took a bite and then chased it with a gulp of water from the bottle she'd given him.

HAM TOSSED THE PHONE back on the seat, hoping the rest of his guys could get up to the mountain in time. He'd called in some favors and rounded up the rest of those in his employ. He'd told them that they were at war with the Bakers. That the Baker brothers had tried to kill them and take over their territory. They'd all sounded ready to fight.

Now, if they could just get there in time. He'd relayed James's description of where the cabin was the best he understood it, and he could only hope they got there before or at the same time as Lee's reinforcements. If they didn't, then James wouldn't stand a chance. And without James and company to protect him, Lee would certainly come if the Russians didn't first. He'd been hoping that James would help him take out the Russians once he located them, but the likelihood of that was beginning to fade fast.

A fox darted across the road ahead of him, and he took his foot off the gas.

But maybe he'd get lucky and Colt would take care of Lee himself. If he did, he'd have to get over his differences with him. Either that or get rid of him. If Colt managed to take down the Bakers himself, then his sense of entitlement might outgrow the boundaries of what Ham was comfortable with.

What about the boy?

He no longer cared about the boy.

He turned the truck down a dirt road, not completely sure of where he was going. He wasn't that familiar with the area, but Ron had said he wouldn't be able to miss the turnoff. And he'd been right. The fallen tree on the side of the road was unmissable. The path he was on now would supposedly take him to a hidden driveway. There would be a chain that he'd have to get past, guard dogs further up.

He would deal with it all in turn and get this next guy to talk, just as he'd gotten the last two to talk. And then he'd have his answer and know exactly what he was dealing with.

82

AS STACEY DROVE HER car north on I-95, she couldn't stop glancing at the destination displayed on the dashboard GPS.

Connecticut.

Was it a coincidence? In her line of work, there was no such thing as coincidence. But she couldn't figure out how that piece fit into the puzzle. Not that she had any portion of the puzzle assembled, but that particular piece was a different size altogether. Vadim was dead. She'd blown his head into mush.

Then why Connecticut? Because the senator is from Connecticut.

A car passed her on the left, and she instinctively took her foot off the gas, slowing her speed and diminishing the time both cars would be beside each other. It flew past, but the passenger side window never cracked, no muzzle peeking out at her. She took a deep breath and accelerated.

But it wasn't sitting well with her. *Could there have been a connection between Vadim and Newell?*

You're going back eight years, she told herself.

She ignored it, a new thought striking the forefront of her brain like a blacksmith beating on an anvil. *What if Newell is behind all this?*

You're crazy, she responded.

What would it do to his campaign?

If they spun you into a Russian double agent who attempted to assassinate the front runner before the primaries?

Holy shit.

Yeah. Holy shit.

So had it been Vadim, the SVR, or the Agency that had introduced me to him?

She would find out tonight.

83

A SONG THAT JACK didn't recognize came in and out of the one working speaker, and even that was intermittent and shrouded in plenty of static. The occasional sign told him he was driving east on Route 33, and that he was passing through George Washington National Forest. He was surprised the radio was picking up anything at all.

The car was toying with his sense of reality as flashbacks came from memory banks he didn't even know existed. So many stories had been written in this car—not this exact car, but close enough. Stories he had completely forgotten about and might never have remembered again had he not come across the old Caprice. Emotions he hadn't felt in a long time were rising to his eyes and threatening to spill down his cheeks. He could almost see his younger self sitting in the back seat when looking into the rearview mirror. Grandmom riding shotgun beside him. They were happy days. Burdened by the loss of his parents, yes, but happy days nonetheless. He missed them. He missed them a lot. As the years went on, it became easier and easier to forget. A glimpse of a picture here or there would bring them back to the forefront of his mind, but this... To feel their presence again, to relive the memories and translate their existence into his current time line, wondering what they'd think of what was going on, how they'd love Joseph, what they'd think of Stacey... It was a whole other level of missing them that daily life rarely afforded, and here, in this car that turned out to be a time machine, he was hearing his grandmom talking to him in her sweet voice, hearing the "zingers" Grandpa would randomly fire off in his teasing manner.

He missed them.

He missed his life before the cruise ship. Before it became this other thing with long tentacles that squirmed into every aspect of his life, changing, corrupting, destroying.

He missed Ivan. Donny.

God, he missed his *daughter*. And what would Grandmom have said about that? He almost felt as if he could turn and ask her.

A tear escaped, and he brushed it away.

He needed to find someone who could tell him where the cabin was. Or at least had an idea of where the cabin was. It would have to be someone who was familiar with Bakerville.

Hang in there, buddy. I'm coming.

He knew whom to ask. Knew how he'd have to ask it too.

He began to pray for the first time in years.

COLT SHOULDERED THE RIFLE and slipped the knife out of its sheath. This was it. He was about twenty yards from Seth, and Seth had just set down his own rifle and looked like he was getting ready to take a piss.

Colt crept slowly through the undergrowth of the forest, silent as a snake, his fingers flexing on the handle, his adrenaline pumping.

A noise.

From behind him.

He turned and saw a deer standing at his five o'clock, thirty feet back. When Colt met the doe's bulging black marble eyes with his own, it took off with a long leap, darting back and forth through the woods like a rabbit.

Colt whipped his head back around to Seth and saw that he'd also been startled by the noise. He already had his rifle back in his hands, and Colt knew he was thinking that it might've been the kid who spooked the deer.

Seth was coming toward him.

"Hey, kiddo, come on out, will ya? You done real good, ya know? So I quit. We all do. You win. Ya hear me? You win the hide-and-seek game, okay?" He was getting closer, his eyes sweeping left and right.

Colt held his breath. If Seth didn't see him, there was a chance that he'd walk right past. Colt could then step out, grab him from behind, and slit his throat. But Seth was walking closer and closer to his position, and he knew the shrubs in front of him weren't thick enough to completely conceal him.

"C'mon, ain't ya hungry? Don't you wanna get some lunch or somethin'? I ain't gonna hurt ya. None of us are. Hell, we even —" His eyes fell on him.

Dammit. Colt reached for his pistol, hoping that the sudden shock of Seth seeing him crouching there would stall him for just a second. It was all he needed. Just one second.

Colt drew the pistol and brought it up at the same time Seth brought his rifle up.

They both fired.

They both missed.

Colt dove to his left and crawled behind a tree as bark splintered around him. He spun around and fired at where Seth had been standing, but he wasn't there, and the bullets struck a dirt rise a hundred feet away. He swept the pistol to the left and to the right, searching for any sign of him. Nothing. He had to be lying on his stomach, below his line of sight and on the other side of the shrubs. He fired into the underbrush and then came around.

He wasn't there.

Colt quickly scrambled back to a row of trees for cover, expecting Seth to start firing at him from his new location. But no more shots came. He tried to hold his breath, to listen to his surroundings, to hear Seth's movement. But all he could hear was his heart pounding in his ears.

85

THEY HEARD THE GUNSHOTS echo back and forth through the hills below them.

"That's Colt's pistol," Michael said.

"And Seth's rifle," James responded.

"Well, if Lee didn't call for backup already, he sure is now."

James called Ham again. "Ham, you have any help on the way? Colt and Seth are shooting at each other, so you can be pretty damn sure all of Bakerville will be on its way up here if it ain't already."

"I called who I could. Give 'em a few hours," came the reply.

James hung up.

Michael squinted up at the sun. "We could take off. Get to the bottom of this damn mountain before they start climbing it."

"They might already be climbing it."

"Then a few hours ain't gonna do us any good anyway."

James shook his head. "Nope." He knelt and raised the rifle to his shoulder, looking through the scope and into the direction he thought the shots had come from. "But we need the boy. If we can't get to the Reds, then he's gonna be our only leverage."

"They don't need to know we lost him."

"What if they find him before we do? Or we start singing when they crush our balls with nutcrackers?"

Michael went silent, and James stared at the path descending the hill, wondering who would be coming first, Ham's backup, Lee's backup, the Russians, or the boy's father. Or maybe the CIA for that matter.

"So then what do we do?" Michael asked.

James stood. "Ain't none of them lookin' for the boy now. Guess we might as well do it. If we find him, we grab him and get the hell out of here."

"Which way you wanna go?"

"Not that way." He nodded in the direction of Lee and Seth. They walked to the barn and the ATVs.

86

JACK KNEW HE WAS close. Had to be. He'd followed the signs all the way into this small town, and the mountains were so tall around him that he felt like they were bending over to embrace him.

The town he was driving through was by no means "downtown." There were no buildings, just empty streets with the occasional house tucked back in the trees with only an old mailbox to signal its existence. He wondered how often these people got mail. It was too cliche. The backwoods, hillbilly, West Virginia town nestled in the mountains. He expected to pass a porch (the house it was attached to in various states of disarray, of course) any moment now, its occupants malnourished inbreds picking away at banjos and chewing straw.

Stereotypes. All from books and TV. Had to be. Because he'd never even been to West Virginia or met anyone from around here (this morning's company excluded, and they certainly didn't fit that image). Hell, the closest he'd ever been to anything "backwoods" was eight years ago when Agent Johnson had stashed him at that house in the Poconos.

He needed to find someone though. Someone he could ask—

There. A person was walking down the side of the road ahead of him. He came to a stop beside them. "Hi, mister," he said, leaning over and calling out the passenger window.

The person turned to face him, and he saw that it was actually a woman.

"Oh, sorry, ma'am. My mistake. I don't have my glasses on." Actually, she was wearing baggy jeans and a short-sleeved collared shirt, and her hair was pulled up underneath a baseball cap. In fact, if it weren't for the twin swells peeking over the top of what he could now see were overalls, he might not have apologized. Maybe some other place he'd have to worry about which pronoun she preferred, but out here? Not a chance.

She stopped walking and stared at him.

"Can you point me in the direction of the nearest police station?" he asked.

She didn't blink, didn't shrug, didn't do anything. Just stood there staring.

Jack looked away, unsure what was happening. Did he look that bad? Or maybe she knew who owned the car? He was about to move on when she suddenly raised an arm and pointed further down the road.

"Make a right," she said. Then she turned and continued walking.

"Thank you." He watched her for a few seconds, wondering where she was heading, how long she'd been walking. He thought about asking if she needed a ride, but decided he didn't have the time to spare. He kept driving, watching her in the rearview as he passed, hoping she didn't whip a .357 Magnum out from her overalls and blow out his tires as he did so.

He came to an intersection half a mile later, noted that there wasn't even a stop sign posted, and eased the Caprice into a right turn. The view was more of the same. Trees on both sides of the road, the mountains just beyond stretching up into the sky and blocking the sun.

There, up ahead and on the left, was a little building. He guessed it was the police station because there was an old cruiser parked in front of it. He couldn't believe how easy it had been to find. One question to the first person he saw and it was just down the road? Seemed too good to be true. Like when he'd survived the fall off the ship. Guess he'd chalk it up to good luck and fortune and maybe even (for Grandmom's sake) a miracle. Either that or it was back to revisiting questions concerning his current state of reality, and he didn't have time for that.

The station looked like a holdover from the Wild West days. Though he wasn't sure if this was considered the West. He thought "the West" referenced everything west of the Mississippi. Was he west of the Mississippi? No, he wasn't. So he guessed he couldn't refer to it as a Wild West holdover after all. Oh well, it resembled the sheriff's offices in those old cowboy movies anyway.

He pulled onto the grass beside the cruiser. It was an old 1980s black and white. He gave the building another once-over, wondering if this was a legit county operation or if someone just walked in one day, found a badge in an empty drawer, and proclaimed to themselves through a dirty mirror, "There's a new sheriff in town." But that would be stupid, right? Who would be paying his salary? And the cops in neighboring counties would no doubt know there was some impostor driving around in a police cruiser. Still, good ol' Theodore hadn't called this "Bakerville" for nothing.

He got out of the car and walked up the wooden steps. Before pushing the door open, he turned and looked at the Caprice sitting there next to the cruiser. Probably wasn't the smartest thing to do, parking a stolen car in front of the county sheriff's office. But he shrugged and entered what really could be the set of a Western flick.

The smell of cigarette smoke hit him immediately. A few windows let light in, and sun rays were cutting diagonally through all the dust and smoke floating in the air. There were a few cells in the back, all empty.

"Help you?" a tired and gravelly voice sounded from his right.

Jack looked over and saw the top of a hat hovering behind a counter. A tower of intertwining smoke rose from the unseen cigarette, extending up to the ceiling, where it turned into a cloud and proceeded to move throughout the room. Shifting his gaze a couple of degrees to his left, he then spotted two socked feet, crossed at the ankles, propped up on the same counter. He walked over, noting the holes in the socks and the unpleasant smell ruminating from them, and then looked down at the fella leaning back in the chair, hands resting on his stomach, fingers interlaced, the brim of his hat tilted down and covering his entire face. An ashtray lay on the floor beside the chair.

Jack stepped back a second and looked down at his own flannel shirt, then back at the sheriff's. They were almost matching. Same colors, just a slightly different pattern. Jack frowned and stepped back to the counter, wondering again at how cliche this all was. That Dean Koontz book he'd started reading on the cruise—*The House of Thunder*—came to mind. Not for how it related to the Trenton Thunder stadium and the false-flag plot to blow it up, but the story itself. He'd finished reading it over the next couple of years, and he wondered if this place, this town, could be some Soviet operation. Wouldn't that be something?

"Am I in Bakerville?" Jack asked.

The man just sat there, not moving, staying still.

Jack wondered if just hearing the name had killed him.

But then the man unlaced his fingers and reached for his hat, pushing the brim up with a long index finger. He had a five-o'clock shadow and was younger than Jack would've assumed, but his face was hollow and gaunt, and Jack wondered if the cancer already had him.

"What'd you say?" the man asked.

It wasn't a "Hey, I didn't hear you, would you mind repeating yourself?" what'd you say. No, it was more of the "I just want to make sure I heard you right" variety.

"Bakerville. This it?"

The socks came off the counter. "Who wants to know?"

That was a yes. "You the sheriff in these here parts?" He wondered if the guy would be able to pick up on the sarcasm in his voice.

"That's right."

Nope. "I'm looking for their cabin on Hollow Mountain. Lee told me to meet him there at four o'clock, and I lost my directions. You can imagine what he'll do to me if I'm late. Let alone if I lost the directions." He tried a nervous laugh.

The guy stared at him as the smoke caressed his face and curled around the underside of his hat.

"I know what you're thinking," Jack continued. "Is this some sort of test? Well, if it were, you'd already have failed it by responding the way you did. Someone comes in here asking about Bakerville, you don't say, 'Who wants to know.' You say, 'Baker-what? Never heard of it. You must be lost. Maybe try the next county over. Maybe the next state, even.'" He put his hands on the counter. "Okay, I'll tell you what. We both messed up, so how about we help each other out? You tell me where the cabin is, and I won't tell him you're not the brightest bulb in the pack. The sharpest knife in the drawer. The quickest bunny in the forest. The fastest ship—"

"I get it."

"Oh, good. I was running out."

"But I have a better idea. How about I just throw you in one of those cells back there until I can figure out just what the hell you're talkin' about."

Crap. Jack was hoping he'd just buy his story and tell him outright. He hadn't, so Jack was forced into plan B. He pulled the pistol from his pants and aimed it at the sheriff's head. "I don't have time for this, Barney."

The sheriff put his hands up.

"Now listen. That piece of shit kidnapped my son and tried to kill me. He's got him in a cabin on Hollow Mountain. He's going to hand him over to some people tomorrow morning. Now, you being a sheriff and all, I can assume you know what kind of 'people' would want to buy a twelve-year-old boy, am I correct?"

No response.

"Can you?" Jack yelled.

The sheriff flinched.

"Yes."

"So you know that there's nothing I won't do to stop that from happening."

He nodded.

"Good. Now I'm obviously not from around these here parts, so I don't know what the hell is going on. If you work for the Bakers or are afraid of the Bakers. Either way, I think you'd agree that it would be in your best interest if I was the one who came back down off that mountain and not them." He pulled the hammer back on the gun. "Now tell me where the cabin is."

The sheriff told him everything he knew.

87

HAM GAVE THE TRUCK some gas, and it jumped up a steep hill, barely fitting between two trees. The path was getting harder and harder to follow, and with all the rain they'd just had, he was afraid he was going to get stuck in the mud.

The truck made it up the hill, and he drove another hundred feet or so before a chain appeared, stretched across the path. He stared out the windshield, his eyes darting left and right, looking for any signs of movement in the scattered woods around him. He didn't see anything.

He grabbed Joanna and opened the door. He climbed out of the truck and walked to the chain, saw that it was stretched between two large trees. He pulled on it. There was maybe half an inch of wiggle. And it was thick. He looked up the path and wondered if he should just walk the rest of the way. Though he had no idea how far the rest of the way was. *Who am I kidding?* After a hundred yards, he'd have a stroke.

He took a deep breath and lifted the axe in both hands, holding the handle in his left hand, his right grasping it under the head. This would be no easy task. Might even be easier to chop the tree down. He supposed he could shoot the chain. He gave another look around, thinking of all the stories he'd heard over the years and wondering how many were true and how many had been exaggerated.

Then a thought occurred to him. Why not call the FBI? Tell them there were KGB operatives who had been hiding in the Appalachian Mountains ever since the Cold War? Anonymous tip. Maybe they'd storm the place and turn the whole thing into a Russian Ruby Ridge. The FBI could do his job for him.

Unless they already knew about it.

He wrapped his fingers around the handle, thinking it through, his heart pounding harder, faster. If the Feds did nothing but get in the way, then there'd be no getting to them at all. He'd be drawing attention from all the wrong people at that point. Still...

He'd try this first. See what was ahead and whom he could get to talk. If the situation was—

The bullet that entered his head disrupted his thought, scattering it with the rest of his brain all over the front of his truck.

The next bullet severed his spine and almost took his head completely off his shoulders. Instead, his head flopped backwards and hung upside down between his shoulders. His glasses sat crooked on his nose. Before he collapsed onto his belly, Joanna still in his hands, he wondered how his truck had suddenly gotten in front of him and upside down.

JACK WAS STANDING HALFWAY up a hill on what the sheriff had said was Hollow Mountain. He looked back down toward the road and the Caprice he'd left parked alongside it. He said goodbye to the memories he might never have occasion for again. "Thank you, Grandmom and Grandpa." He adjusted the belt pack, making sure the water bottle he'd taken from Cullin was secure (he'd poured into it what was left in the plastic water bottle Bernadette had given him). Then he checked JT's rifle, made sure it was loaded. It looked and felt similar enough to Theo's, so he didn't think he'd have an issue with it. He slung it over his shoulder and continued to climb.

After two meals and over an hour of sitting still behind the wheel of the car, he was feeling pretty good. Physically, at least. His eye was still bothering him, but compared to how he'd felt last night—hanging naked over an open flame—he felt like a new man. Still, the sheriff said it would take him the rest of the day to get to the cabin. If, that was, he ran the whole way and was familiar with the terrain and managed to avoid the many pitfalls said to be scattered all over the mountain. The sheriff himself had never been up there, but he'd been close enough to see the smoke from its chimney once. So Jack knew that his feeling good would be short-lived. Soon his legs would be on fire, his heart hammering in his chest, and his whole body soaked with sweat. And he would want to stop. He'd want to rest. But he wouldn't let himself. Not when he was this close. He'd gotten all the way from the campsite in Pennsylvania to this mountain in West Virginia, and he wasn't about to stop now. Saturday morning was still a day and change away, but he had no idea what was happening up there in that cabin after Lawrence's tell-all text.

He climbed and climbed and climbed, and soon he was lost in another world, surrounded by a dark and ominous forest without end.

89

JAMES TRIED TO CALL Ham again. They'd been riding around through the woods, looking for signs of the kid, for nearly an hour. They hadn't heard any more gunshots, nor had they received any updates from Colt over the radio. Maybe Seth had killed him. Maybe they had killed each other. The afternoon breeze moved through the trees around them, swaying branches and rattling their leaves.

"What if something happened to him?" Michael asked, referring to Ham.

"Good question," James said.

Then the cell rang.

James answered it and was greeted by a voice he didn't recognize.

"Who is this?" the voice asked.

James knew this was not good. "Who's asking?"

"Are you with the fat man?"

Michael could hear the voice through the phone's speaker, and he took off his hat and ran a hand through his hair. He cursed under his breath.

"Where is he?" James asked.

"He's all over the place now."

Before James could respond, the voice asked, "Are you the ones we hired to get the boy?"

Michael spun back around and shook his head, urging James not to answer.

But he did. "We are."

"I assume there is a problem, then? If you are trying to find us."

"We have the boy."

"Good. That is good. We will expect to pick him up at the designated location Saturday morning."

"What about the fat man?"

"His body will never be found."

"What do you want with the boy?"

"That does not concern you."

"It does if I'm handing him over to a bunch of fuckin' perverts."

Silence on the other end. Then, "I assure you it is nothing like that. The boy will be taken good care of."

James thought about it. "So we leave the boy at the drop-off location. How do we get our money?"

"There will be no money now. The fat man killed two of our resources. They will need to be replaced. We will keep the money as compensation. Unless you would like us to find compensation in some other way?"

"Maybe."

Michael's eyes widened. "What're you doing?" he whispered.

James waved him off. "You're down two men, and my brother and I just happen to be looking for a new employer."

More silence.

Michael threw his hat at James. "Are you outta your damn mind?"

"Okay, we will leave fifty thousand dollars in the glove compartment of the fat man's truck. It will be waiting for you at the drop-off. There will be a note with another time and place. Meet us there, and we will talk."

"Who are you?" James asked.

No answer.

Michael was pacing. "You'd best start talking, James. What the—"

James picked up the hat and threw it back at him. "I'm gettin' us money. We're gonna need it."

"So you ain't plannin' on joinin' up with the Commies?"

With the phone still pressed to his ear, he whispered, "No, ain't plannin' on it. But it's still an option that's better than gettin' dead."

The voice spoke again. "If you do not show up with the boy, we will kill you and everyone you know one by one over the next two years."

James hung up.

"They're gonna kill us anyway," Michael said.

"Maybe." James got back on the ATV and started it up. He looked back at his brother. "Maybe not."

90

THE WOODS WERE DENSE and dark, everything set at a steep angle. Jack was hungry and tired, his muscles aching a lot sooner than he'd expected. Yet he pushed on. He kept looking at his watch, marking the time and guesstimating his progress.

He thought he should be coming within radio range soon, and he unhooked it from his belt. The volume was turned low, and he turned it up. But then he noticed the red power light wasn't glowing. He pressed the button and changed the channel. Nothing. The battery was dead. He tossed it on the ground and continued on.

After twenty minutes, he found himself jogging in the shade of towering hardwoods, which he thought he could identify as poplars, oaks, hickories, and maples. The ground had leveled out, and he thought he might be halfway up the mountain. But then a gust of wind spread the canopy apart, and he got a glimpse of the peak still so far away.

The birds were singing their songs. Tiny little chickadees were rustling in the undergrowth with small singsong whistles; jaybirds jeered from tree branches; sparrows, wrens, and finches all called out to each other while the occasional hawk looked down from above. Chipmunks darted away from him whenever he got close, hiding under the nearest deadwood. He even spotted a few deer, each of them raising their head before leaping away.

He came upon a stream, just like the sheriff said he would, and he followed alongside it. It took him through fields of wildflowers, evergreen forests, and eventually to a waterfall.

A squirrel ran up a nearby tree. Frogs croaked. He continued on, wondering if the ground would swallow him before he reached the top.

91

HER HEART WAS POUNDING. The GPS said she was one minute away. There were few houses on this road, all of them large. At least half a million dollars. Not estates, exactly. Not like Vadim's, but a lot more than a politician should be able to afford. Though they all seemed to.

She came up on the residence and turned the wheel. There was no gate, no security guard, just a long driveway that led past flowering trees sprinkled over a well-manicured lawn. One of the doors of the four-car garage began to open as she approached.

She pulled in between a Porsche and a Buick, wondering which one he campaigned in, and put the car in park. She sat there for a moment. Still. Trying to anticipate what might be expected of her at this moment. What this little rendezvous before the party was actually about.

The door at the end of the garage opened, and a man appeared leaning against the door frame with a short glass in his hand. He smiled a bright smile, waved her in, and then walked out of sight.

Well, he isn't in a leather thong and wearing an executioner's hood, so at least there's that.

She grabbed the bag from the hotel and got out of the car. She stepped up through the open door as the garage shut behind her, plunging the room into darkness. She entered a hallway and looked left and right.

"Over here, love," a voice called out.

Love? Wonderful. If he wasn't behind this, then she could only imagine what she had supposedly been saying to him. She followed the voice into a large den. Long wooden rafters raced back and forth in the vaulted ceiling. A large stone fireplace was crackling despite the time of year, a large Persian rug circling the room in front of it. Brown leather furniture was scattered throughout the room, and there was even a grand piano over in the corner by the bookshelves. On the walls hung paintings she assumed were valuable, but she didn't give a crap about art and never pretended to know anything about it.

The senator sat on a two-cushion sofa that faced the fireplace. He had his feet up, his ankles crossed. He was in a hundred-dollar pair of jeans and a Polo. It was so typical it almost made her laugh. His haircut matched the Ivy League persona to a T. She wondered if he was a Bonesman. If he was, if he had those kind of connections...

He patted a spot on the cushion that was still visible beneath him. It was a very small spot, and the fact that she was expected to plant her ass there, where it would be touching his lap, told her all she needed to know about what he thought was going to happen. She walked over and sat, and he shifted from his back to his side, pressing against her and letting her know that he was ready when she was. He flashed her a smile that radiated arrogance.

"Where's your wife?" she asked.

His smile faded. "Away. Don't worry, no one knows you're here." He put his hand on her back.

Inwardly, she cringed. Outwardly, she smiled. She was used to this game. After so many years with Vadim and others, it had become part of the job. Not that she wanted this to turn into one of those times. She'd given herself to other men in the name of patriotic duty before, but she wasn't sure what this would be in the name of.

Saving Joseph?

Maybe. Maybe not.

"I can't believe we're finally together," she whispered, looking into his eyes, searching for clues.

"It's been a long time coming," he said, and then he smiled again as if she didn't get his meaning.

She wanted to throw up in his face. Maybe start beating the crap out of him right here and now, get him to tell her all he knew. But then if he didn't know anything, and she really was supposed to blow him to hell tonight... Well, then the dinner would be off, and they'd kill Joseph. She was absolutely sure of that. She could easily take care of him right now. It'd take less than a minute. But they apparently wanted the whole show. It wasn't just about getting rid of him, it was about who they were going to blame and what they were going to use it to accomplish.

She looked at him. He looked just like he did on all the websites she'd seen in her research of him. He looked like Tom Cruise. From that movie where he played the senator. Maybe that was what he was going for. If so, he nailed it. And she was pretty sure he was used to nailing whatever and whomever he wanted. She figured the wife had to know. Hell, she was probably out doing the same. Wasn't that how the games went with these people? They paraded around on moral high ground, warriors for social justice in front of the cameras, and as soon as they got home... Well, here she was, wasn't she?

She crossed her legs and leaned forward. "If you get elected—"

"*When* I get elected."

"Fine. What will you give me?"

"I'll give you whatever you want, wherever you want it."

"Enough—"

"Beating around the bush? I was thinking the same thing." He sat up next to her and drained the glass. Then he set it down on the table beside the couch and picked up another one. He handed it to her. "Go ahead."

She took it and drained it in one gulp. Handed it back to him.

"Seriously," she continued. "If I use my clearance to gain you access—"

His eyes lit up, and he leaned forward. "Please."

She pushed him away. "Listen to me. I want assurances. Whatever you think is about to happen here, once you get tired of it and move on to your next slut—"

He growled and raised his eyebrows while putting his hand over her mouth. "No more talking." He slipped his other hand up her shirt.

She grabbed his wrist, and it was clear he was surprised at how strong her grip was. "What do you want from me?"

He pulled his hand back. "Fine. Fine. Business before pleasure." He stood, picked up his glass, and took both of them over to the fireplace, where a bottle was resting on the mantel above it. He poured more in each glass and walked back over with them. He handed her one and sipped from the other. "I want to know everything. Everything you know. I don't want to be another JFK, making enemies with the Agency and having to look over my shoulder all the time. With them, yesterday's agendas are tomorrow's liabilities and all that, and I want to be a step ahead of them at all times."

"Isn't the director your friend?"

He snorted. "He likes my stance on Russia, but that's about it. As soon as he gets what he wants, he won't hesitate to stab me in the back if the opportunity presents itself."

"Aren't you being a little paranoid? After all, you will be the President of the United States of America. They will be working for you."

He threw back the rest of his drink, turned, and tossed the glass across the room and into the fireplace. The glass exploded. He pointed at her. "Don't play dumb. You know what they can do to someone. Even a president." He started unbuttoning his shirt. "Now that's enough talk."

"You didn't answer my question."

He sighed. "Yes I did. I said whatever you want. You tell me when you want something, I'll get it for you. You'll have the president in your back pocket. You scratch my back; I scratch yours."

"Why me?"

He tossed his shirt on the arm of the couch. He was fit enough. Especially for a politician, but he was no Jack. He was all charm and arrogance and power. That was how he got into the women he lusted for. It was not his body. "Because I want you, and you're available."

She blinked, trying to process his statement. "What do you mean?"

He shrugged. "What do you mean, what do I mean? You are a CIA agent with top clearance who will be very convenient to have around. You are an available asset that I can use, and in more ways than one. Which is why you're here. You do want to be here, don't you?"

She gave him her best mischievous smile. "I drove all the way here, didn't I?" She stood and walked over to him, leaned up, and kissed him while slipping her hand down his pants.

He kissed her back, his breath on fire with alcohol, and she could feel his desire like a force radiating from him. But she was not going to let him have her. She pulled back and looked at the clock. "The dinner is in an hour. That's not enough time."

"It's plenty of time."

"Not for what I have in mind." She ran her tongue around the rim of her glass. "Let me come back afterward."

He thought about it, not wanting to delay the experience but curious to know what it was she had in mind. "Why don't we take a shower now, and then you can come back?"

She shook her head. "No. I want our first time to be very precise."

He looked her up and down and then nodded. "Fine. Follow me back. I'll have to move things around and come up with an excuse for my wife, but that's fine. I'll think of something."

"I'm sure you always do."

"Alright, well, then you better get going, then. You stay here any longer and I can't promise I won't tear your clothes off and take you anyway."

You just try it. "Later."

"Later." He picked up his shirt and put it back on. "C'mon, I'll walk you to the garage."

She got back in the car and backed out of the garage while giving a seductive "until next time" wave to the senator. He smiled back and hit a button that began lowering the garage door. She turned the wheel, swinging the car around so she was facing the street, put the car in drive, and got the hell out of there.

She wasn't sure where she was going. There was still an hour before the dinner started, and so far, there had been no other instructions. She wondered if having sex with him was part of the Russians' agenda. Did they have cameras in there ready to record the affair? What did her leaving early do to their plans? She was almost certain that he was not in on it. She was a CIA operative, able to profile and see through people so well it was like reading their minds. And there was only one thing on the senator's mind, and it would be on his mind all night. At least until she hit the detonator. No, if he knew she would be all over the news tonight, then why have her over at his house earlier? Why risk the attention by bringing an affair into an equation that didn't need one? He wouldn't. People like him didn't get this far in their careers by being careless. Oh, they did whatever the hell they wanted to, but they made sure that all the right people were paid off to look the other way or to keep their mouths shut. He had been set up just like she was, their "meeting" orchestrated by whoever was behind Joseph's kidnapping. Apparently, they'd made him believe that she had access to Agency secrets and was willing to whisper them into his ear at night. She wished she could see those communications.

She took a deep breath and felt a sting in her eyes as she thought of Jack. She kept driving.

92

COLT HEARD THEM BEFORE he saw them. A whole bunch of them coming up the ridge beneath him. The Bakerville gang. Lee's reinforcements. They were like a marching army flashing at moments through holes in the canopy. Either they'd been close enough to come on foot, or they'd parked their ATVs nearby and were hoping to take the cabin by stealth. Either way, once they cleared the trees below him and entered the glade they were heading toward, they'd be ducks in a pond. And he was sure as hell going to take out as many of them as he could. He raised the rifle, switched to semiauto, and waited for the lead person to appear in his scope. From his position on the high ground, shielded by rocks and hidden by brush, he stood a good chance of getting them all before they even located him. They were about fifty feet below him and maybe two hundred feet away. He thought the glade they were moving toward had been made by the Natives ages ago, burning away a section of forest in order to grow grass that would attract deer, making them easier to hunt. If so, Colt thanked them, because they'd also made it easier to hunt men.

The data lines followed the blurred flashes of blue jeans until the trees ended and they intersected over a bearded face. Colt pulled the trigger, and the face disappeared from the scope as the blast rolled down the hills and echoed off the mountains.

He looked up from the scope and saw a dozen or so men swinging their guns back and forth, searching for signs of where the shot had come from. Another head exploded, and Colt gave them another hint.

They all turned, aiming their weapons in his general direction. They didn't know where he was, but the way their friend's head had whipped back told them which direction the shot had come from. They started shooting.

A volley of shots filled the forest, all of them aimed far too low. They thought he was down on their level, in the trees across from the clearing. He shot another one.

That time, one of them must've caught sight of his muzzle flash, because the guy immediately raised his gun and fired off two shots that ricocheted off the rocks around him, making him duck for cover.

Dammit. He'd hoped to get at least three more before they could home in on his location. Now they were scattering out of the clearing and into the surrounding trees, shooting up at him and keeping him pinned down. He took out the radio and called James.

"James, you copy?"

"I copy."

"Bakerville has arrived. I got 'em pinned down by a clearing 'bout half a mile from the cabin."

"Where's Seth and Lee?"

"I don't know. Seth slipped away. Haven't seen Lee." He swung the rifle up and took a few more shots, striking another man and making the rest shrink back for cover. "Where are you?"

"Lookin' for the boy."

"Check under the cabin." He fired another shot.

JACK LOOKED BACK DOWN the ridge, noting how far he'd climbed. The stream was beneath him in a valley, shooting over the side of the cliff and splashing against the rocks even further below. The water snaked away from there, disappearing beneath the forest ceiling and back where he'd come from.

The sun was dropping fast. Soon it would dip beneath the rolling green waves stacked across the western sky. He looked up north, toward the top of the mountain and where he was heading, but all he could see were trees. They were so thick on this part of the mountain that it was impossible to see anything beyond them.

He continued on, and the sound of the waterfall grew more and more distant until it was finally replaced with the familiar sounds of birds and insects.

But there was another sound.

He stopped and stood still, trying to decipher it. It sounded like firecrackers. Way off in the distance, maybe on the other side of the mountain. Or even on a neighboring mountain. But he knew they weren't firecrackers. They were gunshots. But there were too many too close together for it to be hunters.

He forced his weary legs to run.

STACEY FOLLOWED THE DIRECTIONS to the address on the invitation using the car's GPS. She was about ten minutes away and nearly half an hour early when a sound pierced the quiet interior of her car. She tilted her head, trying to place it while at the same time looking at the radio display to see if maybe the radio was on at a low volume. But the radio was off.

A gas station was coming up on the right, and she turned into it, pulling into a parking spot. She quickly got out of the car, ran around the front and to the passenger side. She threw open the door and looked under the front seat. The noise was definitely coming from beneath it, and being this close, she could tell it was a ringtone. There was a cell phone under the seat.

She reached for it. Grabbed it.

Missed it.

She'd never seen the phone before and could only assume that the people who were setting her up had placed it there earlier. Though she didn't know when. Maybe when she was at the hotel. Maybe weeks ago. She swiped the screen to unlock it and saw that there were ten missed calls. All from "private number." She checked the times. The first call had come half an hour ago. Apparently, they'd been trying to get in touch with her since she left the senator's. Maybe they were pissed that they didn't get the footage they wanted and were going to try to make her go back. Maybe they were calling to tell her the deal was off, that she failed and that Joseph was dead.

She shut the door and ran back around. Climbed back behind the wheel. She held the phone in one hand and gripped the wheel with the other. She stared at the blank screen, waiting for it to ring again.

A whole minute passed.

Should she try to return the call? She was certain it wouldn't go through, but what the hell. She hit the phone icon next to the number in the call history.

"We're sorry, the number you have dialed is not receiving calls at this time."

She leaned back in the seat and closed her eyes, the fingers on her left hand drumming impatiently against the steering wheel. She took a deep breath, leaned forward and set the phone in the cup holder in the center console. She put the vehicle in reverse and was about to take her foot off the brake when the phone rang again.

She swore and threw the car back in park and answered the phone.

The voice started speaking right away. *"You were shorter than expected at the senator's."*

"Is that a problem?"

"Not ideal, but not the end of the world."

"What now?"

"Now you go to the dinner in your red dress. You will need to stop somewhere along the way to put it on, yes?"

She held her breath. Had the person really just said what she thought they did? Did they finally make a mistake? The way they asked the question... It was a rhetorical question phrased by someone who knew English as a second language. No one in America used "yes" as a question tag. They used "right" or "isn't that so" or something along those lines. Never "yes." That was not an American construction. Spanish, Italian, and French with a basic understanding of English typically used, "no" as a question tag. And it was the Russians who used "yes."

Her mind reeled, trying to grasp at new pieces of the puzzle, seeing if any of them were corners that would help frame her situation.

Or had that been intentional? Did someone simply want her to *think* she was speaking to a Russian? But then what would it matter what she thought if she was about to be dead anyway? Unless the conversation was being recorded for later use, either as proof of claim or proof of blame. Either way, she'd be the

American agent with prior connections to the SVR and the one responsible for carrying it out.

"Are you listening?"

She blinked. "Yes."

"There is a bomb in your car. You will park the car where they tell you, against the building. The detonator is in the handbag. You will detonate the device when the senator is in close proximity to that side of the room. The blast should level the entire building, but we do not want to take any chances. Wait until he is on that side of the room."

She stopped breathing. So this was it? This was how it would all end for her. She couldn't keep her voice from shaking when she asked, "What then? What about my son?"

"As we said, he will be fine. We will not harm him. He will be looked after."

"You'll recruit him, you mean."

"He will be a valuable asset, motivated by his mother's sacrifice."

"Sacrifice for what? For who?"

"Do not be late. And do not fail. Or he will not be fine. This is the last we will speak."

"What if something goes wrong? What if it doesn't go off or something?"

"If there is a technical difficulty or if something unforeseen happens, then you will get a call on this phone with further instructions. Put the phone in your handbag."

"Why a detonator? Why don't you just do it yourself with a phone call?"

"Goodbye, Anna Aleksandrov."

The line when dead.

95

THEY MOTORED THROUGH THE tree line and up the grassy slope toward the cabin, James looking back behind him to make sure Michael was still on his tail. He couldn't believe what Colt had said, that the kid had been under the house the whole damn time. Yet it was a brilliant move, wasn't it? The kid was smart, and James wondered if he'd gotten those smarts from his parents. If so, then maybe they'd been worrying about the wrong people.

Standing and leaning forward against the handles, he continued to fly up the hill, unable to hear the gunshots over the engine but knowing they must be echoing up and down the mountain all the same. The cabin grew in size as they got closer and closer to it, but the porch and the underneath of it was still out of his line of sight due to its position at the top of the hill.

Then they cleared the slope, the ground turning flat, and the cabin was directly ahead of them a hundred yards away. The porch came into view, but they still couldn't see anything beneath it. They skidded to a stop right against the side of the cabin and hopped off the ATVs.

"You go around the back," James yelled while pointing.

Michael ran around the other side.

"Hey, kid," James called out, bending over and trying to see into the darkness beneath the cabin. "You under there?" Now he could hear the gunshots. Colt was doing a good job keeping the Baker gang pinned down and away from the top of the hill. If they got past him before Ham's help could get here... "C'mon out, kid. It ain't safe under there. We gotta get you out of here before those men get up the mountain."

Nothing.

"See anything?" he called to Michael.

"No!"

He got back to his feet and ran to the ATV for a flashlight. While he was going through the utility box tied to the back of it, he caught movement in his periphery. He spun his head around and saw the kid sprinting away from the cabin, still in his socks. He hopped back on the vehicle and was about to call out to Michael, when he suddenly appeared from behind the cabin, already chasing after the boy.

James started the ATV and accelerated, bringing the front wheels up into the air as the back wheels spun in the grass, searching for traction and shooting him forward when finally they caught.

The boy was heading away from where Colt was fighting with the Bakers, so at least there was that.

The kid was fast, maybe one of the fastest in his grade, but Michael was faster. He'd overtake him before the kid could reach the slope. But James would pass both of them on the ATV, which was his plan. Cut the kid off and let Michael grab him when the boy tried to change direction. James could ride alongside him and try to grab him, but then he'd risk running him over.

He was coming up on Michael, about to pass him, when Michael, in mid-run, suddenly convulsed into an involuntary sort of spastic dance. His shoulders rotated, and his arms flew out as he twisted downward, his legs running out from beneath him. A red mist sprayed the air around his back, and James watched his brother hit the ground, tumble awkwardly, and finally roll to a stop.

James turned and looked behind him. Saw Lee standing beside the cabin and aiming a rifle at him.

A flash, and the rifle jumped in his grasp.

Miss.

James broke off his pursuit of the boy, bringing the ATV around to face Lee. He was about seventy yards away from him.

Lee fired again.

Miss.

James squeezed the accelerator and began moving across the grass at 20 mph.

Another shot, but James had started to swerve back and forth a little, and it was another miss. He saw Lee work the bolt action and look back through the scope.

45 mph.

Another miss. And now the distance was too close for a scope, and James squeezed the accelerator all the way, screaming as the 570cc engine between his legs shot him forward straightaway.

Lee began to backpedal as he fumbled with the bolt action. He raised it and, without using the scope, fired one last shot from his hip.

James felt a pinch in his arm a fraction of a second before slamming into Lee at 60 mph.

Lee disappeared, flying up over top of him. James hit the brake and skidded to a stop. Looked down at his left arm and saw a hole in his shirt and through the outside of his bicep. He held up his arm and saw another hole underneath, right before the armpit. It was a miracle the bullet hadn't continued on into his ribs. Blood trickled into his eye, and he wiped it away with his right hand. He touched his scalp. Lee's rifle must've struck him as he flew overhead. He looked back at Lee. He was lying on the ground, and one of his legs was bent at the knee ninety degrees in the wrong direction. Bones were sticking out of flesh. Yet he was crawling. Trying to get to his pistol, which had flown from his pants while he was airborne.

James revved the ATV, and Lee rolled onto his back. Lifted his head. His beard covered most of his face and sat in a pile on his chest. There was something in Lee's eyes. An icy defiance that seemed to dare James to do what he was thinking.

So he did it.

He ran him over on his way back to Michael.

By then, the boy was nowhere in sight.

96

THE SOUND OF JACK'S thumping feet, snapping twigs, and labored breathing had since drowned out the distant shots. But now, suddenly, there came a new sound. A closer sound.

Engines.

The noise was coming from the other side of a small rise, and he scrambled up in the hopes it would offer a view down to whatever vehicles were making it. Or maybe they weren't vehicles. Maybe they were chainsaws or...

They were getting louder, and he could tell that they were definitely vehicles. And more than just a few of them.

He reached the top of the rise and peered down to his right. To his left, the ground continued to incline and race for the summit, but there was a steep drop the other way, and the noises were coming from down there somewhere. But he still couldn't see them.

And then he could.

Through the trees, he could make out glimpses of movement. They were still pretty far away, and having to navigate the terrain was slowing them down. He needed to get closer, to see who they were. He ran down the other side of the rise, hopping over dead branches and sidestepping bushes. They were about a hundred yards away, coming up on his right.

Eighty yards.

They altered their course and turned right toward him. Then, coming off the rise and onto level ground, he lost sight of them through the trees. He spotted a large boulder and ran for it.

Fifty yards.

The engines were getting even louder. There had to be a dozen of them, all blasting their grumbling chorus off the mountain. He ducked behind the rock and risked a glance around its jagged edge. He got a clear view of them and saw that they were turning again. Still coming toward him but now they would pass about forty yards to his right.

He stood. Counted them as they appeared. One, two, three... Men on ATVs, all of them with guns.

He ran as fast as he could, sprinting straight ahead as the convoy passed.

Four, five, six, seven.

He crashed through the underbrush, certain they wouldn't hear him over the engines.

Eight, nine, ten...

There were only two left. He maneuvered his body sideways to fit between two trees as the eleventh ATV passed.

Hoping he timed it right, he launched himself off the balls of his feet. He would either tackle the driver off the seat, or be run over.

He hit the driver in the shoulder, wrapping his arms around his neck as his momentum took them both to the ground. Jack raced to get to his knees, knowing that whichever one of them got up first would be the one to walk away from this. But the guy was too shocked and confused, his mind bent on trying to figure out what the hell had just happened, to recover quick enough. Jack punched him in the head once, twice. Then he grabbed a rock at his feet and brought it down on the man's head. Not hard enough to crack his skull (he hoped), but hard enough to knock him out. He quickly searched the guy's person and found a radio. He also found a knife and a pistol. He took them and ran for the ATV, which had rolled to a stop ten yards away. He needed to get going before the person driving ahead of him turned around.

He hopped onto the seat. It was another quad, a little different than Theo's, but all the buttons and pedals and levers were all in the same place. He started it up and got moving, making sure to keep some distance between him and the next guy.

He found that an AK-47 was strapped to the side of the ATV, and he suddenly felt better about his odds of making it to the cabin. These guys were not going somewhere to drink beer and shoot targets, they were—

His new radio crackled. He brought it to his ear.

"Hang in there! Ham called in backup for you! We're almost there, and we'll kick the Baker boys in the ass!"

Jack realized it was from someone in the convoy calling ahead to James and company. And the situation became clear. The gunshots he'd heard... Ham calling in reinforcements...

He was driving into a war zone.

97

STACEY HAD STOPPED AT a roadside diner and gotten dressed in the bathroom, so by the time she arrived at the party, she was already wearing the red dress. The private security who had checked her invitation at the entrance before letting her into the parking lot had a lot of trouble focusing on anything other than the low neckline. He didn't check the bag, which she'd discovered had a false bottom installed to hide the detonator. No way that guy would forget her. If he survived the blast, he'd be one of the eyewitnesses who would identify her car as being the one that exploded.

She stepped out of the car and looked up at the building, noting the windows two stories up. It would have to be quite a blast to take out the whole building. She reached into the car and grabbed the handbag. As she went to close the door, she paused, her eyes sweeping back and forth through the interior of the vehicle. Was this the last time she'd ever see it? Times spent in the car suddenly came back to her, and she saw Joseph sitting in the back seat. Jack in the passenger seat.

Jack in the passenger seat. Those times weren't often, because when they were all together, they usually took Jack's car, and Jack usually drove it. Not because he was a better driver (she'd been trained to drive by the CIA, after all) but because she knew it made him feel good to do it. Made him feel like he had some element of control within the family, which was good for him since she knew he was haunted by feelings of inadequacy. He was a salesman; she was a spy. And there was the whole cruise-ship thing she'd always be amending for. But there was one specific memory of when she had driven them all in this car that she was thinking about. A surprise trip to the beach on Father's Day, the car preloaded with food and drinks and Frisbees and footballs. Jack had gotten a pretty bad sunburn on his back, and on the way home he'd lain down on his chest in the passenger seat, trying not to move.

Emotion choked her for a second as her brain softened to the idea that this was it. She'd managed to hold it off for Joseph's sake, but now, with just an hour or so left in the hourglass that was her life, leaks were beginning to spring in her walls. She closed the door and looked up to the sky. To the sun. A few birds fluttered past. *This is the last time I will be outdoors, standing beneath the sky, breathing the fresh air.*

A gasp escaped her throat, and tears welled in her eyes. She clenched her fists and closed her eyes. The tears hit the blacktop. Taking a deep breath, she calmed herself. Then she started walking, the leaks plugged again.

Other guests were arriving, pulling into empty parking spots and leaving their vehicles behind as they escorted their dates across the lot and up the stairs to the main entrance, where someone in a tuxedo held the door open. Stacey fell in with them, noting that so far, she was the only person she'd spotted who was here without a guest. And then she felt it. Like a ton of bricks, it hit her. She was a suicide bomber. Walking to her target. She was the very person she'd spent her life trying to stop. She was the terrorist.

She looked at the people around her. Politicians. They made her sick, every one of them corrupt as far as she was concerned. And a barrier to the nation's safety. They were the ones who were always tying her hands behind her back while demanding impossible results. And for a split second, she was glad they'd all be dead by the end of the night.

She took the elevator to the second floor.

98

JACK FOLLOWED THEM UP the mountain, thanking God that he'd crossed paths with the riders right when he did. Had any detail of the last day taken even a minute longer, he would not have been in position to follow them up the mountain. If Stacey had answered the phone when he called, if the sheriff had five more minutes of information, if the guy in the pickup hadn't dropped him off where he had...

He tried to stop thinking about it as a sign. Maybe the guy in front of him would look back over his shoulder and shoot him in the head, and then none of it would have mattered at all, and he might as well have died back at the campsite on Tuesday.

A call went out over the radio, instructing half of the reinforcements to go help Colt and the other half to head for the cabin. As the ATVs split apart in front of him, Jack tried to guess which direction was which. Half of the convoy veered toward the right, following what might be a path. He went with them.

Five minutes later, they were through the tree line and climbing a grass hill. A cabin came into view.

Jack's heart hammered in his chest. He was so close now, closer than he ever thought he'd be. He could hardly believe it, and for a split second wondered again if he was still hanging over the fire, all of this a dream. Or maybe he was still home and the camping trip hadn't even taken place yet. Or he was five years old, Mom and Dad still alive and well, his entire life since nothing but a bizarre dream. He wasn't exactly sure why whenever something seemed to work out for him, he assumed he could be dreaming. *Maybe because I believed my beautiful wife married me simply because she loved me...*

He ignored his Jerry brain suggesting this was all a simulation in the Matrix, justified or not in thinking it, and focused on the cabin and what could be happening inside it.

There was a body lying in the grass beside the simple structure. It was mangled and bloody, bones sticking out of skin. James turned his head and stared at it as he passed by. It was a large man with a great white beard. He was still breathing, his chest rising and falling as if something was trying to get out of him.

Five of the ATVs came to a stop alongside the cabin. Their riders dismounted, drew their guns, and ran into the cabin. Jack stood back, waiting to see what would happen. He hopped off the vehicle, grabbed the AK-47, and went to the other side of the cabin. He ducked when he heard steps going back outside.

"You take that side. I'll take the side over there," he heard a voice say. Then engines started again, and two of the ATVs raced off in opposite directions. That left three of them still in the cabin.

Jack took JT's rifle off his shoulder and leaned it against the cabin. He set the AK-47 next to it. If Joseph was in there, he didn't want to go in spraying bullets all over the place. He checked both pistols, one in each hand, and took a deep breath.

He crept over to a window, turning the radio low, and put his back against the wall beside it. He turned his head and leaned over, trying to get a glimpse through the dirty glass. Someone walked past, and he pulled his head back. He glanced over the open land before him, noting the trees at the bottom of the hill, how they stretched into a blanket of thick forest that met with swells and swells of others before running against higher mountain ranges in the distance, the sun dropping quickly behind them. How long would Colt and the others be able to hold off Bakerville? And if they succeeded, how long before they'd be back? He needed to do this now.

He ran around to the front of the cabin, ducking low to stay beneath the windows. The two ATVs were down the hill and out of sight. Before going up the porch steps, Jack took one more look at the guy who was sprawled in the grass and struggling to breathe. He was on his stomach now, his head turned toward the side and...

He paused.

The guy was staring at him. One bulging eye fixed right on him, tracking him while his fingers twitched.

The door banged open behind him, and Jack spun sideways, throwing himself up against the cabin wall next to the porch, both guns coming up and ready to shoot.

One of the guys from the ATV walked down the steps, his focus entirely on Bulging Eye in the grass. "Lee Baker, is that really you?" he asked, walking closer to the man. "Well, I'll be damned. It is you!"

Jack waited until the guy was standing directly over the Baker brother before reaching up and climbing over the side of the porch. He quietly straddled the splintered banister and slipped through the doorway unseen.

He swept the pistols back and forth through the tiny cabin, looking for signs of occupants. He knew there were at least two more men in here somewhere.

No one was in the kitchen area or the room off it. He swung around and into a short hallway, doors on both sides. He stepped lightly across the wooden planking, hoping the boards wouldn't give him away. He opened the door on his right. A bathtub.

He turned to the door on the other side. Pushed it open.

The two men had their backs to him. They were talking to someone who was lying in a bed, bandaged and bleeding.

Jack locked eyes with the person in the bed, and when those eyes went wide with alarm, the two men got the signal and spun, raising their guns.

Jack targeted the man on his left first since he was turning around the fastest, a short semiauto in his hands already raised waist high. Both Jack's pistols went off, his fingers squeezing off two quick bursts from each. The first shot, fired from the rider's pistol in his right hand, missed and struck the wall behind the guy. But the second and third shots punched into the man's shoulder and side. The fourth shot, following just a hundredth of a second later, entered the guy's right eye and blew it out the back of his head.

Jack spun out of the doorway and back into the hallway before even seeing the contents of the skull splatter the wall or the body start to fall.

A shot from within the room blew a chunk out of the door frame beside him. His eye went blurry for a moment, and he rubbed it with the back of his left hand.

Another shot and the hallway was filled with splinters. He was about to take a couple of blind shots into the room, when he realized he hadn't seen Joseph yet. It was possible that he was in there. He didn't think it was likely, but he couldn't risk it. He needed to know where his son was before he could just start shooting away blind.

The guy who had gone outside came running back in. Jack shot him twice, and the man went twisting out of the kitchen and into the fireplace, striking his head against the stone mantel and crumpling awkwardly to the floor.

Jack ran down the hall and threw his back up against the kitchen wall. He quickly peered around the corner.

The hall was empty, the door at the end still open.

He had to figure the guys in the room had a radio, and if they called for help, he could find himself held up in the cabin like Butch and Sundance with no more hope of saving Joseph. He thought he could use tape from his belt pouch to depress the transmit button on his radio to block the frequency. But then everyone would just be able to hear them shooting at each other and whatever they might yell out. He could wrap it in the towel hanging next to the sink and then use the pot on the stove to cover it so that no one could hear...

But that would all take time. Instead, he fired a shot around the corner and yelled, "Where's my son?"

"What the hell you talkin' about?" the man yelled back.

Jack thought it could be possible that the guy might not actually know what he was talking about. But he didn't have time to waste, and he needed to take him out before he could call for help.

He bolted out the door, clearing the stairs, and landing in the grass already running. He sprinted to the back window and fired both guns through the empty square in the wall. Then he ran back to the kitchen and looked down the hallway. The guy was lying on his stomach, legs still in the room, his upper half in the hall. Jack shot him in the head. He felt bad, but...no chances. He tossed the empty gun.

He walked into the room, the other pistol now aimed at the guy in the bed, as he searched the small space. No Joseph. But he spotted the glass on the floor and noted the way the window had been nailed to the window frame.

"You the boy's father?" the man asked, and then coughed.

"Where is he?" Jack asked.

"Hot damn," he said, shaking his head. "Can't believe it."

Jack walked over beside the bed and put the pistol against his temple. "Where is my son?"

"We took care of him. Didn't hurt him none. Swear."

"Which one are you? Theo, Lawrence, and JT are dead, so you gotta be James or—"

"Michael."

"Okay, Michael, I'm not going to ask again." But of course that was a lie. He'd ask as many times as it took.

Michael sighed. "At first we thought we was hired by perverts who wanted to do some child sex thing, and we weren't okay with that. We'd never done anything like that before." He coughed, and the spasms made him sit up a little. "But then we hear 'bout your wife and Russians and such, and we know we're in over our heads. We don't know what the hell is going on. And then the Bakers, they decide to start takin' us out. Lee out there shot me. And we're wonderin', are the Bakers workin' for the Russians? No one knows." He looked at Jack. "Do you know, mister?"

Jack took a deep breath and then pressed the gun into the bullet hole in Michael's chest.

Michael gasped.

"I'm running out of time here, Michael, which means I'm just going to have to increase the pain." He stood and covered Michael's mouth with his empty hand while pushing even harder into the wound.

Michael screamed into his hand.

"Where is my son?" He lifted his hand from his mouth.

"I don't know. He took off into the woods. We was chasin' him when Lee shot me. James brought me back here."

"And then he went back out lookin' for Joseph?"

He nodded.

"Which direction?"

Michael closed his eyes, tears of pain leaking down his cheeks. Then he opened his eyes and moved them in a very specific direction. "That way."

"I should kill you," Jack said.

Michael didn't argue with him.

But Jack just left the room instead. He walked to the kitchen and retrieved the radio. Then he went back outside and down the steps. He saw patches of Lee's beard scattered all over the grass. The guy who had come out apparently had himself some fun before making the unwise decision to come back into the cabin. Jack stepped closer to Lee and saw that his tongue was hanging out of a hole in his neck. Like a tie.

He was still alive.

Jack shot him between the eyes.

He didn't feel bad about that one. He tossed the pistol and ran to the back of the cabin for the rifle and machine gun he'd left there. Then he got back on the quad and took off after James and Joseph.

As he flew down the hill, he heard the radio squawk.

"The boy's father is coming for you," Michael said.

99

COLT HEARD THE ATVS coming and so did the Bakers' gang. He watched from the high ground as they turned their attention from him to the newcomers. And that was Colt's opportunity to move.

He backed away from his position, staying low so as to remain out of any crosshairs, and began working his way down the rise where he could circle around and start picking off his enemies from their blindside one by one. He took a quick look at the sky on his way down and noted the sun's position. He figured he'd been here shooting at the Bakers for nearly an hour. He hadn't been trying to kill any of them, just keep them pinned down until reinforcements could arrive. He had been trying to conserve his ammo while getting them to spend as much as possible. Now that reinforcements had arrived, he was free to kill on his own terms.

At the bottom of the rise, he turned and followed along its base, heading for the trees. He'd use his knife to continue saving his bullets. He didn't know where Seth got off to, and he didn't know where Lee was, so he still had to plan for an eventual run-in with those two.

He came upon a small stream and skipped across scattered rocks. Then, once on the other side, he followed it around a ridge. The sounds of gunfire grew louder.

Since the Bakerville clan was focused on Ham's guys, Colt didn't have to worry about making noise. They wouldn't be able to hear him coming over the gunfight. So he ran as fast as he could, jumping over rocks and tearing through tangled foliage.

The first guy he spotted was about twenty yards away and aiming in the opposite direction, his back toward him. Colt put a hand over his mouth and slipped his thirteen-inch tactical knife into the guy's back. Pushed it until the blade punched out of his chest. Then he withdrew the knife, still covering his mouth, and reached around, stabbing under the armpit once, twice, three times. The guy dropped his gun, and Colt spun him around and slammed him up against the tree. He stabbed him in the throat and tore the knife sideways, out through the side of his neck. Colt dropped him to the ground, picked up his gun, and went searching for the next guy.

100

JOSEPH HEARD THE ATV coming long before he got a glimpse of it. He wasn't sure where he was heading, just away from the cabin. The sun was going down, and the forest floor was getting darker. Soon he would have to find a place to sleep and then continue on in the morning. Despite his socked feet, he smiled at the thought of it. He'd find a place he could build a fire. Just like the one they'd built the other day. A Dakota firepit. Underground so there wasn't much smoke. Maybe he'd come across a stream, and he could catch a fish. He was sure finding a worm out here wouldn't be a problem, especially with how moist the ground was. A hook though... He sighed. If only he still had his book. But of course, all that depended on not getting caught again.

He spotted a tree that must've been uprooted in the storm. It was huge, the trunk almost as wide as he was tall. A large portion of the ground was still held together by its roots, leaving a massive hole in the ground. He ran over to it, hopping over sticker bushes, and slid down into the hole. It was so deep that when he crouched down, his head disappeared under ground. And speaking of bait, there were bugs everywhere. Wriggling worms, slithering centipedes, and all other sorts of insects. He wondered if he would get desperate enough to try eating some. But after not being able to get the worm down earlier, he doubted it. Not for a couple more days at least.

The sound of the ATV grew louder, and he risked a peek out from behind the uprooted earth. He saw a headlight flashing between trees. It was coming toward him, but it was far enough to his left that the driver should pass by his position half a football field away.

He ducked back down and rolled into a ball, pushing his back up against the side of the hole.

The engine got louder and louder and then began to fade. He lay completely still until he couldn't hear it anymore. Then he got back to his feet and climbed out of the hole. He looked around, but it was pointless. There wasn't anything that gave him any clue as to which way he should head. He could tell which way the sun was dropping and knew that was west. His mom and dad, the campsite, his house, was all to the east, he was sure. Though maybe not. Maybe they were north. Or south. He actually had no clue where they'd driven him, and he'd been too out of it to search for street signs and other clues.

He needed to find a town or a phone, but had no idea which direction the nearest town would be and which direction would only lead to more wilderness. If he came to water, he could follow water. Water always led to something eventually. But in the meantime, he decided it was better to head in one direction than in many. So he decided on west since he could chase the sun until dark.

He was glad he was free, and truth be told, he couldn't help but feel a little excited being out here on his own just like the characters in his favorite books. At least it was summer. Winter would be a totally different story. Yet he couldn't help thinking about his dad. Where was he? Was he okay?

"I'm coming home, Mom," he whispered. "I'm coming home, Dad."

101

THE ROOM WAS PACKED with round tables, each one with a centerpiece. Stacey didn't have a clue what the occasion was, what the senator had to say. She imagined he was going to say something, because there was a podium with a microphone and a speaker set up at the front of the room. Each table looked to seat about six people, and there were at least fifteen tables set up throughout the room. The tables were filling up fast as the guests continued to come off the elevator. Everyone was dressed for the occasion. The men were in suits, the women in their best Oscar-worthy impersonations. But no one else had a Ferrari-red backless dress painted on them, and all eyes went to her as the newcomers passed her table on the way to theirs.

Stacey watched them watch her. And sure, she'd be lying if she didn't get some sense of gratification out of their envy and lust. As a woman in the spy business, she had learned to view her body as an asset. The number of eyes she attracted just reaffirmed how great an asset it was.

Except that in this case, her assets were working against her. Not that any of these people would survive to talk about it (unless someone were to send photos off into cyberspace). Or maybe they would. The voice on the phone had said the explosion should be enough to level the building, yet they wanted him over by the wall her car was parked against just in case. That got her thinking. What kind of explosives were they using? She figured it could be anything. A nuke even. Though what would be the point in all the foreplay if it was a nuclear bomb? The death of the senator would be lost in the masses of other casualties. No, a false-flag nuclear attack would only serve as an instigation for nuclear war, and she didn't think that was what this was.

She wondered when they'd put it in the car. The same time as the phone? What if it wasn't in the car at all? What if they'd just told her that? It could be anywhere. Could be in the podium, and she was meant to detonate it when he was all the way across the room. If the bomb wasn't that big, he might survive. What if she didn't have the only detonator? What if they had a backup in place to ensure the bomb went off if she got cold feet? What if the bomb was never meant to go off, and the FBI would be storming the room any minute to apprehend her and save the day? Of course, they'd never take her in alive. They'd kill her for "trying to escape" or some such nonsense.

What if.

What if.

What if.

She spotted the senator as he walked through a door across the room. She saw his eyes scan the room, searching for—

Yup. His eyes stopped right on her red dress, and a slight smile pulled at the corner of his lips. It was quite obvious he'd only been thinking of one thing since she left him. And now, seeing her in the dress, even from across a dimly lit room, that thought had just climbed into another stratosphere.

People were suddenly around her, pulling out chairs and sitting at the table. Two men with two women. The men were trying not to stare at her, while the women were watching the men to see if they could. When they weren't watching their husbands (she assumed that was what all the rings meant), they were giving her the evil eye. Jealousy or protective instincts, she wasn't sure. Both, probably. Not that the women were in bad shape. But they weren't in a bright red dress with their assets hanging out.

"You're here alone?" the woman on her left asked. Her tone wasn't mean, but it wasn't friendly either.

She wasn't sure what she was supposed to say because there was an empty seat next to her. So she just shrugged and nodded at the vacant chair.

The woman thought she understood. "Ah. Something came up?"

Stacey decided to play her role. Why not? She didn't like any of these people anyway. She smirked. "You could say that. Then his wife walked in."

The woman's eyes went wide, and she turned her head away.

"If you'll excuse me, I'm going to get something from the bar," Stacey said. "Would you like anything?" But she didn't wait for an answer. She walked through the tables, soaking in all the stares, and approached the bar in the back of the room. The bartender smiled when he saw her coming, and she smiled back. "Vodka on the rocks, please."

He smiled and poured her the drink. "Nice dress," he said.

"Thanks. Probably a little much for something like this. I've never been invited to one of these before. You see a lot of them?" She turned her bare back to him and leaned against the bar as she took a sip from the glass.

"A few."

"So how does it go? Some aspiring politician gets up and gives some lame speech about how he has plans to make the world a better place and he appreciates all the people who've helped get him there?"

"Something like that. Though this is a birthday party for the senator."

She turned and faced him. "Really?"

"You didn't know?"

"I was the date of a guest who just called me and told me he wasn't going to make it. He had to take his mother to the ER."

"Oh, damn."

"Yeah. So here I am. I should probably just leave."

"Why would you do that? Free drinks all night."

She drained the glass and turned around to face him. Leaned against the counter and slid the empty glass in his direction. His eyes couldn't help themselves, and she watched them watch her as her dress did all it could to contain her breasts. She smiled. "Hey, bartender..." She lifted the glass an inch before clanking it down against the bar.

"Sorry," he said. Though it was obvious he wasn't sorry at all. He poured another two fingers.

"Oh, just fill the thing," she said.

He laughed. "Whatever you say." And he filled it to the brim.

"Well, guess I should get back to my table." She started to walk away, then looked back over her shoulder. "I'm sure I'll be back."

"Please," he said. And he actually winked at her.

She drained half the glass before getting back to the table. Her handbag was still where she'd left it, under her seat and leaning against the right front leg of the chair. Not that she'd ever really taken her eye off it. She sat.

The senator was making his rounds, shaking hands and giving hugs. She figured he'd be over by the window in about twenty minutes.

Twenty minutes.

A bead of sweat broke out across her forehead, and she took another gulp of vodka. *Twenty minutes left to live,* she thought. *Shit.* She finished the glass and got back up. Walked to the bar again. "Think I need another one."

The bartender suddenly looked concerned. "You okay?"

"You tell me. You think I'm okay?"

He laughed. "I think you're more than okay. You're like Kate Beckinsale in her prime."

She wasn't sure if he just dated himself or dated her. He was in his late twenties. Probably working nights to put himself through law school or something. "Kate Beckinsale is always in her prime. Fill me up."

He stared at her.

"With vodka, Romeo."

He filled her glass again, and she returned once more to her table. The heels she was wearing a little less sturdy for this round trip.

The waiters and waitresses appeared with large silver trays filled with plates. She almost ran into one before she reached her seat. "Excuse me," she said. The two couples at her table obviously knew each other and were lost in a discussion about foreign oil.

Stacey looked around the room, listening to all the chatter. She saw the senator, that cheating bastard, still making his way through the tables, getting nearer and nearer to the window. She looked at her watch. It was 7:30. She reached down for the handbag when a piece of a conversation from a table behind her caught her ear.

"...we haven't had a night out in six months. How old is *your* son?"

"He just turned five. His little sister will be three next month, so we know what you mean about not getting out."

Laughter.

She sat up and risked a glance behind. Put faces to voices. Her heart started to pound. These people had no clue they were all about to die. For Joseph. Her son. For her hopes and dreams for him. Not that those dreams would be realized in the same way she'd imagined, but she could see him in her mind's eye all the same. Playing high school sports, the prom, graduation, college, meeting the girl of his dreams, starting a family...

But then she looked at each of the faces around her, and for the first time, realized that they had all of the same hopes and dreams for their own kids as she had for hers. She'd never cared before. About the collateral damage. It went with the whole "the ends justify the means" mantra that she'd always lived by. Even when it had involved the life of her husband. She didn't have a problem with Trenton or any other place that required innocent lives to be sacrificed for the greater good. And these people here... Were they even that innocent? Maybe. Maybe not. But was *she*? No, she sure as hell wasn't. But Joseph was. *And so is the boy who just turned five and his little sister*, a voice whispered in her head.

"Did you hear me?" the woman asked her.

"Excuse me?"

"I asked how you knew Doug."

"Oh." She wiped her head. "Work."

"Really?"

She took another drink. "Through work, I should say."

Her brow wrinkled in thought, trying to place her answer with whatever it was she knew of the senator's life.

"Who are you?" Stacey asked. She hadn't meant to be so blunt, but the drink was starting to take over.

"I'm Doug's sister," she said.

"Oh."

"Are you okay?"

But before she could answer, Doug was right behind her, his hands on her shoulders.

"I see you've met Stacey," he said to the rest of the table. "Stacey, this is my sister, Heather, and her husband, Paul. This ugly dufus is my older brother Byron and his wife, Jill."

Heather looked up at him, her eyes lingering just a moment on her brother's hands and the toned flesh beneath them. "She was just saying she knows you through work."

He nodded. "Stacey works for the Agency. She's helping catch me up to speed on what's happening in the world. She's on the same page when it comes to our national interests."

For a second Stacey thought he was going to slip his hands forward and right down the front of her dress. And then the whole table would start laughing, everyone in on the infidelity and thinking it a joke. But he didn't, and they hadn't. Instead, Heather shot her brother a look that threatened recourse if she were to ever find out that the lady in the red dress was anything more than political leverage.

He bent over and quickly whispered in her ear, "I'll see you later."

She smiled and raised her glass.

"He's married, you know," Heather said after the senator had moved to another table.

"Heather," her husband snapped.

"Oh, please," she said, shooting him a daring look. "Look what she's wearing, for god's sake."

But Stacey wasn't listening anymore. She was watching Douglas move closer to the window. He was two tables away now. She reached into the handbag and pulled out the detonator. Set it in her lap.

She drained the rest of the glass, and her head began to swim. The voices around her became muffled and distant. Her mind loosened. *Joseph.* It was for Joseph.

She rested her thumb on the button.

All these people. All their hopes and dreams. Their families. All of it gone with just one small flick of her thumb. What power. What terrifying power.

She wondered what would come next. She never believed anything would come next, but now that thought bothered her for some reason. She'd never see Joseph again. Never reunite with her daughter. Jack...

Or...what if Jack's grandmother was right? What if there was something after all this?

Her head spun and spun.

She didn't want to die. She didn't want all these people to die.

But they'll cut Joseph into little pieces and mail you parts of him for years to come.

She squeezed the detonator, her thumb twitching.

They might kill him anyway. And if they don't, they said they would raise him as their own. Which could be a fate worse than death for a small boy.

She looked back over her shoulder, still ignoring whatever Doug's family was saying, and looked at the bartender as he poured drinks for an older man who had his hand around the waist of an older woman. Doug's mom and dad? Aunt and uncle?

Stacey turned back and interrupted whatever Heather was in the middle of saying. "Do you have kids?"

Heather blinked and exchanged a quick glance with Jill. "Yes," she answered, a little shocked at the sudden question and the blunt way it had been asked. "We both do."

Stacey looked over at Douglas. He was standing at the table closest to the window, his back just two feet from it, her car and the bomb directly below him. He was smiling and shaking hands. "Where's his wife?" she asked.

"Doug's? She's with her father. He's in the hospital."

"And he still had a party for himself?"

This time it was Byron who answered. "His wife is the one who arranged the party. She didn't want to cancel."

Well, she thought, *it wasn't his wife who wrote the note on the invitation, that was for sure.* She figured Doug snatched it out of the pile and had it sent himself. To whatever address she'd supposedly given him, only for it to end up in a Gucci bag outside a hotel room door.

Byron leaned forward. "Are you okay? You don't look so good. Had a little too much to drink, maybe?"

She closed her eyes, feeling every second tick by as if it were a minute. She savored the smell of the food being served, the faint music, the sounds of voices and laughter...and knew she'd never sense any of it again. "I love you, Joseph," she whispered, and she—

Paused.

Her thumb was on the button, but she didn't press it. She couldn't.

She opened her eyes, placed the detonator back in the handbag, and ran a hand through her hair.

"Who's Joseph?" Jill asked.

"I'm sorry, would you excuse me?" She grabbed the bag, stood, and headed for the restroom.

102

COLT STOOD OVER LEE'S body and savored the sight. Bonkers Baker... How fitting that someone had gone bonkers on him. He was twisted like a pretzel with bones sticking out of his skin, his beard was cut, and his tongue was hanging out of his neck. He just hoped that whoever had done it to him had done it before putting the bullet between his eyes. He was a little upset that he hadn't had the pleasure of doing it himself, and he spit on the corpse before entering the cabin.

He caught a glimpse of himself in the reflection of the kitchen window as he passed. There was blood all over him, but none of it was his. He swept the pistol back and forth as he continued out of the kitchen, searching for James, Michael, and the boy.

All he found was Michael.

"Where's James?" he asked as he went to the bed and looked over Michael's wounds.

Michael opened his eyes. "The boy took off. We was chasin' after him when Lee shot me." He coughed. "James took care of him and then went after the boy."

Colt examined where the bullet had hit him. If there was a medic around, he'd probably be okay. But he was no medic. "You need a doctor, Michael."

Michael closed his eyes. "It'll be dark soon. How the hell am I gonna get to a doctor?"

Colt spoke through the radio. "James, do you copy?"

"He hasn't been answerin'," Michael wheezed. "Must be down in a valley or somethin'."

"Well, most of Ham's boys and most of Bakerville all just killed each other. Seth's still out there though."

"The boy's father too."

Colt knelt beside the bed. "What?"

"He's here. The boy's father. He came into the cabin. I told him we didn't know nothin' about what was going on."

"Where'd he go?"

"After his son."

So the boy was out there with his father and James looking for him. And Seth was out there too somewhere, though who knew what the hell he was up to. And then there were the Russians, who might or might not come to kill them all. "C'mon, I'm getting you off this damn mountain." He helped Michael sit up and then wrapped his arm around his back, put Michael's arm around his neck. They limped out of the cabin and to one of the remaining ATVs.

Colt took a look at the sky, noting how close the sun was to being penetrated by the jagged horizon.

103

JACK DROVE SLOWLY, ONE hand on the accelerator, the other holding his flashlight. It was getting dark quick, and the remaining light that still filled the sky was mostly lost in shadow down on the forest floor. He had no idea which direction his son was heading in, but if he had to guess, there was one guess that he thought was better than all the others.

West.

His son knew more about wilderness survival than he did. Yeah, he had been showing him how to hold the knife, and swing the axe, and everything else he'd been reading in preparation for their trip, but Joseph had read a lot more than he had, and he was counting on the fact that his son would know it was better to head in one consistent direction than to just wander aimlessly through the mountains. And with the sun setting, a westward heading would be the easiest way to go.

But still, a general direction out here was no guarantee that he'd catch up to him. He could pass him a mile to the left if their heading was just a few degrees different. So he decided to yell, calling for his son at the top of his lungs and waving the flashlight back and forth. He knew there was the real possibility that James would hear him first. Maybe he already had and was trailing him, waiting for him to find Joseph before coming up on both of them with gun drawn. *Jack, lie down on your stomach with your hands out. Joseph, you come over to me.*

But it was a chance he had to take. The second he heard Joseph's voice call out to him, he would go as fast as he could, and he would be ready. He would embrace his son, and then they would drop to the ground and hide. They would spend all night working their way down the mountain, crawling on their stomachs if they had to.

He called out again.

And again.

The trees stared back at him, their arms outstretched in a clueless gesture under the circle glow of the flashlight.

Somewhere an eagle screamed.

104

STACEY FOLLOWED THE senator's family out the doors and into the parking lot.

"I don't think you should drive," Heather said.

"I'm fine," Stacey said.

"You're not. You drank half a bottle of vodka."

Stacey waved her off. "Child's play."

"I'm serious. You can't drive like this."

"She's right," Byron said. "Give me your keys."

You want the keys to the bomb? She wasn't sure if she'd said that out loud or not, but he didn't blink, so she guessed not. She looked around the parking lot and happened to spot the bartender. "Ah! I'll get him to drop me off."

They followed her gaze and saw the guy walking to his car. When she started walking toward him, they didn't stop her.

"Hey, Romeo," she called out.

The bartender looked up and over the roof of his car. Saw her coming and smiled.

"I think it's your civic duty, especially since you served me, to make sure I get home safely. Or maybe if I get killed, you could be held culpi-ba-ble." She dragged the word out and stumbled over it.

"Yeah, okay. Get in."

Stacey turned and called back to the others, who were all standing around watching her stumble toward the bartender's car. She waved to them. "Hear that? He's gonna give me a ride."

She could hear them all thinking, "He sure is." But they all started moving again, and soon they were getting into their own vehicles.

She dropped into the passenger seat and closed the door, aware that her dress was practically up around her waist. "So," she said, looking over at him.

"So," he answered back.

She crossed her legs, took off one high heel, then crossed the other leg and took that one off too. She sighed in relief.

"Where do you live?" he asked.

She looked out the passenger window and watched Heather and company drive away. "Actually..." She leaned over and kissed him on the cheek. "I think I'm fine. Thanks anyway." She threw open the door and got out. She ran to her car, stilettos in hand. Once inside, she opened the glove box and took out the phone. She had to squint to see the screen, and it was either 14 missed calls or 4141 missed calls. She went to return the call, and stopped just before tapping the screen.

What if they'd done it? What if they'd killed her baby boy?

The phone rang in her hand, and she answered it.

"What happened?"

Even with the synthesizer, she could tell the person was pissed.

"Nothing happened. I pushed the button, and nothing happened, you piece of shit. Where's my son?"

"You think for one second we believe that?"

"I don't care what you believe. What did you do with my son?"

Silence.

"What did you do with my son?" she screamed, striking the steering wheel with her hands and kicking the floor mat with her bare feet. "I'll go to the CIA, the Feds, the *Washington Post.* I'll tell the whole fucking world what you're doing. I don't care who you are. You can be the NSA for all I care, and I'll expose you to the world, motherf—"

"He is still alive. We have not harmed him. But your threats are meaningless. No one would ever find us. You would only be exposing your own history."

"How do you know—"

Again the voice cut her off. *"Shut up and listen. Go back to the senator's house and kill him there. We will not speak again. If the senator is not dead by sunrise, your son dies. Goodbye."*

The line went dead.

105

JAMES WAS WORRIED ABOUT Michael. But if he didn't get the boy, then there would be nowhere he could take him where the people behind all this wouldn't find him and kill him anyway. Ham was dead, and who knew how much of his gang was left? Colt could be dead too. Hell, Michael could already be dead. Leaving just him.

He drove at a crawling pace, the headlights on the ATV reaching out and illuminating the dark labyrinth of dense forest ahead of him. He thought about making a run for it. He could survive out here in the wilderness. Head north or east. He could even go west and cross over the Mississippi, take the old Oregon Trail. The possibilities seemed endless, and all a lot more promising than staying here and messing around with the boy.

But he couldn't just leave Michael. Not when his mother's dying words were for him to care for his baby brother. Which was what he'd always done. Sometimes for his brother, but always for his momma. The thing buried in his backyard that Ham thought was something they'd had in common wasn't actually his doing. He wasn't sure what Ham thought happened, where he got the story from, but James had thought it beneficial to let him keep thinking it. In reality, however, it was Michael who had run over a boy in his truck, an empty six-pack on the floor in front of the passenger seat. The kid had been walking down the side of the road with a fishing pole over his shoulder and never knew what hit him. Michael was hysterical, but James had known the kid. Had even given him a ride a couple of times. The boy's mother didn't have a husband,

and he had been working on getting up the courage to ask her out. Instead, he buried her son in his backyard and never saw her again. He could've killed Michael himself, but Momma said...

He was just about to head back to the cabin when he heard a man's voice in the distance, calling out for his son.

106

SHE MADE IT BACK to the senator's place without driving into oncoming traffic. She was drunk, but she'd always been a functional drunk. Her hand-eye coordination suffered a little, and her reflexes wouldn't be as quick, but she was a trained operative, and the few notches she dropped while drunk still left her head and shoulders above most of the world's population when it came to hand-to-hand combat. Or anything else for that matter. A lot of the things she had done for her country had been done while intoxicated. She was used to it. Well, she *had* been used to it. Since Trenton, her operations had slowed significantly, and she had gotten older. Eight years older. But her mind, if not her body, still moved through the foggy seas as it always had. Though she wondered if she'd even know the difference. Maybe her thought process was only coherent to her current state. How would she even know? *In my defense, I thought I was just getting trashed to push a button.*

Whatever. She replayed the party in her mind, the parts that stuck out and made some kind of sense anyway. The senator knew her name. Not her actual name, but the American name she'd been using since arriving in the States. She wasn't sure why that surprised her. Maybe because it raised other questions about what he knew. Did he know she was married? Would it surprise her if he did? No, of course not. The person on the other end of the telephone knew her actual name. And who else could know that but the SVR and the CIA? Maybe the FBI? But she didn't see the FBI orchestrating something like this. Yeah, they occasionally set people up by recruiting, training, and equipping them into terrorist activities just so they could stop them at the last second and look like the hero. But this was something a lot bigger than that.

Or maybe a lot smaller.

That thought rang in her head like an Oriental gong. But before she could unwrap it, she realized she was already in the senator's garage.

She got out, still in her bare feet, and stepped up through the same door the senator had welcomed her through earlier. She heard music coming from the room with the fireplace, a faint piano mix that she supposed he thought was sexy. Seemed there was a whole routine for this. She hoped she wouldn't enter the room and find other naked women with him. That would complicate things. She was more than prepared to kill the senator for Joseph. She might have been surprised to discover a moral compass at the bottom of her glass tonight, but that moral compass wasn't spinning now. Not for this guy. She'd end his life without thinking twice. For Joseph. For country. For whatever excuse she could get.

That's just the vodka talking.

Is it?

She entered the room with the grand piano and the fireplace and the couch she'd sat on earlier, and there he was. Another drink in hand. Wearing a black silk robe. *He really is so cliche*, she thought and almost laughed out loud. Yet she was glad it wasn't another darker cliche. She'd been to some *Eyes Wide Shut* events before, and she was glad she hadn't walked into that shit. If she had, she would've gotten back in the car and drove it through the garage wall and into the middle of the room before hitting the detonator. Send them all to hell where they could worship their god face-to-face forever.

"I thought maybe my siblings scared you away," Douglas said, walking toward her, the fireplace roaring behind him.

"Nah, they were nice," she said. He laughed and handed her the drink. She took it and was surprised to find that it was warm. "What is it?"

"A little espresso concoction I came across in college."

She smelled it. "Liqueur?"

"Among other things. Thought you could use some caffeine."

She took a sip. It was good, she had to give him that. And it cleared her head a little.

He moved around behind her and put his hands on her shoulders. Slipped a finger beneath one of the straps and moved it over. Kissed the skin beneath it.

She drank more, the heat of it seeming to blow the fog away. As he did the same thing to her left shoulder, she started scanning the room. Looking for a weapon.

The straps were off her shoulders and hanging in the crook of her arms.

There was the fireplace itself. She was sure she could work him into it, but that would be messy and loud. He wouldn't go easily. If she could get him over toward it, she could smash his head against the stone, crack his skull open. Then maybe she could push him into the flames.

He straightened her arms and ran his hands down to her wrists, taking the straps along for the ride. The front of the dress fell away. He reached around, tracing curves with his fingers.

She closed her eyes as her body started to respond. She'd always hated that. The way her body could betray her mind. When alcohol and certain buttons were combined, even with the most vile and disgusting men... But it made the job easier, and it was all for God and country anyway, right?

And this is for Joseph.

She didn't need to allow this though. She could just turn around and throat punch him.

Maybe.

Maybe not. She didn't really know anything about him, and when you didn't know your enemy, the worst thing to do was to underestimate him. What if she turned around to punch him and he blocked it? Then what? What if that was actually a dagger in his robe? What if he'd drugged her drink? What if he had his own plans of putting her in the fireplace when he was done with her?

No, it was a lot easier to take out a target while in the throes of sex. So she let him touch her, and let her body do whatever it did in response. It was what she'd been trained to do so long ago. She opened her eyes and started looking for more things she could use to kill him.

"Wait," she whispered, tilting her head to the side so that her hair hung down over her shoulder.

He kept going.

She grabbed his hands and stopped them from moving. "Where's the ladies' room?"

He turned her around so that she was facing him. He looked her up and down, appraising. "That way. Down the hall on the right." He nodded his head.

She leaned forward and kissed him. "I'll be right back." She walked out of the room, not fixing her dress until she was in the bathroom, letting him watch. There was a sink on top of a cabinet with a center drawer between. There was a shower, a toilet, and a towel rack.

As she sat on the toilet to relieve herself, she moved her eyes around the room. There had to be something here she could use as a weapon. She finished and went to the sink. Turned on the water for some cover noise. She opened the drawer and found some brushes, a curling iron, and other useless things. Must be his wife's. Or maybe his wife didn't even know about this place and it was just where he lived with his girlfriends.

She knelt and opened the cabinet doors. Towels, washcloths, soap, nail polish, hairdryer, petroleum jelly... She found what she was looking for.

A nail file.

Stainless steel, tapered into a point. She'd take him to bed and let him get on top of her. When he closed his eyes, she'd shove it into his throat. Then, while he was holding his neck, confused and shocked at the blood squirting all over the place, she would grab the bedsheets and wrap them around his head. From there, she would be able to do whatever she wanted to him. Stab him through the ear, bash his head into the nearest sharp object, strangle him, suffocate him...

She flushed the toilet, turned the water off, and slipped the file down the crack of her ass. She'd have to keep her glutes contracted and keep his hands away from them, but she was confident it would work.

Then what?

She didn't know. They'd find out somehow and let Joseph go like they said they would. And then she would... *Go back home and pretend nothing happened and wait for the FBI to come breaking down my door? Or do I go on the run? Get a new identity and disappear? Could I do that? Leave Joseph behind? Do I have a choice?*

She shook her head. First things first. She opened the door and walked back into the room.

And found the senator lying on the floor next to the couch, his eyes closed.

She walked over and started to kneel down to check on him, thinking he'd passed out or maybe had a heart attack, when a voice startled her.

"So this is what you do, huh?"

She looked up and watched a man step forward out of the shadows next to the fireplace.

It was Agent Johnson.

107

JACK SAW IT FOR just a second—a flash of light in the distance, fractured by a thousand obstacles that filled the space between them. He braked and shut off the headlights. Turned off the flashlight and slipped off the seat. He took his knife out and started moving through the dark, working his way through a sea of tall ferns, ducking low so that they brushed his elbows.

Why wasn't the light still flashing?

Because whoever was behind it heard you hollering and shut it off, same as you.

Which meant they were hunting each other. Had they just heard his voice, or had they seen the light too? They could be walking straight into each other.

He heard a twig snap not that far away. Maybe within twenty yards. Could the other guy see him? His palms were sweating, his grip on the knife slippery.

He could shoot in the direction of the sound, but if he missed, he'd be giving away his location. Or worse, it could be Joseph out there.

He could think of only one thing to do. He turned his head back toward the way he'd come and softly called out, "James?" He wasn't sure if the trick would work or not, if he could successfully "throw" his voice, but it was worth a shot. Maybe it would sound like he was further away than he really was.

"That you, Jack?" a voice came back.

Jack recognized the voice from the radio. "You took my son and tried to kill me," he said, turning his head again.

"I'm sorry about that."

"Are you? Then what are you doing out here looking for him?"

"Actually, I was just 'bout to head back. My brother's been shot pretty bad, and he needs my help."

"Yeah, I saw him."

They were both silent for a minute.

"You've got a smart boy," James said.

"There's nothing in this for you anymore. They're just gonna kill you when you hand him over."

"Wasn't plannin' on givin' him over. Just needed him to buy us some time to get outta here."

"Could still work."

"Unless they find him first."

"Well, if they find him first, we both lose," Jack said.

"What would the Reds want with your son, anyway?"

"Leverage. To get my wife to do something for them."

"To further the Communist agenda."

"I guess."

Another pause. "I got no love for the Commies, Jack. And I really wasn't all that thrilled with this business of kidnappin' your son to begin with. Now if you're willin' to let bygones be bygones, I'll leave you to findin' him, and I'll be gettin' back to my brother."

Jack's head spun. Was the guy being sincere? James's best chance was to run, and having Joseph with him wouldn't be good for that. He'd just slow him down. And this guy didn't seem insane like Cullin, someone who just wanted to kill people for the sheer pleasure of watching them die.

Jack didn't really have a choice unless he was willing to get into a gunfight right now, in the dark and unable to see anything. He needed to find Joseph and get off this damn mountain as soon as possible to try to stop Stacey from doing whatever it was they wanted her to do. If she hadn't done it already.

"Your wife works for the CIA. Is that right?" James asked.

Jack knew Lawrence had texted him everything he'd said. "She used to."

"Well, Jack, I'm pretty sure my best chance at getting outta this whole mess is if you do too. You were supposed to be dead. You ain't. Neither's your boy. If the two of you make it out of here, maybe you can help bring the wrath of God down on these KGB f—"

James stopped talking in mid-sentence.

108

"WHAT THE HELL DID you do?" Stacey asked.

Johnson held up a syringe. "He's just sleeping." Her mind was reeling, and he could see it in her eyes. "I went to your house," he said.

"What?"

He reached into his pocket and pulled out a cell phone. Held it up.

Stacey stepped forward. "That's my cell."

"Yeah. Jack called."

She blinked, and her knees went week. The room seemed to spin. Her heart skipped a beat. "What?"

"He left you a message." He tossed her the phone.

She caught it out of reflex and held it in two shaking hands. She moved her thumbs over the screen and then brought the phone to her ear. Her eyes tracked Johnson as he maneuvered the senator's body onto the couch, but her brain wasn't processing it. All of her attention was on the voice coming through the phone.

When the message ended, she played it again. This time with tears running down her face. She walked over to the nearest chair and sat. "He's alive," she whispered.

"Well, he was when he left the message, but who knows what he's gotten himself into since," Johnson said, walking over to her.

She looked up from beneath a lake of tears and had to blink to bring him into focus. "Why?" She shook her head. "I mean, what...do you want?"

"I want you to not kill me. That would be the first and only thing I really want."

The cold, black-op spy-bitch act was gone. She looked away. "I'm not going to kill you, Agent Johnson."

"Good. Not sure if I totally believe you, but it's still nice to hear."

She looked back at him. "So after I called—"

"I knew something was wrong, and there are a few scenarios that come immediately to mind when people like you say they're in trouble—"

"I never said I was in trouble."

He held up a hand. "You were drunk. More drunk than you are right now." He looked back at the senator. "Were you really going to—?"

"Nail him?" She leaned forward and reached behind her. Brought out the nail file. "Yeah."

"Then what?"

She shrugged.

He walked across the room and to a sliding glass door. He opened it and stepped out, then returned with a small duffel bag. He threw it at her feet. "Get out of that thing."

She unzipped the bag and saw some of her clothes folded neatly inside. "Thanks," she muttered, and began to slip out of the red dress.

"Damn, Stacey, right here?" Johnson asked, a little embarrassed and shocked.

Stacey looked up at him, only in the black lace panties, and gave a tired smile. "Shame, insecurity, sex...when you've been through what I've been through, trained for what I was trained for, those things tend to lose their meaning."

He walked away as she pulled on a T-shirt and a pair of jeans. He went to the bar that was beside the kitchen. "What was he drinking earlier?"

She stood and buttoned the jeans. "I didn't see—"

"When you were here. Before the party."

She wanted to ask him a hundred questions, but now was not the time. "Rum, I think."

He grabbed a bottle and walked to the kitchen. He poured out half the bottle into the sink and then came back to the senator. He spilled some of the rum on his robe, poured some into his mouth. Then he stood the bottle on the floor beside the couch and positioned his hand around the bottle's neck.

"You think he'll fall for that?" she asked.

He pulled a thong out from his back pocket and placed it on the arm of the couch, next to his head. "Well, we'll just have to hope he values his privacy, won't we?"

She smiled. "Where did you get those?"

"I picked them up on the way over."

"You took the tag off, right?"

He walked in front of her and looked her in the eye. "Look, I can't say that I like you very much. I know what you did."

For a split second, she felt the instinct to plant a knee between his legs and strike his nose with the palm of her hand on his way down. But it vanished just as quickly as it came. "Then why are you here?"

"I'm here to help Jack and Joseph. Just like I did before."

"Why? Aren't you exposing yourself?"

"To whom? The Agency?" He laughed. "They don't care about me."

"They know you were the one who called that radio station."

He shrugged. "That was a long time ago. I've moved on. I'm not worth the expense."

"So then what's your plan?"

"First, we have to get rid of your car."

"There's a bomb in it."

He blinked.

"Yeah, I have a detonator in my handbag. I was supposed to blow up the party. I didn't. They gave me one more chance to kill him before tomorrow morning."

He grabbed her elbow. "C'mon, we have a lot to do and very little time to do it."

As she followed him out of the house and to her car, she asked, "What if they're watching?"

"Then they're watching. Nothing we can do about that. Now let's go. We've got a plane to catch, but first we need to put your car at the bottom of a lake."

"A lake?"

"There's one on the way. I'm parked down the road off to the side." He pointed. "Just follow me."

"But—"

"We'll talk after the lake. No time now."

He turned and ran down the driveway, disappearing in the dark.

Stacey got in the car.

Jack was alive.

She whispered a thank you into the night.

109

JAMES KNEW THE BOY'S father was just in front of him, that he was trying to throw his voice. It actually worked the first time. The guy was smart. James could fire his gun at his position if he wanted to, shoot him dead. But he didn't want to. There'd be no point. All the guy wanted was his boy back, and he couldn't blame him for that. Besides, if the guy got his boy back and reported the whole thing to the police, then maybe the Feds would come down here and exterminate these Russian bastards. They'd never find him, and if they got the Reds off his back, then he wouldn't have to spend the rest of his life looking over his shoulder. The FBI wouldn't give two turds about some non-militia West Virginian hillbilly who disappeared into the wilderness with his wounded brother.

"So we good?" the boy's father asked.

"Well, Jack, I'm pretty sure my best chance at gettin' out of this whole mess is if you do too. You were supposed to be dead. You ain't. Neither is your boy. If the two of you make it out of here, maybe you can help bring the wrath of God down on these KGB f—"

Something rustled behind him.

He turned.

Saw the boy standing there just two feet in front of him while simultaneously feeling an explosion in his guts.

He looked down and saw something coming out of his stomach. His eyes followed it all the way into the boy's hands.

They stared at each other without speaking.

James could bring his gun up and blow the kid's head off. Could reach forward and strangle him. But why? He never wanted to hurt the boy, and the boy was just protecting his father. He smiled.

The kid took a step back, but he didn't let go of the wooden spear.

"Damn, that hurts, boy," James whispered. For a second, he saw uncertainty flash in the kid's eyes, and he thought maybe he was going to pull the spear out of him and stab him again. He held up a hand, palm out. "It's okay, kid." He knelt to his knees. "It's okay."

Now the boy did let go.

James watched all the emotions play across the boy's face. Anger. Fear. Guilt. Sadness. Excitement. "It's okay. You done good." He plopped down onto his butt and waved the pistol at the boy. "Go on, git."

The boy just stood there.

"C'mon, move it, boy. And don't look back."

The kid walked a wide arc around him, studying him, not trusting that he wouldn't shoot him in the back. Then he finally did turn. "Dad?" he called out.

James got onto his knees and started working his way back toward the ATV.

110

DAD?"

Jack stood up straight. "Joseph?" He started looking around in the dark. "Where are you?" He thought he'd heard talking but wasn't sure. Now it sounded like Joseph's voice was calling out from the same area James had been in.

"I'm over here."

Jack could hear someone walking through the underbrush, coming even closer. Would James shoot them both as they embraced? He couldn't rule it out. "Joseph, listen to me. I'm going to shine my flashlight at a spot in the forest for a second, and I want you to run to that spot as fast as you can, okay?" They'd present a much harder target this way, moving quickly through the dark.

"Dad, it's okay…"

His voice sounded soft, injured.

"I stabbed him. He crawled away."

Jack didn't fully understand what he meant, or if James was somehow tricking him, but he still didn't trust—

And then Joseph was right in front of him, lunging forward, arms wrapping around his waist. He buried his head in his stomach, and Jack held him tight.

No shot came.

Jack knelt, dropping the knife, and took Joseph's face in his hands. He stared into his eyes, the last moments of twilight offering just enough light to catch a sparkle of tears running down his son's face. "Are you okay?" he stammered, his hands going up and down his back, into his hair, around his face.

Joseph nodded.

Jack hugged him again and couldn't stop himself from crying. They held each other for what seemed like a long while, neither wanting to let go, fearing that if they did, one of them might disappear again.

Jack couldn't believe it. Just couldn't believe it. He'd done it. Had made it all the way from Pennsylvania to this damn mountain in West Virginia in time. Had found the cabin. Had found his son. It was a miracle.

He looked up to the stars, he guessed to offer up a thank you, but all he saw was the dark underside of the forest's leafy roof. He picked up the knife and put it back in its sheath. Then he took Joseph's hand. "You said you stabbed him?"

Joseph nodded.

"With what?"

"A branch that I sharpened into a spear."

"My own Robinson Crusoe."

"I..."

There was a lot of emotion in his voice, and Jack thought he knew what he was feeling. The same way he'd felt after killing the guy in their garage eight years ago. Just add a twelve year-old's innocence to the equation. "What?"

It took him a minute. "I don't think I needed to."

Jack didn't think so either. If James wanted to shoot them, he would've done it by now. But he couldn't let such a thought torture his son. "That man. All those men... They tried to kill me, Joseph. They kidnapped you and were planning on handing you over to some very dangerous people. For money. All for money. You didn't ask for this. I didn't ask for this. They are the ones who asked for it. And you know what? You reap what you sow. So don't let it bother you. You didn't know if he was going to shoot me or not. And you weren't going to take the chance. I would have done the same thing."

"You would?"

I have. "Absolutely." *Don't you remember your mother shooting your might-be biological dad right in front of you?* "And besides, if he's well enough to crawl away, then maybe he'll be okay."

He looked down.

"You did real good, Joseph. I'm proud of you. You're a survivor. Just like all those characters in your books. You escaped, and you saved your dad."

The white of his teeth appeared as he smiled.

"Now what do you say we get the hell off this mountain?"

III

THEY STOOD BESIDE THE Ford Edge, Johnson's Impala behind them with its headlights on and illuminating the gravel lot and the water beyond it.

"How am I going to explain a missing car?" Stacey asked.

"Report it stolen."

"From where?"

"That's all stuff we can figure out later." He looked at his watch. "We have to go."

She nodded.

"I don't know how deep the lake is or if it has a drop-off, so I want to get some speed behind it. Maybe the momentum will float it further out before it sinks," he said.

"What kind of bomb do you think it is?"

He stopped. "What do you mean?"

"You don't think..."

He stared at her; then he stepped away from the car, suddenly looking at it differently, as if seeing it for the first time. He opened the back and looked around. Then he looked under all the seats. Then he got on his back and slid beneath the vehicle, pulling out a small flashlight and examining its underbelly.

He rolled out from underneath and stood, thinking.

"What?"

"We could call it in. Get the bomb squad out here."

"No. Not yet. Not until I know they're safe."

He nodded. "You have the detonator?"

She held up the handbag.

"Okay, c'mon." He started jogging back to the Impala, crossing in front of the beams. He got behind the wheel and closed the door.

She got into the passenger seat beside him. "What are you doing?"

"If we detonate the bomb underwater, USGS could get a reading on it."

"Depending on how big the bomb is."

"Right. Or—" He put the car in reverse, turned and looked back over his shoulder, his right hand on the back of the headrest behind Stacey's head. He hit the gas, and the Edge suddenly started to shrink in the high beams. He whipped the steering wheel and swung the car around, threw it in drive, and took the road out of the park. When they were about a mile away from the Edge, he stopped. He looked over at Stacey. "Hit it," he said.

"What?"

"Just do it."

"But—"

"Stacey, hit the damn button."

She took the remote detonator out of the handbag. She looked at him and held her breath. Pressed the button.

Nothing.

No lightning, no thunder.

"Maybe we're out of range," she said.

He turned the car around and slowly headed back the way they'd come. "Keep hitting the button."

She pressed it every second or two with no results. She kept doing it until the Impala's headlights were back on the Edge. "How close do you want to get?" she asked.

"How close were you supposed to be?"

"Fifty or sixty feet on the other side of a brick wall."

He drove a little closer.

She fidgeted.

"Hit it again."

She held her breath and pressed the button. Still nothing. "Maybe it malfunctioned," she said.

"Maybe. Maybe not." He turned the car around and sped as fast as he could through the park. "I want you to tell me everything. From the beginning."

112

JACK BLEW INTO THE flames, trying to get the kindling going. They'd dug a hole with some rocks and the stock of the rifle and had gathered a few handfuls of whatever tinder they could find in the dark. He used the lighter to ignite it, and now it was just a matter of getting the tinder to burn long enough to light the sticks they'd layered over top.

Jack hadn't wanted to leave the ATV behind, because it was the quickest way down the mountain. But he didn't want to use it at night either. Not without knowing who was still out there. With the headlights on and the engine purring, they'd be easy to locate. But he didn't want to risk going down the mountain on foot either. Not in the dark, not with Joseph in his socks. All it would take was one twisted ankle and their journey out of the wilderness would be a whole lot more complicated, and he didn't come all this way just to die in the escape.

"You think there might be any Sasq—"

"Don't say it," Jack warned. "Just saying the name might alert them to our presence."

"I think you're thinking of ROUS, Dad."

"Rodents of Unusual Size? I don't believe they exist."

Joseph laughed. "Great. Now we'll have ROUS and Sasquatch to fight off."

Jack winced. "Oh, you did it. You said the name out loud. We're done for now."

The ATV was about a hundred yards behind them. They'd hop on it at first light and work their way south. He wasn't sure where they were in relation to the path he'd followed Ham's guys on. He could probably find it if they worked their way back to the cabin, but he didn't know what was going on up there and didn't think it worth the risk.

"Did they treat you okay?" he asked Joseph.

"Yeah. They didn't hurt me."

"They feed you?"

"Yeah."

"Good." The sticks caught, and he added some broken branches. He hadn't vented the whole like they'd done the first night, but they weren't cooking anything either. They just wanted some heat while they slept without creating a blinding light in the middle of the woods. If it hadn't rained the day before, he'd put a rock in there, but the last thing he needed was for it to explode and have them both die of stupidity. He rolled onto his back. "How'd you make the spear anyway?"

"With Hugh."

It took Jack a second to remember what he was talking about. "The knife? You have the knife?"

"I slipped it into my pants before falling asleep. They never searched me or anything. I used it to break the window. I wrapped a blanket around the handle and hit the glass when it thundered."

"You did that?" He raised his eyebrows. "Maybe you didn't need me after all. You probably would've walked all the way home."

"Maybe if I'd slept in my boots too."

They listened to the fire crackle.

"Dad?"

"Yeah?"

"How did you get here?"

"Well, now that is a long story that I will gladly tell you in the morning. But right now, I just want to fall asleep thinking about everything I'm gonna eat when I get home."

"I want an Italian hoagie," Joseph said.

"Good choice. Think I'll go with pizza, wings, a cheese steak and fries. With a movie, of course."

"Can't have pizza without a movie. How 'bout *Jeremiah Johnson.*"

Jack lifted his head. "Seriously?"

"Yeah."

"Haven't you had enough of the mountains? How 'bout *Cast Away* or even *Robinson Crusoe*? At least they're on an island."

"With Pierce Brosnan? No thanks."

Jack didn't know how many twelve-year-olds knew who Pierce Brosnan was and wasn't sure if he had rubbed his own generational playlist off on his son, or if Joseph had seen the movie just because he saw and read anything having to do with the character.

"*Into The Wild* then?" Joseph asked.

Jack groaned. Joseph had been begging them to let him watch it for months. "I don't want to see another tree for a year. But maybe."

"Yes!"

Jack looked at his son in the soft light, afraid that if he fell asleep, he'd only wake up to find him gone again. So he stayed awake as long as he could, past 2 a.m. according to his watch. He thought about Stacey. About what this was all about. He thought about his mom and dad, his grandparents. He listened to the forest. And then, without even knowing it, sleep took him.

113

STACEY LEANED HER HEAD against the window and looked below. Johnson was in a seat at the back of the plane, talking on his phone. She'd filled him in on the calls while he drove them an hour west to a small airport and to this waiting jet. They'd been in the air for ten minutes, and for the first time since she'd gotten that call on Tuesday, she felt safe. No one could touch her up here. And though she wasn't sure what Johnson had going on, she guessed that he had at least some support of the federal government on his side. How that had happened, she was too tired to find out. She relaxed, thankful that her husband and son were still alive, and that she was on her way to them. The drinks and adrenaline were taking their toll now, and she knew fatigue would be sending her to dreamland at any moment. She looked at the world below while she waited for it to pick her up.

Pockets of glowing lights dotted the rural space beneath them, and she began to think about all the people down there those lights represented, each with their own story and at one place or another within that story. There were people down there on their way to their honeymoons. People celebrating promotions. Birthday parties. Women giving birth, not knowing until now that it was even possible to love someone so much, while others sobbed as their hopes and dreams were carried away forever. There were people dying after a long and terrible fight with cancer. Others were slipping away gracefully in old age, generations surrounding them and sending them off. There was a woman getting raped, calling out for help that wouldn't come. Criminals plotting, always plotting. Children were sleeping, dreaming of adventure, while other children were too afraid to sleep, either from imagination or something much more real.

So many people. So many stories. She saw them all from thirty-four thousand feet. Saw the police closing in on the person who had just held up the local convenience store, the owner on his way home to his wife and family, glad to be alive. Saw the homeless looking for food and shedding tears of appreciation when a stranger brought them a meal and a blanket. Saw the baseball games and thousands of fans cheering, while further away thousands of other fans were mourning. Light and dark. Good and evil. The best and the worst. She knew Jack would see a giant cage over all of this, the real bad guys sitting in some James Bond-type command center and orchestrating all the misery for their own gain. Control, power... She couldn't deny it. She'd seen enough. Had played her part in it even.

The party tonight. What she thought was going to be a political ass-kissing event, but turned out to just be a birthday party. No strippers, no naked people in animal masks, no sushi girls or faux corpses, no Skull and Bones or Masonic rituals or other occult candle-lighting ceremonies. Just a guy—yes, a seedy guy with many issues, but still just a guy—at a birthday party thrown by his wife, who was in the middle of her own story arc, not present at her unfaithful husband's party because of her own father's illness.

She'd been close to ending them all. Whether or not there even was a bomb was beside the point. She almost pushed the button, fully believing that it would be the last thing she did.

But she hadn't.

And maybe not pushing it had breathed a little life back into a soul so calloused, so professional, that she was starting to retain some feeling in those moral limbs. Or it could just be the alcohol and the emotional cyclone she was currently caught up in. But she didn't think so, because now she was thinking of all the times she *had* pressed the button. In the name of national security. In the name of the greater good. In the name of Uncle Sam. Of freedom. Of whatever the hell she thought it was at the time.

She thought of Trenton and wondered why she hadn't seen all those people the way she was seeing the world below her now. A tear formed in the corner of her eye. Perhaps the heaviest single tear she'd ever shed. It was a tear that, when it struck the armrest and exploded, seemed to explode her whole life with it.

She fell asleep.

THE HELICOPTER'S ALMOST READY," Johnson said as he handed Stacey a Styrofoam cup of coffee. "Sorry, it's instant."

She didn't care if it was poured out of an old leather boot as long as it was hot. She took it from him and brought it to her mouth, feeling the steam as it rose against her face. The night had slipped by like a time-lapsed daydream as she went in and out of consciousness. She'd hardly been awake when they landed and a waiting car drove them to a motel. When a knock at the door woke her up, it had taken more than a moment to piece together where she was and how she'd gotten there. And now, at 5:02 in the morning, standing in a field as a helicopter was being prepped behind them, she sipped the coffee and watched the new dawn break over the Appalachian Mountains.

When she didn't respond to him, Johnson asked if she was okay.

"Yeah." The FBI jacket Johnson had also given her rustled against a cool morning breeze, and she crossed her arms. She looked at him. "Sorry, last night..." She dropped her chin to her chest and massaged her temples with her free hand, arms still folded. "I think I only got half of what you were saying. How did you—" She looked around and gestured at the half-dozen agents running back and forth. "Who are these guys?"

"THU," he said.

"Tactical Helicopter Unit? With HRT? How the hell did you pull that off?" She looked at the black Bell 412 helicopter. "When did it get here?"

"Last night. They've been pretty busy."

"I don't understand."

"Jack's message, that he thought they'd kidnapped Joseph to get you to do something for them..." He took a sip of his own coffee. "I checked your online activity and saw that you'd been looking into Douglas Newell. I figured the only reason you'd be taking an interest in him was because he was your target or your suspect. Either way, I figured that's where you were heading. I just had to find out where he was."

"Looks like you got there just in time."

He shook his head. "Not if there *was* a bomb and you *had* decided to press the button."

"That's true," she whispered. "You don't think there was a bomb?"

"No."

"Why not?"

But before he could answer, a man in camouflage ran over to them and shouted, "Ready to go!"

They ducked into the helicopter and watched the ground fall away, the remaining agents moving back and forth in their makeshift command center.

"I still don't understand," Stacey shouted into Johnson's ear. "What are they doing?"

"You'll see," he hollered back.

The helicopter banked right and climbed above the mountains of West Virginia.

114

JACK'S EYES WENT IMMEDIATELY to the spot where Joseph had fallen asleep, to the patch of grass beside the fire across from him. But he wasn't there. Before he could even blink, however, he felt the presence of another body against him, and he looked down to see that his son was curled up against him. Jack sighed with relief.

He looked at his watch. It was just after five. His stomach growled, and he sat up, stirring Joseph in the process.

Joseph yawned and rubbed his eyes. "What time is it?" he asked.

"Time to get moving. With any luck, we'll be home watching *The Last Starfighter* tonight."

"If by *The Last Starfighter* you mean *Last of the Mohicans*, then I'm in."

Jack stood. "*The Last Boy Scout?*"

"Huh?"

He smiled. "Fine. If we get out of here, *Last of the Mohicans* it is." He rolled down the sleeves of his shirt as he noted the fog enveloping the forest. "You cold?"

Joseph was just realizing that he'd been tricked out of *Into The Wild* but managed to nod while rubbing his arms. "It should be warming up soon though."

"Whatever you say, Davy." And he started walking back to where they'd left the ATV, whistling the Davy Crockett theme song as he went.

When they were both on the ATV, all the guns loaded and in the right positions, Jack started it up. "I don't really know where we're going," he said over his shoulder. "But I think if we head southeast, it might take us off the mountain and into town." *And to my stolen car.*

Joseph nodded and wrapped his arms around his waist. "Hey, Dad?"

"Yeah?"

"Are you being like Mel Gibson right now?"

Jack turned and looked at him. "What do you mean?"

"Like in all his movies, he's going after someone who was taken from him and kicking ass."

Jack couldn't help laughing, and as he thought about it, he figured this was a little like a Mel Gibson movie. Except that in those movies, the person Mel cares about is usually killed, and he's going for revenge. He didn't care about revenge. He just wanted to keep his son alive.

"Like *Mad Max* and *Ransom* and *Blood Father*?" Joseph asked.

"When did you see *Blood Father*? Whatever. Sure, just like those. I've been kicking ass up and down these mountains all week. And don't say ass."

And in the morning light, Joseph noticed the cuts and bruises, his father's bloodshot eye. "I prayed that you would find me. I knew you would."

"Well, as long as this isn't *Edge of Darkness* or *Braveheart*, I think I can handle this." Then he realized that Mel died in over half of the movies just mentioned. Hmmm. "Okay, hold on."

He hit the accelerator, and they started moving down through the mist, weaving back and forth between the trees, following the heading on Jack's watch.

115

JOHNSON LEANED OVER AND raised his arm across her body, pointing out her side of the helicopter. "Look," he said.

Stacey looked down and saw an opening in the canopy. As they got closer to it, she could tell there was a structure there. And a moment later they were over top of it. It was some kind of compound. She could see fences with barbed wire and what she assumed were multiple utility sheds surrounding half a dozen cabins. There was even an old guard tower in the one corner. "What is it?" she asked. But before Johnson could answer, she spotted movement.

People walking around in blue jackets. Big yellow letters on their backs. There was a crowd of them over by one of the cabins, circled around a person on their knees, their hands behind their back.

She saw a body lying sprawled on the ground, an AK-47 lying next to an outstretched hand. The grass around the person was red.

And then they were past it, moving deeper into the mountains.

"DRGs? From the Cold War?" she asked.

He nodded. "Leftovers from the Illegals Program."

"Were they—"

"The calls to your phone came out of those houses."

She tried to digest that, what it meant.

"We've had our eye on them for years. Until now, they'd just been operating locally. Mountain-type crime, mostly."

"Mountain type?"

"Drugs, moonshine, the occasional hit on some other bootlegger. As far as we know, anyway."

"You've been watching them?"

"They've been on the Bureau's watch list. As soon as I heard Jack's message, I made some calls to see if we knew of anything in the area. This came back. We got a drone out here right away. Live feed captured them burying a body. It was enough for probable cause."

"How do you know the calls came from there?"

"Called in a favor to the NSA on that one. They matched your received calls with outgoing calls from the area."

She eyed him with skepticism. "That's really fast work," she said.

"Not my first time at the rodeo, Mrs. Green."

"They didn't find Joseph?"

"No. I don't think he was ever there."

"Those are the people who threatened to kill him. If they didn't have him, then he might be okay?"

"Depends on the kidnappers, I guess. Jack said they're supposed to hand him over tomorrow morning. We'll keep a presence in the area in case they show up, but I doubt they will. I'm hoping we find him before then anyway."

"If they have him, why wouldn't they show up?"

"We started monitoring radio frequencies in the area. Sounds like there was a good fight up on one of the mountaintops last night. Rival gangs, it sounds like."

She looked at him, waiting for the part that made it relevant.

"They mentioned trying to find a boy."

"They lost him?"

"If it is him they're talking about, then it sounds like it's a possibility."

"So my son could be out there in the mountains alone?"

"Could be."

She looked out at the ocean of green and tried to determine if that was good news or bad news. "How the hell did you manage to call in a favor to the NSA? Just what have you been doing the last eight years."

He just smiled.

116

THE MORNING MIST WAS thinning, and so far there was no sign of anyone pursuing them. Jack was getting hopeful that they'd be in town in just a few more hours. Unless he was miscalculating their route and they were just heading deeper into the wilderness. But he didn't think so.

They'd seen deer, rabbits, chipmunks, even a flying squirrel (something Jack had to admit was something he'd always wanted to see for himself). If it weren't for the dire circumstance that led them here and the trauma they'd experienced, they might be tempted to slow down and make a day out of it. Maybe stop by a stream and soak their tired feet. Or pick some berries. Try to trap some lunch. It was beautiful up here, and Jack was able to appreciate it more now that Joseph was safe in his care again.

He maneuvered the ATV around some rock formations that were coming out of the ground like giant teeth and down a small slope to a spot where the ground was free of trees and rocks for a good hundred square feet. He rode out into the middle of the little hollow and stopped. "Look over there," he said over his shoulder, pointing into the trees to their left.

Joseph looked over and saw what his dad was pointing at. A black bear. It was halfway up a tree. "Just a cub," he said.

"Does that mean mama's around somewhere?"

"Probably."

"Oh, by the way, your theory about black bears being friendly and all. Yeah, I'm gonna have to disagree."

They both heard a noise over the idling engine and swung their heads around to their right.

Mama.

He felt Joseph's hands grip him tighter.

"We're between her and her cub, Dad. That's no good."

"I know," Jack said.

Mama bear started walking toward them.

"Can we go, please?" Joseph asked.

Jack was about to respond by hitting the accelerator when the bear suddenly stopped about forty feet away. It looked left and right, breathing out of his nose. Then it started pawing at the dirt, growing agitated. It took one cautious step forward as if she feared some invisible trap had been set for her, and then took her big paw back.

"Is she scared of the ATV?" Jack asked.

"I don't know."

Jack was afraid that if he took off, the bear would chase them. If they spilled on the uneven mountain terrain, the beast would be right on top of them. He applied the slightest pressure to the accelerator, and the four wheels began to turn ever so slowly.

The bear stood up on its hind legs and then dropped back to the ground, slamming its front legs into the grass with such force that Jack could feel the ground shake even while sitting on the running ATV.

The bear did it again. Stood tall, roared, and then dropped onto its front paws.

"Whoa," Jack said, suddenly looking around. "Did you feel that?"

"Yeah." Joseph was looking around too.

"Hold on!" He hit the accelerator, but it was too late. Something beneath them cracked, and the front of the ATV dropped beneath the ground.

They sat still, not moving. The front of the quad's nose was up to the handlebars inside the mountain.

"Don't move," Jack whispered. He shut the engine off for fear the vibrations would shake them loose. There were boards beneath them, wooden planks long buried that had cracked under their weight. Jack's head spun, imagining what could be beneath them. What someone would want to cover up. *Hollow Mountain*, he recalled. Like a honeycomb.

"Dad," Joseph whispered.

"Yeah?"

"It's walking away."

He turned and saw that the bear was circling around the clearing, heading for its young. "Good." He took a breath. "Now listen. We're on top of some kind of hole or something. Someone covered it with boards, and we just broke some of them." He felt Joseph nod against his back. "I think if we can climb off the back, the ground should support just our weight."

Another nod.

"We'll go one at a time, okay?"

Another board cracked, and the hole swallowed the handlebars. They were almost entirely vertical now. There was no more time.

"Go now!" Jack hollered. He turned his head and watched through the corner of his good eye as Joseph climbed over the back of the ATV and dropped from sight behind it. "Joe?"

"Here. The ground is real mushy. I don't think—"

His word got lost in a scream as the mountain opened, and they fell through.

Falling.

Falling.

Jack couldn't believe this was how it was going to end. After getting Joseph back, they were both going to die after all. Falling into a crack on the side of some obscure mountain in the middle of the wilderness where their bodies would never be found, their bones destined to rest in isolation until the end of time. At least they'd be together. Father and son. Forever.

Stacey...

THE PILOT WAS KEEPING the helicopter so low that Stacey was afraid he was going to snag a tree with one of the landing skids. Streams, rocks, cliffs, and game trails all raced by beneath them. She tried imagining Jack being out here on his own. It was such an absurd thought—Jack in the mountains—that she found herself smiling trying to imagine it.

The helicopter banked, throwing her against Johnson. She recovered, Johnson not even acknowledging the contact, and watched as they rose alongside another mountain, heading for its peak. Then they were over the top, and the helicopter was casting its insect-like shadow on a grassy plateau. There was a hunting cabin at its center, and Stacey couldn't tell if the topography was natural or if it had been cleared out by humans a long time ago.

There were more FBI agents walking around the cabin, and Stacey assumed they'd also been dropped off by helicopter. She saw a couple of quads, but didn't think they'd had time enough to drive to the location.

The pilot took them down, the skids kissing the ground with hardly a nudge, and Johnson jumped out. He turned and offered her his hand, which she took to be polite, both of them knowing she didn't need it.

As they walked toward the cabin, the metal bird rose back into the air.

"Where are they going?" Stacey asked.

Johnson twirled his finger. "Search and rescue."

A man dressed in dark fatigues came jogging over to them.

"What do we have?" Johnson asked.

"A mess is what we have," the man answered. "Bodies scattered all down the mountain's side."

Johnson pointed behind him to a body that was sprawled on the ground beside the cabin. "Who's that?"

"Lee Baker."

"That the older one?"

"So says the locals."

"No sign of the others?"

"Nope."

Stacey stepped closed. "What are you talking about? Who is that?"

"We think it's the leader of one of the two rival gangs the Russians were using to kidnap Joseph."

She walked past them and to the body. No one had bothered to put a sheet over him. She studied the lifeless face before moving her gaze over the rest of him. "Looks like he was run over, cut, and then shot."

"Corresponds with the tire tracks," the agent said, pointing to a group of twin tread marks.

Stacey looked around and could see them everywhere now. They came or went from two different directions. "My son was kept here?"

The agent nodded. "From what we were able to piece together from the radio transmissions, yes, he was here. And your husband was too. We think they rode off on an ATV."

"When?"

"Last night."

She looked up into the morning sky and spotted the helicopter circling in the distance. Then she looked back at Johnson. "What happened here? What the hell is going on?"

"There's coffee inside if you want some," the agent said. Then he turned and walked over to a couple of other agents who were busy looking at a map sprawled out on the seat of a quad.

Stacey followed Johnson into the cabin, and the first thing she noticed was that there was food here. Someone had been cooking. She thought that was a good sign. Hopefully Joseph's captors had been taking good care of him. She took her second Styrofoam cup of coffee from Johnson and sipped. Then she looked him in the eye. "So?"

"So far, we know that the calls came from that compound. And we know the occupants of the compound were from the

Illegals Program, hiding out in the mountains since the Cold War. Who activated them and what they were trying to accomplish—" He looked around and shrugged. "But it looks like those agents hired some of the local riffraff to do their dirty work. They were supposed to kidnap Joseph, and I assume kill Jack in a way that looked like an accident, and deliver him to them tomorrow morning."

"How'd they get here from the campsite?"

"We're still putting that together. I assume they loaded their ATVs onto a truck and drove to the mountain before taking the ATVs to the cabin."

"You said rival gangs."

"Yeah, according to the local authority, if this region had a godfather-type figure, it would be that Lee Baker and his two brothers. They even call the area Bakerville."

"And the other gang?"

"We're not too sure about them, but we think their leader was found at the compound. That's who they were burying." He shrugged again. "The sheriff said a guy came in matching Jack's description, asking how to get to the cabin. He didn't say much at first. Until we told him that Lee over there was dead. Then he wouldn't shut up."

Stacey stared at him.

"What?" he asked.

"I'm having a real hard time believing you put all this together from Jack's voicemail yesterday."

"Well, you called me before that, didn't you?"

She studied him. "Just who exactly are you, Agent Johnson?"

"Thought you knew, CIA woman."

"You didn't really go off the grid blowing whistles, did you?"

He smiled. "Well, *Anna*, let's just say some of us keep our own tabs on some of you."

"I don't understand."

"If we find your husband and son, maybe we can all sit down and talk about it."

She looked away. "So what now?"

"Now we wait for a sighting."

HE DIDN'T STRIKE HIS head on an outcropping on the way down or shatter his legs on a rock floor. Instead, he fell into a freezing cold, as if the hole had been a portal to outer space. Sudden pressure in his head. His fall slowing to a stop. Suspended in darkness.

The cold was so numbing that all he could do was float there in the void and hope his motor functions came back before he suffocated. Somehow he knew to hold his breath. He thought of Joseph. Where was he? He tried to turn his head, though it was still pitch black, and he wouldn't be able to see anything anyway.

Was this hell? Outer darkness? The bottom of the Atlantic?

His arms started to move, his legs. He looked up and saw a shimmer of light far off in the distance, and he realized that he was indeed under water. He kicked and felt himself rising, his lungs starting to burn. Was that the moon he was swimming toward?

His head broke the surface and he gasped for air, his arms splashing in the darkness. "Joe," he hollered. His voice sounded different, a hollow echo.

He was in a cavern.

He called for Joseph again. Was he pinned beneath the ATV at the bottom of this underground lake, struggling for air, hand outstretched and waiting for—

"Over here," Joseph called out.

Jack turned and swam toward his voice. His hands found him in just a few strokes. "Thank God you're all right," he whispered, giving him a quick hug as they treaded water.

"It's so c-c-cold," Joseph said.

"I know." He looked up and saw daylight coming through the hole they'd fallen through. But they were too deep for the light to offer any real sense of their surroundings. "C'mon. Let's find the wall. Keep a hand on me."

They swam in one direction for what seemed like ten minutes. Maybe it had only been one, Jack wasn't sure. But thinking of time made him think of his watch, and he held his wrist up and pressed a button on its side, illuminating its face. It was no flashlight, but it did provide a glow, and they saw that they were just a few feet from the edge of the cavern. They made their way to it, feeling around until finding a fissure they could use as a handhold.

"Must be flooded from the storm," Jack said. "Lucky for us."

"How d-d-do we get out?"

"They call this Hollow Mountain because it's so full of caves that it's practically hollow. A sheriff told me there's an underground river that runs through it. Maybe it flows through here." He shivered. "Stay here. I'm going to swim around and see if there are any ledges."

"Don't go," he objected.

Jack opened his belt pouch and took out the flashlight. "I'll keep the flashlight on so you know where I am. I'm not going far." He pushed off the wall and started to swim. He didn't know how long they'd be able to stay down here in this water before they got hypothermia or drowned. He had to find a way out. Or at least a way out of the water.

His hands struck something floating in the dark, and he shined the light on it. A piece of wood from the broken planking. He hooked his arms over it and kicked with his feet, conserving energy. "Found a piece of wood," he reported, his voice echoing.

No response.

He turned and aimed the light back where he'd left him. "Joseph?"

"I'm h-h-ere."

And the silver glow picked him out from against the wall. Jack continued searching the perimeter, his numb fingertips brushing smooth stone. He swept the beam of light across the rock, hoping for an exit.

Minutes passed.

"You still with me?" he called out.

"Y-y-y-y-y-yessss."

Not good. If Joseph lost his grip on the wall, he'd be too tired and numb to tread water now. He had to find something fast. He was on the cavern's side at about Joe's ten o'clock.

His eyes were beginning to adjust, and the world around him started to materialize, bad eye and all. He continued making his way around the perimeter of the flooded chamber.

He heard something. Splashing, it sounded like. Coming from up ahead at Joe's two o'clock. "Hey, I hear something," he called out.

"W-w-what?"

He kicked his feet and floated the board across the room, the sound getting louder. As he got closer to it, he moved the flashlight around and saw a large fissure in the rock. He figured the water must be flowing through it and spilling down into a lower chamber on the other side. Maybe the river he'd been told about. He looked for handholds. There appeared to be plenty.

He put the flashlight in his mouth and swam closer. Shaking from the cold, he reached up and grabbed an outcropping. He pulled himself up and out of the water, climbing until he could squeeze his body through the crack and drop down into the next chamber if he wanted. There was no light on the other side, and if he committed to it, there might be no way of getting back. Yet they couldn't climb out of the cavern, and the only people looking for them were the people trying to kill them.

He jumped back into the water, grabbed the piece of wood, and swam back to Joseph. "Okay, buddy, we're gonna swim over to that wall, and we're gonna climb through a big crack, okay?"

He nodded.

Jack got him onto the wood and swam him to the wall with the fissure, the flashlight beam like a laser moving all about. "Okay, you're gonna have to climb up there. Can you do that?"

"I c-c-c-an't see."

Jack aimed the light so Joseph could see the crack and the handholds.

"I'll give you a boost," Jack said. He put the light back in his mouth and interlaced his fingers, letting Joseph stand on his hands. The boy reached up and pulled himself into the crack. Then Jack climbed up, and the two of them were standing in the wall, listening to the overflowing water pour into the next chamber. Jack went to take the flashlight out of his mouth, but it slipped through his fingers and plummeted downward with the water. The light winked out as it sank. "Crap," Jack said. "Oh well. I still have my watch."

Joseph just shivered.

"I'll go first," Jack said. He maneuvered around Joseph as they switched spots, almost slipping a few times in the water that was flowing over their feet. He grabbed the sides of the fissure and lowered himself down, the water striking him in the face as he hung, suspended, his hands holding the slick rock.

How far did it drop? He hadn't been able to tell before losing the flashlight, though he didn't think there were any rocks at the bottom of it.

His fingers were losing their strength, and now he wouldn't be able to pull himself up even if he wanted to. His hands slipped, and he was away.

He landed in water that was once again deep enough to tread. He swam away from the roiling water and immediately felt a current trying to pull him away. He reached out for a handhold and found one just in time. Was he in the underground river? If so, maybe it would carry them out of the mountain. *Or maybe there is no way out of the mountain.*

He ignored the thought. There was no use dwelling on all the bad possibilities. They were committed, and whatever it was going to be it was going to be. "Okay, jump down, Joe," he called out over the sound of the water. "Just like in a pool!"

"Are you s-s-sure?"

"Yeah!"

He jumped.

Jack heard the splash. "Joe?"

No response.

"Joe?"

"Over here! Where are you?"

Jack hit the light on his watch and spotted Joseph's outline just in time to reach out and grab him as he was passing by.

He held his son. "How you holding up?"

"Just f-f-ine. You?"

Jack smiled. "We're gonna ride with the current, okay? Hopefully it'll carry us right out of the mountain."

"Sure wish you hadn't dr-r-r-ropped the f-f-flashlight."

"Yeah, yeah." He wrapped his arms around him tight. "Keep your head up. Here we go." He pushed off the wall and let the water carry them into the void.

HE HEARD A SOUND above him and managed to look up. A shadow hung in the sky, silhouetted by the sun. Like a giant locust, it just hovered there, beating its wings.

James tried to sit up, but the pain rebuked him, and he lay back down on the seat of the ATV. The stick the boy had thrust into him was still protruding from his stomach. He'd been afraid to take it out. He'd gotten back to the quad, intending to get to Michael and the cabin, but he'd fainted and had been in and out of consciousness ever since. He felt semi-delirious and knew he was dehydrated. The bullet hole in his arm didn't help any either. He'd never make it anywhere in this condition. He watched as men began sliding down out of the sky. They came to him and inspected his wound.

"How did this happen?" one of them asked.

"Fell off a ledge and landed on a stick," he lied. He didn't miss the big yellow letters.

"What are you doing out here?"

"Looking for my brother. Have you seen him?" He was doing his best acting job, but the pain was making it hard to concentrate.

"Let's get him to a doctor," one said to the other. Then he spoke into a radio.

The helicopter drifted away and then descended behind some trees.

As they carried him on a stretcher, he thought about the boy and his father. "Before I fell off the ledge," he said, "I saw a man and a boy. They looked like they might be in trouble."

"Where did you see them?"

He closed his eyes. "I don't know. Not far from here. You haven't seen them either?"

They didn't answer him, just spoke into the radio again.

James watched the clouds roll by overhead and hoped Momma would understand that he tried... He wished he had a toothpick.

STACEY HEARD THEM CALL it over the radio. They'd found someone with a significant gut wound who needed to be transported to a hospital ASAP. She also heard them say the person had mentioned a man and a boy being in the area.

"ETA on the other chopper?" Johnson called out to one of the men in the cabin.

"Ten," a voice called back.

Johnson spoke into the radio. "Copy that. Maybe make one pass on your way out. Over."

"Roger that. We'll make one circle at a hundred feet. Over."

"Copy."

Stacey ran a hand through her hair and tried to remain calm. It was obvious that Johnson wasn't telling her everything, and she wasn't sure why. But seeing as he was the only hope she had right now, she thought it best not to push him on it. She'd find out later. Maybe after she found out just who the hell he really was. A friend at the NSA? Enough pull to get Hostage/Rescue out here on a moment's notice? An FBI raid on a Cold War KGB installation in the middle of the Appalachian Mountains? No way. Somehow, he knew what was going on. More than she did. *And thank your lucky stars for that, right?* Maybe. She began to wonder if maybe Agent Johnson had ulterior motives. Could he possibly be setting her up somehow? All this to end with her in handcuffs? Instead of the CIA or the FSB setting her up, might it be the FBI coming to hold her accountable for all her sins?

Johnson noticed her staring at him, and he looked away.

No, Stacey thought. She called him, and he'd stopped her from killing the senator.

Or maybe that was the plan all along.

She was beginning to think like Jack. Like her Jerry. She decided to run with it, playing it out. Agent Johnson looking for revenge, like he was Elliot Ness and she was his Al Capone. Or John Dillinger to his Melvin Purvis. Or, more accurately, she was the CIA psychiatrist played by Patrick Stewart in *Conspiracy Theory*, and he was Federal Agent Lowry—who turned out not to be with the FBI but from a secret agency that watches other agencies. In the movie, the secret agency was using Jerry to stop Patrick Stewart. She almost laughed at the irony of it. What if the FBI (or whoever Johnson worked for) set her up? There was no car bomb, which Johnson had somehow guessed, and—

She froze. Could it have been Johnson's synthesized voice on the other end of the phone? But as she looked around at the sweeping mountains, she couldn't figure out what the point in his bringing her out here would be.

Johnson walked over to her. "Listen. I need to tell you something."

She turned her body to face him. Was this when all the agents would come running out of the cabin and tackle her to the ground, cuffing her hands behind her back?

"After Trenton—"

Her heart stopped, and her breath caught in her throat, but she forced her eyes to reflect none of it. She waited for the gavel to drop. But before he could continue, the radio sounded.

"We found a clearing nearby. There's a big hole in the ground at its center. From here it looks like the hole had been boarded over. Could be something broke through it. Over."

"Can you see into the hole?" Johnson asked.

"Negative. It's too deep. Over."

"Where's that other chopper?" he called out again.

"One minute out," said someone coming out of the cabin.

Johnson spoke into the radio. "Give us the coordinates and proceed to the nearest hospital. Incoming team will take over. Over."

The coordinates came back, and Johnson wrote them down on a notepad. Then he turned and walked back into the cabin. "Get me that sheriff. We need to know more about this mountain. And get a dive team ready just in case."

Stacey came up behind him. "A dive team?"

"The sheriff said the mountain is like a honeycomb of caves and caverns with an underground river connecting most of them. Some of them may have flooded."

"What if they weren't the ones who fell through?"

"Do you want to take that chance?" he asked.

No. No, she didn't. The thought of them trapped inside the mountain, lying there with a broken back in the dark, not knowing that anyone was looking for them..."I want to go there," she said. There was no negotiating in her voice.

He stared at her for a moment, considering it. Finally, he said, "Okay." Then he instructed the incoming THU pilot to set down on their location for a pickup.

A minute later, a black Bell 407 was hovering above them, its rotors beating the air.

121

JACK HELD ON TO Joseph as tight as he could. The current had gotten stronger, and now they were moving fast. Where to, he had no idea. Hopefully straight to the waterfall the sheriff had told him about. He prayed that they wouldn't end up in another closed-off canyon. Just the thought of having to hold his breath while swimming through some underwater tunnel, hoping he could make it to the next air pocket, was enough to induce a panic attack. But to do it with Joseph? No way. He'd seen all those movies, and he wasn't going to watch Joseph do a Kurt Russell from the *Poseidon* remake.

They couldn't see anything, and that alone was terrifying. They could slam into a rock or drop a hundred feet at any given second, but all they could hear was the rushing water rolling off the cave walls, and all they could feel were the icy waves slapping them in the face. Jack had yet to feel the bottom with his feet. That could be a good thing, the floodwaters carrying them over top of jagged outcroppings, but if they ended up in another pool where the waters had risen above the exit, then they'd be faced with the aforementioned situation. And Jack might just prefer hypothermia to drowning.

It felt like they'd been moving for hours through a blackout version of some water park attraction. Like Sesame Place meets Space Mountain. But again Jack knew it had just been minutes. The absence of light did funny things with time, and he wanted to check his watch just to give himself a handhold on reality, but he was afraid to loosen his grip on Joe to do so.

Then the sound of the water began to grow louder, echoing around them in a deafening roar. He tried to imagine the scene in his mind's eye, what could make the water sound so loud. It had to be blockage. The water was rushing into a wall or rocks or pouring down into more water. Maybe the cave was bottlenecking, the water roiling through the smaller space.

Things started moving even faster, and it felt like they'd been shot out of a sling. His head went beneath the water even as he tried to keep Joseph's elevated. They were spinning, beginning to tumble. His grip was slipping, the force of the current trying to tear them apart.

He struck a wall, and the force of the impact knocked him free of his senses and all bodily control. His arms flung wide, and Joseph was pulled away.

His motor functions came back a second or two later, and he waved his arms, trying to catch his son. But he was pinned against the wall, white spots flashing in his head. Then he was sliding alongside the wall and rushing out of the mountain toward sudden daylight.

He flowed out of the cave and squinted against the brightness. He turned back and saw one of the mountain's many mouths shrinking away as he continued to be pulled downriver. Evergreens grew all around the opening, stretching up toward the sky and making the gap nearly invisible from the outside. The light was too intense, his right eye throbbing, and he turned back around. He forced himself to look for Joseph and quickly spotted him some fifty feet ahead, about to round a bend. Jack saw that the water they were in was going to merge them into a much bigger and more powerful river.

"Joe!" he called. He thought he heard the boy's voice over the water rushing in his ears, but he wasn't sure. And then he was around the bend and thrown into the larger river. "Try to grab on to something!" he yelled. Rocks flew by him on all sides, the river winding, dropping, winding more. It might have been fun if they were in a kayak with life vests and helmets.

Then he heard it, and there was no mistaking what it was.

They were going over.

122

WHERE DOES THE UNDERGROUND river let out?" Johnson asked the sheriff over the radio. The pilot was taking them down over the clearing, the hole in the ground just ten feet below them, the surrounding forest pressing in close to the spinning blades.

"*Hold on. Let me get you in touch with someone who knows the mountain,*" the sheriff said.

"Anything you know, I need to know right now. Could be that someone is down there."

"*Down in the caves?*"

"Possibly." He held the radio to his ear to get the response.

"*Well, like I said before, they're probably flooded. If they're lucky, they fell into the river connects to all the others. River could carry them straight out.*"

"And if they're not lucky?"

"*If they're not lucky, then they could be trapped in a cave with no way out.*"

Johnson looked at Stacey, but she couldn't hear the other side of the conversation over the sound of the chopper.

"Where does the underground river exit the mountain?"

"*I've never seen it myself, but I hear there's a cave on the west side. It connects to the river and flows down the mountain, continues for miles before joining another river.*"

"Thanks. And get me that guy."

"*You got it. Oh, there's a waterfall. Pretty steep one too. I've seen that from a distance.*"

"Thanks. Over." Johnson nodded to the men surrounding them, and they immediately began getting into position.

"What are they doing?" Stacey asked Johnson.

"Fast-roping."

"Into the canyon?"

He nodded. "These guys are trained the same as Delta. Don't worry, the pilot was a Night Stalker before joining the Bureau. They're trained to fly in spots no one else would dare try squeezing into."

She watched the men around her clip onto the ropes and disappear out the side of the helicopter. She looked over the side, past the landing skids, and saw four ropes hanging down into the black hole. The operators were already down there, and she could see the beams of flashlights crisscrossing back and forth from within.

"Anything?" Johnson called over the radio.

"It's filled with water. No answers to our calls. Looks like there's a vehicle at the bottom. Maybe twenty feet deep. Probably an ATV."

"No sign of them?"

"No."

"Are there any other ways out? The local sheriff said it was possible they could ride the underground river all the way out of the mountain."

"It looks like there's a crack in the wall that may lead into another chamber."

Stacey sighed in relief. There was still hope.

"All right," Johnson said, "bringing you back up."

The four operators rose out of the darkness and back to the hovering helicopter.

"Let's find the river," Johnson said.

The pilot lifted them up out of the clearing and headed west.

123

THE ROARING GREW TO an impossible, constant thunder, and just before he went over, Jack caught a glimpse of Joe's hand sticking up out of the rapids, hoping for someone on the other side to take it and pull him to safety at the last second. Then his hand dropped from sight, and Jack screamed his name.

Jack's stomach tightened into a fist and shot up into his throat as he was carried over the edge and flung into the frothy cascade of plunging water. As he fell, and his mind seemed to escape the constraints of time, he thought of Michael Douglas. Of the movie he'd watched a hundred times with his grandfather. *Romancing The Stone*. They'd had it on VHS, but he wasn't allowed to watch it alone, not without Grandpa sitting there with a ready remote for strategic fast-forwarding. Released in March of 1984, it was one of those PG movies that you wouldn't dare show your kids today (the PG-13 rating would come with *Red Dawn* in August of the same year after the May release of *Indiana Jones and the Temple of Doom* led to a decision to adopt a rating somewhere between PG and R). Of course, that hadn't stopped Jack from popping the tape into the VCR when no one else was home. But it was still a grainy VHS tape on an old projection TV. It wasn't until he'd seen the movie much later on 1080p Blu-ray that he realized just what his grandfather had been fast-forwarding. He wondered if some of those old movies would have to be re-rated by the Motion Picture Association after 4K restoration allowed you to see with clarity things never seen before. Like the opening of *Jaws*. PG for sure.

As he got closer and closer to the point of impact, more knowledge of *Romancing The Stone* flashed through his mind at lightning speed, and he remembered an article about how Michael Douglas's stunt man nearly died while filming the waterfall scene. There were platforms attached to the car that they were supposed to jump from in order to clear the car and the whirlpool below, but one of them malfunctioned, and the stunt man went straight down with the car. He later told how it took every ounce of energy he had to break free of the whirlpool. Ironically, Jack thought, the name of the character Michael Douglas played was Jack. Or maybe it wasn't so ironic, he supposed. There seemed to be an overabundance of characters named Jack, so the odds were probably better than he supposed.

He wondered how many more times he was going to go over a —

The force with which he struck the surface stunned him and shot all thought from his brain. The sheer energy of water rendered him powerless against it, and it pushed him down to the bottom of a pool that had been hundreds, if not thousands of years in the making. He felt his body strike objects. His knees, elbows, feet... Was it the ground or rock or ancient trees that had been swept over and caught forever in this churning prison? There was no sense of up or down, and all he knew was that he was spinning. Rolling, end over end. He opened his eyes, but saw only confusion. His lungs started to burn. He needed to find up. Now.

As he thrust his feet out, hoping to make contact with something that would orient him, he thought of his son. Was he here with him in this washing machine, tumbling just inches out of his reach? Or had the whirlpool released him already, and his boy was now heading further downstream without him? Jack kicked, and he kicked, afraid that he was just propelling himself down and away from the air he so desperately needed. He was so very close to inhaling. The stuntman's words played back in his mind, "every ounce of energy..." He kicked his feet as hard as he could, moving his arms, not caring what direction he was going in. If he swam down to the bottom, then at least he'd know where the bottom was. He just needed to escape the whirlpool. It didn't matter in which direction.

He stopped tumbling. The roaring in his ears lessened. He looked around and saw the sun up through the water, behind a liquid veil.

His head broke the surface, and he inhaled with a loud, violent gasp. He coughed, and then inhaled more precious air. He looked around, barely noticing his more peripheral surroundings, his eyes searching the surface of the river for small splashing hands. Looking back toward the waterfall, he saw just how remarkable it was. It shot out into the air, propelled by the force of the floodwaters, and crashed with unforgiving violence into a rainbow mist of frothing mayhem. It looked to be about forty or fifty feet high with piles of rocks at its base. Had it not been for the flood shooting him out past the rocks, he might have been crushed against them. Hell, if not for the flood, they might not have survived the fall into the cave at all.

But where was Joseph? He called out at the top of his lungs even as the river continued to carry him down the mountain. "Joseph!" He called out over and over again, his eyes still focusing on the water immediately around him.

Then he heard a voice.

He turned every which way, trying to locate it.

There. Off to his right along the bank. There was a group of rocks, and Joseph was kneeling on one of them, waving his hand.

Thank God. Thank you, God, was all Jack could think. He closed his eyes, overcome with both relief and the terrifying sense of just how close he'd been to losing his son again. He started to swim, working his way toward the river's edge. But the water was still moving too fast, and he wasn't able to get to the rocks Joseph had found safety on. He floated past him.

"I'll meet you further down," he yelled, and swam harder. His shoulders were on fire, his hamstrings tightening and nearing spasm. He rolled onto his back and just floated along with the current. Joseph would be fine, he told himself. He was a mountain man. A real Jeremiah Johnson or Daniel Boone. He watched the clouds drift on by, felt the sun warm his face.

The river was quick but gentle, and as he looked to his left and to his right, he saw the wilderness pressing in. Big rocks littered the banks, and the river flowed around them, winding through the forest like a slithering snake.

Once his muscles relaxed, he started moving toward the edge again. Eventually, he came to a fallen tree and was able to wrap his arms around one of its submerged branches. He pulled himself along it, hand over hand, until his feet could touch the ground. He walked out of the water and collapsed. He still had the belt and his knife around his waist but that was it. No gun, no radio. He rolled onto his back and called out for Joseph. He didn't think he'd drifted too far past him, and was expecting to hear him come running through the underbrush at any moment. He smiled, unable to comprehend their escape. He thanked God again. "Joseph! I'm over here!"

Still nothing.

He got onto his side and forced himself to his knees. The forest was dense with evergreens, and it reminded him of pictures of the Canadian wilderness. Of grizzlies catching salmon out of streams. The river bent behind some large rocks about a hundred feet away, and he couldn't see beyond them. Getting to his feet, he called out again, but again he got no response. He stumbled back upriver.

He stopped. Listened.

There was a noise... A thumping noise. Like the bass turned all the way up on some top-of-the-line car stereo of some college kid's souped-up Honda Civic. It got closer. Louder. And then a shadow fell over him, and he looked up. Saw a helicopter appear over the tree line and shoot past him before banking and coming back around.

124

IF IT WEREN'T FOR the sunlight glinting off the water through the trees, Stacey might never have spotted the river. As they flew over it, they began following it downstream to the waterfall.

"Look," Johnson pointed out.

Stacey saw what he was talking about. There it was. The smaller river coming out of a cave nestled into the side of the mountain and flowing about seventy-five yards before merging into the larger river they'd been following. She could tell that the water level had risen above normal because the tall grass along the bank was mashed down and bent and covered in mud. How small this little underground river usually was, she couldn't begin to guess. Maybe a little stream, a trickle of water that merely wove its way through a stony bed.

The pilot navigated the river, taking it slow, following the bends, giving them an opportunity to get a good look below. They came upon the waterfall, and she couldn't help bringing a hand to her mouth. Could they have survived that? The pilot expertly brought the helicopter around and hovered at the base of the fall. They all peered through the churning water, exploring the nearby rocks and shores, searching for any sign of her family. They stayed there for a good three minutes, hanging mere feet above the rapids and staring into the mist before turning and continuing downriver.

Was it possible? Stacey wondered. That they could've made it out of that cave and down the waterfall? She craned her neck to search below, but the forest was so thick here that she couldn't see anything but the winding river and all its many rocks.

"Up ahead, on the right," one of the pilots said. "See him?"

Stacey and Johnson looked and saw a man standing on the bank of the river. As they got closer, the man looked up.

Stacey's heart leapt in her chest, and she gasped. "Jack," she whispered.

125

JACK WATCHED THE HELICOPTER begin to descend fifty yards further downriver where it was wider and the trees weren't pressing in as much. The downdraft made a circle of white in the water below it, and even at a hundred and fifty feet away, Jack had to cover his face with his arm against the spraying mist. The pilot had the helicopter's skids about a foot off the surface of the water, holding it with perfect steadiness as men began jumping out and into the knee-deep water near the shore. They were dressed in black and had semiautomatic rifles.

Jack began to backpedal. Were the Bakers this well connected that they had a hit team with a helicopter at their beck and call, or was this the Russians? It didn't look like the Russians. It looked like a CIA death squad to him. The helicopter rose back into the air, the men it had left behind beginning to walk toward him. He turned to run.

"Jack, wait!" a voice called out.

He turned back and saw the four men, walking shoulder to shoulder, begin to part. Two people in plain clothes appeared behind them, one of them a woman, her hair blowing in the breeze. He squinted, sure that his eyes hadn't fully adjusted to the light yet or that his injured eye was in some way distorting his view. Because the woman looked just like—

"Jack!" she called out.

His jaw went slack, and without even realizing it, his legs began moving. Before he could comprehend what was happening, he was holding his wife in his arms, running his hands over her face, through her hair. She was doing the same, neither one of them sure if they could really trust that this was real. They kissed and embraced. Then she pulled away and looked into his eyes.

"Where's Joseph?"

Jack turned and pointed upriver. "We went over the waterfall back there, but he got out okay. I saw him climbing on some rocks as I was swept by. I just got out. Was about to go look for him when you showed up."

She didn't wait for another word, just started moving in the direction Jack had pointed. "Joseph," she called out, navigating the rocks and heading behind the tree line.

"Hey, Jack," said another voice.

He looked up and spotted the plain-clothed man stepping forward with an outstretched hand. Jack blinked, momentarily confused. And then it hit him like a thunderbolt. He was eight years older, of course. Had a different hairstyle and some white in a short beard, but it was him alright. Agent Johnson. "What the hell are you doing here?"

"That's a long story, so why don't we get your son and get out of here before I start telling it?"

"Yeah, yeah. Of course." Jack started walking after Stacey, but he held Johnson and the four armed men in his quizzical gaze for just a moment longer. He caught up to Stacey, and they both moved quickly behind the tree line, running alongside the river and calling out for their son.

"I don't understand," Jack said, growing worried. "He saw me go past him. He should've headed downriver after me."

"Maybe he fell or got hurt," Stacey said.

"Maybe," he muttered, and picked up his pace, ignoring the muscles beginning to knot in his legs again.

They followed the edge of the river for another five minutes, climbing slopes and circumnavigating large boulders and debris from the storm until they rounded a bend and could see straight to the waterfall.

"You went down that?" Stacey asked.

But Jack didn't answer. He was too busy looking around. "Where the hell is he?"

Stacey turned in a complete circle, her eyes absorbing the entire scene.

A blast exploded behind them.

Instinctively, they both ducked behind a nearby rock, their feet splashing in the water.

"That came from the woods," Stacey said.

They could hear Johnson and the other men yelling.

Another crack echoed through the forest.

Jack took off, trudging through the water toward Johnson, using the rocks as cover. He slipped and went down, started to get carried away by the current, but grabbed a branch and pulled himself back to his feet. He looked behind him and saw that Stacey had gone straight into the woods and was currently weaving her way through the trees. He stumbled out of the water and went after her.

Another shot.

Why weren't Johnson and his men firing back? But he knew the answer. He ran through the trees and cleared the river bend and could see three of the men in fatigues, ten yards away and crouching behind rocks and a fallen tree in the shallow water along the bank. They were aiming into the woods, while the fourth of them was floating, spread-eagle on his back in the water. The current was keeping him pressed against the tree, but soon he'd be carried around it and drifting away. Jack ducked to the ground and tried to peer through the woods in the direction they were facing. Stacey was a few feet to his right, behind an adjacent tree.

"I think they have him," he said to her.

"Who?" she whispered back.

He brushed his wet hair back out of his face. "Joe."

"*Who* has him?"

He thought about it. Could be the Russians. He didn't think it was James, not after what had happened last night. Colt, then?

And then a voice cried out from the shadows of the forest and removed all doubt.

"You killed my brothers, asshole!"

Seth.

Jack followed the voice with his eyes, realizing the sole remaining Baker brother must have been tracking them. And sure enough... "Oh, god," he gasped.

"What?" Stacey asked.

Eyes wide and watering, Jack pointed. About a hundred feet behind the tree line, he could just make out Joseph tied to a tree and facing the river. Seth was behind the same tree, using it for cover. Had Johnson's men returned fire, Joseph would've surely been hit. Which he assumed meant that they'd seen him. But he couldn't just assume. He had to make sure they knew. He waved at Stacey. "Do you see him?" The look on Stacey's face when she turned toward him told him that she had. "We need to tell Johnson not to return fire," he said.

The helicopter circled above, but Jack knew they had no shot through the trees. He picked up a rock and threw it at the men held up along the bank. They looked his way, and he waved. "He has my son tied to the front of the tree he's behind," he yelled in a whisper.

Johnson nodded. "We see him," he said back.

"What do we do?" Stacey asked. But she wasn't really asking him. She knew infinitely more than he did. She was thinking out loud, going through her options. She looked at him. "You think it's just one guy?"

He nodded.

Seth's voice echoed back. "If I see any of you tryin' to circle 'round me, I'll slit the boy's throat."

"What do you want?" Jack yelled back, not caring that it might give away his location. And in fact, a shot sounded, and a chunk of the tree between him and Stacey exploded.

"I want a trade," he answered. "You for the boy. Father for son!"

If the Baker brother would honor such a thing, then Jack would walk out to him right now. He knew for a fact that Cullin would shoot Joe in the head, laugh, and then shoot him between the legs and laugh some more. Maybe Lee would too. So how could he trust Seth?

Johnson got their attention and tossed a radio to them. Stacey caught it as another shot sent everyone back down for cover. She held it to her ear and heard the pilot say he was somewhere behind the shooter's position and that his co-pilot was fast-roping down. He'd work his way toward the shooter and try to get a clear shot from behind.

"What's going on?" Jack asked her.

She signaled with her hands what they were planning.

"*Be advised, Alpha Two is on the ground. Over,*" the pilot said.

126

JOSEPH WAS STILL WET and shivering, and his back hurt from slamming into something along the bottom of the river, but he was otherwise okay. He could see the men in black ducking for cover along the riverbank. His dad was with them, so he guessed they were the good guys.

He'd been working his way downriver, chasing after his dad, when this bear of a man came barreling out of the woods beside him and tackled him. Before he even knew what was happening or could get a look at the man, he'd had his hands tied behind his back with a piece of rope. After being pulled to his feet and spun around, Joseph noticed the man from the cabin. The one with the shaved head who looked like an MMA fighter. Joseph didn't have any idea how he'd found him or where he'd planned on taking him, but when they heard his dad's voice calling out for him, the man had pressed a knife against his throat, right on top of the scar. He'd felt his skin open a little, blood running down his neck.

"If you make a sound, I'll cut your head off and toss it to dear ol' dad, and when he goes to catch it, I'll shoot him," he'd said. So he hadn't made a noise, just let himself get pulled along and away from the river.

But when the helicopter appeared, the man's plans seemed to change, and instead of making a run for it, he decided he'd rather make a stand. So he'd untied his hands and shoved him against a tree, using the rope to hold him there.

But Joseph had held his arms out at his sides a good four inches while Seth tied it off behind him, the muscles in his shoulders screaming as he strained against the rope while trying not to give away what he was doing.

It seemed to have worked. When he relaxed his arms, he could feel the rope go slack a little. He kept pressure against it, keeping it tight, waiting for the right moment.

He heard Seth demand a trade, but knew it was crap. He'd just shoot his dad when he got close. He had to do something. If he could make a run for it, maybe it would give the police a clear shot, and they'd take Seth out before he could shoot him in the back. Maybe not. But he couldn't let his dad die. He'd risk his own life to make sure of it.

While Seth shouted at the men across from them and took an occasional shot in their direction, Joseph began relaxing his arms.

The rope dropped a few inches. Slowly, he began wriggling his arms, and the rope shimmied down some more. Seth wasn't looking. He was too preoccupied with the activity along the riverbank.

He bent his elbow and moved his hand up under his shirt. Along his belt. He began working out the pocketknife with his fingers. He held it in his fist, finding the lever and pressing it. The blade swung open. The rope was down around his stomach.

Movement to his left caught his eye. Someone was moving through the trees, coming toward them. *No*, he thought. He almost shouted for them to get back, not to trust this guy, but then he saw who it was, and he froze.

It was his mom.

127

CROUCHING LOW, STACEY DARTED from one tree to the next despite Jack's pleas to stay put and to wait for the operative who was coming up behind Seth. She couldn't just sit there and wait, though without a weapon she wasn't sure what she'd be able to do. Maybe she just wanted to make eye contact with her boy, to let him know that she'd come for him. If things didn't end well, at least he'd know she'd come.

So far the guy hadn't noticed her flanking him. His attention was on the THU operatives on the riverbank. But she knew all it would take was one snap of a branch to bring his attention to her—and his rifle with it.

She was about fifty feet away and could see Joseph, her brave boy. He was moving his arms ever so slightly, and the rope was shimmying down his body. She watched him take something from his pants, and then the blade of a knife appeared. She was both filled with dread and awe. Her beautiful, brave boy. What was he going to do? What was he thinking? He was twelve years old. He should be crying and wetting his pants, not pulling out a knife.

She moved a little closer, to the next tree. His face...there was no fear in it. Only determination.

He looked her way, and their eyes met.

It was a moment in time that seemed to stand still, as if the universe was put on pause, yet their minds still free to play on. So much was communicated in that twinkle of an eye, so much love, hope, and understanding. Yet there were questions too. Questions that would take years to unwrap. Years... She needed them to have that time. As painful and impossible as those questions might be to unearth and explore and even dodge and deny, they needed the time to do it. For a second though, she thought he was about to call out, and then it would all be over.

He didn't. Instead he looked away, pretending as if he hadn't seen her at all, afraid that his attention might make the man behind him look over in her direction. He brought his arms up and out of the rope but continued to hold the rope in place so that it didn't fall to his feet. Not yet.

The man was leaning against the other side of the tree so that she couldn't see his face. And he couldn't see hers. He fired another shot at the river.

And that was when Joseph made his move.

She watched it all in slow motion. Half of her crying out for him to stop, the other half cheering him on, hopeful. Without realizing it, her feet propelled her forward, out from behind the tree and toward her son as he let the rope fall.

Joseph spun to his left and back around the tree he'd been tied to, knife swinging in a wide arc at the man's exposed back, kidneys, and ribs.

She heard the man cry out and saw the barrel of the gun that was on the other side of the tree go pointing into the air. Then Joseph was running. But not toward her. He was running for the river and the men with guns, and she understood why, even though a boy his age shouldn't have such situational instincts. He knew that running to his mother could get them both shot. So instead, he was running away from her, hoping to keep her concealed.

But she wasn't. She'd left the trees and was already halfway to him when Joseph sprinted past his captor. She turned her head and watched him run, and all she could think was, *Don't run with the knife in your hand.* But he was no small child anymore, was he? Just in the last two minutes alone, she'd seen that he was older than she'd ever imagined.

The man stumbled from behind the tree and started chasing after Joseph. She knew that the operatives wouldn't have a shot with Joseph blocking the target. She ran after them. Thought of screaming to get the man's attention, but knew that would just get her shot and that the man would still be able to shoot Joseph anyway.

She ran harder.

Just as the guy reached out to grab Joe's shoulder, a blur of movement crossed Stacey's periphery and slammed into the man, lifting him off the ground.

Jack.

He'd tackled the bald man, leveling his shoulder into his ribs right where Joe had stabbed him. They went down together, the rifle bouncing off the ground away from them. Joseph stopped and turned.

"Go," Stacey yelled to him, pointing toward the men in the river.

Joseph looked at her and then back at his dad then back at her again. Finally, as much as his eyes said he hated it, he obeyed. He turned and ran for the water.

Stacey went for the rifle.

128

JACK ROLLED ON TOP of Seth and threw a punch at his face. But Seth blocked it with his large forearms and lifted his leg into Jack's groin, thrusting him forward and over his head. Jack landed on his back but quickly got to his feet. He took another run at Seth, but Seth just grabbed him, halting his momentum like he were a brick wall. He punched Jack in the face while still holding him with his other hand.

Jack knew that his close proximity to Seth was the only thing preventing Johnson's men from taking Seth out. He had to get away from him, to give them a clear shot. Even as Seth's fist was bashing his face, he saw Johnson leaving the bank and making his way toward them, the three operatives on his heels, rifles raised, knees bent in a crouch. Tactical.

Seth whipped out a knife and thrust it into Jack's side. Jack screamed, pulled out his own knife and returned the favor, sliding the six inches of high-carbon steel into Seth's gut. They stumbled away from each other, each one holding their wounds, blood seeping between their fingers. But before anyone could get off a shot, Seth was running again.

Jack braced for the impact, but the bull ran straight past him, and Jack was again between Seth and Johnson's rifles. He turned to see where Seth was going. Was he making a run for it?

And there was Stacey, her back turned toward them, bending over and making sure the rifle she picked up off the ground was loaded. She slammed the bolt home, sliding a round into the chamber, and started to swing back toward them. But before she could bring the gun all the way around, Seth took her to the ground. Again the rifle flew.

Jack turned and ran, knife ready and like a heat-seeking missile. But he felt like he was running in a dream, his feet stuck in mud. Too slow. He watched Seth raise his knife.

Johnson and his men all appeared to be in the same quicksand, so close but still too far and not gaining ground fast enough.

Joe was behind them all, hands balled into fists at his sides, his mouth open, yelling, though Jack couldn't hear anything other than the blood rushing in his ears.

Seth's knife plunged into Stacey's stomach. One. Two. Three times. Trails of blood clinging to the blade and splashing the ground. Her eyes went wide, the man's weight trapping her beneath him. She punched and slapped and pushed on his chest, but his huge frame wouldn't budge.

Seth put the knife to her throat and lay on top of her. He licked her face and started to cut.

Jack screamed, still five feet away.

STACEY FELT THE KNIFE press into her neck and knew this was it. She was aware of Jack and Johnson's team in the background, blurred and out of focus behind the frame of this man's face, but they were too far away to stop him. At least they'd be able to kill him now, and Joseph would be safe. That was all she'd wanted. She relaxed and waited for the blade to sever the muscle in her neck, to open her throat and empty her of her life force. She felt his tongue on her face and thought of all the things she'd done with men and women over the years. Perhaps men and women more vile than this man. She'd never know. If she could only do it all over... But would she? Joseph filled her mind's eye. Her brave little boy. *No*, she thought. *He's a man.* And he would be fine. She opened her eyes and looked at the man who was ending her life.

The knife sank deep, and she felt it start to slide.

Then she went blind.

At first she thought she was dead. Then thought that her own arterial spray had shot into her eyes. But she felt the man's head strike the side of her face and his body go limp on top of her. She brought a hand up and wiped her eyes and saw that half the guy's head was missing. His skull was cracked open like a ceramic pot, and what was left of his brain sat in the bone bowl like a gob of jellyfish. She pulled a flap of his skin off her forehead and pushed him off her. She rolled away from his corpse just as Jack came sliding on his knees beside her.

She went to wrap her arms around him, but pain in her stomach doubled her over, and she clutched at the damage done there. Jack was yelling something, but she couldn't tell what.

Her vision faded, and everything became distorted, as if she were sinking underwater. Or fading into oblivion.

JACK LOOKED UP AT Johnson, who was on the radio, asking the operator who had just fast-roped down behind them if he'd taken the shot.

"*Negative,*" came the response.

Holding Stacey in his arms, Jack looked around for where the shot could have come from. And there, up in the trees atop a hill on the other side of the river, he caught the glint of sunlight off a scope.

Johnson saw it too and began raising his pistol, though it was probably more of a reaction or a message to the others than an actual attempt to use it.

"No," Jack said, reaching up and putting his hand over the pistol, lowering it. "Let him be."

Johnson looked at him with a hundred questions, but when he looked back to the hill, the person was gone.

Jack picked Stacey up in his arms and carried her down to the river, Joseph walking beside him, crying.

COLT LOWERED THE RIFLE with a sense of satisfaction. He didn't know if he'd gotten the shot off before Seth damaged the woman beyond repair, but he had definitely put that asshole down once and for all. No more Bakers. No more Bakerville. And whatever double-crossing scheme they'd cooked up with the Commies, he was having the last laugh, wasn't he?

The boy looked to be okay, and that was fine with him. The boy was a survivor, and he respected survivors.

He ducked back into the woods just in case the boy's father changed his mind about coming after him. He'd seen him stop the man from raising his gun, which he took as a "let him be" gesture.

Colt knelt in the thicket and watched them for a while. The helicopter came back and descended on the banks, the pilot resting the skids on top of the water. Colt was impressed, the guy was good.

The men in fatigues, some sort of Special Forces unit it looked like, helped the woman onto the chopper, then the boy, his father, and the plain-clothed man. One of them climbed into the co-pilot's chair and another hopped in the back. Then the helicopter rose into the air and flew away, leaving two of the operatives behind with their fallen brother and Seth's body. That meant another helicopter was probably on its way.

He got to his feet, checked the sun, and set a course. He didn't know what happened to James and wished them luck, but now he was leaving all of that behind. Michael had succumbed to his injuries overnight, and he'd buried him. Maybe someday he'd look up James. See what happened to him. Send him a letter letting him know where his brother was resting.

He headed north.

132

AFTER GETTING MEDICAL ATTENTION himself and being cleared for release after stitches, Jack had worked with Johnson to acquire a rental car. Thankfully, Jack still had his license on him. Johnson had said something about having someone take Stacey's car back to their house, though he wasn't clear on where she'd left it.

When Jack went to get the rental from the place across the street, he'd found that there was a Starbucks next to it. He'd gotten only his second coffee since the bad batch he'd made Monday morning. He sipped it as he hobbled back through the hospital, his entire body feeling as if it had been steamrolled.

When he got back to the waiting room, a nurse told him that Stacey was ready to see him. He thanked her and spent a couple of minutes with Joseph before going to see his wife.

Ten minutes later, he motioned for Joseph to come into the room, and his son obeyed. Though there was a slight hesitation in his step, as if he feared getting too close to his mother might kill her. Like he had a communicable disease that she was susceptible to. It was fear, Jack knew. Fear that this could be a final conversation and not sure how to go about it. Not wanting to.

"It's okay, Joe," Jack said. "She's going to be fine." He put his arm around his shoulders and, forgetting about his own wound, pulled him in tight. He winced.

Stacey opened her eyes and looked at them standing there beside the bed. Her throat was wrapped, and Jack was sure that Joseph was thinking of the old story about the girl with the green ribbon around her neck. Only it was white gauze keeping his mom's head on her body. God, that story had messed him up as a kid. He wasn't sure why he'd read it to Joseph when he was younger. Probably thought it'd be fun to see his reaction.

"Hi, baby," she said, reaching out and taking Joseph's hand. Her eyes went to her son's neck where the same knife that would've severed her head had traced an old scar on his, and when her eyes darted from the small bandage to Jack's eyes, Jack gave a subtle nod.

What did Joseph remember of that day when he had been here in his mother's place, lying on a hospital bed with a white ribbon around his neck? Well, if anything would jog his memory, it would be a fresh cut on top of an old wound, the similarities of which he wouldn't be able to miss. And now it wouldn't just be the mirror that would taunt him with clues, it'd be every time he looked at his mom and saw her scar staring at him too.

Jack ruffled Joseph's hair. "Okay, sport, give us a minute."

Joseph leaned down and kissed Stacey on the cheek.

"I love you," Stacey said.

"Love you too, Mom." Then he turned and left the room.

Jack sat on the edge of the bed.

"Did he say what happened?" Stacey asked, still a little drowsy.

"Not all of it. I don't want to push him. He'll talk when he's ready."

"You don't think we need to worry about...you know. If anything happened up there."

Jack shook his head. "No, I don't think so."

"He's so strong," she whispered.

"Definitely stronger than me."

She gave him a disapproving look and squeezed his hand. "You literally climbed mountains and took on gangs to save our son."

"And now I think I could sleep for a month."

She smiled. "Thank you."

"I did what any father would."

"If every father were Mel Gibson."

He laughed, loving how the three of their minds shared a common wavelength, even if it was something as insignificant as movie references.

"My Jerry has really turned into Jerrymiah," she said. Then she broke eye contact. "Speaking of Johnsons, did you talk to

Johnson?"

"A little."

"Where is he?"

"Out there in the waiting room with Joe."

She looked back at him, her eyes probing for something, but he wasn't sure what.

"What?"

"Nothing."

But something twinged in his gut. The way she was looking at him...it was the same way she'd looked at him eight years ago when she'd walked into their bedroom the night of Trenton. "What did they want you to do?"

"What do you mean?"

He sighed and stood. "Seriously?"

"Did Johnson say something?"

"No, but it's not hard to put together. They were supposed to hold him until Saturday, so either you were trying to get rid of me"—he managed to keep himself from adding "again"—"or someone was using him as leverage."

She stared at the wall across the room.

"So who was it? The Russians again? The FSB? Another former husband? The CIA?"

"I don't know," she said. She closed her eyes. "It's a long story."

"I bet. You called Johnson?"

"I found his card in your drawer."

"If it weren't for him and his FBI friends..."

"Yeah," Stacey said, quickly imagining a very different ending to the story. "Jack," she said, squeezing his hand again and staring into his eyes. She started to cry.

"What?" He thought this was the moment where she told him that it had been her who had tried to get rid of him after all, that she had to in order to save Joseph. Again.

"My injuries..."

Jack watched the tears run down her cheeks and cling to the underside of her jaw.

She took a deep breath, as if the words she were trying to speak had gotten stuck and could only be blown out. "I can't have children anymore."

Jack felt like he'd been slapped. *Children?* They'd just crossed into the forties. Had more kids even been something they—his mind reeled, not sure what to do with the information. But then he felt it. Felt it deep down in his soul. Bethany. Their daughter. Somehow she was in the equation, her absence suddenly front and center. His own eyes started to water. They'd had a larger family for a short period of time, and they'd loved it. They probably would've never tried to replicate that feeling again, but now came the keen awareness that it was no longer a possibility at all. And they were left grieving the loss of something that they realized too late that perhaps they'd wanted.

Jack didn't know what to say, so he brushed her hair back, wiped her tears.

A knock on the door.

They both looked over and saw someone bring in a bouquet of flowers.

"Where would you like them?" the person asked.

"I'll take them," Jack said. He wiped his eyes and stood, holding out his arms. "Thanks." He brought them over to the bed. When the person left, he asked, "Who the hell knows we're here?"

"Maybe it's the wrong room?" Stacey wiped her eyes.

Jack picked the envelope out of the arrangement and handed it to her. There was no name on the front of it.

Stacey tore it open and peered inside. She frowned.

"What?" Jack asked.

She slowly pulled out its contents. A glossy four-by-six of Yul Brynner and Ingrid Bergman.

Jack leaned forward. "A movie poster?"

Anastasia. 1956.

The picture began to shake in her hand.

"I don't get it," he said. That there was a correlation between his wife's real name and the name of the movie's title, however, he did get. Was it a message from the Russians? Letting her know they were still out there? That maybe she still had something to do?

When she looked up from the picture, the color in her face was gone, like she'd seen a ghost. "Go get Johnson."

Jack didn't hesitate. He darted out the door.

JACK LED JOHNSON BACK into the room, and before they even got to Stacey's side, Stacey asked, "What were you going to tell me? Up at the cabin before the helicopter came?"

Johnson looked momentarily confused, wondering what he'd missed.

Stacey handed him the picture of the poster. "You know something about the people behind this, don't you?"

Johnson took the picture and studied it.

"*Anastasia*," Stacey said. "Based on the seventeen-year-old Grand Duchess Anastasia Nikolaevna of Russia."

"Played by Meg Ryan in the cartoon movie?" Jack interjected.

Johnson ignored him, thinking. "1918. The Imperial family... The czar and his ten family members were killed by the Communist revolutionaries who had them under house arrest. Shot, clubbed, stabbed. Their bodies hacked to pieces, burned with acid, and buried in an abandoned mine."

Stacey looked at him, wondering how he might have come to know that.

"I read Radzinsky's book."

"That was almost thirty years ago."

Jack looked back and forth between them.

"I didn't read it thirty years ago," Johnson said.

Stacey seemed to let it go. "So you know that there were supposed sightings of Anastasia throughout the 1920s and 30s."

"Fueling the theory that they'd let at least one of the children escape."

"And paving the way for impostors pretending to be the youngest daughter."

"And screenplays."

"It's more complicated than that though," Stacey said.

"It always is when there's a cover-up."

Again Stacey stared at Agent Johnson.

He sighed. "I know about the different theories, that Lenin ordered the execution because he wanted to prevent the Czechoslovak Legion from rescuing them. That the Soviets claimed they were killed by left-wing revolutionaries and later tried to deny they were even dead. That Stalin prohibited any discussion of the event.

"In 2007, the bodies of Alexei and either Anastasia or her older sister were found in a separate, unmarked grave. DNA testing confirmed that all four grand duchesses had been killed in 1918. The fraud, Anna Anderson, who claimed to be Anastasia, was cremated in 1984, but DNA testing in 1994 showed no relation to the Romanovs."

Johnson walked away from the bed and went to the window. He stared out at the Virginia traffic.

"What does this have to do with anything?" Jack asked. He felt his heart begin to beat faster, the tension in the room growing, but he didn't know why. "What? Is this like the books that guy was sending you before? Are you supposed to be Anastasia? Is it a threat or something?"

"I was Anastasia, but I wasn't the real Anastasia. I was Anna Anderson. An impersonator. He thought it was so funny and that he was so clever with his nickname. But like the cartoon movie, I began to feel that Rasputin's curse had extended to even pretenders."

Jack was almost beside himself. He hated that his wife had this whole secret past with previous husbands and countries, and now her and Johnson were circling something they both seemed to know but wouldn't come out and say. "So who the hell sent the damn picture?"

Johnson answered as he continued to stare out the window. "We have reason to believe that you may not have succeeded in killing Fedyenka."

Stacey blinked. Apparently that was not the answer she'd expected, their dance circling different ideas. "No. I shot him."

Jack tilted his head. "I thought you said you hit him with a fire extinguisher."

Johnson turned from the window and looked at Stacey. "And he spent the next five years recovering from it. Had to learn to walk again."

"No," Stacey whispered.

"The guy who was sending you the books? He's still alive?" Jack stood.

"It's why I didn't think there was a bomb in your car," Johnson explained. "This was never about starting or preventing a war. It was always personal."

Tears filled her eyes. She fought against the very idea of it. She'd seen the back of his head break apart. The explosion... She caught her breath. "Did he even want Newell dead?"

He turned and looked into her eyes. "I don't know."

Jack looked back and forth between them, trying to fill in the gaps. *Who the hell is Newell?* His brain was overheating, melting. Had he just heard that his wife's former husband's jealous compatriot had been planning his revenge on her for the last eight years? And like before, good ol' Jack had been on the board simply by association? Just a pawn to be sacrificed or a nuisance to be removed?

"Agent Johnson," Stacey said, "or whoever you are, would you give Jack and me a moment?"

"Sure. I'll check on Joseph for you." He walked out of the room.

Jack stared at his wife and felt all the foundations he'd rebuilt over the last eight years begin to crumble. His life was teetering.

"Jack," she said calmly, "look at me. And listen to what I say."

He blinked and finally managed to hold her stare. "What?"

"We have something we need to do now, and I need to know you're with me on it."

"Do what?"

"There's a clear and present danger to our family, Jack."

If she'd meant to associate the Jack Ryan movie/novel with his own name, identifying him as Harrison Ford, then she certainly got what she'd wanted as he quickly made the deeper inference to *Patriot Games*, where Ryan's family is targeted by terrorists. Her meaning couldn't be clearer. "You need me to be Jack Ryan now."

"No," she said. "I need you to be John fucking Wick."

The look in her eyes scared him, yet he felt a fire beginning to rage in his own gut. Still, he couldn't help himself. "I guess you'll be Salt, then. Not Salt from Salt-N-Pepa. Angelina—"

Despite her injuries, she managed to reach up and grab his head. She lifted herself up and kissed him hard on the mouth.

When she let him go and collapsed back to the bed, he said, "Time to get our *Red Dawn* on."

She tried to nod but winced and brought her hands to her throat. Too much talking. Too much moving.

"Which means you need to focus on recovering," he said. "Get some sleep. I'll get Joseph and me a hotel."

"Have someone look at that eye," she said.

He waved her off. "I was just gonna get an eye patch." He kissed her again and said he'd call her in a bit. Then he went out to get Joseph. After all, there were Italian hoagies that needed to be eaten and *Into The Wild* to be watched. Whatever the hell had just happened in the hospital room could wait until tomorrow. For now, he was going to enjoy his son, who happened to be safe and sound beside him. Then he would sleep. And if upon waking, this all turned out not to have been a dream, then he'd worry about this Fedyenka asshole and whatever the next chapter of his life was going to look like then.

He told Johnson that he'd talk to him later, and he walked with his son, hand in hand, out of the hospital. As they approached the rental car, Jack looked across the parking lot and to the tree line across the street. "Joe, look," he said, pointing.

Joseph followed his father's finger and saw it. "What is it?" he asked.

"It's a gray fox."

The story continues in...

MAN IN THE FIRE
Coming Soon!

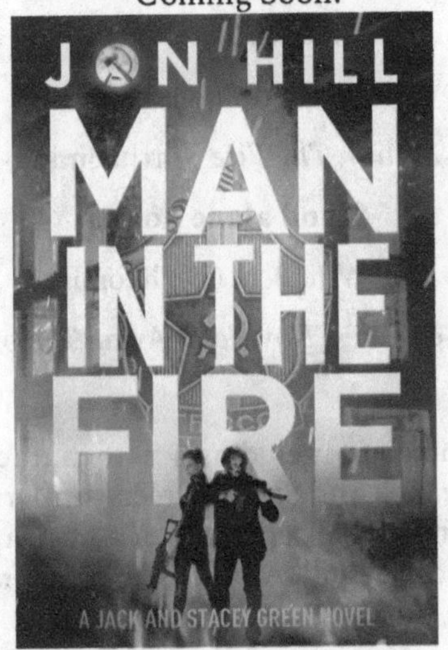

Also By Jon Hill

The Jack & Stacey Green Thrillers:

Man In The Water

Man In The Woods

Man In The Fire (forthcoming)

Stand alone novels:

My Wife Beth (forthcoming)

Seagull: A Novella of Avian Terror

Much more is on deck, including a new character series (that will merge The Jack and Stacey Green thrillers and My Wife Beth into the same world), episodes of a post-apocalyptic story along the lines of Seagull. A futuristic conspiracy story set in Antarctica, and much more.

Be sure to visit www.jonhillwrites.com to get on the mailing list and get a free copy of *Seagull*, to contact me, and for the inside scoop on current and upcoming projects!

IF YOU ENJOYED THIS story, then might I ask for just a couple more minutes of your time? If you wouldn't mind leaving a review, I would so much appreciate it! And feel free to hit me up on social media an let me know! I'd love to converse! Thank you in advance.

And don't forget to get on the mailing list for your free ultimate beach read and news on new releases and other projects!

About The Author

Jon Hill lives in Pennsylvania with his wife, children, and dog (princess) Leia. He's been on three cruises, which inspired his story *Man In The Water*. He loves to read and write, preferably on stormy days, and spends too much time watching movies when he should be writing. He is an avid football fan and misses the days of pick-up tackle football and two-on-two sand volleyball. He still gets to play basketball on occasion, but he's not that good at it. He works out and hates running, but since his wife is a runner, he finds himself trying to impress her by delivering race times slower than their elementary school daughters. But he can still beat them all in a sprint, so at least there's that.

He is busy working on the next novel.